Inca Gold

All That Glisters

Sybil Beaton

Order this book online at www.trafford.com
or email orders@trafford.com

Most Trafford titles are also available at major online book retailers.

Printed in Victoria, BC, Canada.

ISBN: 978-1-4251-9100-9 (sc)
ISBN: 978-1-4251-9160-3 (dj)
ISBN: 978-1-4269-0036-5 (eb)

*Our mission is to efficiently provide the world's finest, most comprehensive book publishing
service, enabling every author to experience success. To find out how to publish your book, your
way, and have it available worldwide, visit us online at www.trafford.com*

Trafford rev. 08/19/2010

www.trafford.com

North America & international
toll-free: 1 888 232 4444 (USA & Canada)
phone: 250 383 6864 ♦ fax: 812 355 4082

For David,

who alone knows what he had to put up with

AUTHOR'S NOTE

The situations described in these pages are all too real, but this book is a work of fiction. The characters, events and politicians are imaginary though some names may bear resonances of real people. I am greatly indebted to friends who share my love for the countries portrayed, to whom I extend my especial thanks, as also to countless advisers, friends and cousins, in particular to:

Ruth, Gillie, Sophie, Linda and Bill, my nephew Martin,
and especially my 'technical adviser' Jennifer.

* * *

Chile is fortunate in the number and variety of her offshore islands, particularly those in the Patagonia region. But, although based in the area around Coinco, this account does not claim to be factually accurate. Nor are any of the characters in the story, living or dead, based on real people but are entirely fictitious, existing only in the imagination of the author.

Dramatis personae

Hamish ex-copper and currently a vicar; born in Outer Hebrides and educated in Glasgow

Katie Blair, wife of Hamish, Chilean-born, now living in Cheshire with Hamish and son Matthew

Vanessa, Katie's Chilean cousin - organising the cruise - and husband, Jaime Fuentes

Freddie, Uruguayan oncologist, and wife Ursula; also on board

Aidan Johnson, former CID cop, seconded to Interpol from Glasgow

Benz Tring, former DI, supposedly on loan to CIA drugs fraud administration

Jocelyn, and other assorted Chilean and Peruvian cousins on cruise (such as Argos)

Tony Mackenzie (former British museum curator, now freelancing) and his wife Sheila

Srta Consuelo Gonzalez Ballunde (and Peruvian minder) of the Peruvian contingent

Watanabes, Señor & Señora (so-called husband-and-wife team of the Peruvian group)

Sherwin, American archaeologist (retired professor on holiday)

Tyler, Head of American Peace Corps in Chile, friend of Sherwin's

Anna, Australian pharmacologist attending international conference, now on board

Nigel, another Australian pharmacologist on board

Raùl, (Adonis) young Chilean scientist smitten with Anna

Ari, Vanessa's indebted young nephew in hock to the Peruvian drug mafia

Paulina, Chilean girlfriend of Raùl whom Ari is interested in

Lorca, Tony's cellmate while in prison off Chiloé (& his mother Señora Lorca)

Catriona, Hamish's first girlfriend from South Uist and later in Glasgow

Captain, First Mate and Manuel, PR man/purser all on *SS Skyros*

Sundry villains, fishermen, stewards and others (eg Señora Valdemar)

Time: March, 2001 Place: *SS Skyros*, up and down the southern
Chilean coast

PART I

"…*and wine that maketh glad the heart of man;*" Psalms

CHAPTER ONE

Southern Chile, March 2001

If Katie had realised then how many of his nine lives Hamish was to use up during this holiday she would certainly have had second thoughts. As it was, she blithely rushed to the travel agents for flights once he had changed his mind and relented; and then immediately e-mailed her cousin Vanessa in Santiago cancelling her earlier regretful refusal of the invitation to join their special new-millenary cruise party.

The hubbub of sixty or so assorted passengers from all over the world, gathered together on the MV Skyros two-thirds of the way down the Chilean coast, was deafening. One of the less ebullient couples, Katie and Hamish Blair from the north of England, was meeting all her Chilean cousins and friends for the first time, much to their bemusement and, in the case of the non-Spanish speaking Hamish, mostly incomprehension. He began to wonder whether he had not been right after all to persuade his wife to refuse the invitation when it first plopped through the letter-box so unexpectedly all those weeks ago.

Having spent nearly all his boyhood in and out of boats, Hamish had retained his love of the sea despite a rather tough spell training on a minesweeper when in the Officer Training Corps; this was while he was still at university in Glasgow. Coupled with Katie's description of the birds, scenery and their likely fellow-passengers, the idea of a cruise had tempted Hamish. He badly needed a break after his recent heart scare and he wondered whether this might fit the bill.

"But I have to say the thought of setting foot in one of your banana republics when we have perfectly good holiday spots in our own country really makes me hesitate. What's so special about your Chile anyway?" (only half-teasingly).

Hamish had indeed taken some more than subtle persuading and it was only when he spotted Katie's ill-disguised disappointment that he had finally given in.

"You know I don't like foreigners. I can see absolutely no point in travelling halfway round the world when we have wonderful scenery, and fishing on our own door-step in Scotland, especially the outer isles. But I suppose I'm being selfish. Let's give it a whirl. You deserve a break, and I do realise this really is a once-in-a-lifetime chance for you, - for us rather. But revisiting your native country after so long may be something of a letdown. You'd better take off the rose-coloured specs and prepare yourself for a bit of a shock. As for meeting myriads of far-flung cousins, I'm not so sure but I suppose..." his voice tailed off. After all, their one-surviving child had as good as left home and was now virtually independent; and Hamish was overdue a sabbatical. Besides, he and Katie had started bickering over trifles, something they had never done before - a sure sign they needed a break.

Having yielded against his better judgement, Hamish was determined to make the best of it, all the more so in view of his doctor's warning after his recent mild angina. Maps were consulted, finances examined, several visits to the local library were fitted in; and he enlisted for evening classes in Spanish South American-style for good measure.

Some weeks later a group of nearly sixty cousins and friends mostly of Chilean origin were finally foregathered in Puerto Montt, on the Patagonian coast, at the start of this cruise together with a dozen other motley tourists. Organised by Vanessa, an Anglo-Chilean cousin of Katie's, the trip had originally been intended to celebrate the new millennium by sailing as far south as icebergs would permit in order to be amongst the last to witness the setting sun on the year 2000; hence the first to welcome in the new millennium. But "owing to unforeseen circumstances" (as the travel brochures say), the trip had had to be postponed for a year for a variety of reasons, some quite beyond their control; the halving in value of the Chilean escudo for one. (Which at least made the trip affordable for the Blairs, Hamish reflected.)But here, at last, they all were - thanks to Vanessa's dogged determination and administrative skill.

Surveying the scene and his fellow-guests Hamish hoped he hadn't made a dreadful mistake. To his dismay he saw they were about to be harangued. His heart sank though it wasn't Vanessa who had risen to address them, but one of her cousins from Uruguay. At the other side of the bar Katie, engrossed in conversation, managed to catch her husband's eye and flash a sympathetic smile.

"Just before it was due to close, last Sunday in fact," Freddie began, "three or four of the most valuable and outstanding artefacts at an exhibition in the Peruvian National Museum in Lima simply disappeared." He made a dramatic pause. "An act of brazen daylight robbery! Nobody saw it happen and it was a while before it was even noticed and the alarm raised."

By now an audience was flocking into the saloon of the MV Skyros, their mini-cruiser, which was moored in the outer harbour of Puerto Montt, over halfway down the long Chilean coast. The saloon smelt of furniture polish, fresh seafood and suntan lotion; anticipation was in the air. Passengers crowded in to listen to this fascinating story which so far had only been sketchily reported in the Peruvian press in a small paragraph which had concluded: *The Minister is confident the police will soon have the criminals responsible brought to book and the exhibits restored to their rightful place in the museum.* Of course no mention at all in the Chilean dailies.

"All we've heard so far," Vanessa confirmed to Freddie, "is from my cousin up in Lima who said the exhibition had mysteriously been closed a week early 'for undisclosed reasons'. No-one could find out why. There wasn't even a word on the radio or in the Chilean newspapers about it so what you're telling us now is all news."

Freddie, an oncologist from Uruguay, had come straight down to Chile from Lima where he had been attending a medical conference. His wife Ursula had joined him in Peru, from their home in Montevideo, and they had then travelled on south together. A supposedly international symposium had gathered cancer specialists from throughout the Americas in a splendid new location just outside Lima; it had been opened with fanfare by the ageing President. Impressive, and useful for contacts, but while in Peru Freddie was in fact more interested in seeing this exhibition whose fame had extended far and wide. Talk of it was on everybody's lips, and though determined, he had been thwarted at the last minute by the robbery. Even the symposium, glittering as it was, hadn't compensated for that.

It emerged from Freddie's account that the exhibition had been loaned by one Señor Muji Gallico, a mega-rich Peruvian, famous for having assembled a priceless collection of Inca gold and jewellery unmatched anywhere in the world. He was also, 'not unnaturally' according to Freddie, known to be extremely reticent about letting even the experts view his treasures (whose provenance was often shrouded in mystery).

"This was a double disaster with loss of face all round, for the Museum but above all for the Peruvian police," Freddie continued. "Even the President felt personally let down and loudly demanded instant action from his police, amid many face-saving declarations and promises of speedy and terrible retribution for the culprits."

The story of the President's humiliation was especially enjoyed by the many Chileans on board: most Chileans seemed to have a love/hate relationship with Peru stemming from the 1920 fruit wars and the everlasting border skirmishes which had recently flared up again around the El Teniente silvermines and in the Atacama desert. Tension was also high with their Argentine neighbours in Bariloche high up in the Andes over a border dispute. But Peru and Chile were hardly 'buddies', as Vanessa termed it, over the exporting of their respective silver and copper ore; and now there was talk of oil being discovered along their respective frontier so this might well prove to be another explosive flashpoint in their mutual rivalry. Whatever, they lost no chance to ridicule each other and here was a 'golden' opportunity. There was always the risk of trouble brewing over fishing rights though here Peru seemed to concentrate more on its squabbles with the United States and, less recently, with Japan than with Chile.

"What price the President's re-election now?" they crowed. "This'll just tip the balance. See if it doesn't."

After the recent humiliation in Europe of their own President General Pinochet, most of the Chileans were only too happy to see Peru's embarrassments in their turn, and to get their own back. True, their fiasco had originated at the hands of an obscure Spanish magistrate and was certainly not planned by the host government, or so it was alleged, but it had still given rise to a huge dent in Chile's public esteem. England's name was anathema and the Argentines and the Peruvians loved it.

Tucking into the *pisco sours* circulating freely, Freddie had continued his story, in English now in deference to the North American contingent just arrived. Raising his voice further as other passengers flooded in:

"Yes, it was rumoured that Gallico kept his collection in his own private Fort Knox of a mansion in Miraflores, a smart Lima suburb where he lived surrounded by guard dogs and every electronic security gadget known to man: laser beams, the lot. The Minister for Culture, himself a friend of Gallico's, had had a hard job twisting the millionaire's arm to persuade him to show his treasures to the unwashed in celebration of the millennium, and speculation was rife as to the inducements or political favours he was alleged to have offered. What was especially curious, however, was that as well as the gold, a few pieces of erotic pottery, depicting weird sexual encounters, normally held in his strongroom and never before on (even limited) public view, had also apparently disappeared. At least according to the *cognoscenti* and again without trace, at least so far."

"In keeping with good Catholic tradition," Ursula, Freddie's wife, had added dryly, "such pseudo-pornography was shown in a separate room from which we women were naturally strictly barred."

Which presumably at least meant that the felon was not a woman, thought Katie overhearing. But later as new developments came to light she began to question even this assumption. Katie, revelling in being back "home" - her native Chile - and speaking Spanish again, albeit the Chilean variety, was plunging into the conversation with gusto. She sincerely hoped Hamish didn't feel too left out and that the few language lessons he had managed to squeeze in before leaving would stand him in good stead.

"It appeared the thieves left no clue and annoyingly got away scotfree. So far the only leads the police have are a mysterious telephone warning, allegedly received two days before the robbery along the lines of: "You're so smart, you think you've got it all sewn up? Just you wait!" Freddie continued. "And, later, some incoherent blabbering from one of the guards about the Señor Ministro and his last-minute confusing changed instructions."

"They were so taken offguard they had no chance of tracing the anonymous telephone caller, certainly not of recording it, and their contacts in the underworld all strenuously denied having any idea of who the caller might have been or of whether he, for they were sure it *was* a man, could be connected with the Peruvian mafia, or indeed a ring of international art thieves known to be operating in the vicinity."

"According to the newspapers," he went on, "the majority plumped for North Americans being implicated, the usual cop-out as they make such convenient scapegoats and this shifts the blame away from the locals."

"You mean no-one had any concrete leads at all? Not even after those rewards, huge ones I gather, had been offered? Incredible! I heard they went into the thousands - dollars of course, enough to tempt the middle classes as well as the *rotos*. Anyway, what about finger-prints?" one of the Chileans asked.

"No, none. The only other lead came from the owner himself - under some police questioning after the theft. He admitted, very reluctantly, that each of the stolen *objets d'art* possessed a curious virtually unidentifiable mark in a certain place not known to anyone other than himself. The Peruvian officials scoffed at first; later, however, they were hoping this fact might make it even more difficult to dispose of the stolen goods on the open market provided the relevant information could be circulated, through Interpol, to the appropriate police forces right across the continent in time; the USA included. Although it's becoming increasingly clear that they must have been stolen to order and are unlikely to appear on the open market."

"That special unknown identification mark, er..." interrupted a hesitant young voice, "wouldn't be something like this?" One of the late arrivals to the party, the slight young man sidled up to Freddie and showed him a card with a monogram of an *m* super-imposed on a *g* about half the size of a baby's little finger nail. Freddie looked incredulous and his face blanched. Not willing to show he was stumped, he scrutinized the new arrival: "Wherever did you see that? Did the police show it to you or how did you come by it?" he demanded.

The young man hesitated, turned bright red and mumbled something about his sources being confidential; in the confusion he withdrew quickly, clearly feeling he had received the confirmation he sought. At Freddie's enquiring look, Vanessa whispered a name into the Uruguayan's ear. The knowing ones all nodded sagely passing on titbits and gossip to each other about the young man while Katie continued none the wiser, wondering what was so significant about the alleged special mark. She glanced across to Hamish to see if he had noticed as he too seemed curious about this enigmatic chap whom Vanessa obviously knew quite well. From the other side of the gathering Hamish quietly took all this on board as he wondered if he should go up on deck to light his pipe, or bide his time until more people began to circulate, making his absence less conspicuous.

CHAPTER TWO

Born in Ecuador but with a Peruvian passport, educated in Lima and married to a Chilean of a well-established farming family also of British descent, Vanessa felt thoroughly cosmopolitan. A 'citizen of the world', she had long cherished the idea of reuniting her extended circle of friends and relatives on such a cruise. Originally she had intended it to celebrate the millennium but, after several unforeseen last-minute hitches, they had all succeeded (or almost all) in embarking a year late on this mini-cruiser. They still intended to celebrate, she told her party, spending a week at sea sailing down to the Antarctic Circle - as far as they could get in the time. The San Rafael glacier was their particular goal, then as far further south as they could reach allowing time to stop off at some of the islands *en route*. This would be the last sailing of the season because, now that March was here, ice-floes were already threatening.

A feat of organisation on Vanessa's part but a shame, she felt, that not everyone who had booked was actually able to come. In the event, three couples had let her down at the eleventh hour; otherwise their multicultural and multilingual group would have occupied virtually the whole of the main deck plus half the deck below. Nevertheless, Vanessa had succeeded despite her husband Jaime's sour predictions and was triumphantly determined that her group was going to have fun. It would not be for lack of trying on her part if they didn't: it was all part of the challenge and particularly sweet if it proved her sore bear of a husband wrong.

A smouldering junoesque beauty with a redhead temperament, Vanessa was used to digging in her toes especially where her husband was concerned. With her multi-national background and extensive travelling under her belt, she felt confident about coping with allcomers from wherever, quickly able to put them at their ease and dispel local tensions especially Peruvian/Chilean ones.

"The family will now see for themselves what I've been planning over the last couple of years," she told Katie. "Sometimes against considerable odds, I may add, as for instance when we had that change of government, with political upheavals resulting in fiendishly restrictive travel laws being introduced, and then the escudo plummeting in value...".

She was particularly pleased to have lured these cousins of hers from Scotland, (or really now Cheshire, she should say); -her first cousin Katie, whom she hadn't seen for years, plus husband Hamish, an unpretentious and probably rather dull vicar in his early fifties. All she had heard about him was that he originated from one of the smaller Hebridean islands way up to the northwest of Glasgow, that this was virtually his first trip abroad and that he spoke with a strong Scottish accent when he did speak, and he smoked a foul-smelling pipe. But, strangely, Katie seemed to adore him.

"Fancy Katie marrying a vicar of all people," Vanessa had remarked to her husband when Katie's letter cancelling her earlier refusal had arrived. "I gather he's been ill so I fear he'll be duller than ever. I only hope he won't need too much looking after."

Jaime murmured something about giving the fellow a chance and they left it at that. However, as soon as Katie and her tall, rather gauche husband arrived at Santiago airport Vanessa was relieved to see Hamish looking reasonably fit. While the menfolk sorted out the suitcases Vanessa was determined to find out more about him.

"How ever did you, living in the smart home counties and with your background, come to meet someone from the remoter Hebrides? South Uist I believe you said (wherever that may be)?" Vanessa questioned Katie when she first had the opportunity. Later back in their smart Santiago duplex, while Hamish was being taken on a tour of the garden and swimming-pool by Jaime, she returned to the attack.

"That's rather a long story," Katie replied, "but, briefly, you'll remember that after Eduardo Frei came to power so unexpectedly in the 1960s a lot of Chilean latifundistas got fed up and went abroad, leaving their farms to rot in the hands of the *rotos,* just taking whatever they could with them in the form of US dollars. Some people - like Cousin Antonia - were really quite smart and managed to smuggle out huge quantities of cash and even gold and jewellery, but my parents were not among them. Alas."

"Yes, we were in Peru then - happily for us, and the Peruvian dollar was quite strong on the exchange rate so we didn't do so badly. But my two aunts who remained in Santiago never stopped moaning about the new government and the *reforma agraria* which they said was going to ruin them."

"Well, my father wasn't so quick off the mark either," Katie continued. "But eventually when he realised what was up, what it really entailed and that he would lose all his capital if he stayed, he decided to quit too. Since my mother's family had some money, shares and things, tied up in England they decided to go there until everything quietened down under Frei, when of course they intended to return and resume their comfortable old lifestyle in Santiago or on the *fundo*."

"I suppose that would have been round about 1966/67 time?" Vanessa queried. "Your parents must have had a dreadful time adapting to such a different kind of life, and the worry must have…".

"Yes. And of course things didn't quite work out like that, did they? Hardly a week went by without a gloomy letter from one or other of the aunts telling us about the huge rise in the cost-of-living, no meat in the shops except of course on Fridays when a consignment of broilers would arrive from the States. (For a so-called Catholic country too!) No petrol, so virtually no cars: only people who could afford to buy fuel on the black market had those. And no little luxuries, like paper hankies or sticking-plasters, flown in from BA or Panama, either. Tia Susie couldn't afford to get to her weekly bridge session so was miserable, and even Tia Lucie couldn't afford the alpaca wool she used for knitting those dreadful cardigans she used to give you at Christmas, so altogether life was pretty bleak all round."

Vanessa nodded sympathetically and waited for her to go on.

"But not really all that much better for us in England, though I'd just gone to boarding-school and so didn't notice it so much. My sister of course continued to be a pain, a typical teenager wanting everything and at once, not noticing how the parents were scrimping to let her have it, and then moaning about having to stay in the miserable English climate, and why couldn't we return home. Etc. etc."

"It's rather remarkable that less than half a century on we've made so much headway," Vanessa murmured, looking out on to the manicured lawns and swimming-pools of her neighbours all around. "In fact here in Chile we've got a thriving economy now, second to none throughout South America, virtually full employment and…," she smiled at Katie not wanting to rub it in too much. She quickly brought the conversation round to Hamish again and asked how they had met, being from such totally different backgrounds and parts of the world.

"We were living in Marlow at the time and all the young men I met were so stuffy and unadventurous, and pompously self-righteous. Then one day when I went for my usual pre-lunch swim I dived in without looking and practically went head-first slap into this chap doing back-stroke coming at me from the other end. As it was we ended in a tangle of arms and legs and, of course, profuse apologies. It turned out he was on a training attachment to the local police athletics centre at Bisham Hall not far away. Since they didn't have a pool he used to slip over to the public baths in Marlow for a quick dip before their mid-day meal whenever he could get transport. So that's how we met," she ended; rather defiantly Vanessa thought.

"But how did you get to know him? And what did your parents say?" Vanessa was full of questions but Katie merely smiled and promised to conclude the story later. She was anxious to catch the mail, having promised her son a letter at the first opportunity, and was also a little anxious about leaving Hamish to the tender mercies of his gruff host, Jaime.

Conversation at lunch was stilted: Vanessa officiated, helped by the maid whom she summoned by tinkling a beautiful silver bell, and Katie and Hamish were on their best behaviour. They took care not to catch each other's eye as Vanessa sought to impress; especially when she saw fit to scold the maid for something trivial.

Afterwards, however, over coffee Vanessa relaxed a little. She filled in the background of some of the other passengers they were going to meet on the cruise. As well as Cousins Freddie and Ursula from Uruguay, Vanessa's sister and two nieces from Ecuador, plus one or two cousins from the USA, the Argentine and Peru, various Santiago friends and unknown Antipodeans were also joining what was a mainly Spanish-speaking group. Vanessa anticipated much cross-cultural joking and leg-pulling in the days ahead. Veterans of many sea cruises, she and Jaime had already been on a similar trip to the one they were embarking on now, so she knew what was in store for them - or so she thought.

However, by the time they reached Puerto Montt next day, after a breath-taking flight down from Santiago, they were all less tense and Hamish was beginning to think he might not have made such a mistake in coming after all. The scenery alone was going to be worth it. And, who knows, he might see some spectacular birds as well.

CHAPTER THREE

On board the *Skyros*, Hamish, the dour Scot, had already made his number with the jovial barman despite their lack of a common language. Thankful, now that the season of Lent was upon them, that he had decided not to give up his evening dram, Hamish was doubly glad later when he tasted some of the more unusual Chilean wines, that he had decided not to give up drink at all for Lent. There were plenty of other things he could go without instead. Or, more to the point, good intentions he could carry out. Meantime drinks on the house were circulating freely and *empanadas,* a typical Chilean pastie, were being offered as more people arrived on the scene. Vanessa was still doing her best to introduce them all; Hamish and Katie were joined by several hitherto unknown cousins from Peru and the Argentine and the noise grew deafening.

Earlier Hamish, unnoticed, had slipped away to inspect the top deck where several mysterious-looking parcels shrouded in sacking had come aboard along with the fresh fruit and provisions. More from curiosity and to get some sea air into his nostrils than from anything else, he clambered from deck to deck noticing plenty of action but nothing untoward. He succeeded in rejoining the party before anyone had missed him, even Katie who was immersed in conversation with newly reclaimed relatives.

Of course they were all still talking about the robbery and speculating about the ultimate destination of the loot. Someone had even suggested a wealthy Chilean upstart collector who had had his eye on it for some time and was known to be desperate to get his hands on genuine Inca gold as so much nowadays in the museums was alleged to be counterfeit. Ribald suggestions were made of the purloiner's "doing a Schliemann" (acquiring the famous Cretan - or, in this case, Inca - gold necklace to adorn his beloved and manipulative '*nouveau riche*' wife) to great shouts of laughter and raucous, libellous, remarks.

Then there were the North American private collectors, not to mention the great and often wealthy museums all over the States. And private individuals on the European continent too. In the hubbub of the first evening's lavish hospitality - free drinks all round, and very good pisco sours they were, followed by even better food - Hamish turned his attention to being neighbourly and practising a few words of halting Spanish. He was quite unable to follow much of the rapid exchanges but Katie could always fill him in later, he hoped. The Chilean sense of humour had him floored and though nearly all of them spoke English, they interlarded it with so many words which were not in his dictionary that he was quite at a loss. Katie explained where she could, that is when she wasn't too doubled up with laughter herself.

Nearly everyone spoke American-English or English, some with an Australian or South African accent, and there was a variety of South American versions of Spanish, as well as a smattering of Brazilian Portuguese. But happily for Hamish the *lingua franca* was English (though not everyone connected with his Hebridean accent at first).

Most people were only too happy to lay the blame for the gold theft if not at the door of the Peruvian President, then at least at someone else's with plenty of clout.

"It's common knowledge," one of the cousins from Buenos Aires interrupted, "that our supposedly outgoing President hankers after gold - in any shape or form. And if and when he loses the upcoming election, boy, is he going to need it? They say that, among the ostentatious ornaments in the presidential office, on his desk he has a bowl of apples - solid golden apples, and very beautiful ones, to wow his visitors with."

"Must weight a ton…," Hamish thought.

"That's why they nicknamed his palace the 'garden of the Hesperides'," another know-all interjected. "It's rumoured that, even privately, they eat off gold plates, with a footman behind each chair at table; presumably to see they don't get nicked by the guests."

"With these elections in the offing," the first cousin pontificated, "and inflation back home running at between 120% and 160%,".… "for which he's undoubtedly responsible," someone else piped up; "this villain has at last realised the only worthwhile commodity for him to have (in case he has to scarper *pdq*) is gold. Gold in any shape or form, bullion or ornament. Apart, of course, from the secret numbered bank account in the name of his dear wife, darling Bella, in Switzerland."

Hamish could hear sniggers in the background.

"Libellous but true," added the speaker's husband.

Hamish was listening amazed, though pretending not to show any interest. Katie exchanged a glance with Vanessa who winked at her as if to say 'Men! we women know better.'

"Not as bad as our lot in the Argentine. What about *our* so-called President? And the beginnings of *his* collection? They say it was commandeered from some of the '*desparecidos*'?" another chipped in. "I heard that on really good authority, a cousin of Galtieri's."

"Not to mention also the winnings from those of his fellow-putchistas whom he'd managed secretly to blackmail and relieve of their ill-gotten gains?"

"But to return to the artefacts," resumed Freddie loudly, "or, rather, Peru and its President. I've heard those in the know hint that some extremely rare and beautiful Inca jewellery is amongst *his* collection, including the hollow gold facemask of the famous 'Inti Rama' descended from the Sungod himself. You know, the one that was supposed to have been found in Cajamarca right up in northern Peru - where they were trying to assemble enough gold to ransom the captive Inca from the marauding Conquistadores. Yes, filling that cave with artefacts supposedly made by the most skilful Inca artisans ever, from beaten gold inset with huge sapphires and rubies. And the most delicately wrought…"

"I saw it once, the hoard." Vanessa interjected. "It really is a magnificent sight; I was lucky enough to see it among the Sipán treasure on display in Lima - in the late eighties, I think it was."

"Quite breathtaking," Freddie agreed, shaking his head dreamily as he recalled the unbelievable beauty of the workmanship and the lustre of the gold despite the elapse of time.

"What about the Chavìn animal jug he's supposed to have 'expropriated' from the Cajamarca Museum too?" interposed Sherwin, one of the Americans on board, a retired professor. "I'm told that's not been seen in public for some time, and no explanation…".

Various members of the audience chipped in with anecdotes about their own particular Peruvian artefact, allegededly true, some highly embellished and fanciful, each one 'improving' on the one before.

Returning to the 'Lima heist' and allowing for the hyperbole and potential libel, always prevalent in such gatherings, Freddie's story made riveting listening to those others in the bar who were outside the group but managing to eavesdrop. As more and more people joined the party, they all crowded round to hear, begging him to recap what they had missed. Each recap seemed to boast more and more superlatives, Hamish noted dryly; and was yet more libellous. He hoped there were no secret policemen from the DINA in the offing.

"What's more," said Freddie, thoroughly enjoying his large audience, "at the press conference when the news broke, a newspaper reporter, less sycophantic and rather more daring than the rest (must have been a Brazilian), asked a question of 'the coprophilous Minister'. Since no-one had the faintest idea what he meant there was a hush, then a hubbub while the aide, put on the spot and guessing wildly, explained to his boss that it surely meant 'security-conscious'. Whereupon the said Minister beamed and "begged him to proceed". It wasn't until the next day's headlines that a furious Minister ordered his minions to track down the cheeky pressman and 'have his guts for garters,' to use his phrase. It was assumed the aide got the immediate chop too."

The canny ones in Freddie's group of listeners broke into roars of laughter knowing the Minister's reputation while newcomers sought to find out what all the hilarity was about. Meanwhile Hamish had a quick look in his Spanish dictionary and discovered the word meant 'delighting in dung or filth': no wonder the Minister was hopping mad, he thought, particularly as it was probably absolutely true, what with the erotica he was alleged to hoard and so forth.

As the sun was sinking behind Tengo Island across from Puerto Montt, the narrow channel between it and the mainland was illuminated in a glow of apricot shot with gold. The silhouette of the mountains overhanging the port stood out sharply, there was no cloud and the weather omens were pronounced good. While everybody was admiring the sunset Vanessa quickly totted up numbers: her group was all miraculously safely aboard and they were now only waiting for one or two other stragglers before setting sail.

They were assembled in the main bar of their cruise-ship, moored in one of the sheltered bays along the Chilean coastline. After an effusive welcome from the Captain and the PR man-cum-purser it was Vanessa's turn to address her group. No sooner had she started than a loud juddering thud overhead interrupted her introductory briefing. She had worked for many months to gather so many of her extended family for this cruise and was on the point of full-scale introductions when the incident occurred; nothing was going to stop her now. But the noise was momentarily deafening. A crane hoisting one of the lifeboats aboard had malfunctioned and let slip its cargo prematurely, with a lurch and a thump, and a series of consecutive thunderous jolts, right onto the deck above them - or so the Purser hastened to explain.

After a second or two Jocelyn, one of the younger cousins, broke the stunned silence with "Oh my God, it's either a tonne of potatoes - or *choclo* - or perhaps a body? Or both?".

Little did she know how near the truth she was but everyone who was familiar with Jocelyn's sense of the dramatic just burst out laughing. When the mirth had subsided Vanessa returned to her programme, now aided by the arrival of yet more *pisco sours* and further refreshments.

*   *   *

Hamish was everyone's idea of the typical lanky auburn-haired Scot, not quite so fiery perhaps, really pretty easygoing; some might even have considered him taciturn. Asked to describe her husband, Katie after some thought said he reminded her of a copper beech - despite its not really being native to Scotland, and certainly not to the Hebrides where he hailed from. He was after all once a copper (she enjoyed her private pun) and truly auburn into the bargain, with magnificently burnished bushy eyebrows and lashes. His lean frame betrayed wiry strength which went right down to his fingertips. His spatulate nails and strong fingers made his mother-in-law comment he should have been a 'cellist or, better still, a double-bass player. But, although he had an ear for music, that would have been quite beyond the means of his crofter parents, to their regret, and hence quite out of the question. Sturdy and dependable, and rather introspective, Hamish liked playing his cards close to his chest. He was always the soul of discretion, very occasionally bending to the wind of expediency but never so as to compromise his principles, which he defended fiercely.

Among all the men of Katie's acquaintanceship, Hamish was the only truly considerate one, she said, always thinking of her wants and other people's welfare before his own. To her he seemed the model of compassion, not sentimental but a true liberal, invariably patient and, like the beech-tree, versatile. His crowning defect was his obstinacy particularly where a matter of principle was concerned but, after nearly

15

quarter of a century's wedded life, Katie reckoned she at last knew how to deal with that. With few knotty preconceptions and hang-ups (except against "ruddy furriners") his mind was nevertheless, she maintained, flexible enough; and ultimately imaginative enough in its insights. Though he was - just - in his fifties his abundant auburn hair had scarcely begun to thin; and he had retained his lanky athletic figure. Perhaps he was no longer so fit as he had once been but he could still play a good game of tennis; swim a mile, and walk straight up a mountainside, or so it seemed to his short-legged wife. His sunken cheeks, however, accentuated by the deep lines on his forehead, told a different tale betraying his recent health problems, ruefully registered now by Katie.

Hamish's diminutive wife Katie, Vanessa's cousin, though a strong swimmer like her husband, did not share his passion for the sea. But she was relishing this opportunity to return to her native country after so long; she had so many relations here and had not seen Chile for over thirty years (when on a brief return visit with her father in the sixties); and she still suffered occasional pangs of homesickness. In her adoptive country ponies had been her thing and at the posh English boarding-school which her parents had seen fit to send her to, she hadn't empathised with her teachers so she had taken refuge in sport. A natural gymnast, she had been good at all their school games, captain of cricket and netball and brilliant at diving. What she lacked in height her nimble feet more than compensated for by their agility. She smiled as she remembered her mother's aghast expression when she read her school report:

"Katie excels at physical exercise; she is a natural gymnast and a proficient spin bowler and fluent with the bat. Consideration should be given to the advisability of further coaching in the nets with a view to possible selection to represent her county on leaving school. Unless of course she opts for a more academic career, in which case she would need to apply herself rather more seriously than she has seen fit to do so far. Whereas her arts subjects, notably the pianoforte, could pass muster, Latin and Mathematics both leave much to be desired." And so on.

Had he still been alive, her father would have been horrified. He considered cricket most unladylike for girls and would probably have put a stop to her playing it; though he might have decided to demonstrate his broadmindedness by allowing it now and then provided of course her shorts reached below her knees. As it was, her mother had no real problem dissuading her from a career in gymnastics or games, Katie's own inclinations lying elsewhere. Her natural preference lay in the arts, but she had already decided she wanted to do something "useful" with her life, either train to become a social worker or a hospital almoner or something similar. She chuckled to herself as she remembered her mother's total incomprehension of anyone wanting to do anything so strange, especially a good-looking girl like her with a dowry and fine marriage prospects,... but Katie stopped her wanderings down memory lane short when Hamish reappeared at her elbow saying he was just going up on deck to catch the last of the sunset.

"You've only got five minutes before dinner," she reminded him. "Don't be late or all the lobster will go."

CHAPTER FOUR

Impressed by the speed at which Katie had adapted to a totally different lifestyle as wife to a rural vicar with its host of attendant duties, and realizing it must have taken its toll, Hamish let his gaze linger on her as he slipped back into the crowd. Sleepy Cheshire seemed light-years away from quicksilver Chile with its mercurial people and changing scenery, and he was now glimpsing a different creature from his ever-busy 'English' wife.

Feeling his scrutiny, Katie looked up. Hamish felt an electric impulse flickering through his body as their eyes met across the saloon on his return from up on deck. He sensed Katie was sending him a complicit message across the sea of volubly chattering cousins and smiled to himself. Even after quarter of a century he still reacted to her look, though recently they had been so busy their relationship had come under strain.

A month ago in their busy rural life Katie had nearly reached breaking-point, he realised now. And Hamish himself had felt drained as he never took time off and had four far-flung parishes to cover. As a result of recent reorganisation within the deanery he had acquired a further two new parishes within his ministry and had only just been sent the promised curate to help him cope with such a large area. When he was not actually working in the parish or at meetings he was at the hospital visiting, or writing sermons, and they scarcely saw anything of each other for days on end. Except at mealtimes: they used to make a point of catching up with each other and the children then, and they rarely if ever missed the chance to sit down together, to eat and catch up.

But first they had had to endure the dreadful shock and trauma of their firstborn's tragic death. Winifred had been a premature and delicate baby. Always a little backward, she was nevertheless the pride and joy of her father until, quite out of the blue, she had succumbed to the relatively rare, or at least still not universally known and recognised, phenomenon of 'cot death'. Both parents were absolutely devastated. Of course they had had to submit to an enquiry, several enquiries in fact, and all the red tape that that had involved so it was some months before they could grieve in peace. Katie noticed that the parents of other children of the same age, some who had been to antenatal classes with her, and who were at first extremely supportive, slowly began to distance themselves as an unaccountable feeling of guilt took hold. But the Blairs did not hold this against them; it was all too easy to understand their confusion and inability to express their sentiments, at the same time as wanting to move forward with their own children's lives.

As the other parents rushed to nursery school on the morning run with their boisterous four- and five-year-olds Katie and Hamish continued silently to mourn their beloved Winifred, channelling their grief and energies into parish work. Luckily Matthew, born two years later, survived and grew into a resourceful and affectionate lad. His parents took great care not to spoil him and were relieved to see him making friends easily at school. He did not seem to mind not having any brothers or sisters at home to play with as he had so many mates outside, and grew up to be quite the extrovert, unlike his father. In this he was his maternal grandmother's pride and joy.

But that was a good twenty years ago now. Hamish had borne his loss stoically and silently and found solace in his religion. Katie, on the other hand, reflecting on how emotionally drained she had felt these last few months - running on empty - realised how badly she had needed to replenish her batteries, her motivation and her inner thoughts. Even Khalil Gibran - her erstwhile guru - failed to restore her. She had not liked to admit to her husband that for a while she had no longer found true solace in her Bible. More recently, however, her faith was gradually restored as she felt more at one with Hamish and with God in their shared tragedy. At least they were able to talk to each other frankly about their feelings of guilt and deprivation, and comfort each other when things got unbearable. And happily Matthew was a real joy, and so spontaneously affectionate.

For years, as she had admitted to Vanessa, Katie had secretly been yearning to revisit her native country even though everyone she knew warned her about the profound (and often unwelcome) changes she would find. Now, at last, she was going to see things at first hand. She would finally be able to make up her mind for herself even if she didn't get to see all she wanted to.

Katie screwed up widely spaced green eyes, set in her round freckled face, against the waning sun still slanting into the saloon. She hoped fervently that the sea air would do Hamish a power of good, and maybe gain herself a tan as well. What better use of his savings could they make at this juncture? they both badly needed this change of air and a chance to unwind and relax. Besides, they'd only be away for less than a fortnight, barring accidents; and it looked as if everything was covered at home.

Settling into their seats in the dining-saloon, Hamish and Katie brought their attention back to Freddie who was relishing the last of his pisco sour before turning to look at the wine-list. Realising they were not going to hear any more sensational disclosures, the audience had broken up and drifted into the dining-saloon along with them. For those seated at his table Freddie found he couldn't resist gilding the lily.

"It appears the thieves left no clues; annoyingly they seem to have got away scot-free," he continued, lowering his voice. "So far the only lead the police have was a mysterious warning telephone call allegedly received two days before the robbery along the lines of: 'You're so smart, you think you've got it all sewn up. Just you wait!'"

Freddie paused to let late arrivals get seated and the waiters get by.

"In the event the police were so taken by surprise they were unable to react fast enough or in fact do anything sensible at all. They put out a few feelers of course but did nothing commonsensical like wheeling in the 'usual suspects' or offering a tempting reward. Their bovine inertia seems, not surprisingly, to have drawn a complete blank so now they're left to scratch around in the dirt like headless chickens," Freddie finished triumphantly.

While Freddie held the floor Hamish and Katie inspected the other passengers. She was fascinated by the garb of some of the youngsters and speculated with Hamish on the relationships of some of the older "couples". Freddie was a youthful sixty, his goodlooking wife Ursula somewhat younger. A second wife perhaps? He had grey curly hair cut *en brosse* and a distinctive Hapsburg lower lip which emphasized his mobile face. Ursula was stunning in a Latin American way, but nice, not haughty like some of the other cousins.

Circulating among them after coffee, Katie smiled wryly as she listened to Jocelyn complaining about her maid never dusting under the beds properly. She talked vaguely about having to sack her on her return to Santiago but everyone knew she wouldn't. As a part-time social worker and wife of a vicar, Katie couldn't afford the luxury of someone to clean for her mother, let alone for herself, but she remembered her mother's stories of how she had been brought up surrounded by servants in Chile so she bit back the facile remarks rising to her lips. It would have been tactless in the extreme for her to criticize one of the more flamboyant and extrovert members of the party before they had even embarked on their little jaunt, and she felt sure Vanessa would never forgive her. After all, this was one of the perks of an otherwise often unbearably curtailed lifestyle and by all accounts Jocelyn was an exemplary hostess, wife and mother, to say nothing of tactfully keeping an eye on her own busy socialite mother as well.

"In other words," as Vanessa said, "a typical 1980s Chilean upper-class wife with time on her hands," and who was she (Katie) to pass judgement on that?

By now Jocelyn had moved on to the subject of the children, wondering how the maid was coping, this being her mother's bridge evening so *she* couldn't possibly be expected to help out today. "And you see, darling, my Tonino will almost certainly be entertaining business chums up at the golf club so he can't be expected to be at home either."

Katie wondered privately whether he might not more likely be at some expensive restaurant entertaining his mistress but banished this unworthy thought, exchanging a conspiratorial smile with Vanessa. These Chilean men she seemed to be hinting, and Katie looked round to reassure herself, to her relief catching sight of her Anglo-Saxon surrounded by other men who were obviously sharing a rather dubious joke judging by the hearty laughter and sly glances all round.

The hubbub at dinner had been so great they scarcely noticed when the gangplank was raised, an hour late, and the crew cast off with very little ceremony. Deep night had fallen when, with a couple of hoots on the ship's sirens, they were away - to Hamish's relief. Katie was enjoying herself enormously but all too soon it was time to turn in if they were to be up in time for the morrow's arduous programme. Just as they were unlocking their cabin door humming a snatch of a Chilean *refalosa* to themselves they heard another large shuddering thump, a shout and some scuffling which was then shushed.

By the time Hamish reached the top deck everything was peaceful again and he thought no more of it. He lingered for a moment watching passing ships and trying to identify stationary lights on shore but soon gave up. With a last look round, having identified Arcturus in an unfamiliar position, and deciding that it was all much better than he had feared, so far at least, he turned and went below. By now it was too dark to be able to see anything out of the porthole in spite of the bright starlight, and the Undurraga they had drunk at dinner had been both excellent and plentiful.

*   *   *

Hamish had been gratified to find that their cabin, a *de luxe* one, was on the main deck not far from Vanessa's and the purser's office. It was distinctly luxurious, far roomier than they had expected and the bunkside lights actually worked. He was also delighted to find the bathroom so well appointed, with the correct shaving point. There was plenty of room to stow away the great collection of pills and medications he had grudgingly been forced to bring with him, and already he felt relaxed and ready for the fray. He only hoped he didn't get button-holed by too many nosey-parkers wanting to engage in conversation but word had already got round that he was a solitary individual who preferred to be left in peace. He suspected his wife of colluding with Vanessa over this!

"What did you think of Freddie and Ursula?" she asked him later in the cabin. "And did you find any other congenial people to talk to?" Whenever Katie had checked, Hamish had always seemed to be immersed in conversation and certainly not the sore bear she had feared he might have been.

"Oh, the barman seemed a decent enough chap and that other Scot - the genuine one, not your phoney Chilean one - was quite jolly. And I liked the American ex-professor; at least he talked English - of a sort - and was amiable and not too talkative. And above all, he didn't talk politics. Freddie's a queer fish though, not quite sure what to make of him but good enough company for now, which is more than can be said for some of your female cousins (not wishing to cause any offence, but aren't they rather a shallow lot; not a thought in their heads except where they're going to find a reliable maid or the smartest shoes or dressmaker?). And that polo-playing guy from the Argentine, what was his name? Please don't expect me to make polite conversation with him any more."

"Haven't a clue," Katie replied sleepily. "I couldn't stand his line-shooting either."

It could have been so much worse, she thought as they prepared for sleep.

CHAPTER FIVE

Of the eight other strangers supposedly sharing their deck, it turned out two were from *down under;* one was the retired American professor from Harvard with not a single word of Spanish, and the other five were Peruvian. Manuel, who doubled as interpreter and PR frontman, was severely put out when, at the last minute, one of the Peruvians never arrived to claim his cabin, the last of the single ones which had been greatly in demand.

"Lopez Jimenez? Never heard of him." The others all shrugged evasively when questioned by the purser. The two Peruvian women exchanged enigmatic looks and the men succeeded in looking so shifty when disclaiming all knowledge that Manuel remained unconvinced. Feeling uneasy, he made a mental note to refer to the Captain. After all, this meant quite a shortfall on revenue which they could ill afford especially when there had been a substantial waiting-list of disappointed punters after the single cabins.

Two of the Peruvians who did check in, an ill-assorted couple travelling under the name of Watanabe, were of Japanese descent. They were very secretive and appeared to speak only limited Spanish. Though the husband had some fragmented English, he was too bashful to use it. His wife, with her broad flat forehead and shrew-like eyes, long straight raven-black hair and a bovine expression, stuck to her husband's side like a leech and was never heard to utter. Except, that is, in their cabin when Katie overheard her issuing what sounded like peremptory orders, supposedly to her unfortunate husband. Quite out of keeping with her public persona, she thought. Katie was sure she also heard her swear in American English, rather dispelling the myth that she spoke none.

Consuelo, another of the Peruvian contingent, with a cabin next-door to the Watanabes, was the woman whom Vanessa thought she recognised from their Lima school-days. A beautiful leggy blonde who went by her mother's maiden name of Gonzalez, she turned out to be a cousin of the outgoing President. She was coy about her origins, refusing to let her passport out of her sight even though Manuel promised to return it promptly. The others alleged her to be so stupid as to be unable to refill her stapler unaided but Vanessa, vaguely remembering the gossip about her from school, suspected that this was only a ploy to hide a razor-sharp mind - at least so far as Number One was concerned.

Consuelo Gonzalez' protector, an overbearing, swarthy and thickset man who sported a monogrammed silk shirt and a flashy tie, didn't look as if he had ever been to sea before and was certainly not relishing the prospect. His head, just separated from his shoulders by the merest suspicion of a neck - a bull's neck - added to his belligerent stance. But his flickering eyes missed nothing and the naked woman on his tie seemed to quiver whenever his emotions were aroused.

According to his compatriots, Señorita Gonzalez' protector claimed to be descended from one of the original *conquistadores* although he was suitably short on detail as well as in stature. He reminded Vanessa's husband Jaime, a staunch Chilean, of Dylan's 'Aguirre on his duchess-faced horse' referring to the conquistador's equestrian statue down in Valparaiso. Aguirre, the notorious seeker of El Dorado, was an arrogant Peruvian Conquistador, so Jaime's fellow Chileans did not always appreciate the origins or the irony of this remark. And the horse being an import from northern Spain, unknown in the South American continent at that time, was even more heavily resented.

The protector's pudgy short-fingered hands, resembling a bunch of chipolata sausages, were never still and looked as if they yearned to be at a slot-machine or else counting out ill-gotten escudos or million-dollar bills; but they certainly would not rest comfortably on the reins of a horse. Or even on a beautiful girl's thighs? Katie wondered. He never left Señorita Gonzalez' side and his eyes followed her wherever she went but it was not her beauty he chiefly appreciated.

"I bet he even follows her to the bathroom," Katie muttered but was disabused by Vanessa. They didn't in fact have a double cabin; instead they shared a suite with two small interconnecting cabins separated by the shared bathroom, all quite chaste - or seemingly so. Moreover, Señorita Gonzalez' cabin also had an interconnecting door with the Watanabes, Katie and Hamish's nextdoor neighbours, so was well supervised.

Further down the other corridor, judging by the noise, must be Vanessa's two voluble nieces from the States - complete with boyfriends, and hangers-on, Katie and Hamish surmised. Then there were the two Australians; a couple of South Africans; and the American professor, Sherwin something-or-other, who was reportedly a retired palaeontologist or anthropologist. At least none of the smaller children was on their deck, still relatively peaceful, but the sounds of another heated discussion, this time in Japanese, broke the calm. Elsewhere a guitar could be heard picking out some of the more melodious Chilean folk songs they'd heard the night before over dinner.

Apart from the Captain's more spacious double cabin, that seemed to account for their deck, Katie noted to Hamish.

*   *   *

Day two dawned bright and clear, dispelling their worries about the forecast, low cloud and mist yielding to rain. Hamish studied the guests on the decks below as he leant over the ship's rail, content to be seabound again. Comparing notes with Vanessa's husband Jaime, also early up on deck, Hamish had been pleased to discover that, despite their very different lifestyles, they had many tastes in common including a passion for birdwatching.

"Yes, I took early retirement from the Scottish police force when it was offered," he told Jaime. "Having reached the level of Detective-Chief Inspector, I realised that was as far as I was likely to go especially when they brought in, over my head, a new Chief with radically different views, with whom I feared I would not always agree."

What in fact Hamish did not spell out to Jaime was that he had perceived a total difference in ethics and moral outlook between himself and his new boss. When it arose unexpectedly, therefore, he had gratefully accepted the chance of early retirement on reaching the age of forty. This had enabled him to answer a late vocation and train for the ministry, thankfully with Katie's full support. Ordained after four years' hard study, he had become a much-loved and conscientious parish priest in a remote part of rural Cheshire, responsible for four small churches - now rising to six - and working nearly a hundred-hour week.

"In fact this is my first proper holiday for over twelve years," he confided to Jaime, "and even now I'm having misgivings about leaving my group of parishes in the hands of our newly arrived curate. Poor woman, talk about a baptism of fire. But it was Katie who finally persuaded me by telling me sternly that it wasn't as if I was actually consigning them to outer Hades... but I still fear perhaps I was being selfish."

Jaime explained to his new friend that he had spent a couple of years at school at Glenalmond, where he had developed a taste for Scotland. This was at the outbreak of World War II before his Chilean mother had refused to risk her precious boy any more in submarine-infested seas. He told Hamish how he had grown to love the rugged scenery, the shinty, the salmon and, amusingly, the haggis, then unknown in Chile except in the form of a kind of faggot... eaten only by the really impoverished and certainly not by Jaime's grandiose family, not even the maid.

"My great-grandfather was a knowledgeable and influential arboriculturist who, amongst his many other achievements, introduced the seeds of the monkey-puzzle tree into England via Kew in the 1890s." Jaime liked to boast of his English antecedents; and his grandfather and father had maintained their lifelong interest in trees, an interest which he had inherited.

"In fact, one of the reasons why I love the *Skyros*, apart from its being such a comfortable and well-appointed ship, is its wonderful panelling. If you look around you can see a huge variety of different Chilean natural hardwoods, not those ghastly imitation woods so beloved of the current generation. And they have a distinctive smell, not that anodyne non-smell of plastic wood." Hamish found himself sympathising with Jaime's impatience with the brash younger generation as they went together on a tour of inspection, Jaime pointing out all the different kinds of timber and enumerating the origins of where the trees mostly grew.

'*With its four decks which can accommodate up to 100 passengers and 30 crew, the ship, though small by modern standards offers every comfort and amenity...*' its glossy brochure announced. '*Every cabin has its own window, or porthole in the case of the lower Athens deck, and the sundeck gives a wonderful opportunity for admiring the breathtaking scenery.*'

For those with nautical inclinations like Hamish and Jaime, the state-of-the-art instruments and sophisticated communications systems up on the bridge also provided much to examine. The captain and first mate seemed not to mind when passengers crowded on to the bridge to look at the charts, gasp at the scenery and give spurious advice on navigation generally. Perhaps it was just as well the sea was like a millpond that first day out, as access to the charts would have been seriously impeded, if not impossible.

Brought up as he was on small sailing-boats and with only limited experience in the Navy branch of the Officers Training Corps during his short spell at Glasgow University, Hamish was absolutely fascinated by being given a free rein on the bridge. He looked forward to giving the ship a more thorough inspection the next day; and on his way down to the deck below, the *Parthenon*, he was delighted to discover there was a 'smoking' as well as a non-smoking bar together with more deck space, which he planned to use later when enjoying his pipe.

CHAPTER SIX

That afternoon, despite the sunny start, the wind had freshened by the time he got back out on deck and most people were retreating below. But Hamish, accustomed to the strong Atlantic winds in his native South Uist, was happy. He felt thoroughly at home in the lowering, pewter-coloured skies and stiff breeze, and roamed around inspecting every inch of the ship. As the sky darkened persistent groans of thunder began to be heard. There was an unexpected short sharp shower sending everyone scurrying when the rain turned to unkind hailstones.

Hamish sought shelter on the bridge where the first mate beckoned him in. He was amazed to see, reflected in the glass, one of the sailors, a Chilean of Araucanian-Indian extraction - as the mate explained to him - furtively paying homage to his deity Pillán when he thought no-one could see him. Pillán, the mate explained, was the god of thunder and the cause of earthquakes and was a malignant spirit who took possession of the souls of those killed in battle. Since earthquakes were quite frequent in this region (they were not far from the San Andreas faultline) many of the indigenous people, whilst paying lip service to the Roman Catholic church, still took care to propitiate their own local and household gods whenever they thought it expedient and they were unobserved.

"Homage takes the form of a libation of pisco over the side accompanied by some mumbo-jumbo in the Quechuan language," so the mate elaborated condescendingly. It was obvious he was above such superstitions he implied, but Hamish couldn't help wondering if secretly back home he mightn't himself indulge too.

Gradually the weather improved as the sun chased the black clouds away and people returned to sit out on deck, carefully drying off the wooden deckchairs first. The rest of the afternoon proved relatively uneventful enabling the passengers to concentrate on the fantastic scenery, very similar to a Norwegian fjord - as many commented.

Having left the Quitralco fjord behind, they were now well out into the Gulf of Alcùd; by now everyone was enjoying the sun on deck and watching the playful dolphins disport themselves alongside the ship, later seeing shearwaters and grey-headed albatross as well as other less spectacular seabirds.

"Did you know that the Imperial cormorants were once called gunny cormorants as they provided the vast stocks of *guano* which first brought Europeans to Chile?" Jaime loved to ask ignorant *gringos* like Hamish who were expected to challenge this statement.

"You Europeans don't realise how valuable a commodity *guano* became once it was transformed into fertilizer, but quite a lot of people out here made their fortunes out of it, most of them of British origin. And among them Vanessa's and Katie's grand-father," Jaime grinned triumphantly as if distancing himself from 'you Europeans'.

Hamish digested this information silently and decided on his own line of attack.

"I've been told that, similar to where I come from in the northern Hebrides, pelagic birds in these parts, the Austral Zone, often spend as much as six months on the wing before returning to their nests with food for their mates and offspring. Indeed, the stormy petrels only come ashore to breed in fact. But that doesn't apply to the largest of them like the albatross, for example, does it?"

"No, but bet you don't know the average wingspan of an albatross here, do you?"

"Yes, but you're going to tell me anyway," thought Hamish.

"Round these parts it's alleged to be twelve foot - allowing for vagaries in sailors' methods of measurement. Even the giant petrel has an eight-foot span - far more than you get up in the fringes of the Arctic, believe me."

"And do you know the minimum wind speed at which an albatross can take off?" Hamish countered. "And, more importantly, do you know how many are being killed each year by long-line fishermen?" He had just read that, 'on the lookout for an easy meal, albatrosses are attracted by the slowly sinking bait and are then drowned after being caught on the fishing hooks of lines which careless or ignorant fishermen have failed to reel in'. The press had frequently been alerted by single-handed sailors and recent racing competitors, and a campaign to ban the worst excesses and the casual use of plastic, just chucked overboard, was slowly gathering momentum worldwide, so he had heard.

"These lines are cast at night when birds are not feeding and by day all they can see is the bait," Hamish persisted. "Normally the albatross would live to 60 years or more but, according to the latest statistics published, up to a hundred thousand birds a year are being killed. Imagine! so that's why numbers keep on dropping so dramatically," he continued, not allowing Jaime to interrupt. "Those lines can constitute something of a hazard for single-handed sailors too as they are almost impossible to see and avoid at night, and it's so easy for them to get fouled up round the rudder, they're becoming really dangerous."

"No, I wasn't aware of that danger," Jaime admitted, "but I do know that the albatross can't fly if the wind speed falls to below 11 mph; and they could fly up to something like 50,000 miles without landing - in the right conditions."

Having blinded each other with science, Hamish's bona fides as a bird lover were established and Jaime stopped treating him as a complete ignoramus. Hamish still thought the golden eagles of his native North Uist took some beating even if their wingspans couldn't quite compare, the ospreys too, but being a peaceable man didn't voice his thoughts.

Jaime was not used to being challenged on his home territory but here was obviously someone who cared about nature and birds so Jaime called a truce. Hamish had established his credentials. Unfamiliar with this terrain, to his surprise Hamish found everything enchanting, even the people, although he was normally not gregarious especially with "*furriners*". Passengers were exchanging knowledgeable snippets of information in various languages and congratulating themselves on knowing so much about the local flora and fauna, comparing birds and trees, then binoculars and cameras, and finally (voices lowered) the different nationalities especially the women. Of course the Chilean fair sex was far more beautiful than the Peruvian. And so on. And of course some Scottish ladies made the exception prove the rule…especially if they were of Chilean origin.

Hamish took the opportunity to question Jaime about the acrid smoke they had seen rising from a pile of burning rubber tyres just beyond the harbour the day before. All the way from the airport and halfway down the coast the evil smell had been all-pervasive; clouds of black smoke had hovered uncertainly over the road leading down to the docks and the whole busload of passengers had craned their necks to see what was happening but to no avail. Eventually the driver, despairing of ever getting through had backed up and taken a sneaky little side road which had brought them through higher up and round onto the docks from another direction.

From something the driver said they realised the men, who wore fishermen's oilskins and boots, had been blockading the road in furtherance of some grievance. Some kind of strike was obviously being organised though it all looked rather chaotic and amateurish with people milling around all over the place. Different people were yelling at each other, some with megaphones, but to little effect and most of the men just looked mulish, letting their colourful banners trail in the dirt without a concerted effort to get their message across.

The strikers' faces as they realised they had been outmanoeuvred were comical in their fury though Katie couldn't help a pang of sympathy for them. They ranged from menacing as they jumped up and down in their rage to vapid as they were forced to accept the new situation. Several passengers inside the bus felt distinctly uncomfortable, cowering at the noisy exchanges of views and the threats returned by their driver who obviously despised them.

"Those layabouts," he muttered, "they don't know when they're well off," displaying the landlubber's scorn of seagoing folk. A few stones were thrown, rather half-heartedly, but the driver put his foot down, the tyres squealed as he thrust the gears into reverse and ten minutes later the passengers were all safely deposited on the quayside beside their mountains of luggage and so relieved to be there they asked no questions as they hurried on board to find which cabin they had been allotted.

"What was it all about?" Hamish now asked Jaime. "Why were they going out on strike and what was the final outcome? What did they hope to gain?"

Jaime explained that some Peruvian interlopers had infiltrated the local band of fishermen and stirred it all up, encouraging them to defy the bosses and overlords who had a stranglehold on local distribution. Discontent had started when the inshore fishermen learned that deep water fishermen were being allowed to take fish inshore so the locals started to boycott their catch. But this had swiftly been exploited by the Peruvian mafia it was whispered.

The police had arrived, the inshore fisherfolk protesting loudly had been made to disembark various sackloads of evil-smelling merchandise and all this in double-quick time as their boats had to get out of the way of the passenger ship which in turn had to be made ready for sailing on the evening tide. The Peruvians had spread rumours that there were bodies inside the sacks, a sailor had plunged a jack-knife in and a foul-smelling viscous liquid had emerged, evil enough to frighten off the more faint-hearted. The next thing the owners knew was that everyone had downed tools, the fishermen, the dockers and the sailors, and the shop stewards emerging from nowhere had taken over. It took some pretty tough talking and a series of threats, no pay and so forth, to get the port workers and the crew, evidently few of them unionised, to resume work in time for the ship to be prepared for that evening's sailing. Even physical manhandling had been on the cards when the police arrived but mercifully this idea was abandoned as the strike started to crumble. But the discontent continued to rumble; they were still grumbling hours later, some looking very sullen. As for the fishermen, they were left to sort out their own grievances amidst a pretty hefty police presence.

"But last seen," Jaime said, "to my amazement the blockades had been lifted and they were shaking hands all round." He reckoned the Chilean fishermen would have got the worst of the bargain (knowing the crafty Peruvians) and feared somebody must have bribed someone somewhere though he reckoned they would never know exactly.

The policeman in Hamish was relieved to have sorted out this little conundrum which his lack of Spanish had so frustratingly prevented him from fathoming at the time.

CHAPTER SEVEN

Katie had stayed in the cabin to write to their son whom they had left in charge of the vicarage (not without certain misgivings on Hamish's part he had to admit) and wrote:

15th March, 2001
on board SS Skyros

Darling Mattie,
It seems an age since your solemn face saw us off at the airport - for which Dad and I thank you enormously. So much has happened and we have been plunged into the middle of nearly 50 cousins and various other cosmopolitan passengers on this ship, from the US, Peru, Japan & so forth. You name it. All jabbering at once in a dozen different lingos; even the various Latinos speak different patois but we're managing to make out. Dad is doing brilliantly, healthwise and linguistically: his few Spanish lessons seem to have paid off, at least they've given him a bit of confidence though of course he doesn't say much, as usual.. But he seems to understand more than he lets on.
As you can imagine, he's also extremely tactful with our hosts Vanessa and Jaime who are obviously beginning to like him very much though they were rather distant at first. When you remember what a snob Vanessa is (like all the Fuentes), that's high praise. [Don't repeat that!]
We did get rather a rude awakening on our arrival at Santiago airport, something which caught us totally unprepared. After the initial niceties and embraces, Jaime (whom you would probably consider slightly to the right of Genghis Khan) subjected us to a tirade about the

inhospitable behaviour of the English - this made Dad wince - towards someone who had been a guest in their country. We were gob-smacked. "I would never have imagined the Brits capable of such ungraciousness towards a former President and moreover a friend of your very own Mrs Thatcher!" or words to that effect. While we carefully avoided looking at each other, he went on in the vein of "Whatever would your country have done during the Falklands war without General Pinochet's aid? And what about old-fashioned good manners?" Completely disconcerted, it was a moment or two before we could fathom what he was driving at. Dad, however, - trust him - made a huge diplomatic effort. "Yes, I can see that must have been extremely upsetting for you," and then muttered something about events being rather forced upon us by an over-zealous official in Spain and nothing personal being intended, initially at least. He managed to calm them down after emphasizing how grateful the UK as a whole was to Chile, blah-blah.

Since we had secretly applauded the extradition request I avoided Dad's eye and held my breath. We both made a mental note never to talk politics in South America again no matter what the circumstance, at least not with Jaime, but I'm sure we won't stick to our resolution when talking about the States, or Peru, etc. to the others. They all seem to have very robust right-wing views on politics and I foresee fireworks. Thank goodness Dad's here to pour oil on troubled waters... It would hardly have been politic to kick off the holiday on the wrong foot with hosts we scarcely know and who otherwise have been extraordinarily hospitable. I had forgotten how touchy Chileans in particular are in matters of national pride.

I could see Dad wondering how to change the subject but he needn't have worried as Vanessa quickly brought our minds back to the present and to hurried last-minute preparations for the cruise. The tickets needed to be collected urgently and we had to buy currency, mosquito repellent, lip-salve, etc. etc. Vanessa was insistent on this and chivvied us all the way. Then we realised we hadn't brought enough film, and so on. It's really quite a relief finally to have left Santiago! And apparently without forgetting anything vital. So far.

We had a breathtaking flight down to Puerto Montt yesterday, stunningly beautiful. Although a bit foggy to start with, it soon turned clear and sunny and our views of the Andes were fabulous although they do look quite brown lower down, probably as a result of the last (quite recent) earthquake and the 1960 tidal wave. You can still see the effects all along that coast, even after all these years. We saw several volcanoes, some still active and with the occasional plume of smoke, which made Dad's eyes bulge, and we were only half-an-hour late landing which was quite good considering the chaos.

It's much cooler here, cloud and a brisk wind, but of course we are at least 1,200 kms. further south of the capital and the weather system is quite different.

I enclose a brochure of the luxurious cabin we have on the main deck (for our sole use). Incidentally, ALL the decks are carpeted: can you imagine? Dad snorted when he saw it and remarked to Jaime "Not very nautical, is it?" with which Jaime mercifully agreed. You'll see it's nearly all of different kinds of wood, despite the fitted carpets, and every known modern fitment, the lot. Not like our poor grimy little boat. And so spacious, comparatively speaking! At least Dad can stand upright without fear of cracking his skull.

Sorry, there's someone at the door and we're due to go ashore any minute now so I must stop. More in my next... Dad sends his love; mine too.

Bye for now. Remember to refer to Geoff if there are any problems at all.   Love, Katie-Mum

PS. Dad says thanks a million for finishing clipping that wretched hedge- a load off his mind, which means he's been able to relax properly and stop fretting about the garden. Thank you, my darling, from me too."

*   *   *

Just as she was addressing the envelope Katie heard another quick knock on the cabin door simultaneously pushed open by Vanessa, who muttered an apology. Stopped short by the array of pills by Hamish's bedside, Vanessa asked anxiously how ill he was. Katie reassured her and then, to her amusement, learned the real reason for Vanessa's unexpected visit.

"How long has Hamish been a vicar?" Vanessa asked and, on being told it was nearly ten years, continued: "Oh, I see. I thought it was much longer. And what was he before he went into the church?"

Katie always thought it was such a funny way of describing people who had been ordained but answered perfectly seriously, "A policeman". She was amused when Vanessa, blushing, came clean and admitted to Katie how, had she known at the outset that her husband had first been in the police and then had become ordained in the Anglican church, she probably would have had second thoughts about including them in the party. Even a bank manager would have been preferable, she admitted, not meeting Katie's gaze.

"A policeman? That would explain it." Vanessa had tried to hide her surprise and not sound too condescending. In Chile one only ever hobnobbed with the Chief of Police, anyone else being definitely socially inferior. Apparently the Captain had received some intelligence over the radio of a British ex-cop on his passenger-list whom he was supposed to contact in the event of liaison with Interpol becoming necessary. Quite why this occasion might arise had not been spelled out but the Captain, understandably, assuming it was something to do with narco-trafficking had quizzed Vanessa since she was the most likely to know who it would be.

"Yes, although he did reach the rank of Detective Chief Inspector quite young," Katie started to explain to Vanessa, "after the quite nonsensical reorganisations both internally and across the region, some fourteen years ago now, which resulted in a new boss taking over, with totally different ideas, and methods. Hamish knew he'd reached the moment of decision: to get out now or to stay and fester. Fortunately the opportunity to retire early with full pension rights was offered him so he jumped at it. It really was a godsend as for some time he'd been mulling over the idea of training for the lay ministry but knew we could neither afford it nor give it the time he'd need."

"So?" prompted Vanessa.

"Yes, so…" continued Katie, "this forced his hand. He realised it would give him the chance to do what he really felt he had a vocation for but would never otherwise have the courage or the means to pursue. And provided I supported him…".

"And did you?"

"Well, at first I had dreadful doubts, but soon I could see it would be the making of him, and 'd give him such peace of mind and a proper sense of achievement that I gave in and backed him up. So here we are and that's what happened."

What Katie omitted to add was that Hamish, having received what he had to admit was a glowing testimonial from his new boss, had been slightly mollified when matters finally came to a head. She knew he had been determined to stay in the force to nail some of the drug bosses in the Glasgow underworld but that, for some unspecified reason which she was only to learn much later, he had suddenly changed his mind. According to Hamish, his integrity and personal commitment to duty were exalted unusually fulsomely in this testimonial (even by the standards of the boss's known hyperbole), and he noticed that, unbidden, his length of service had been rounded up to the twenty years needed for an extra gratuity. When his conscience moved him to point this out he had been abruptly cut short and told not to make a fuss. *Sic gloria tempus mundi.* Was this another way of quietening him he wondered, buying his silence over the shortcomings of his own police colleagues. But he did not express any of this to Katie who happily remained unaware of his being potentially compromised.

Katie hoped Vanessa would quickly ignore Hamish having ever been in the police force. Though still rather nonplussed, she appeared satisfied with the explanation, wondering aloud what kind of 'back-up' Katie had been called on to give her husband, but impressed all the same. Lowering her voice she then told Katie it was better not to mention her enquiry to him, at any rate yet, and Katie, only too anxious not to get Hamish involved, readily agreed. As soon as Vanessa left she donned her walking-shoes ready for their visit ashore and went in search of Hamish. She found him where she expected to, on the bridge of course, talking animatedly to the first mate.

Chatting with Vanessa and thinking back to their early days together had reminded Katie what a complete contrast her own background had been to Hamish's. By English standards in the postwar fifties, she would have been regarded as extremely privileged whereas his early life on South, and later on North Uist in the Hebrides was austere to say the very least.

"Do you realise how lucky you were having such a stable and harmonious home life even though I know it was tough?" she asked him now as they went back to the cabin for their binoculars.

"Och, aye," he agreed, a little surprised at such a question. He knew her parents, by contrast, had both been born into the same kind of *latifundistas*, upper middle-class landed gentry who owned vast tracts of rich farming land in Central Chile, but he guessed what she was driving at. She had told him how in the fifties they had actually lived in Santiago very comfortably, surrounded by servants and every luxury, on the proceeds of their distant farms which were worked in a desultory kind of way by their agricultural tenants known as *"rotos"*. Absentee landlords such as Katie's parents had had it all their own way until the early sixties when Eduardo Frei was unexpectedly voted into power on the strength of his promises of 'land reform' among others.

With feelings of mixed loyalties Katie had told Hamish the story. How in vain Frei, poor man, tried repeatedly to push his Reform Bill through the Chilean Parliament but opposition in the Senate was always too strong for him to get more than an emasculated version through and, when at last it was voted into law, his reforms proved virtually impossible to implement.

Making a brave start by repossessing the worst-run of the absentee landlords' properties, she had told Hamish, had proved fatal. Though idealistic and honourable in intention the effort was flawed in execution and Frei ended by saddling himself with an intolerable burden of debt. On many *fundos* (large farms) what machinery there was had been left to rust and litter the yard, anything serviceable having already been stolen. The *'rotos'* had broken into the cellars and drunk all the wine, much of it vintage, and then under the influence had done even greater damage.

Some of Katie's cousins had been apoplectic: "Hardly a bottle, even of the Reserva, remained unbroken and the overpoweringly rancid smell in the cellars was legendary. Absolutely impossible to eradicate, my dear, and the fractured glass…,". Katie well remembered her cousins' tales of drunkenness and wanton damage to their vineyards with workmen lying stoned all over the place, snoring their heads off, impossible to rouse. And the danger to the farm animals of all the broken glass and splintered wood not to say lack of being fed.

"So you see, the *roto* simply cannot be trusted when it comes to giving him anything breakable at all, let alone valuable farm machinery. Frei must have been mad to ever think it would work," they had admonished Katie, whose sneaking sympathy for the poor man had grown, a sympathy she would never have dared admit to her parents.

According to the newspapers of the time which Katie promised to show Hamish later, President Frei's government had reportedly insufficient capital to invest in new - or even in good secondhand - working machinery and so the ultimate state of these farms tended to be far worse than when originally expropriated. Added to this was the fact that Frei's government was being sued by the landlords whose properties had been expropriated. Although a lawyer himself, the incoming President was quickly bamboozled by the legal experts employed by the Opposition. His new Bill was in tatters as they ran rings round him while the government was virtually bankrupted - to the delight of neighbouring countries like Peru and the Argentine Republic which feared copycat legislation being tried there. And which cashed in by selling the starving Chileans food, at an inflated price.

For many, such as Katie's family, Frei's downfall was a hollow victory, however. The canny few had already exchanged their tangibles for gold and fled the country, having first deposited their wealth in countries like Uruguay or Switzerland where not too many questions were asked, happy to receive gold no matter whatever its provenance. Katie's father had not been so quick off the mark, though he did opt to spend some time in Britain ostensibly for the duration of his children's schooling; reserving judgement as to when to go home afterwards. He had sufficient investments in London for the short term and was still determined to return to Chile once his finances had sorted themselves out and a less hostile government was back in power.

And then, shortly after Hamish had come onto the scene, Katie's father had had his fatal heart attack and her mother had been left to fend on her own. Katie had regarded this blow as the end of the world and would never forget how bleak life had seemed then; with no light at the end of the tunnel. One moment comparative affluence, and the next what seemed like abject poverty staring them in the face. While Katie's sister complained so annoyingly: "Mama, why can't I take a taxi? Buses are so dirty," - and so on, *ad nauseam* it seemed to her elder sister, her only solace was the budding friendship which was developing with this strange Hebridean who had sprung out of nowhere.

Although she still had many relatives and good friends back in Santiago, Katie's mother realised that when finally, in the late '60s, the Junta regained power and some of her less rightwing, more liberal, cousins started mysteriously disappearing, she would be a marked woman if she returned home. Besides, it was unlikely she would be able to reclaim any of her husband's former property, or even her own parents'. At least not without expensive lawsuits and a considerable greasing of palms. She would therefore be virtually bankrupt and at the mercy of her relations, and even then not certain of success - not a nice prospect with two children in tow. She yearned to return to her native country but forced herself to be practical. After all, even if she was obliged to claim assistance she would never actually starve in Britain whereas in Chile, with no such social welfare programme, she couldn't be so sure. Besides, the fear of having to spawn on relatives gave her pause.

Katie was in fact rising eighteen but her mother still insisted on regarding her as a child; her younger sister was just fourteen and seemed happy enough at her English day school. Their father having prudently taken out an educational endowment when he knew his health was failing, her younger daughter should at least be able to finish at her school provided Katie was able to support herself in the meantime. Another two years and then perhaps time to reconsider, thought Katie's mother.

Katie had recounted all this to Hamish shortly after they first met. She wasn't sure how much of it had sunk in since their lives had followed such totally different paths. She had the feeling he was paying rather more attention to her face, certainly to her figure, than to her words but at least he managed reassuring and sympathetic remarks at the appropriate moments. And he agreed with her that his own life of austerity was not without its compensations. At least in the remote islands of Uist they hadn't had that kind of upheaval to cope with and his frugal habits were so well imbued he had learnt to live on next to nothing, so he hardly missed life's little luxuries, the kind that Katie used to find indispensable.

Although hardly methodical (the artistic side prevailing, she said to herself), Katie nevertheless enjoyed making lists. She supposed she must have inherited this trait from her very efficient father, the only good characteristic she seemed to have gained from him, she thought ruefully. In her moments of introspection she acknowledged that she really took after her rather spoilt mother and lacked a real sense of "throughput". But she had also inherited her mother's intuition amounting to psychic powers, as well as her looks and considerable charm and artistic abilities. She realised her Latin temperament made her seem very different from English girls of her age but that this must be what had captivated the young Scotsman who had never met anyone quite like her.

*   *   *

Aware that this was all over a quarter of a century ago, Katie brought her mind back to the present and the exciting things they had in store. Handing Hamish his binoculars she followed him down the gangway on their way ashore to inspect the local birdlife.

CHAPTER EIGHT

As they progressed further south along the Corcovado Gulf the water gradually darkened but was still clear enough for the occasional shape of a playful dolphin to be glimpsed from the bridge. Through his binoculars Hamish could just catch sight of Chaitén on the mainland surrounded in haze. He fancied he saw a thin plume of smoke curling up from the volcano, but was assured by Jaime that it was virtually extinct and in any case the dangerous side was on the Argentine frontier! The little town of Futaleufù lay directly in its path but since the volcano had been dormant for hundreds of years, if not thousands, no-one ever gave it a thought.

Shortly before lunch they dropped anchor in Castro harbour to take on fresh fruit and delicious fresh lobster and bucketsful of *mariscos* (shellfish as Jaime informed Hamish). Small boats ferried those passengers who wanted it to go exploring. Making the most of their unexpected shore-leave, the passengers sauntered round the wooden-built fishing village pausing to admire the unusual painted wooden church with its intricate spire also carved from wood and the houses on stilts by the river's edge, a precaution against the fierce tides. Swollen by the freezing Humboldt current these tides had been known to sweep away everything in their path as had happened again two years previously, with devastating results.

"How amazing the speed, the speed with which they seem to have rebuilt everything," Katie marvelled to Hamish. "And how picturesque it all is now. I must say I don't quite see myself living in one of those houses perched so perilously on rotting wooden stilts out there. They seem to be just waiting for the next deluge." She thanked her lucky stars she didn't have to. They had once been threatened with floods in Marlow when the River Thames had burst its banks but luckily the sandbags had done their job though the nauseating smell had lingered for days; she didn't envy these poor people.

Everything was to be viewed against the constantly changing colours of the Andes which provided a dramatic backdrop of early morning azure, transmuting from grey to blue then green as the clouds passed overhead and the sun came lower. Hamish stopped to take a photo. The treeline, lower down, boasted some unfamiliar species worthy of examination Hamish thought as he trained his binoculars on them. And the fringe of trees round the water's edge was an unnaturally vivid green. He would have to inspect that as well. It could be phormiums growing there with their tough evergreen leaves or some other hydrophilous plant native to Chile. An unusual shrub with red trumpet-shaped blooms each with a scarlet and yellow throat caught his eye.

"Some kind of fuchsia perhaps?" he asked Katie. He caught its unusual fragrance as the breeze wafted it to him and picked a stem to take back for identification, regretting not having brought his book on wild flowers to add to their pile of luggage. Although he couldn't possibly admit it, Katie had been right when she had suggested bringing it.

Realising how unfit they were, Katie and Hamish puffed up the steep trail with some of the other ship's passengers to the local peak where they had a magnificent view of the whole peninsular and of their ship, now a tiny dot, moored in the bay below. Not only could they just trace the sea-route they had followed but they could vaguely make out where they were heading for and also some of the scattered islets they would have to weave in and out of.

Thinking of Mount Olive and the important part mountains and hills had played in the Bible, in the Old Testament as well as the New, Hamish realised what an advantage height gave and how one gained a sense of perspective being able to distance oneself from the clamour and bustle of the world around. Lovely material for a sermon on his return, he thought. No wonder Jesus had retreated frequently to small mounts or hills, or even a fishing-boat, to avoid some of the throngs, if not exactly today's tourist crowds.

Hamish took a deep breath of mist, inhaling the aroma of the herbs growing wild all about and focussed his binoculars, still ruminating on a possible sermon. Great activity centred on the *Skyros* and the few passengers left aboard were savouring in advance the many different delicious types of seafood being carried aboard and stowed away down in the hold. Turning to descend, the Blairs (Hamish and Katie) were thrilled to catch sight of some miniature scarlet begonias at the edge of the stream. There were other unidentifiable blooms nestling there, also brightly coloured, which after various dangerous manoeuvres Hamish managed to pick and present to his beloved.

"Quick, let me have the binoculars: there's some kind of songbird trilling away over there, rather like Shelley's skylark but bigger."

"It's a funny thing, each time you manage to see the damn' bird it goes behind a bush or a branch and you lose it. It's almost as if it knows you're trying to watch it."

"Here, let me have a look. I've no idea what that is…"

Hearing the ship's warning hoot they realised with alarm they were in danger of being left behind, and scooted back down the trail just in time to leap aboard the last dinghy ferrying them back before the ship cast off. A near thing; they vowed to be more careful next time.

As they regained their cabin they caught the sounds of a spat. "I told you, you shouldn't have given that cabin to…," Jaime rumbled. Then, hearing Vanessa's raised voice, they realised their cabin must be sandwiched between the Peruvian group and the Fuentes.

"I wanted them to be near Freddie and Ursula so that…Anyway, it's none of your business. It's *my* group."

Katie thanked providence that Hamish was normally so placid it would take a mountain to move before he so much as spoke roughly to her, let alone shouted. She wondered why Vanessa was getting so worked up but remembered what she had said about it having taken her over a year to perfect her plans and how uncooperative and sceptical Jaime had been. And how grumpy when he realised it would cut across his fishing holiday.

*   *   *

Together Hamish and Katie Blair scrutinized the passenger-list, recognizing more of the names now.

"Vanessa told me that she spent her schooldays in Lima where in fact she still has several good school-friends. She persuaded Manuel, the PR chap-cum-purser to give her the lowdown on the Peruvian contingent as she was sure she recognised one of them from school, the good-looking blonde with the conspicuous jewellery. But she's decided to bide her time before making her number with her," Katie told Hamish.

"Probably sensible if she's being shadowed that closely - a sure sign that the Peruvian mafia have their fangs into her. It wouldn't do to arouse their suspicions unnecessarily. Besides, with that huge group of hers, Vanessa must have more immediately pressing concerns."

"Even so, that body-guard chap strikes the fear of God into me - a real bull in a china shop!"

"Yes, you'd better steer well clear of him too, my darling. I don't want you running any unnecessary risks, however pure your motives may be."

Katie decided to change the conversation and drew Hamish's attention to a couple called Mackenzie, a loudmouthed English pair from one of the lower decks who appeared not to be able to hold their drink very well. "And we could well avoid those two as well, I reckon. She asked me loudly whether I was English yesterday and I rather prevaricated in answering."

Even though they now lived in England the Blairs still regarded themselves as Scots, or at least certainly not English, and did their best to escape the opprobrium usually reserved for the boorish English abroad (and nowadays the multitude of corny jokes about their name which assailed them wherever they went. Not even 'the Reverend Blair' saved them though Hamish hardly ever used his honorific). Natural modesty and police-ingrained caution meant that they preferred to keep a very low profile and, with Katie being something of a linguist, they usually got by comfortably enough without attracting attention even though their travel opportunities had been very few of recent years. Now that their only child, Matthew, was at last virtually independent and off their hands (though he still lived at home between jobs), they hoped to remedy that situation.

Mercifully the young in the party were all accommodated together on the lower decks away from the old fuddy-duddies, in the cheaper and less well-appointed cabins. The latecomers were also down there but the hard core of Vanessa's friends was all together on the upper decks.

Watching Katie in animated conversation with her cousins that morning Hamish had been relieved to note the tension and worry lines in her forehead had softened. At last her impish look had returned. Exchanging knitting patterns and cooing over the youngest member on board, young Baby Leon, seemed to be absorbing her. Had anyone in England dared suggest before their departure that Katie, normally totally immersed in parish life and its social problems, would look so relaxed so soon in such a scenario he would have been given short shrift. According to Hamish's churchwarden, Katie was absolutely indispensable in the parish: perhaps this had been part of the trouble. If he had not been so bound up in his own work with its endless diocesan meetings, parish committees and innumerable problems and commitments including hospital visiting - on top of all-consuming financial worries which seemed to beset every parish church these days - Hamish would perhaps have noticed before how strained she was looking.

And then there had been his attack, true not a severe one happily, but nevertheless enough to make him sit back and take stock. Did he really have a right sense of priorities? Or was he too bound up in himself and his soul-saving? And was he piling too much onto his longsuffering wife? Recently he had even been getting her to make some of the sick visits as she was so much better at this than he, so instinctively able to empathise and say the right thing that he gladly accepted her offer whenever he could. This was one side of his work he had less aptitude for, he had to admit, though it irked him to do so.

It was so good to see his beloved carefree and relaxed again, he realised he was glad he had yielded to her persuasive powers. He had really not wanted to come but now he was pleased they had despite the occasional moments of embarrassed discomfort caused chiefly by clashes in culture. And although Katie had warned him, he had been unable to prepare himself for some of the extreme rural poverty he was witnessing.

"Far worse in Bolivia, in Brazil and even in parts of the Argentine," she reminded him. "As for the slums round Lima, you simply wouldn't believe the deprivation and dirt some of those people regard as normal. Clean water? Forget it. In fact, Chile has a very good record compared with most of its neighbours. Remember that. And its public education is second to none. Its universities too."

Not only that, but the sickening sense of superiority displayed by the top social classes in Chile, Hamish found quite shocking. He well remembered the look on his wife's face as Jaime had pronounced nonchalantly on their way in from the airport:

"Of course I'm a pretty tolerant guy. You've only got to compare the way these peasants live..,".

"Who's he kidding? 'Exist' he means, not live," Hamish had thought. Even in South Uist the crofters enjoyed a better standard of living than what he was witnessing here. He hadn't dared look at Katie as he let his eye rove over the slummy over-crowded suburbs sprawled alongside the riverbed on Santiago's outskirts around the airport. Quickly they had passed on into an up-and-coming area, one of the newly-fashionable *varios* (districts) where Jaime had remarked:

"Here, for example, they at least have some pride in keeping their front gardens neat and tidy and the streets relatively litter-free."

"That's because the people who live here can afford to water their plants and also to pay the dustmen to remove their garbage," retorted Vanessa, who normally didn't take issue with her husband in such matters.

Jaime frowned at this letting the side down while Katie, surprised, thought back to the days when no-one had ever bothered to grow flowers out front (if indeed you had an 'out front') knowing they would all be picked overnight as soon as they were in bud, and on the market stalls or street pedlar's stand before one could say "bloom". Things had at least progressed since then, nearly half a century ago. The newly thriving middle classes who grew flowers in their (fenced) front gardens were now at odds with the oligarchy who needed the poor and down-'n-outs more than ever to keep their economy ticking over and their dirty jobs done for them, so as to keep their way of life nice and comfortable. It was the poor working endless unsocial hours who had continued to put money into the pockets of the erstwhile mega-rich even though they now numbered fewer than before. Still, most of them - while sitting on their undeclared original Goyas and Velasquez and Sèvres porcelain - actually paid taxes these days, whereas before they had always seemed able to wriggle out of them, usually by knowing someone who knew someone related to the Minister of the Interior.

Hamish had realised that this was not the moment to voice his concerns so turned instead to current preoccupations, thankful to let the women sort out the practical preparations for the journey. Thoughts of rich men, camels and needles flitted through his mind as Katie stole a look at him to gauge his reactions.

Still staring stonily at the miserable huddles of human habitation, Hamish couldn't resist asking Jaime:

"How do they cope for sanitation? Do they have el-sans, or running water even? Or cooking facilities?"

Vanessa suppressed a snort: "They wouldn't know how to use it even if you did give them sanitation; not that lot. And there's plenty of firewood for them to nick for cooking. And potatoes too," she added for good measure, "and even the odd chicken if they're quick enough to catch it…and don't get nabbed in the process."

Hamish had realised there was no point in pursuing this conversation either and was content to let silence fall. For the time being anyway.

$$* \qquad * \qquad *$$

That had been three days ago: it now seemed like a lifetime and Hamish was shocked to discover how quickly he had put it all out of his mind and was indeed even now revising his opinion of Jaime. Earlier that evening, having climbed up to the ship's top deck, he was luxuriating in the powerful scenery not unlike the north-western isles of Scotland though more majestic, thankful he had remembered to bring his good binoculars. He took the opportunity to ask Jaime for identification of the trumpet-shaped flower he had picked during their brief visit to Coinco, which now lay withered and inert in his palm.

"Oh my God, I've no idea of its proper botanical name but as kids we all used to call that 'blood-and-pus' because if you let it touch a raw place on your hand or anywhere it went bright red and yellow and smarted like the devil. You don't want to keep that." So saying Jaime snatched the limp flower and threw it overboard. Slightly taken aback, Hamish returned to his binoculars while Jaime went below. His spirits soared as he watched an albatross with its ten-foot wing span circling the ship, beautiful and yet somehow sinister and haunting. But he shivered as its shadow fell across the deck.

"A good south wind sprung up behind; the Albatross did follow, and every day, for food or play, came to the mariners' hollo!" The Ancient Mariner's words sprang to his mind just as he noticed the wind shifting round. Perhaps it was as well they weren't heading out to the Pacific proper where the twelve-foot wing-spanned albatrosses could be glimpsed if one was lucky. They were awesome enough like this he thought. His cheerful mood gave way temporarily to a more sombre one as he scanned the towering mountains on the far coast. They were already blocking out the sunlight and leaving the foreground black. Just the very tops were

glinting white reflecting snow in the weak sunlight from the north but cloud was sweeping in and it was getting noticeably colder. It still smelt distinctly autumnal though he knew winter was well on its way.

Then, quite unbidden, the following lines from Pablo Neruda came into his mind and buoyed him up again. Luckily his Spanish teacher had insisted on his having at least a nodding acquaintanceship with Chile's most famous and prolific writer of the moment. Katie, who had just joined him on deck, was used to his coming up with unexpected lines from Wordsworth, or Shelley, but this was a new departure and took her by surprise. Of course he had only read it in the English translation when he had been trying to get a feel for the country he would shortly be visiting, but it was a sentiment which gladdened his heart: *"Latin America is very fond of the word 'hope'. We like to be called the 'continent of hope...'. This hope is really something like a promise of heaven, an IOU whose payment is always being put off."* There spoke Neruda the sage, not Neruda the foreign-office diplomat, thought Hamish while Katie looked pensive, her mind on Neruda the Stalinist; and Neruda the Deceptive as so many of the young idealists following him came to feel ultimately.

Another riotous dinner followed that evening which completely banished this rather cynical frame of mind. Katie and Hamish were joined by Ursula and Freddie who were in festive mood. After several schoolboy type jests the men swapped anecdotes about the War, in which their fathers had both served, though only from 1941 on. They agreed in deploring the baleful influence some of the North American Air Force men who brought the Flying Fortresses over to Lossiemouth had had on the local girls. They discussed the even more obvious evidence of the fascination the Yankee troops exerted on the girls in the south of England, in ports like Southampton, during the massive build-up to the Normandy invasion. A sudden surge in the local birthrate nine months later had taken no-one by surprise. Talk then turned to the Falklands War while Freddie explained why large numbers of his friends back home had supported their neighbours in the Argentine. Even so, Uruguay - though fearful of its larger and more powerful neighbour - had nevertheless later chosen to go against it in rooting for Great Britain. And how, surreptitiously, they too - like Pinochet - had been of great help to Mrs Thatcher, now of course Lady Thatcher.

The Blairs exchanged covert glances. Hamish hoped Jaime was out of earshot or he might get another blast of pro-Pinochet propaganda when they were next together. But Vanessa and Jaime were surrounded by family and completely absorbed, able to forget their organising responsibilities for the time being.

Pleasantly wearied from a day of new experiences and much chatter, they all decided to turn in early to be ready for the morrow's fresh excitements, little doubting what they had in store. The noise level gradually subsided as people drifted back to their cabins replete and wearily contented.

Having never set foot in the Indian sub-continent, Hamish supposed conditions there were not that much different: sublime scenery intermingled with extreme squalor. And amidst it all moments of unexpected spiritual experiences prompted by the soaring beauty of the mountains, almost unbearable for their poignancy. He couldn't help feeling elated one minute by the sheer majesty of his surroundings, and the next miserable at the evidence of man's inhumanity to man, though he supposed that numbers here were nothing in comparison with what he might find in Calcutta for example. Seeing Katie's happy expression he resolved not be a killjoy, however, but to enter into the spirit of the party. He later tumbled into bed confused but cheered: the bonhomie had been infectious.

CHAPTER NINE

For as long as he could remember Hamish had suffered a recurrent anxiety nightmare which, though totally unpredictable in its many chameleon forms, was more likely to occur when he was beginning to relax after a mini-crisis of some sort. (Perhaps that was because he was more prone to indulge a little on those occasions and then to suffer indigestion, Katie suggested). Recently he thought, thankfully, he had grown out of it but that night the dream came back, this time with a distinct variation.

He was being chased by a swarthy aquiline-nosed Asiatic-looking individual (probably an Amerindian, he realised) who was throwing darts at him which glinted in the sunlight; or perhaps it was moonlight? His feet were glued to the ground as he struggled frenziedly to get away, and the man was gaining on him, rapidly. The missives turned into golden Inca manikins which started to rain down furiously on him as his legs were still pinioned and he found himself unable to move an inch. Katie later accused him of having grabbed all the bedclothes and thrashing them and then suddenly lying inert on top of them with only his eyes fluttering and cheek muscles twitching.

In his dream he watched, fascinated, as first one and then another crimson rivulet oozed slowly drop by drop from holes in his forearm, presumably made by the darts. They gradually transformed into bell-shaped trumpet flowers gleaming viscous and deep red but retaining their shape as each petal petulantly dropped to the ground and lay in its own scarlet pool, the trumpet meanwhile turning gold.

When Hamish woke up in a muck sweat gasping for breath Katie was already awake beside him with a glass of water. If she had waited till morning he would certainly not have remembered his dream in such detail but because it was so vivid he recounted it to her there and then, hoping to lay the ghost so that it never returned.

Reading his guide-book as he smoked his after-breakfast pipe, Hamish decided that if they ever got as far as Quellon, the southernmost town of Chiloé Island glimpsed out to starboard on the way through the Channel, he would buy Katie one of their distinctive ponchos which Vanessa had told him about. Its design was unusual, black and white geometric patterned bands on a grey woollen background sometimes enlivened by a scarlet *copihue*, allegedly exclusive to the south of the island - the same island which was now sheltering them from the main force of the ocean and which he hoped they would have time to explore. He might also fall for one their typical woven baskets which they had admired in the market at Puerto Montt. Vanessa had told him then, sharply, that they were half the price in Castro where they were made and could easily be found at the Feria Artesanal most days of the week, so not to buy them here.

For his part Hamish was determined to track down one of the Nercon churches whose interior, frescoed with a specially prepared white paint supplemented with guano and grey line drawings, was reputed to resemble marble. He had heard they were almost unknown outside the island but well worth the extra trip for the *cognoscenti* so he decided to try to bend the Captain's ear to see if this could somehow be included in their return itinerary.

After having sampled the delights of sightseeing in Castro and a late lunch, the ship pushed on to Coinco and Puerto Aisén which they reached in the early evening. The helmsman skilfully skirted round several small heavily wooded islets off the Chiloé archipelago and after further deft manoeuvring of the ship they moored for the night in a completely secluded unspoilt bay alongside some sulphur springs. At first the country looked totally uninhabited but gradually they could make out a cluster of low wooden shacks with pale grey roofs centred round the pontoon and, back behind it, an unostentatious covered swimming pool beside the steaming springs. Hidden from the sun now, the water surrounding the boats along the jetty was black and menacing and virtually motionless. The only sounds in the deserted landscape were from birds, eerie in the stillness, and the occasional plop of a fish.

Hamish and Katie quickly decided to go ashore as soon as a gangplank of sorts was lowered to explore the birdlife before it became too dark to spot some of the shyer songsters hiding in the hibiscus hedgerow. A shame most of the scarlet begonias would be over as they were reputed to be stunning in this region when they bloomed *en masse* but the phormiums and other humidity-loving plants might still be flowering, less spectacularly of course, but worth hunting out. Garlanded with binoculars and carefully avoiding puddles, they trudged up the steep hillside breathing in the dank smell of damp undergrowth while searching for signs of birdlife.

Just as dusk was falling and they had given up hope of seeing anything out of the way they were lucky enough to spot a rufous-breasted thrush tanager. As Katie snapped happily away on her new camera hoping there was enough light she noticed a commotion down near the sulphur springs. But they decided not to bother to investigate, at least not yet. When they got down to the landing-stage in the almost dark they could see nothing unusual. The place which had been a hotbed of activity a few moments earlier was now virtually deserted, just a few wicker lobster-pots and fishing nets with their coloured floats and other fishing paraphernalia and one or two scantily dressed children aimlessly kicking a football around in what passed for a play area.

They stopped to inspect the albino sheepdog guarding a small intensively cultivated vegetable plot. As they marvelled at his white velvety coat and brightly coloured studded collar and the huge variety of the vegetables being cultivated, many totally foreign to them, an overpowering smell of sulphur filled their nostrils and a voracious wave of midges swarmed all over them in the evening twilight. The hum of mosquitoes could be heard too. They understood now why Vanessa had been so insistent on their buying repellent before leaving the capital. Turning tail they fled back to the ship, but not before they had noticed the gardener trying to negotiate a very narrow path leading down to the ship's gangplank with a rickety cart piled high with produce. A curious time to be restocking, they thought, but then logical perhaps if they were to leave early in the morning.

But there was a slight change of schedule next morning (day three) to the delight of Sherwin, the American professor, but the disgust of the Peruvian mob who protested strongly; and the ship didn't leave after all. Sherwin, the retired archaeologist who had already whetted their appetite for exploring, had been telling them about some stone-age tombs in the vicinity which had apparently recently been discovered but were not yet open for inspection by the general public. However, with the help of his professional contacts Sherwin was determined to make the most of this unscheduled stop. Expressing his appreciation of the opportunity to study an unusual rock formation not far from the jetty he scurried off, binoculars, camera and notebook in hand.

The Peruvians, on the other hand, were obviously in a hurry to reach the next port-of-call where they allegedly had urgent business. They started to agitate and heckle the Captain asking repeatedly what the reason was for the delay but to no avail. The Captain was polite but firm in his insistence that they would cast off as soon as everything was shipshape and not before. To placate the passengers and take advantage of the unplanned stop he offered instead the choice of a visit to the fishfarms way out in the lagoon which they could visit by motorlaunch or a swim in the warmer "Termas" sulphur pools just behind the shacks abutting the jetty. This could be combined with a climb up to the top of the nearby hill which offered a stunning view.

Or sunbathing on deck, an option taken up by the brassy English couple (not of their party as Katie had discovered) who had obviously had far too much to drink the previous night and presumably needed to sleep it off. Katie noticed that the man, probably in his early forties, walked bow-leggedly and with a slight limp but she couldn't decide whether this was just the effect of overindulging or of an accident, or possibly of polio in his childhood. Had it not been for his triangular-shaped face and heavy jowl, he could easily have passed for an oriental. His wife, however, was the English-rose type slightly past her prime (though still in her thirties; that fair skin doesn't stand the sun or age well, she thought cattily), but she must have been pretty once in a vacuous kind of way. Now she looked faintly dissolute, maybe just hung-over, her little eyeteeth visible when she parted her lips, accentuating the creases round her mouth. Her expression hinted at permanent disappointment though she was pretty enough whenever she smiled. And she nagged her poor husband for good measure. ("I wonder why he puts up with it," thought Katie.) This was the couple she and Hamish had earlier decided to give a wide berth to so Katie was glad to leave them dozing.

Most people opted to go to the fishfarms but Hamish chose to swim in the sulphur pools instead. Though not brightly sunny, the weather was still warm enough and the mist had cleared. At least the water in the pool would not be anything like as cold as in the sea itself where it would be decidedly fresh. But he decided first to take his binoculars and camera to where he thought he had spotted a rare Andean hummingbird the day before. Disappointed not to find it, he climbed further up the steep hill which overlooked the bay for a final glimpse of the distant mainland volcanoes Minchinmaida and Corcovado, to his surprise already laced with snow.

Spotting a young American couple from the ship stumbling unwillingly up the path from the base of the Minchinmaida with their headsets clamped firmly over their ears and their eyes glazed behind wraparound fancy sunglasses, Hamish couldn't help feeling rather sorry for them. But sorrier still for their parents who must have forked out a tidy sum for them "to see the world" only to find they had come back with postcards, not photographs of what they had supposedly enjoyed seeing. As they gradually came within earshot he was intrigued to hear one drawl to the other, for a moment lifting his earphone: "So that bitchy Peruvian dame didn't get to her rendez-vous after all, I guess."

Hamish longed to ask them if they meant the blonde Señorita Gonzalez, alias Ballunde, or the Japanese/Peruvian Señora Watanabe - not quite the same kettle of fish to his book though both might fit the description - and how the Americans knew about the strange rendez-vous. But they passed him without registering and were soon lost to their inner musings - or, rather, their state-of-the-art iPods - scarcely casting their eyes on anything but the ground in front of them.

It reminded him, incongruously, of a time when he was still a student on a rock-climbing holiday in the Lake District. He had spotted a couple who, confronted with the most breathtakingly beautiful view above Derwent Water, had continued to sit in their car with the windows steamed up listening to frenetic pop music with their eyeshades on. He had longed to batter on the window to point out what they were missing but knew it would be badly received. Then as now he had given up, but he was still curious about the 'bitchy Peruvian dame' and the significance of her rendez-vous.

As he descended Hamish was wrenched back to the present when he saw, or thought he saw, a knot of people gathering around the back of the men's changing hut by the sulphur pool. As the unmistakable fumes drifted up to him he saw one man running and shouting orders, another humping something heavy onto the vegetable cart, and the rest looking simply bewildered. Was it an hallucination produced by the all-enveloping swarms of gnats making him imagine it all? Or something with a perfectly simple explanation? He caught up with Manuel the PR man, normally so smiling and affable, and asked him what was going on, only to be brushed aside with a muttered apology and a hasty getaway.

A few minutes later Manuel sought him out discreetly to make a fulsome apology and explanation: it seemed one of the Peruvian party, the sixth and most shadowy one, who obviously must have unobtrusively claimed his cabin minutes before they sailed after all, had slipped on the wet stones and cut his head open and had had to be taken further inland for medical attention. His head was bleeding profusely and with no vehicle handy and indeed no viable track, this had posed logistical problems, but in the end everything had been sorted out with the help of a fishing-boat which was able to ferry him further down the coast to nearer the medical centre. From there motorised transport would be available. Reassured, Hamish made to return to his cabin.

Stumbling down the mountain path he missed his turning and came across a fast-flowing stream. With faith in his boots he squelched across just as an arrow of translucent ultramarine tinged with russet skimmed across the water a mere couple of metres from his nose. His heart leapt as he realised this must be the Chilean version of a kingfisher about which he had read but had never expected to see as they were reputedly extremely shy. The shimmering colours were different but the swooping flight and dominant beak were unmistakable. His mood started to lighten as he tried vainly to focus his binoculars back onto the bird only to be distracted by the more frenzied gesticulations around the sulphur baths again.

He abandoned all thought of swimming and hurried back to the cabin where his wife - who had preferred the fishfarm visit by motorlaunch - awaited him in a state of high excitement.

*   *   *

On their way out to the fishfarm (which had proved to be something of a disappointment, Katie told Hamish), Jocelyn's camera had slipped over the side into the water. Since it was an expensive new digital given her by her husband, she jumped to retrieve it, herself slipping half-overboard as she did so. She had reckoned without the extreme cold of the water - the Humbold current, straight up from the Antarctic - and had had to be rescued and hauled back on board by boathooks and the crewman acting very promptly. Even though they were some distance from the salmon-pens all the splashing had thoroughly upset the fish there; they started leaping out of the water as people crowded to the other side of the launch to watch them, nearly capsizing the boat.

Then the engine stuttered and cut out and was found to be flooded, so by the time they managed to restart it with a spare part ferried out by rubber dinghy from the main-land, they were a great deal later reaching the salmon and then dry land than anticipated; and a great deal colder and wetter (especially Jocelyn). Some passengers were in a hugely emotional state, chattering nineteen to the dozen in voluble Spanish... and some were just thankful to be back on board in the warm with tempting smells of food wafting in from the dining salon and no serious mishap to report. Which was why Katie had only just got back ahead of Hamish and was dying for a shower but also anxious for news of Jocelyn and of her camera, and bursting to tell her husband all about it. Though happily strapped to her wrist the camera had nevertheless been fully submerged and might have suffered in the seawater. So Katie forgot to ask Hamish how he had got on and whether he had swum. He reminded her that, its being supposedly waterproof, the camera shouldn't have suffered too much from its lagoon dunking since the water there was scarcely saline. Katie only hoped it had been worth all that effort to salvage it and that her cousin would suffer no ill effects. Hamish bade his time, listening to her breathless staccato story sympathetically and deciding to keep his own until later when he could have Katie's undistracted attention.

In an attempt to catch up on his schedule, the ship's captain had decided to leave immediately after a late lunch for the long haul to the glacier and not to spend another unscheduled night in Puerto Aisén. Since the going outside the lee of the island, with access from the open Pacific, was forecast as rough with 12 knot tides, the Captain decided to issue all the passengers who wanted one with a knockout pill to see them safely through the night in the assurance that they would have reached calmer waters by breakfast time. (Hamish wondered what "'Elf and Safety" back home would have thought of this). The sight of the San Rafael glacier with its towering ice floes would then hopefully obliterate any unpleasant memory of earlier queasiness from their minds.

So long as they were still within the lee of the island the sea was smooth though not many people chose to go up on deck. Not another ship in sight and, with the approach of twilight very few birds, but Hamish was content to stare out into the distance with just his pipe for company. With nothing on the horizon he felt he could identify with those ancient mariners, *'We were the first that ever burst Into that silent sea.'* He felt at peace with the world and thankful they had made the effort to come so far. Gradually the wind freshened and white caps started to skitter across the waves as it grew distinctly colder so Hamish went below to rejoin Katie in the cabin.

That night there was less than a full house for the excellent buffet supper, all sorts of exotic fish and strange fruits which even Jaime hadn't seen before. The other Chileans all disagreed about the local names and Vanessa feared they would come to blows but the excellent Rapél Valley wine came to their aid, mellowing the belligerent ones. A stunning display included angelfish (sometimes called "twin-peaks") and garfish, two different kinds of eel, sea urchins as well as lobster, crabs and langoustines and the usual varieties of coastal fish including some which appeared to have no name or equivalent in English. Katie smiled as she watched Hamish being initiated by Ursula into the arcane mystery of tackling sea urchins. Just when he thought he'd finished one she said:

"Oh no! the real delicacy is the little bean-shaped thing which runs around inside it, like a Mexican bean with the colouring of a ladybird. Which you have to grab with your fingers - so - and pop into your mouth like this!" Ursula moved deftly then smacked her lips appreciatively.

Hamish didn't really fancy the prospect of an insect-like grub rolling round inside his stomach; he looked up and saw Katie staring at him, daring him to do just that so he took a deep breath and bravely copied Ursula. But he wasn't to be let off the hook just yet. The next trial was what the Chileans call *'locos'*. Ursula had looked the word up in her dictionary but could only find the usual meanings of 'mad' or 'crazy' which Hamish felt probably did apply to him, so he shrugged and went for it anyway.

"They look a bit like a lump of mozzarella, and are usually chewier, but I'm told they taste like abalones, which probably accounts for the Japanese going mad for them. The only drawback is you have to cook them for just the right length of time: too little and it's indigestible, too much and it goes rubbery and loses its subtle flavour. Haven't you seen the Watanabes and the others making a beeline for them? At the buffet lunch the other day they polished them all off before any of the rest of us could get near them. To my disgust. But," (looking around the table), "the Peruvian mafia doesn't seem to be with us tonight, does it? Must be why we've got a look in. I wonder where they've all got to?"

Ursula instinctively lowered her voice as they all looked round, examining the half-empty dining room. A pity so few of the passengers had made it as the number of diners scarcely did justice to the food or the legendary Chilean harpist who serenaded them with everything from Villa-Lobos and classical works to South American folk-songs.

Successfully ignoring the buffeting of the wind and waves above deck as the ship emerged from the shelter of the fjord into the full force of the Pacific's Humboldt current up the Morelada Channel, the harpist kept his small band of admirers captivated even when a sudden lurch made him lose a chord. So enthralled were they no-one else noticed that none of the Peruvian party had appeared, nor Sherwin nor the loud English couple, Tony and Sheila. Only the hardy Australians used to worse seas than this, and half of Vanessa's party, Hamish included, braved the conditions. Katie, a poor sailor, was glad to accept the offer of a *Stugeron* and retired below before the full force of the storm hit them, leaving Hamish to linger. She was asleep well before Hamish put out the light, he having ascertained by a visit to the ship's bridge that the passengers were in capable hands. He had gone up to admire the scenery so reminiscent of parts of the waters off his native Western Isles and to enjoy a last pipe but had been unable to see anything owing to the sea mist and the mountainous waves. Even the new moon hadn't helped visibility much.

"You have to go further south than this if you want to see our version of the Shetlands." He jumped as Jaime loomed up on him breaking into his thoughts. "Yes, we have our own Shetland Islands of the South but they're quite a lot nearer the Antarctic. You English," (Hamish flinched; he never liked being taken for English especially by his so-called fellow Scots and especially when they got the islands wrong), "never realise quite what distances are involved. You'll see. Goodnight," and Jaime lumbered off to his cabin leaving Hamish to linger a moment longer.

Hardly surprisingly, once the Australians had turned in, there did not seem to be anyone else about on deck on this foul night to share his nostalgia and marine smells, (even the stack-gas made him feel nostalgic), in fact his enjoyment of the scene, before the swell became too strong and he could hold firm no longer. Once they were totally out of the lee of the island, even Hamish decided it must be time to go below.

But as he still dallied on the bridge absorbed in trying to find the Southern Cross and then trying to identify Formalhaut, he overheard a whispered urgent conference between the Master and the first mate, apparently unaware that he was close by. His feeble grasp of Spanish meant he could only pick up the odd word such as "cadaver", "policia peruana", "oro" and "anoche" (which he took to refer to the night they had spent near the sulphur springs) but already his curiosity was aroused. He wasn't sure what "otros viajeros" meant but when the word Interpol came up he understood only too well. If Katie hadn't been sleeping so soundly and with such a mischievous look on her face when he returned to the cabin he would have woken her to ask. However, he decided it could all wait until morning.

CHAPTER TEN

Day four dawned shrouded in fog and quite sunless but at least the sea was now eerily calm and opaque. On deck, ghosts loomed from behind ventilators and vanished just as mysteriously, provided they didn't trip over a chair or a ring bolt, when sharp expletives would sing out against the background moan of a foghorn.

Hamish couldn't help sympathising with Vanessa when he overheard Jaime tell her, "You can't possibly have the group photo in this: you'll have to postpone it, at least until tomorrow. Not unless the weather cheers up before we reach the San Rafaele." She looked regretful, but reluctantly had to concede.

A light drizzle kept up monotonously, however, and few people ventured up on deck even when they unexpectedly put in at a tiny fishing village, allegedly to take on more water and 'mariscos'. Hamish wondered who the hardy fisherfolk were who had gathered these shellfish in such rough weather the day before. The young Señora Watanabe slipped ashore unobtrusively but was back ten minutes later, water funnelling off her cape and sou'wester. Hamish was amused to note how her normally mincing steps were made cumbersome by her clinging yellow waterproofs and the bucking gangway. She pretended not to understand English when Hamish asked her companionably whether she had managed to make her phone call from such a tiny port but scuttled away furtively without answering, her tight little mouth clamped shut. The ex-policeman was surprised at how scared she managed to look. It did not escape his notice either, even though the fog was still quite dense, that other people had slipped on board too, hunched up against the incipient drizzle, one of whom went straight to the master's cabin.

Katie joined him as they went below for a succulent breakfast, Hamish wondering idly if this could be the Interpol agent, but keeping this thought to himself. No point in alarming Katie unduly, especially as they were supposed to be here for a rest. He turned his mind to conscientious sightseeing and noticed that the ship, having now left the Pacific behind, had entered a fast-flowing river which eventually led them into a kind of lagoon where at last the drizzle stopped and the fog slowly began to lift. Hamish spotted a spectacular waterfall on the ship's leeside and, as they got closer, several smaller brooks cascading down the mountainside and tumbling into the sea lake, frothing as they did so.

"Funny," he remarked to Katie. "As we were churning along, all those little mountain streams looked from a distance like so many cream-coloured lacy frills all looped onto a ribbon. Against the black velvet of an Elizabethan doublet. You know - just like the one in that picture of Walter Raleigh on our calendar. Or the Earl of Essex (his illustration's in that book I'm reading). Then as we got nearer all that foam started to look exactly like the head on a frothy pint of Guinness. Almost a disappointment now to see what it really is. Although still rather spectacular," he added hastily as a Chilean cousin walked past, busily eavesdropping.

Hamish reminded his wife to get her camera and come up on deck. Suddenly the glacier was at last fully in view; the sun graciously fulfilled expectations and shone, fitfully at first, but gradually gaining in strength. The sight of the aquamarine/turquoise glacier in the distance was stunning and the differing colours reflected by the watery sun into a rainbow were dramatic. By now the entire ship's complement was gathering on the foredeck, necks craning, cameras clicking, tongues chattering excitedly, binoculars pinned against faces, all eager to enjoy the trip's highlight. For most people, even including the Australians, this was the furthermost point south they had ever been, at least 150 miles further south than the southernmost tip of New Zealand, yet still some 700 miles from Ushuaia and Puerto Williams (at the extreme tip of the South American Continent), as the Captain pointed out to his passengers over the tannoy.

"Except for those who - like us - have actually been as far south as the Tierra del Fuego," chipped in one of the annoying Argentine cousins. Vanessa scowled at the insinuation of it being their property, always a sore point. Unnecessarily provocative thought Katie, but happily none of the Chileans rose to the implied challenge which mention of this disputed territory often sparked off.

"I hope to goodness they don't go on to talk of the 'Malvinas' now seeing me here with Vanessa. That would be too much," Katie remarked to Hamish, looking round anxiously.

But with a sharp communal intake of breath and a surge to get a closer view, commonsense prevailed. Although the noise of crashing ice was now deafening they were not to be disappointed by the spectacular sight amid the shifting light reflections.

Without warning a tremendous boom reverberated throughout the ship as a huge chunk of blue, green and white ice crashed into the water nearby, sounding like a giant cannon. It slowly sent up a majestic spume of multi-coloured spray before it dropped back into the ocean, the sun visible through the vapour in the form of another fragmented rainbow. An enormous wave like a tidal tsunami rocked the ship; and people clutched each other in bewilderment, some nearly knocked flying. Manoeuvring so as to avoid the semi-submerged floes all around them, the helmsman skilfully steered his way through as the passengers held their breath. As soon as they got close enough to drop anchor some of the crewmen launched a dinghy and managed to hack off lumps from the 10,000-year-old ice rock into silver buckets. Twelve-year old malt whisky was then distributed in glasses sporting the ship's crest, each containing a lump of ancient ice, to everyone on board: the ensuing toast to the new millennium must have been heard the other side of the sound as it reverberated off the mountains opposite.

Small groups of passengers now began to disembark into the motor-launches towed along astern of the cruiser to go and inspect more closely the awesome sight - the glacier towering above them, suffused as it now was with sapphire blue and mysterious silver lights which projected ghostly shadows onto the water.

But it transpired there were only three launches in working order, the fourth having been hastily shrouded on deck, evidently suffering some setback on the way down. Encased in black plastic tied in with a red and white diagonal striped tape, it now boasted a large makeshift notice in Spanish, English and Japanese DO NOT TOUCH. As people crowded around gawping at it, chattering excitedly, Hamish too was preoccupied with wondering why. To his dismay he found himself separated from Katie in the scrum and wedged in by Tony, the obnoxious Englishman who still smelt of stale drink. As Hamish clambered aboard the launch, somebody cannoned into him sending his sunglasses flying into the drink. A sleek sea-lion chose that moment to inspect proceedings and Tony drunkenly swore he could see Hamish's glasses on the end of his wet nose. Katie, knowing Hamish hadn't got a spare pair, marvelled at the good grace with which he accepted Tony's raucous assertion and then clumsy apology as they settled into the boat. He even pretended to inspect the sea-lion for his sunglasses. She meanwhile found herself with Tony's wife in the other launch: rueful looks were exchanged but it would have been too disruptive to have attempted to change boats, not to say dangerous.

Towering over them as they threaded their way through the icebergs towards the monumental glacier several bizarre shapes, again of different sizes and colours, were threatening in their overhanging proximity. Sheila shivered as she looked up at them. She understood now why the Captain had insisted they did this trip before noon, before the sun had had time to cause too many to crash down upon the hapless sightseers dwarfed by this immensity of nature; and before it had moved round to cast even more profound shadows over the small boats.

It wasn't until they were back in their cabin preparing for lunch that Hamish explained why he had changed his opinion of Tony, who had clearly engineered their being thrown together in the launch (and was later suitably apologetic about the lost sunglasses). Katie meantime admitted that Sheila wasn't nearly so bad once you got to know her a little: in fact, really quite likeable if you could put up with her awful neighing laugh and inane chatter. She knew that her husband always liked to see the best in everyone whereas she (she blushed to admit it) was inclined to be blinded by outward appearances and to make snap judgements, often wrong as it turned out. So she was intrigued by what Hamish had discovered about the awful Tony though it would still take a lot of persuasion to make her change her mind about him.

"Tony related quite a complicated story to me. He said that, after graduating well in art history in Sheffield, he had been for ten years a curator at Nottingham Museum. They had been ten good years but, like most regional museums in Britain, since it was chronically short of funding he could see his days there were numbered," Hamish told Katie.

"Was that when he went to London and met Sheila?"

"Yes. He had drifted to London in search of at least enough pay to live on but as soon as, rather impetuously, he decided to get married (against his family's advice and with dire warnings from them about repenting at leisure) they had a rough time and still no money of course, which made it worse."

"I know, Sheila told me about it," confirmed Katie. "She said they couldn't afford to start a family, and sounded pretty fed up about it."

"He subsisted on freelance work, writing for learned journals and doing valuations for Sothebys, probably also for Christies; and maybe other leading auction houses too. But money must have been tight, very tight. I gather he was occasionally consulted by private collectors interested in acquiring South American or, more specifically, Nazca and Mochica pottery which he'd got to know quite a lot about, especially the Mochica. You probably know more about this than I do: I must admit I'm completely zero when it comes to pottery and so on." Hamish was reaching for his Hamlyn edition of *Precolumbian Terracottas* as he spoke.

"He even tried to get a slot on the *Antiques Roadshow* but was turned down as the Beeb already had their longstanding specialist readily available. Tony was pretty gut-wrenched about that. Understandably, as it would have opened so many doors."

"Aren't Nazca and Mochica quite different periods and workmanship?" queried Katie. "From the little I know about it, I seem to remember the Mochica civilization - or Moche, or whatever they call it - after where its centre was - goes back as much as a hundred years BC; whereas the Nazca's not really that old. In fact, it's much younger; I think it stretches up to as recently as the Inca conquest in the fifteenth century. I s'pose they've got quite a lot of overlap in the similarity of their pottery design - though I know they used colours quite differently. But to the uninitiated it probably all looks similar enough. At least to the average layman like you and me."

"I don't know about that. All he told me was that he'd been off to Milan to consult some private collector there who allegedly had some priceless stuff including a polychrome ceramic vessel representing a jaguar. It had unusual geometric motifs all round the edge, of a kind he'd never seen before; it only stood about five inches high but was said to be unique. From northern Peru (present-day Ecuador), supposed to be. But, I gather, the Italian sent him off with a flea in his ear. Said he wasn't prepared to sell to an unknown bidder, and even if he changed his mind it wouldn't be to Tony. So Tony was very disgruntled about that… especially as it appears the piece was an absolute one-off. Chance of a lifetime in fact."

Hamish found an illustration in his book of a vaguely similar piece from Costa Rica to show Katie. "Rather like that, he said, only smaller."

"Sheila told me that in desperation she had got a job as a waitress and Tony had turned to a millionaire collector in London. Of dubious character so it seems, whom he eventually persuaded to give him a commission. Which was to try to verify the provenance and authenticity of some gold pieces thought soon to be coming on to the market, again from Peru, as apparently it had suddenly started to be flooded by fakes. Some of these artefacts were extremely rare and included one notable piece of erotica which nobody is supposed to have seen before…. Or at least admitted in dealing circles to having seen. So his millionaire friend was deeply suspicious about it, but all the same dead keen if it was proved to be genuine."

"That's just it. You remember Freddie was telling us it was even being whispered among the *cognoscenti* that the odd exhibit in the famous Gallico collection had been replaced by a clever fake; how he knows I've no idea. And it's apparently well-known that some unscrupulous museum keepers in Peru have turned a blind eye to the substitution of copies - not even particularly well-made copies at that - of one or two of the least reputed artefacts, which, allegedly of course, have disappeared into the maws of the more avid private collectors. Never to be seen again probably."

Katie who had been fiddling with her camera, suddenly clicked it shut, shaking her head in wonder and dismay at what she had just learned. "Come on, we'll be late for lunch if we don't hurry," she urged, having inspected her last picture.

"Just a sec," Hamish continued, anxious to finish his story. "Tony confided that since the National Museum in Lima and the Arequipa Museum were the only officially recognised owners of such exquisite pre-Colombian gold artefacts in Peru (apart of course from Señor Gallico), and since both denied all plans to sell, he was stumped. He appeared to have drawn a complete blank."

"But wasn't that when…?" Katie interrupted.

"Yes, he was still hopeful he might, with luck, be able to track down one of the famous pieces of gold with extremely beautiful *repoussé* decoration, supposed to be a unique Mochica gold puma skin, which used to belong to the Moche museum in Sipán up north. So he put out feelers. Nobody was quite sure of its whereabouts now as it had been stolen some years ago in a murky incident which had implicated just about everybody who'd ever come into contact with it. The usual thing. It wasn't even as if anyone knew what it had been used for - probably ceremonial as the Moche were known to worship the jaguar and, presumably, also its cousin the puma."

Hamish was still determined to finish his story before they made their way along the corridor to the dining-salon.

"But he'd had a tip-off from a friend in Arica, the northernmost port up on the Peruvian/Chilean frontier, of more smuggling activity into Chile. He said similar pieces of decorative gold work were being carefully concealed amongst the contraband tobacco which seems to cross the frontier at will - all under the control of the Peruvian mafia (who are said to 'own' the customs and excise there) and who get their own specified cut, of course."

"Do you think that could have anything to do with our Peruvian contingent on board?" Katie burst in excitedly. "They keep on mentioning 'gold' whenever I manage to eavesdrop on them and they're not speaking that outlandish mixture of Japanese and Peruvian-Spanish?"

"Yes, I do. Just wait. Which is why Tony elected at short notice to pursue two of the most notorious members in this field known to be operating in Chile." (The Watanabes in the nextdoor cabin, Katie decided. Unless one of them was Lopez-Jimenez, the last-minute no-show who was supposed to have had the horrid accident outside the sulphur baths in Coinco.)

"And hence with his friend's help Tony's last-minute decision to come on the *Skyros* cruise. Even though sending for his wife at the eleventh hour - as much for camouflage as anything - and having to pay her full air fare must have caused a severe strain on their exchequer; not to mention quite a lot of gossip among the neighbours at home. It was only by virtue of the fact that all drinks on board are included - as Tony explained - and that he had found slightly cheaper cabin rates that he was managing to keep afloat."

"That would explain why he is so desperate to get results. And also why he's so determined to get his money's worth on the boat," Katie rejoined, before adding: "I suppose to justify the expenses he hopes his London patron is eventually going to meet?"

"Got it in one. He was pretty sure he was onto something juicy and if he played his cards right he hoped he might make it pay off. After all, the piece is supposed to be unique. And nobody seems to know where the hell it's got to."

So saying, they finally set off for lunch.

CHAPTER ELEVEN

Having vainly attempted to contact Señor Gallico while in Lima to negotiate a purchase if indeed anything there was to be sold, Tony had unwittingly signalled his interest to the mafia bosses in Peru. Unaware of how efficient their networks were, he imagined that two thousand miles away in southern Chile he would be out of their clutches but this was to underestimate the Peruvian mafia (in reality controlled by the even harder-nosed Japanese mafia).

The beautiful blonde's protector, whom Tony had taken for merely a bent policeman, turned out to be much more sinister - and powerful - than that. This much Tony had just gleaned from a coded message sent him via the Captain's radio. He had earlier faxed a coded report through the post office in Coinco to his Lima contact and this reply warned him that, owing to the vagaries of satellite communications, the 'protector' was still awaiting instructions as to whether or not to threaten (or "neutralise") this troublesome nosey Englishman. So to be extra vigilant! To this extent Tony could be grateful for the bad weather and poor radio reception they had been enduring the last couple of days, he acknowledged as he scowled at the watery sun, "but it won't last. One man's meat…,".

The coded message had also advised Tony to make discreet enquiries of the 'Interpol agent aboard' but since he had no idea who this might be and no way of finding out short of asking the Captain outright, he was stumped. Until he hit on the idea of approaching the man rumour said was an ex-copper back in Scotland, or possibly even 'from Scotland Yard'.

Katie and Hamish chuckled for a moment over poor Tony's conundrum, sympathising with his predicament. But the realisation that Hamish's past might catch up with him and draw him back into getting involved in police matters again suddenly struck a chill into Katie. The prospect especially alarmed her when she remembered he had come out here essentially to recuperate and get away from all his preoccupations back home. Would he be strong-minded enough to resist such a challenge?

"On no account are you to get involved in this," she told him sternly as she noticed his nose twitching with anticipation.

"Don't worry, I shan't," he laughed, realizing it would be totally unfair to her for one thing. And really stupid to risk setting back his convalescence for another.

Hamish had no idea how this piece of intelligence, his police background, had circulated but came to the conclusion that Vanessa at least must have been privy to it and had probably mentioned it to the Captain when going through the passenger-list. How "Señora" Watanabe was involved in it all, Hamish could only speculate; presumably she represented the Japanese mafia, said to control everything. And how did they manage to communicate with the other *mafiosi* on shore, he wondered. Satellite would be far too indiscreet and open to prying eyes (assuming it worked here), with all that cumbersome equipment. Even using the Japanese language was hardly foolproof.

On Hamish's probing to find out what made Tony so certain about the protector, he had hesitantly continued to explain. Hamish also asked him about an altercation he had witnessed during their brief visit ashore when Tony had appeared to brush off, rather angrily, remarks made by Ari, one of the younger members of Vanessa's party. Normally Hamish would not have displayed such curiosity about an incident which really didn't concern him, but in the circumstances and because he had seen Vanessa and Jaime in earnest conversation with Ari whom they appeared to know well, he thought it worth investigating.

Tony explained that Ari, who in fact was Jaime's youngest nephew, usually lived in Puerto Rico but had spent some time in Lima before coming south on the cruise. Ari too had initially felt the expense of the trip well beyond him and it was only because Uncle Jaime had offered to subsidise his fare that he had been able to meet up with his cousins on board so, without realising, he had joined the same flight as Ursula and Freddie to travel down from Lima. He was obviously completely *au fait* with the details, such as were known, of the gold heist but also seemed to be in cahoots with some of the Peruvian contingent. "Hopefully not the Mafiosi set," whispered Tony.

For some reason not immediately apparent, Ari must have been nominated by Señora Watanabe to warn Tony off from interfering in their patch but history did not relate quite why or how - yet. Or, rather, Tony had not yet fathomed it. He related to Hamish how he had not taken kindly to being told what to do by a spotty youngster he'd never set eyes on before who, moreover, on enquiry appeared to be skint. Even if he was the nephew of the organiser of the large group obviously so much in the Captain's favour, Tony still didn't see why he should comply with this gratuitously offensive command. But being on foreign soil, he decided to be more circumspect in future, still continuing to keep a lookout out for any suspicious behaviour on Ari's part; and also keeping a wary eye out for the Peruvians, particularly the mysterious Lopez Jimenez.

Katie who had asked Jocelyn about Ari and found out the brief essentials of his background, had not thought to brief herself about his powerful protector as well. She assumed, however, that she now knew what had made Hamish so pensive as, back in the cabin, they prepared for lunch. Delicious *humitas* and seafood had been promised. That at least should take his mind off things for now.

*   *   *

"Poor man. That's obviously why Tony was so interested in Freddie's story of the theft at the exhibition in Lima," Katie remarked to Hamish, noticing for the first time how grey his sideburns had become. Perhaps he should take a tip from his wife and give them a dash of colour.

"I was getting rather fed up with Tony hanging around our group on that first evening, listening in to Freddie's story and so forth, and pretending to be in the know and making snide comments. But I had no idea then how much danger he was in. And I definitely didn't take to Sheila whom I took for a blowsy barmaid out on the scrounge. I'm sorry about that now as in fact she's really rather nice, and pretty naïve. She obviously has a helluva lot to put up with and without much support from her family I gather. Or any from his. And she's certainly having to box above her weight now."

"Whatever do you mean by that?" Hamish was intrigued by his wife's unusual turn of phrase, unusual for her who loathed boxing, that is. Katie promised to explain later after lunch but was determined not to miss out on the tempting looking fishy hors d'oeuvres. Years of habit had made her instinctively cautious about discussing police - or for that matter, parish - affairs anywhere where she might conceivably be overheard; a trait which Hamish applauded and encouraged.

The Blairs made a point of chatting to the Mackenzies (Tony and Sheila) as they settled down to their succulent buffet lunch in the dining saloon but tactfully rejoined Vanessa's party for coffee after. By now they seemed to be on nodding terms with most of those on board and had found several agreeable companions in the group including Freddie and Ursula, who proved a valuable source of information on Peru as well as their native Uruguay, and were always good for a wisecrack. Ursula's dry wit delighted Katie and Hamish enjoyed swapping reminiscences of service in the British Navy with Freddie who, in spite of his Uruguayan passport actually held dual nationality and so had served in the Royal Navy in the closing months of world war hostilities.

Freddie seemed to have kept up with some of his British naval friends, one of whom was now a Rear-Admiral in charge of a big naval hospital in Pompey, with whom he regularly exchanged Christmas cards. He also appeared to be very well connected in Lima, with politicians as well as with the medical confraternity; altogether several irons in the fire. Perhaps this accounted for his hotline to some of the Peruvian government Ministers and his evident ability to keep abreast of things, Hamish decided.

After their boozy lunch, rounded off with *aguitas* (Chilean herbal teas), they all dispersed to their cabins. Although still early afternoon, the wine was having its effect. Hamish sat down to read his book but had just drifted off when he was roused by an urgent knocking. Katie was painting her toenails and was annoyed at being disturbed. She reluctantly opened the door to reveal a distraught Tony clutching a fax which, it transpired, warned him in a cipher message that he was about to be framed for the murder of one of the Peruvian thugs. Although Hamish was *au fait* with most of Tony's story, Katie only knew the snippets Hamish had had time to pass on to her. So Tony repeated his story to her while Hamish prepared to light a pipe which always helped him to think. Then, remembering where he was, he hastily stuffed it away again.

Even Hamish was unaware of the most recent development, however. It appeared that while in Chiloé, Tony's suspicions of "Señor Watanabe", the junior of the mafiosi on board, had been heightened when, trailing him by binoculars he had seen Watanabe leave the ship furtively carrying a smallish bundle wrapped in heavy-duty plastic which nevertheless seemed to weigh quite heavily. Following him down the shoreline to the makeshift jetty where the fishing-boats were tied up, Tony watched him climb into a very dilapidated dinghy after a short parley with its owner and the exchanging of what Tony assumed were dollars (far more negotiable than escudos). They then set out towards the middle of the fjord. Tony had then lost sight of them but ten minutes later the boat reappeared pulling hard for shore.

Deciding to inspect further, Tony quietly tiptoed down the wooden platform alongside the jetty hoping to catch up with the fisherman and was just in time to glimpse some kind of fracas between him and his erstwhile fare. Edging forward for a better view he nearly trod on a moorhen nesting at the water's edge, the squawking giving him away. He retreated quickly but not before he had been spotted by Watanabe, who must have kept this gringo under observation until he was safely back on board before apparently losing interest in him. Tony thought the Peruvian then followed him back onto the ship but couldn't be sure though he still felt uneasy.

When, however, this same Watanabe's body was later found face down in the reeds at the sea shoreline, stuck fast in the mud between the changing hut and the gang-plank, with a knife in his back, Tony was absolutely dumbfounded. His knees buckled as he heard the news. The man had stayed on shore! All suspicion naturally focussed on the man who had been seen following him the previous day, acting so furtively - according to yet another fisherman, (a discreet hint from the first mate bringing Hamish up to date here). The small knot of fisherfolk and gardeners who had gathered at the scene, all curiously subdued, melted away as soon as the *guardia civil* arrived, noticeably scared.

Fortunately the Captain had had the foresight to cast off as soon as he got wind of trouble and before the police arrived on the spot: it would hardly do for his passengers to learn of such sordid goings-on (panic could very quickly set in), his ostensible reason being fear of missing the tide - and hence his schedule.

"Señora" Watanabe - who it later transpired was not the dead man's wife but his partner in business and sent to spy on him by the mistrustful higher echelons of the Japanese mafia - did not react to his death as hysterically as Tony had feared she would. No sooner had they set sail than she emerged from her cabin dry-eyed and sharp-nosed. To his amazement and no little concern, she eyed him speculatively and then smartly disappeared. She soon turned up again on deck with a bunch of faxes in her hand looking distracted but hardly emotionally upset. This made Tony wonder whether it was in fact Lopez Jimenez and not Watanabe who had bitten the dust as there was still no sign of the former. The other Peruvians, even Consuelo's minder, although they obviously disliked her, treated "Señora Watanabe" with some deference - which only served to increase Tony's misgivings and make him wonder what their relationship with her was, as also with the defunct man (whom he now was beginning to be convinced must have been Lopez Jimenez, the alleged no-show).

The fax in Tony's now shaking hand announced, in cipher, that the knife had been bought locally in Chiloé and the shopkeeper had testified to its having been purchased by a 'gringo', a gringo with a slight limp. It was small comfort to Tony that in this part of the world which was currently waging a fishing-war with the Peruvians, it was not only the Anglo-Saxons who counted as gringos but the Japanese and even some Peruvians as well. The term could even have been applied to young Ari, though that might be stretching it since he spoke perfect Peruvian Spanish, hardly looked European and didn't really have a limp.

"I'm pretty bloody certain," Tony blurted, "this man who owned the dinghy, the fisherman, was furious at not being given a big enough cut in on the deal and was the one responsible. But how, without the local flaming patois, am I ever going to make them understand this, let alone believe it? "

Hamish privately agreed. Even if he'd had fluent Spanish Hamish thought there would have been precious little hope of his not being fingered in some way. Foreigners made such convenient scapegoats and the nearest British Consul was 700 miles away in Puntas Arenas; besides, what could *he* have done even if he had been nearer the scene? How to prove that the accused, Tony, had never carried a knife, was totally lacking in any proficiency with knives or indeed with any such weapon, having in fact never even owned a penknife? It simply wasn't his genre. He would also have been quite unable to find and buy any kind of knife unaided in such a godforsaken spot....The language alone would have stumped him. But of course no-one trying to pin the blame on him would ever stop to listen to that.

As they were deliberating what to do there was another knock on the door. Sheila stood there in great agitation hoping to find Tony to warn him that some very officious and disagreeable fellow speaking halting English had come to their cabin accompanied by a crew member, slightly less forbidding but still granite-faced, who said he had a warrant for Tony's detention. Since Sheila's shower was already running she had pretended Tony was under it and promised to relay the summons to present himself immediately to the Captain's cabin. Sheila had not seen the fax and since delay would be fruitless and might only serve to increase suspicion and exacerbate feelings she pleaded with Tony to go straight away and explain the mistake which must obviously have been made.

With misgivings Hamish agreed this might be best and offered to go with Tony to talk to the police but Katie intervened. Since she was the only one who had fluent Spanish she should be the one to go. (Damn her toenails!). Besides, she had already made her number with the Captain whose wife she had chatted to at length in harbour and whose children were exactly the same age as her cousin's children. She also secretly hoped in this way to prevent Hamish from becoming too closely embroiled in the affair. So in the end it was Katie who, against Hamish's better judgement, accompanied a shaken Tony and tearful Sheila (who refused to be left behind) to the Captain's cabin where the *Guardia Civil* awaited them impatiently, smoking furiously, while Hamish went on up towards the bridge to think, taking his pipe with him.

As he puffed away Hamish spotted young Ari, skulking in the shadows, and realised that if he were to interview this rather dissolute-looking young man, tact would have to be of the essence given his relationship to Jaime and the paramount need for Hamish not to antagonise his erstwhile hosts. So he decided to delay taking action even though he was distinctly curious about Ari's rather officious warning off of Tony. So preoccupied was he, he had even managed to singe his spectacular marmalade eyebrows in the process of lighting up. Still engrossed, he initially missed the signs of something unusual happening up on the bridge.

When Hamish eventually arrived up there he discovered that there was a stranger talking to the Captain and the first mate in heavily accented and halting Spanish. Waiting for a moment as he tried to identify the accent, Hamish was sure he recognised that voice. As he puffed away he was disconcerted, amazed rather, to realise from the way the man, obviously suffering from blocked sinuses, cleared his throat that the voice did indeed belong to his old friend and police colleague Aidan Johnson. He'd heard that Johnson had apparently been seconded to Interpol since they had last worked together on the NCS (National Crime Squad) a quarter of a century previously but had hardly expected this turn up for the book. Obviously Tony's intelligence was way in advance of his, Hamish realised. At first he wasn't absolutely certain but that way of sniffing and repeating the question coupled with a kind of 'hrrmph' when Aidan wasn't convinced by the answer was unmistakable.

Johnson still hadn't seen him so Hamish bade his time listening in until the first mate caught his eye. "Ah, a compatriot of yours, I believe?"

Aidan Johnson's amazement and delight at seeing his old mate was unfeigned and Hamish quickly brought him up to date with Tony's story and the background as seen from an insider's point of view while Johnson, having assured himself of Hamish's discretion, explained why his services had been called for and what he had gleaned so far.

The Captain returned to his cabin with obvious relief while the first mate, who allegedly had virtually no English, was distinctly curious as to what was going on. He returned to his duties on the bridge with not a little amusement at these *gringos*, assuring them of his cooperation should it be needed and muttering under his breath in the choicest local Chilean about their strange habits and expressions.

Relieved to be able to reclaim his cabin, the Captain found that the police must have finished their preliminary interviewing of Tony since, leaving the ashtrays full, they had all departed, presumably in the police launch for the nearest station. It was a pity in a way that the Interpol agent had not arrived on board earlier since he could have dealt with the truculent and often vainglorious local force which, the Captain well knew from experience, had to be handled with kid gloves (and the odd hundred escudos or two) if their feathers were not to be ruffled. But at least they had stopped short of demanding proper bribes from him once they had realised that he was *persona grata* with their Commander-in-Chief.

Sometimes in fact they even fed him little tidbits of useful information such as news of the impending arrival in the region of foreign dignitaries or of Argentine snoopers on the lookout for drugs or illicit cigarettes. In fact, they had even been known to look the other way if one of his passenger's visas was not entirely in order. He felt by now they had established a perfectly workable *modus operandi* to the satisfaction of all concerned, so was able to tolerate more easily the Napoleonic gestures of the *gauleiter* and the ignorance of his 'foot-soldiers' in a mutual feeling of superiority over these pathetic 'gringos'.

CHAPTER TWELVE

Hamish could see that Katie was trying to disguise her apprehension that Aidan, whom she had never met before, would gradually involve her husband more and more in this shady matter. She obviously considered it should really be no concern of his, Hamish's. But, despite the state of his health, she knew her husband would not be able to resist being first intrigued by and then subtly dragged into the action; and it was obvious she was torn between fears for his safety and not wanting to stifle his natural instincts.

Katie listened anxiously as, in low voices, they brought each other up to date. Hamish already knew from Freddie's satellite conversations with Lima that the 'coprophilous' Peruvian Minister of Justice had had to resign over the fiasco of the gold theft as his enemies in the fragile coalition government sought to discredit him and through him the Prime Minister/ President. It could only be a matter of time before the Communists, sensing their advantage, pressed for new elections if and when the Justice Minister's handful of supporters withdrew from the government. So time was of the essence if a political débacle was to be avoided.

Aidan now showed Hamish a newspaper cutting from the Santiago 'Mercurio' describing how two wellknown Chilean art thieves had been wheeled in for questioning and detention despite supplying strongly supported alibis; and told him how slurs in the Argentine press had implicated *their* President who was now threatening to sue for libel and have the offending newspapers shut down. So things were not standing still. This Señor Gallico must really wield some clout. But what his erstwhile colleague then told him made Hamish's hair stand on end.

By now, to ensure not being overheard by any English-speaking passenger within reach, they had retired to the cabin provisionally allotted to DCI Aidan Johnson, not far from the Captain's, and had taken the precaution of taking along a bottle of Scotch. Hamish felt in duty bound to explain to Aidan that he had promised his wife not to become too closely involved but that that wouldn't prevent him from taking a passive observer's role and passing on any intelligence he might happen to glean of course.

Aidan said that the *Skyros'* sister ship on her return voyage to Puerto Montt had berthed at Coinco near the sulphur pools the day following Watanabe's disappearance and subsequent supposed murder, and the next day on heaving up their anchor line which had become fouled, the crew had brought to the surface some partially decomposed pieces of a gruesome looking body, probably another fisherman's to judge by the tattered remains of oilskins. First reaction, not unnaturally, was that this was Watanabe (supposedly the man who had disappeared) but on closer inspection it soon became obvious this could not be so if only because of the advanced stage of its decomposition.

The same applied to the missing fisherman who had been reported *desaparecido* the previous year, so the Chilean police who had now arrived on the scene were totally confused and bewildered. 'Bodies' were not very frequent in their line of work: to have two - and possibly a third - all at once and at this time of year, the quiet season, threw them completely. If the remains were not Watanabe's - obviously as they had been there some time and, besides, were certainly not Asiatic - whose were they? Initially they were assumed to belong to the brother of the man who rowed the Peruvian Watanabe out to the fjord: he was known to have disappeared six months previously at the beginning of the tourist season and without any obvious explanation. The local police had maintained a wall of silence and the widow, not having any influential connections, had had to content herself with a complete brush-off. Being only semi-literate and lacking in male support, the poor woman had had to grieve unconsoled and ignored by officialdom as well as by her dead husband's debtors.

The victim was also thought to have been very thick with Lopez Jimenez - the mysterious no-show on the passenger list - but the results of *DNA* tests were not yet conclusive. (Things moved slowly in this godforsaken backwater, it seemed, even worse than in the Western Isles! Even with satellite communication things took their time, Aidan complained). However, it was common knowledge that this fisherman - the long-dead one - had been mixed up in some kind of smuggling ring. Cigarettes perhaps? hardly. Drugs most likely, but because customs men in the archipelago were stretched to the limits and the lengthy indented coastline was difficult to patrol, there had not been enough manpower or evidence to haul him in. Besides, the police on this island all came from the same extended family with links into the excise service and it would have been difficult to convince them of the saneness of making an example of one of their own boys - particularly where some held the view that drugs for one's personal consumption were OK. What was so wrong with smoking home-grown grass anyway? Or if not home-brewed, from only just down the road? (and from there it was only a short step to peddling the hard stuff) they asked; and refused to be convinced by what they saw as North American and European hypocrisy.

"Latin America," Johnson sniffed but was corrected by Hamish "No, no. South America - it's different. Well, at least down here in Patagonia it seems so. At least we don't have to contend with all that Mexican and Costa Rican riffraff as well."

"Don't tell me there's any difference in brands of corruption here. I've seen too much of it, I know: they're all as corrupt as each other from Panamá to Tierra del Fuego," Aidan countered.

Hamish drew in breath but thought better of making a cheap geographical point, and they agreed to leave it at that, Colombia, Panamá, Peru, the lot; conveniently forgetting what went on in their own part of the world where they hailed from, one from the Western Isles and the other from south of Glasgow.

Aidan then turned his attention to chivvying his police contact in Puerto Montt by satellite communication for a definite identification of the *DNA* which they hoped they would get from a hair sample taken from the newly recovered corpse. "Today, not mañana," he pleaded.

*   *   *

Meanwhile Tony knew he was in for a rough time. Although the Captain had managed to keep to his schedule and cast off from Chiloé more or less on time without waiting for the police to arrive, it was not long before a motorized police launch drew alongside and four swarthy customs police clambered aboard, puffing and groaning up the rope ladder. Once safely on deck they lost no time in officiously making for the bridge and the Captain.

Tony had realised of course that it would only be a matter of hours before the police caught up with him and, after a brief initial interview, he was not surprised to be manhandled into their boat and forced to accompany them to their local station ashore. As he was not officially one of Vanessa's cousins' group he felt unable to call on their network of influence and Katie was finding it hard to keep up interpreting for him especially when, in his agitation, he kept on jumping from one story to another. And the police were getting decidedly fidgety and officious.

As he was being fingerprinted Katie did learn one thing which was to prove significant later. When leaving Chiloé the *Skyros* had threaded its way through a lobster-field dotted with colour-coded floats, each one the property of a different owner. Tony had commented to Sheila on them and she had pointed out one which instead of being a round balloon lying on the surface of the water, had been a stick supporting a triangular dayglow orange pennant quite unlike the others and much more visible from afar: he now repeated this observation to the police. What he did not say, however, was that the pots looked to him to have been modified in some way or other - he couldn't put his finger on quite how - but the officer was obviously not interested in what he had to say about lobster-pots, just concentrating on finishing the finger-printing, roughly yanking Tony's thumb down onto the pad and not caring about how much magenta ink got splashed around. Not even when Tony pointed out one of the fishermen's boats which was bobbing up and down on the tide surrounded by the pots did the corporal bother to raise his eyes to register the fact.

Although affecting to note it, the interrogating officer obviously did not register it either. Disdainfully concentrating on the mad Englishman's supposed motivation for following Watanabe, he was convinced by the other fisherman's description that it was indeed Tony who had trodden on the moorhen's nest and so - ergo - was the culprit. QED. Sceptical about the gringo's unsupported story, the officer used his authority to arrest Tony formally on suspicion. He was to be transferred to the nearest jail as soon as appropriate transport could be arranged. The Captain, however, was authorized to send a radio message to Punto Arenas on his behalf to alert the British Consul of this.

Sheila was now in tears and in a dire quandary: whether to stay on the cruise or try - with no Spanish and precious little cash - to travel to Puerto Montt for help. There was no point trying to go with Tony in the launch (even if there had been room) as, having no Spanish, there would be nothing she could usefully achieve and she would only risk adding to Tony's worries. It did not take Katie much to persuade her to stay where at least she had some support and certain board and lodging and the possibility of seeing Tony later, albeit under guard. Quarter of an hour later, weeping noisily, she was led back to her cabin where she collected Tony's things and said a hurried farewell to him. Katie meantime rushed back to find Hamish who had noticed that they were making a marked change of course, presumably heading for land somewhere different, somewhat earlier than officially scheduled.

"Whatever have you done to your eyebrows?" was the first thing Katie said as she studied the singe marks which Hamish had vainly tried to hide. "They look awful."

"What's that? Oh…". Hamish, deep in thought, was still pacing the deck, absent-mindedly and rather sheepishly rubbing his forehead. He was pondering the significance of the statements (shown to him by Aidan Johnson) which had been made by those crew members who had not been given shore leave on arrival at Chiloé.

He noted Katie's reappearance with an absent-minded embrace, avoiding her question, and returned to his reverie. Of the all-male workforce, those who had been in the galleys or cleaning cabins all had alibis; those provisioning the cruise-ship had all worked within sight of each other and noticed nothing except for one who had heard a bit of a splash as a vegetable cart had seemed to get derailed just below the gangplank, but then had thought nothing further of it.

"Otherwise nothing to report," so said his friend Johnson who had decided to go ashore as soon as they returned to Chiloé, where he hoped to link up with the local Chilean gendarmerie. He then intended to question the other fisherfolk and the staff at the baths; he also hoped to talk to the owners of the vegetable plots nearby. You never know, something untoward might emerge from the questioning, particularly if he had the right interpreter alongside him, he said giving Katie a meaningful look.

By now it was obvious to Hamish that they were shortly about to berth near Coinco in the Quitralco fjord again. Presumably for the police posse to take Tony ashore, and then who knew where? He wondered whether the white albino German shepherd-dog was really a guard-dog for the allotments or just a mascot and then he remembered the huge studded collar it had worn. Attached to this collar had been an inch-long Inca gilded manikin, traditionally manufactured from gold but presumably a bronze or painted version. It had seemed to have particularly strongly flashing eyes but that was probably only because the gloom would have accentuated them. He decided to have another, closer, look when he went with Johnson as witness and note-taker on their excursion ashore, as they were to accompany Tony from the local police lockup to the jail some distance away. But first he would have to square it with Katie. Unless Katie opted to go instead, to interpret.

The Captain was now agitating to get moored and shipshape and the crew was fully occupied: so, rather than using a crew member as interpreter for the local patois and Katie not being conversant with this particular dialect, Aidan agreed to Hamish's suggestion to take Jaime with them to the police station. He had of course first to swear him to secrecy on the background details to which he would of necessity now become privy but Jaime knew the score and was naturally discreet so, once the Captain, who had known Jaime for some years, had vouched for him this posed no problem.

Although a large rather lumbering man, and far from inconspicuous, Jaime proved an ideal choice. Being third generation Chilean and well-travelled in his country, he knew the history and idiosyncrasies of the different tribes and ethnic backgrounds of the people living in the region, their animosities and feuds. Inclined to be patrician in his outlook he nevertheless had enough empathy with their problems to understand their evasiveness with the customs men for instance, and even to sympathise with it for he was well aware of the ingrained habit of graft among local excise officers. Whereas he could be impatient with the maid in his Santiago apartment or the caddie at the golf club, here he was sympathy and tact itself. Initial suspicion gradually gave way to a more trusting and relaxed atmosphere but still nothing much in the way of new information emerged from their painstaking interrogations. That is, all except one trifling detail which was later to acquire some significance.

Once back on board Jaime asked Aidan whether he had spotted the wife's uneasiness at some of the questions being put to her husband, owner of the albino guard-dog. It transpired that the man, Pedro Valdemar, had only turned to market-gardening a year previously after losing two fingers in a boating accident. It had been enough to make handling the boat, the lights, the warps, and the chains which moored the many small craft to the jetty too difficult. Not to mention the lobster pots. So he had reluctantly turned to vegetables for his livelihood instead. Although digging was hampered by his injured hand he still found this easier than fishing. Besides, his wife had grown excessively nervous at Pedro's being out all night and in all weathers since the 'accidents'. On enquiring what accidents, Jaime had learnt that her sister and her cousin had both been widowed within the last year and that the fishing fraternity was growing nervous at the heightening toll of unexplained incidents, all of them taking place at night and all of them so far unexplained. The police apparently, thoroughly uncooperative and incompetent as usual, pooh-poohed any idea of foul play and refused to investigate further.

But when Aidan tried to pursue this line with Señora Valdemar she clammed up on him completely. Jaime had tried patiently and tactfully to return to the subject but it was obvious from the terrified looks the Señora cast in her husband's direction that they would get no more information of value from her. Someone somewhere had put the squeezers on them, he decided.

CHAPTER THIRTEEN

Meantime Katie, not finding Hamish in their cabin, collected her camera and sun-glasses to go up on deck and bumped into Vanessa whom she had not thought to burden with the latest developments given her cousin's other preoccupations. But now that Jaime appeared to have become involved (as well as Hamish, despite his promise) Vanessa's curiosity had been aroused especially now she knew something about Hamish's police background.

On the verge of tears, Katie beckoned her into the cabin and after some prompting, *sotto voce*, recounted everything she knew and her fears for Hamish if he got dragged in too far. Mindful of the normal tendency of Chileans to "*copuchar*", that is to gossip, (literally to "windbag"), she begged Vanessa not to divulge any of it. She was well aware that she must avoid raising suspicions amongst the passengers on board, most particularly her Peruvian neighbours.

But on this occasion she drew trumps. It so happened that the Consul in Punto Arenas was yet another distant cousin of Vanessa's who was originally to have joined them on the trip but who had had to cancel at the last moment owing to pressing business. It could be that he was still in Puerto Montt since that was where his business had taken him and Vanessa promised to find out (discreetly) through the good offices of Manuel, the purser/PR man. She also volunteered some interesting information just gleaned from her morning's conversation with Manuel.

Evidently the blonde Peruvian's father's name, according to her passport, was not Gonzalez but Ballunde, the same name as the previous President's. Having learned this, Vanessa had then contrived to fall into conversation herself with Señorita Ballunde - quite naturally for she too was distantly related to Ballunde through her mother (Katie had forgotten how interwoven, even incestuous all these relationships tended to be)! Of course Vanessa had not let on but, both being keen followers of fashion with an eye to the smart accessory, as was evident from their respective turnouts, they had got along like houses on fire; especially once they established that, although not exact contemporaries, they had indeed been to the same exclusive school in Miraflores, a smart Lima suburb. Vanessa was particularly fond of good sometimes rather ostentatious jewellery and her husband Jaime liked to see his striking wife doing him credit, and was also generous - to good effect. She was able to give her new friend the address of an obscure jeweller in one of the Santiago slums, an unlikely quarter, who made and stocked beautiful lapis lazuli brooches from Chilean-mined stones. She showed the Señorita an example of her own which Jaime had bought at a knockdown price, and lost no time in admiring her friend's gold necklace which sported a scimitar-shape manikin whose eyes were particularly dark claret-coloured rubies, pigeon's blood she called them, surrounded by fiery diamonds.

"And what's more, I've earrings to match!" Consuelo Gonzalez concluded triumphantly, rumbling in her handbag to produce them. Vanessa was then rewarded by being told who had given them to her. Katie was fascinated by this revelation but Vanessa broke off to caution Katie (in return) about repeating this information or ever approaching the Peruvian direct since her protector was always hovering and might well think this too intrusive; or, at the very least, indiscreet. It was all right for someone with mutual family and school connections to strike up a relationship but for a "gringo" as Katie, to her chagrin, was now classified, and whose husband was always prowling around on deck in cahoots with the First Mate, this might and probably would be viewed with grave suspicion. In fact a definite no-no.

Just before she left Vanessa added:

"I remember once hearing a rumour that Señorita Ballunde's uncle was in fact the brother-in-law of Muji Gallico's steward (an extremely wealthy and influential man), and in all likelihood the illegitimate son of ....," and she breathed the name of a person famous in Peruvian politics. "Of course her father was well-known in his time. This might account for her preferring to use her mother's name and not her father's: not surprisingly in this all-enveloping world of the Peruvian mafia. Perhaps she's not so daft after all. And more interestingly perhaps, it's obvious she has loads of clout even if she does have to wield it at secondhand through her minder on occasions. At all events she's obviously hand in glove with the Captain - and not just because of her glamorous looks either. You should see them closeted together!" she added.

"Perhaps she's related to him too," Katie suggested mischievously but Vanessa said gravely "no, there was no chance of that, the Captain's family all came from Chiloé and were of Greek extraction, and all seemed to live within a stone's throw of each other on one of the larger islands. And in each other's pockets as well," she added.

*   *   *

Reflected in the now calm sea, hues of the setting sun intermingled deepest amethyst with periwinkle. Looking at this dramatic backcloth from the upper deck, Katie gasped at its beauty. Directly overhead the cotton-wool clouds, resembling a hare's scut, were slowly dispersing wispily. The pouting powder-puffs gradually melded to pink, and the pink to red as Katie felt her heart surge. Back home in Cheshire 'red in the morning' would have been a warning but here in the southern hemisphere she hoped exactly the opposite would apply, though she feared not. The sun now glittered on the mountain-tops like a cherry tomato on top of a slice of crusty terrine, she thought hungrily looking at her watch.

Viewing the Andean peaks, swept up into breathtaking meringue cones after the recent snow, Katie held her breath. She had never seen quite such heart-clenchingly powerful scenery. Surely this could not bode any harm for them, or indeed for anybody, but she still worried absurdly for Hamish in his weakened state. She knew he would be unable to resist if push came to shove and Interpol begged for his assistance. Not a vain man, but he never could resist an appeal to his better nature, his conscience he called it. 'His duty to God and his fellow-man'.

PUERTO MONTT

GULF OF
ANCÚD

CHILOÉ

Castro

Queilén

Quellón

PACIFIC OCEAN

GULF OF
CORCOVADO

▲ MINCHINMAIDA
VOLCANO

CHAITÉN

CHILE

ARGENTINA

ARCHIPELAGO

Puerto Aisén

TERMAS DE
QUILTRALCO

SAN RAFAEL

Approx Scale

0KM   100KM   200KM

PART II

"..and rubies courageous at heart," Robert Browning

CHAPTER FOURTEEN

Humming to himself, Sherwin, the retired archaeologist, was just returning on board well content with his little excursion out to the dig when he nearly collided with Vanessa. Retrieving his spectacles he addressed her:

"Hi there, Ma'am. This unscheduled stop has been a godsend to me, I'm telling yer. I found my little dig site quite easily and the guys up there were more than happy to let me poke around. Not like back home these days. There was even one guy who spoke English - sort of. He not only explained exactly where they had found the artefacts, and showed me the sites, but he let me take pictures of some of them *in situ* too. Then I was able to sketch the layout and…," he was bubbling over with excitement. The wrong side of seventy but very fit, Professor Sherwin had the enthusiasm of a teenager. His muscular legs bulged under his baggy shorts and his eyes darted around seeing everything.

"Some of that stuff is sensational, I promise you. And what's more, Mrs Foreman, have you seen that ornament round the neck of the guard-dog, the one with the white velvety hair, up on the vegetable plot?" he asked, changing the subject suddenly. "It looks just like one of the Sipán exhibits in the Muji Gallico exhibition your friend Freddie was on about. I can't help thinking they must have gotten a camera installed inside it, the way those eyes keep swivelling around watching you. Eyes of the manikin I mean, not the dog. Those rubies look exactly like bloodshot eyes: most arresting. Enough to stop any villain in their tracks."

Vanessa, intrigued first by his enthusiasm then by his curious remarks, admitted she hadn't (without letting on what she had just learnt about the Peruvians on board), but promised she would go and have a look before it got dusk and the midges too voracious. Satisfied, his white hair waving in the breeze and his rimless glasses making him look like a Patriarch, Sherwin set off towards his cabin for a shower.

As Vanessa was edging carefully down the gangway on her wedge-heels she met her husband and the two police investigators on their way back.

"Whatever have you been up to?" she asked her husband, noticing his smug expression and curious to see him in such company. Aidan nodded agreement as Jaime looked to him for permission to explain. Talking softly, he steered Vanessa back to their cabin.

*   *   *

"Great news, darling. Two things, but first...," Katie announced as Hamish pushed open the cabin door. He looked intrigued.

"First, Jocelyn's camera hasn't been harmed at all by its seawater soaking. In fact she's even been able, with the help of Manuel's sidekick - you know, the official ship's photographer - to develop the film she had inside her camera. She's just been showing me her photos. Apparently he put it straight into distilled water and only lost a couple of exposures. Isn't that marvellous?"

Hamish, preoccupied with searching for his tobacco pouch for a smoke on deck later, mumbled: "Great. And the other?" Then remembering why he had been so keen, added: "I'd be interested to have a look at them. You went very close to the lagoon where the lobster pots are, didn't you? I wonder if she took any shots near there?"

"Yes, she did - you'll see, and... Oh, the other. Well, apparently Ursula told Vanessa - in strictest confidence of course - what she thinks is in Freddie's bag, the one he has stowed safely away in the hold under lock and key."

Hamish was now fully alert although he had been unaware that anything had been secreted down in the ship's bowels, anything of such value that is. "Go on, what is it?" he prompted. But Katie was not to be hurried.

"Apparently while they were in Lima at the medical conference Freddie somehow got hold of some radio isotopes for treating one of his gynaecological patients back in Uruguay, but had no idea how he should transport them home. The airlines, for obvious reasons, aren't knowingly going to allow them on their planes; at any rate BA wasn't, and he didn't want to let them out of his sight so he was faced with a conundrum. Whether to smuggle them on board without declaring them and risk having them confiscated and probably a fine as well, and be accused of upsetting the aircraft's instruments, or to try to courier them across by train with all the endless paperwork that that would involve as well as the possibility of their not being kept at the right temperature and so on. Which, naturally, he was reluctant to do as (a) it would have cost a packet and (b) he didn't want them to fall into anyone else's hands. And, I suppose, (c) - having once been radio-active, I suppose they might also still be dangerous."

"By far the most important reason," Hamish rejoined. "Not something you would actually want to carry around, not even in the securest of containers. Why on earth didn't he arrange…?"

Anticipating his question, Katie continued:

"He didn't really feel he could trust the courier companies in Peru, not with their reputation; he didn't know anyone who was going straight back to Montevideo, and in the short time they had to make enquiries it proved impossible to find a solution, so Ursula assumed her husband had had to bow to the inevitable, decline the offer and leave them behind. But no! According to Vanessa, he had found some clever way round by secreting them in special lead-lined containers in the bottom of his Gladstone bag along with his other drugs and medical samples and things." She paused.

"So far so good," she continued, Hamish looking increasingly sceptical. But Katie made sure he was following her and went on: "Ursula would have been none the wiser had she not, when they were standing in line at the airport check-in, tried to shunt his bag along in the queue. She tried nudging it with her foot and to her amazement it weighed a ton and wouldn't budge. As soon as Freddie caught sight of her touching it he grabbed her arm and told her sharply to leave his bag alone.

"Why, what on earth have you got in there? The Elgin marbles?" but he only scowled. She was so surprised - this was quite unlike Freddie - that she meekly obeyed and nothing more was said until they were safely on the plane. Then when she tentatively started to question him he told her brusquely to drop it, so she did. But not without wondering what the hell he could have in it: surely isotopes even in the securest of lead-lined containers could not weigh that much."

"More than you might think though. But why the uncharacteristic behaviour?" wondered Hamish out loud.

"Precisely," Katie nodded.

Hamish still had a bad conscience for allowing himself to get caught up in the mysterious goings-on which Aidan was investigating, though Katie seemed to have accepted that inevitably he would. However, her sandy-coloured eyelashes, normally only really noticeable when wet, told another tale. Had she been weeping? Fiddling with his tobacco tin he bit his lip: he knew she was unhappy about the risks to his health if he became involved and he had more or less promised her he wouldn't. No more had been said about promises but he was still very conscious when soul-searching; after his heart scare he had begun to realise how much he had been heaping onto Katie in the parish. Not only had she taken on the Mothers' Union with all that that had involved, but she was also very active in hospital-visiting, in smoothing down ructions with their temperamental organist who was something of a *prima donna* when it came to choosing the music, anthems especially; and in arranging flower- and coffee-rotas for the church. And making sure the Chuchwarden kept the sidespersons' list up to date and the church fabric in good repair and the church clean; as well as generally keeping people up to the mark. As if this wasn't enough she also seemed to have streams of visitors to lunch, tea and, occasionally, to supper as well as keeping an eye on the children and the house. And of course he relied on her to remember important anniversaries like his Mother's birthday and the dates of diocesan meetings and so on. The Archdeacon needed to be kept informed of contentious matters likely to arise; here again Katie performed an invaluable service, and more tactfully than he would, Hamish realised.

She drew the line at gardening though, and occasionally Matthew would have to help out; but Hamish always managed to turn the compost heap and keep the hedges trimmed. No wonder she was looking rather peaky; she had needed a holiday as much as he (and perhaps more) and could do without this extra worry now. In all honesty he couldn't attribute his recent increasing peremptoriness to his health alone. True, he was overworking but he had to admit he liked laying down the law. He had grown up in a *macho* environment where the womenfolk were subservient to the men; and his mother - though never demonstrative and certainly not effusive - had spoiled him into the bargain, even when times were extra hard. More than his younger brother (but not so as his father would notice): there was no denying he had been her favourite, he remembered wistfully.

His Victorian grandfather had had all the women in the house trembling when he roared and Hamish had seen nothing wrong with that. Catriona, the girlfriend from nextdoor, who he had been to school with and whom he later knew at Glasgow University, seemed to accept this as normal behaviour too. In fact, it wasn't until he had met Katie that he had ever questioned his own attitude and even now he sometimes reverted to his bad old habits until he was shamed out of them. Normally Katie, who herself had grown up in an anti-feminist society where the women were naturally submissive - but had rebelled against it - would have shouted back, but since his illness she had been mildness itself. He thought now how he was still sometimes guilty of exploiting her patience and her loyalty; and in being too severe with Matthew as well. Or perhaps he just expected too much of a teenager (though in fact Matthew had just had his twentieth birthday, a month before they set out).

While Hamish was still lost in thought, Katie promised to get the photos from Jocelyn after dinner to show her husband.

"Why are you so keen to see them?" she teased. "No mermaids or naked girls here I promise you. Even Chile doesn't produce that - not without being forewarned anyway."

CHAPTER FIFTEEN

Vanessa had been hobnobbing with the Captain up on the bridge when Katie joined her on deck. Vanessa had learnt that the albino dog guarding the market garden which backed onto the jetty at Coinco did in fact have a very special collar. Studded with what to the casual observer looked like coloured stones, it was in fact set with a cornucopia of precious and semi-precious jewels all set in gold. This was reckoned to be as safe a hiding-place as any given that the hound was young and had very sharp teeth, and all the locals were in the know and promised their cut if they kept their mouths shut. If, however, word got around or anything untoward were to happen it was hinted that vengeance of a particularly nasty kind would be wreaked on those judged to be guilty of an indiscretion, even remotely. And everyone knew what that meant... No wonder Señora Valdemar was so nervous, as Jaime had observed.

And how had the first mate got to know about it, Katie asked. Why, he was a cousin of Señora Valdemar's, of course. But nothing would ever be avowed openly, Vanessa warned. Secrecy was the order of the day. Mafioso secrecy.

"You said hiding-place. Did you mean just for the necklace or is there something else hidden as well?" Katie had asked Vanessa, agog.

"Well, it seems there is also a minute key secreted inside the necklace but nobody's too sure what it's for, or where exactly it's hidden either," Vanessa paused.

"And those two huge rubies, are they real as well?" Katie pursued incredulously. "Or are they television eyes remotely controlled by the so-called gardeners? They can't possibly be genuine that size, could they?"

An elderly member of Vanessa's group coming up on deck interrupted with a query about the day's programme before Vanessa had a chance to answer so Katie, still intrigued by what she'd just learnt decided, tactfully, to return later. Now that both Vanessa and Jaime were in the loop so to speak she felt she could talk more freely with them but, even so, discretion was of the essence. Besides, she needed to find Hamish to warn him about the secretive comings and goings in the Peruvians' cabin next to theirs which had ended in something heavy, very heavy, being furtively dragged past their cabin in the early hours and along the corridor, *bumpety bumpety bump,* with much shushing amid whispered warnings. Hamish had been snoring at the time so she was pretty certain he hadn't heard, and she'd forgotten to mention it to him earlier as he was still asleep.

✶ ✶ ✶

Warned by Aidan, Hamish had taken to locking the cabin door from the inside as well as from the outside so when, a few minutes later, Aidan knocked he had to wait a minute or two. Standing there he noticed shifty comings and goings down the corridor; while a slight figure heavily muffled in anorak, scarf and boots emerged stealthily from the next door cabin. Aidan was unable to identify it because of its large pair of sunglasses (even though the light below deck was dim), but he realised he was being closely observed from one of the peepholes elsewhere so turned away. Curious, he thought.

"You were quite right, old chap," he told Hamish, "about the results of the DNA. It *was* the second fisherman's brother all right. Results have just come through - and not before time," he added. "The body was pretty badly decomposed as well - as we knew it would be. It must have been there in the water for at least three months and probably longer, and was superficially unrecognizable; in fact it was so bloated as to make it almost impossible to realise it was once a human body." He paused, shuddering.

"But I'm getting absolutely nowhere with that other one I told you about. And the Peruvian gangster, the probable member of the Sentero Luminoso, the one who tried to knife you - the one who framed your English friend Tony - we've still got nothing out of him, at least nothing that makes sense. Could he have been in league with your nextdoor neighbours, our mafia friends, I wonder. We do have some sort of a lead into their background which my 'oppo' on shore is following up. Otherwise nothing useful - except for one throwaway remark he made which did seem a bit bizarre in the current context and might possibly give us a clue."

"Oh, what was that?" Hamish was curious.

"How on earth could he possibly have known the Minister would be interested in lobster pots in Coinco bay. Does he really think the Minister has nothing better to do than…"

"Just a mo," broke in Hamish excitedly. "Did he really say the Minister? And if so, which one? You see I think it was one of the Minister of *Justice's* minions who came snooping down here when really you would expect it to be Fisheries to be interested, wouldn't you? Much more logical. And the lobster pots; Tony said there was something fishy about them. The fact that *he,* the corpse, got mistaken for the brother of the union chap who was stirring up that trouble with the fishermen, and then stupidly got himself topped in a monumental cockup - when really they should have been after the other one, the Union chappie - all makes me think…"

"Hang on, hang on - which other one?" Aidan interrupted, confused.

At that moment Katie, flushed with her news of the hidden mystery key, returned.

* * *

Before slipping off again Aidan warned Hamish that things appeared to be stirring in Santiago according to news just in from his informants there. Nobody was too sure of the provenance of the other rich haul of gold artefacts in Lima but it was obviously from somewhere very exclusive, probably a reclusive millionaire collector's hoard; but someone who had, strangely, not publicized his loss. It was hinted that the insurance had not been claimed either in order to avoid unwelcome publicity: or more likely enquiries into its provenance. Very odd. Obviously not part of the Muji Gallico collection although Gallico himself, whilst collaborating, would have preferred to avoid the intrusive publicity over his loss too.

Everyone was agreed on this but it was impossible to control leaks especially to the bloodhounds from the press, and particularly in Lima. And once it got out to the news agencies there would be no holding it especially if mention was made of the homo-erotic pieces. But who was this other mystery millionaire connoisseur? If, indeed, it was just one individual. And who was he in collusion with? He must have had help from someone close to things, probably someone in government, Aidan surmised. Perhaps even the Minister himself, he hinted, though which one? And if a Peruvian Minister, how did his agents manage to evade their Chilean counterparts or at least avoid ruffling their feathers? Diplomatic niceties needed to be observed particularly closely at such moments if they were to have any chance of international cooperation.

So the Chilean government might be in on the act too: hardly surprising since events were occurring on its territory which could be having a negative impact both internationally and locally. With the Peruvian President looking desperately for a scapegoat it was quite likely that fingers would be pointed at the régime in Chile - totally opposed, ideologically speaking, to its own. It would be handy for the Peruvians to have yet another stick to beat Pinochet with, not that that would carry much weight down here in the Chilean south, according to Johnson; nor yet internationally if his information was anything to go by.

But it might have some impact on local voters in Peru if it meant the Chileans were made to appear the bad guys. This would cast the Peruvian President in a rosy glow - quite an unusual turn-up for the book and oh! how tempting.

$$* \qquad * \qquad *$$

Rebuffed by his pretty cousin who had never had any trouble in acquiring admirers, Ari retired to his cabin to lick his wounds. He had not really been too committed in his flirting but now his pride was hurt. His démarche had partly been intended as a smokescreen to deflect Freddie's obvious puzzlement over his, Ari's, interest in the Peruvian artefacts. But there was no gainsaying the girl was pretty. If he succeeded in appearing head over heels in love with Marietta people would be less likely to query why he, a late addition to the party, had come at all.

In fact, when Aunt Vanessa had heard he was out of a job and kicking his heels in Lima, up from Puerto Rico, and had invited him to join the group it had seemed like an answer to prayer. It wasn't until he went to the bank to increase his overdraft and met with a curt refusal from the manager that he had had to sit down and take stock of his situation. And then out of the blue good old Uncle Jaime, sensing his embarrassment, had quietly slipped him the return fare with a note telling him to repay it whenever he could but not to worry unduly. Ari had heard that he was sometimes impulsively generous but had never suspected Jaime of such sensitivity; this was enough to make him completely revise his opinion of his crusty old uncle.

If he played his cards carefully Ari might, he just might, succeed in contacting his *oppo* in the smuggling ring and taking some lucre off him before things got completely out of hand. But what was the best way to make contact without arousing undue curiosity or suspicion? They would not necessarily know he was down here - yet - but he knew all the passwords and could always invent some plausible story about having been sent at the eleventh hour to avert some fiasco - some over-zealous anti-drug officer arresting one of their contacts, catching him red-handed before the loot had been stashed in the agreed fashion. That might work.

But now that that wretched Interpol agent had so annoyingly, and so mysteriously, appeared on board he would need to think on his feet and be super-alert if things were not to go horribly awry. He couldn't afford any more stupid blunders such as had happened with the other Peruvian fisherman, brother of the first one, and he would have to devise a foolproof scheme for muzzling that sharp-toothed dog and getting hold of the gold key without arousing suspicion. After all, there was hardly likely to be another bloody-fool Englishman on hand ready to take the rap for his miscalculation, was there? Nothing so convenient next time...

Doing a furtive *recce* of the cabin plan in Manuel's office, Ari was completely thrown when he spotted his sister's name plus supercilious boyfriend on the passenger list. It had never occurred to him they would be here, Georgie and her macho Enrico. Uncle Jaime had never mentioned it, nor had his aunt. If Georgie spied him before he had worked out a plan of campaign he would be spiked. Best to throw them off the scent by playing the gigolo again, putting to use his darting sloe-eyes fringed by girlish eyelashes, which he had frequently been told worked like a charm. To action! But who was to be the victim, his next conquest, now that Marietta appeared impervious to his advances? That dishy blonde Peruvian surrounded by minders would make the best possible camouflage but even he, Ari the flamboyant, would need a hell of a lot of nerve, if not luck, to pull that one. It might be safer to try first the raven-haired beauty, the young Chilean lass who went around in a group of well-heeled international jet-setters. At least it didn't look as if she had a protector in tow and her young scientist friend did look rather wet and not really committed, always wandering around in a dream. Not too much of a threat there, he reckoned.

CHAPTER SIXTEEN

Lingering wisps of wood smoke and the darting call of the Andean humming-bird greeted a clear dawn the next morning. Hamish crept down the gangplank to go ashore for his first pipe of the day. Raising his binoculars he thought he caught sight of a rose-breasted thrush tanager in the hedgerow but then decided he was too far south for that. Cautiously winding his way down from the quayside trying to catch another glimpse, his spirits lifted and he wondered why he had felt such a sense of foreboding the previous evening. The air smelt fresh and dew had made everything sparkle.

Each side of the pathway a solitary tree stood sentinel in the morning mist as he picked his way past a dilapidated building smelling of damp stone. A cloud of dazzling white blossom-like flowerets silhouetted against the dirty wall pulled him up short. Such beauty. The tree's delicate black twigs emphasized the purity of the flowers as he gazed, spellbound, at the dewdrops glistening in the early sun like a scattering of diamonds. Diamonds reminded him of the guard dog's studded collar: very odd that. There must be a simple explanation, but he was blowed if he could think of it..

He had succeeded in putting out of his mind his earlier irrational fears about wanton stabbings and malefactors when his eye fell on a scarlet copihue, Chile's trumpet-shaped native flower; and this served to enhance his more cheerful frame of mind. Queer that such a beautiful plant should be a parasite, he ruminated. He stopped for a moment to admire the brilliant sheen of its slender petals. A momentary shudder and he was dimly reminded of a long hidden memory; it must have been a dream.

As he pondered he heard a rustling in the hedgerow and, suspecting a snake, stayed stock still for long enough to pinpoint the cause. The overnight rain had suspended a necklace of translucent pearls to the top twigs of the hedgerow. Illuminated in the rosy glow of early morning, a small urchin, barefoot and grimy in a tattered tee-shirt and holey shorts, was cowering in the stunted bushes trying to avoid getting splashed by the dew. By his feet the furtive violets hid their heads in the purple grass which curled over his grubby toes. Eyes luminous and with a finger to his lips imploring silence, the lad thrust a crumpled and rather muddy bit of paper at Hamish, croaking "Señor 'Amish?" with an interrogative stare. Recovering from his surprise, Hamish nodded but hesitated before finally taking it. When he looked up from it the urchin had vanished.

The church bell, louder and clearer than before, now that the sun was stronger, tolled for early Mass. Glancing at his watch Hamish realized today was some kind of local Chilean saint's feast-day, normally celebrated with gusto throughout this part of the land. That would explain the myriads of national flags and bunting he now noticed hanging limply all around awaiting the morning breeze. How odd that no-one on board had thought to mention it the previous evening, Manuel when announcing the day's programme, Vanessa when marshalling her troops, or any of the many other Chileans on board. The only thing which had been mentioned was that it was Freddie's birthday and a rather special one so Vanessa had been in cahoots with the chef arranging a cake to celebrate. It would have to be pretty large to go round the whole ship's complement, Hamish thought, but the chef would surely be up to that judging by the huge quantities of luscious food he managed to produce on a daily basis.

One or two Lowry-type stick figures were threading their way towards the church and a thin curl of smoke above the baker's announced that the first festive empanadas were already in the communal village oven next door to the barber's. Though he still couldn't catch their distinctive smell Hamish realised he was salivating in anticipation. Curious about his missive, he glanced at it again but seeing it was all crudely written in Spanish and faintly in pencil, he thrust it into his pocket and strode back to the ship's gangplank, his heart lifted by the birdsong pouring forth all around him now.

Perhaps that bird **was** the rather elusive great kiskadee with its pied head and rufous wings - that would indeed be a first, and a triumph. What a pity he hadn't got his camera with him. A bit more interesting than the *lbj* (little brown jobs) he was surrounded with back home. But the finch-like tanager seemed more likely; he really must find a local bird-book. Puzzling about the identity of the bird temporarily drove his secret message to the back of his mind as he sought to pinpoint the avian visitor.

Back in their cabin after lingering over a delicious breakfast, Katie brought him up to date, telling him about the guard-dog's collar (though she forgot to mention the minute gold key supposedly secreted inside it), and Vanessa's take on Señorita Ballunde after the suspicious movements in the nextdoor cabin. She started to burble on about an encounter she had just had with the ship's mysterious assistant public relations man who doubled as purser and general factotum.

"Yes, that purser or whatever he is, that smoothie anyway. Not Manuel, but the other one, the side-kick. He was being hotly pursued down the gangplank by the chief steward, the one with such deft feet and agile limbs - you should see how he shins down the companionway, just like a cat burglar. And those deep lines in his forehead; such mournful eyes too. Like Mel Gibson, or... You hadn't noticed? Oh Hamish, you never notice anything - about people, that is."

"That's what I need you for," smiled Hamish catching her wrist and brushing the palm of her left hand with his lips - so lightly she wasn't sure if it was intentional. His eyes, however, confirmed his meaning. "Anyway, why was he being chased and what else did he say, this mysterious P.R. chap?"

But Katie was determined to tell her story in her own way. "Something glinted in the sun as the side-kick ran ahead. I think it was a meat cleaver or a chopper or something nasty; anyway the way it was being wielded looked serious. From his screams it appeared to be a matter concerning our Señorita Gonzales alias Ballunde... a matter of honour maybe... I'll bet you didn't even notice her jewellery either...the great rocks that flashy alleged blonde from Peru, I mean...".

Hamish was used to Katie's oblique changes of tack and usually managed to follow - eventually - but this time he was completely thrown. Until something stirred at the back of his mind. The mention of jewellery again and of that 'blonde' he'd seen hobnobbing furtively with the chap who looked like a discontented gargoyle, he was sure now he *had* seen her somewhere before. But the 'blonde' had not been Consuelo Gonzalez Ballunde, of that he was sure. So who could it have been? and why would this blonde be involved with a man wielding a meat cleaver? Was it really her or just her double, or someone impersonating her? That way she had of fingering her heavy gold chain, of twisting it and twirling it round and round flashing the huge rubies on her ring finger: what and who did that remind him of? Even his unobservant eye had been caught by that, unobservant that is to female mannerisms and coquetry but not to the odder quirks or compulsive tics of a more general kind. Frowning, he asked:

"What on earth happened to the chap being chased by the meat cleaver? and the blonde? why 'allegedly from Peru'? Don't you think she hails from Peru after all? Are you sure it was Señorita Gonzalez Ballunde you saw, not that other sophisticated blonde we saw at the docks?...I hope to goodness she didn't get hurt?" he added, looking up at Katie's expression, and almost as an afterthought, "and are *you* all right, my darling?".

Katie, stifling her annoyance, didn't answer immediately. Hamish studied her face for a moment, noting how the wrinkles at the corner of her eyes had deepened since his health problems had intensified. He had begun to feel increasingly guilty at involving her in matters which threatened to get out of hand particularly since he had promised to take things easy, and made a new resolution to keep out of anything stressful. His heart quickened as he looked at her again: he loved the curve of her neck as it sloped towards her shoulder and with his finger he gently traced the delicate line round to the nape of her neck, which he brushed with a light kiss. Mollified, she flashed him her sunny smile but refused to be deflected from her story, though she noted with relief a more carefree expression than recently.

Ignoring her husband's first question, Katie answered the next.

"N,noo, she seemed OK. But you know, you might be right after all; it might have been the other blonde, the one from the Argentine, not the Peruvian. But...," still hesitating.

Though improving, Hamish's Spanish was very sketchy and he relied on his wife who had travelled extensively throughout the Americas and was well able to distinguish regional accents: Ecuadorian from Colombian, Chilean from the guttural Argentine with its slurred 'js' and Bolivian from Peruvian. If anyone could detect an Argentine accent she could. But it wasn't the nationality so much as the identity of the blonde he was puzzling about. And what damage the meat cleaver might have done - of course.

"No, **she** was Colombian or Venezuelan or possibly from further north. But this woman might have **lived** in the Argentine (retaining her upper-crust Peruvian accent and vocabulary all right); though she's not necessarily blonde..." she added inconsequentially and then tailed off as another thought struck her. "But you're right, I don't think it was Señorita Ballunde after all."

Hamish grunted, pursuing his own line of thought while Katie continued:

"Another thing I meant to ask you before I forget. Your friend Aidan, has he always talked like that?"

"How d'you mean? like what?" Hamish was thrown.

"You know - in stepping-stones - so you have to kind of jump to follow him."

Hamish privately thought that was rather rich coming from Katie, an arch jumper from stone to stone, but he replied mildly:

"When particularly? When I first met him he had the reputation of the quickest brain in the Force...,".

A peremptory knocking at the door drowned the rest. José, their normal cabin steward stood there looking very sheepish. Immediately behind him and prodding him forward was a fierce-looking man in uniform with shiny buttons and smart gold braid on his epaulettes who then pushed him aside. Hamish thought he probably wore some form of police insignia but couldn't be sure as the man spun round, drawing himself up to his full 5ft 4ins with the light from his signet ring flashing disconcertingly. In the corner of his right eye, which was glittering like one of the poisonous ladybirds they'd been warned about, a livid scar was throbbing. Perhaps he was not as confident as he appeared. Detecting Scarface's pungently perfumed aftershave, Hamish couldn't prevent his nose from wrinkling in distaste. He took a small step backwards; the scent hadn't quite succeeded in camouflaging the waves of stale garlic wafting up towards him.

"Yes?" Hamish asked politely, towering over him as he stood up. "What can we do for you?"

"Mr 'Ameesh Blair?" and when he nodded, "You come with me".

"Just a minute," intervened Katie recovering from her shock. "Why? Who are you?" She felt her pulse beating strongly and in rapid Spanish continued:

"What do you want with him, and where's your authorisation?"

The man straightened and squared his shoulders, surprised at her fluency which he obviously hadn't expected.

"You Meesus Blair Tomson, right? Well, you come too. Translate," and with that he grabbed her wrist and tried to pull them both through the door and along the corridor. But Katie stood her ground and continued to ask for his papers. The peephole on one of the cabin doors opposite flickered as the intruders finally yielded and grudgingly produced identification.

Hamish was sure the voyeur was one of the Peruvian mob, gloating. Perhaps it was they who had tipped off the police in the first place. He had just had time to grab their passports before they were hustled out of the door but his precious binoculars were still lying on the bed together with the contents of the pockets he had previously emptied. He hoped they would not be searched when they got to wherever they were headed for as he still had the boy's mysterious note on him somewhere, which he'd quite forgotten about and which Katie hadn't even seen yet. As soon as they were prodded outside he demanded their cabin key and, returning, unobtrusively managed to wedge the note in the door jamb after quickly retrieving his wallet with his old Renfrewshire police credentials before locking the door. Those credentials whose importance Katie was later to exaggerate when she was called on to translate them. He prayed they wouldn't see the date and realise he had retired from the force, nearly ten years ago now.

They were being pushed into a van, presumably a police vehicle, which had been brought up alongside the quay. The driver saluted their captor smartly so Katie decided now or never to risk all and flourished the police credentials before they were taken too far, loudly demanding that they examine the papers there and then. After a second's stunned silence and suspicious peering at the foreign writing, then much muttering and scratching of heads, a quick consultation on the walkie-talkie which substituted for a mobile phone; some blustering, remonstrances with sour expressions and darting of eyes, more jabbering, another moment's fraught silence while his forehead started to glisten…and then a torrent of profuse apologies and an immediate change of attitude. And tone.

If the agent had been capable of blushing he might have gone pink beneath his swarthiness but instead perspiration began to bead under his moustache. A blast of garlicky verbiage was followed by oily deference as he grovelled and blamed a case of "wrongful identification". The officer wheeled round to put the blame on José who had sensibly disappeared, and contented himself with castigating the driver instead.

Many flowery and obsequious compliments were then launched at them and after a minute's confusion they were accompanied back on board with vehement assurances of punishment for those responsible for the clerical error and an offer of yet another *pisco sour* (at eleven in the morning!).

Yet Hamish was not altogether convinced that it **had** been a mistake, especially when, on returning to their cabin, he noticed that it had obviously been searched. At any rate the scrappy piece of paper had fluttered to the floor but had apparently been overlooked - happily. Perhaps the offer of a drink had been meant to prolong the time available for examining the cabin. His binoculars for one were not quite as he had left them and his diary had obviously been thumbed through; Katie's things had also been disturbed albeit only cursorily. One of the cotton reels from her sewing things had rolled into a corner under the bunk and Granny's silver thimble appeared to have been carefully inspected.

Before Katie could expostulate he put his finger to his lips and steered her into the bathroom where, under cover of the running taps, Hamish explained that they had probably also been bugged. Half an hour later he had located the appliance, an unsophisticated battery job hidden in the shaving mirror light, which he was able to neutralise with a tweak of Katie's tweezers, making it seem as if it had just been inexpertly installed.

"I distrusted that man from the moment he pushed his way into the cabin - with his swagger and his Napoleonic gestures. Did you notice how his toes turned up at the end? I'm always suspicious of men who prance along on the balls of their feet like that, making their shoes turn up like a clown's."

"You and your premonitions," laughed Hamish. "But thank goodness you sized him up so quickly. It wouldn't have been so easy to make him eat humble pie if he'd actually got us as far as the police station in that smelly little van of his. Then I think we really would have been in trouble."

So much for his good resolutions, Hamish thought wryly. Surely he could do better than this but Katie seemed to take it in her stride. She was obviously gratified by his appreciation of her quick thinking and flashed him a smile.

After a speedy shower and still puzzled by events, Katie and her husband repaired to the cocktail bar for a round of gossip before tackling a delicious looking buffet lunch temptingly set out in the dining area. A pyramid of mouth-watering seafood topped with huge local crayfish and fresh mayonnaise; an amazing variety of freshly caught fish was on offer together with an assortment of salads of differing hues, each anointed with a different dressing. Stuck for choice they looked round for someone with local expertise to consult. They met up with Freddie and Ursula and were able to compare notes on their day so far, careful not to let on anything about the police incursion. Freddie had still been unable to glean any definite news about the heist in Lima but was confident there would be further developments before too long. All his informants were positive of this and said the capital was still buzzing with rumour and counter-rumour. One thing was certain that when the time came heads, important ones, would roll.

CHAPTER SEVENTEEN

Ari had decided on his plan of campaign. Having scrupulously studied Señorita Ballunde's entourage he had been discouraged, but now he had found, or so he thought, just the girl on one of the upper decks. She looked ditzy enough to fool the unsuspecting and glamorous enough to seduce any unattached male. At least she would be the perfect foil should his sister Georgie and her nosey boyfriend come prowling. And would relieve him of the implied need to squire Vanessa's lumpy niece. What he had not reckoned with, however, was Paulina herself.

Curious how someone so alert at the card-table, quick to read every smallest hint and nuance, could nevertheless remain impervious to other people's reactions in a more everyday situation, Paulina thought. Preening himself, Ari seemed unaware that she exhibited not the slightest interest in him: she had probably not even registered him.

True, she seemed always to be hanging around in that moneyed crowd of young Santiago twenty-somethings, all dressed in the latest expensive *farnientes* fashion and talking nonsense, and - true - she hung around the neck of that young scientist Raùl. But he seemed to be a bit of a cat-that-walked-by-itself and, although he went along with some of it, he did not appear to be really enamoured. Just the opportunity for a dashing young opportunist to step in and filch her from under his nose, thought Ari. By playing poker with some of the crew down below in the belly of the ship, he had managed to pick up some useful gossip and win back enough dosh for his immediate needs, but not nearly enough to repay his mounting debts and for his forthcoming schemes. He knew he needed to work out his plans in the minutest detail.

*   *   *

Refreshed by an afternoon nap free from dreams, Hamish felt ready to rejoin the fray; his blood was up and he felt rejuvenated. The rest and sea air were obviously doing him good and he was enjoying the fresh feeling of autumn. Though the day was sunny and bright with fluffy clouds overhead, it was distinctly cooler.

Hamish mentally reviewed the past twenty-four hours and all the incongruous things which had happened to him. Without thinking he pulled his wallet out of an inside pocket and the piece of paper with the cryptic message, as yet still undeciphered by Katie, fluttered to the floor.

"My God," he thought, "I quite forgot. I must get this translated *pronto*," and turned to his wife, appealing to her.

Written in a spidery hand in rather faint pencil and ill-spelt Spanish, Katie was at first nonplussed, then at last, painstakingly, able to make out the following for him:-

JC NOW TRAC(K)ED TO GOLDEN QUELLON (CHILOE);
IMPERATIVE MEET YOU THERE 2200 hrs LOCAL TOMORROW.
LEEWAY HALF-HOUR MAX. USUAL PRECAUTIONS.
(signed 'Roger B Tring')

A faint *Tuesday* had been scrawled at the top so that meant a rendez-vous on Wednesday, **today** Hamish realised confusedly looking at his watch. In six hours' time. But who the hell was Roger B Tring? Oh, of course. In the Force he'd always been known as "bent string" alias "knotty" as his surname was Tring, Benz Tring. Indeed, Hamish had never realised he had a first name or that it was Roger but suddenly it all came flooding back, their early days of training together at the police college in Kincardine Bridge, halfway between Edinburgh and Glasgow; the rivalry and the banter. He had never especially liked Tring but had had to respect him as he was so smart and obviously streets ahead of the rest of them, intellectually if not physically.

Their wariness of each other had been evident as each vied for the top prize; they both yearned to pass out first for a variety of reasons but in the end Hamish had been eclipsed, probably rightly he grudgingly felt although Tring must have been a good year younger than him and would therefore have had another chance. Still, rather galling in the event when he had so hoped to see the proud smile on his parents' faces.

A lot had happened since those carefree days though, plenty to catch up on but for the present he must find out what on earth this rendez-vous might signify and, more importantly, where exactly it was supposed to take place. If he could get to it then he might also find out the why and the wherefore though he remained sceptical as to its ultimate value, at least to himself. He supposed Tring had been seconded to either Interpol or the CIA in another capacity but how on earth had he managed to track Hamish down, Hamish whom he hadn't seen in years? Must obviously be through Aidan - but why would they be in touch unless they were both working together, under cover of course. Having both been seconded by Interpol for example. He must find out, but he supposed he'd have to wait until Aidan returned from his mysterious rendez-vous ashore.

"Who on earth is Roger B Tring?" queried Katie, totally at a loss.

"A friend of Aidan's - I'll tell you more later," Hamish replied hoping she wouldn't insist on more details now. Happily she was anxious to get going herself so accepted his temporizing.

But what or who did Tring mean by JC for a start. Obviously not Jesus Christ, but how about Jimenez Cruz, pseudonym of a well-known figure in the drug world and one not averse to blasphemous gestures? And where on earth in Quellon was this meeting to be? And why "golden" Chiloé? Although small in comparison with the mainland around Coinco, it nevertheless covered some area and how was he to discover - discreetly - exactly where the clandestine meeting was supposed to be, even assuming the ship's next (unscheduled) port of call was to be within striking distance, without alerting all and sundry? And earlier than originally programmed. As far as he could find out they were not scheduled to call in at Quellon until their return trip in two days' time. But perhaps there had been a change of plan that Vanessa was not yet privy to and Manuel, who was toeing the party line until he was told otherwise, had kept mum about.

Maybe Aidan would be able to cast more light on the scene; after all, he should know of Tring even if they weren't actually in cahoots and working together. They must have overlapped or been almost contemporaries at the police training academy in Marlow. Indeed, it *must* have been through Aidan - who else? - that Tring had hoped to make contact anyway. And why with him? Why not just with Aidan? and what an odd unreliable way in which to do it. Totally contrary to the police manual, and as if he was hoping it would be intercepted. And why sound so mysterious? Was it a trap?

Tilting his chair back and steepling his fingers, Hamish trawled through his memory bank. Why did this chap Tring, his ancient rival, imperfectly recalled from distant days, seem so sure that they were destined to meet up again? It did seem distinctly odd. And why ever did he entrust his message to such a crazily haphazard method of delivery? Had he not been able to locate Aidan? And why write it in Spanish when it might be intercepted and read locally? Almost as if he was inviting a leak. Perhaps he was and thereby wanting to incriminate Hamish, but why? It all seemed distinctly fishy to him. Fishy? That was it: the fish pots, what was in them and why had that fisherman come to such an untimely and smelly end? A thought suddenly struck him; he must alert Aidan to it and without losing any more precious time. What an idiot he was not to have thought of that sooner.

It would be good too if Aidan could make the Tring rendez-vous as **he** was here legally and carried far more clout whereas Hamish was allegedly only on vacation, and totally without any police responsibility any more or indeed any authority whatsoever. Besides, he had promised Katie not to get too heavily involved at least not in the sense of courting unnecessary danger. And in a strange country and without the lingo… and with no legal standing. It would look distinctly odd for him to be seen sculling around the dockside wherever they tied up in Chiloé, obviously on the lookout for someone, and probably dressed conspicuously as well. If "JC" turned out to be the local drug supremo it was a decidedly risky venture and best left to the proper police or at least someone with some genuine business and/or police protection. After all, his sleuthing days when he could sink into the background were long gone, Hamish reflected ruefully. In any case he was a man of the cloth now, no longer a cop, and with different responsibilities, not least to his family.

Earlier in the day as he slunk back aboard after his pre-breakfast pipe, Hamish had thought he was being observed by someone, a shadowy member of the Peruvian group perhaps, unless of course it was an off-duty crew member having a fag on his way ashore. It was impossible to identify the man - or woman - who took good care to keep away from the light and had a fisherman's cap pulled well down over his eyes, but the furtive way he - or she - moved vaguely disturbed the policeman in Hamish.

However, hurrying to Aidan's cabin, he pushed it to the back of his mind and concentrated on his recent missive. Aidan, annoyingly, was not in his cabin; the Captain thought he had slipped ashore again. Being very close to land by now he must have used the dinghy with the outboard motor as the life-rafts had all been safely stowed back on deck, all that is except the malodorous one used as a coffin for the poor unfortunate fisherman whose early demise had started the ball rolling. Strange that Hamish hadn't heard the splash when Aidan launched it but he was probably in his cabin having his doctor-prescribed nap then. However, the Captain, gruffer than usual, declined to enlighten him further and the First Mate who was obviously avoiding his gaze, was ostentatiously studying the next day's charts in deep concentration.

As Hamish peered at the charts of Chiloé island and Isla Guafo over the Mate's shoulder, he realised they were not where he thought they were - or should be. Before he could comment,

"Yes," the officer said, his mouth puckering wryly, "we *are* coming astern of that buoy there," prodding it with his finger "and we *are* berthing at Quellon tonight instead of the day after tomorrow. For a number of reasons," he added hastily before Hamish could draw breath to question him further.

With a meaningful look in the Captain's direction he stepped away from the bridge out onto the deck, followed by Hamish, where he continued in a low voice:

"The police are really getting up the poor man's nose; not only the Chilean but the Peruvian as well; and he's got Interpol to contend with in the person of your friend, and now the CIA are trying to get in on the act. Things are getting quite out of hand. What started as a nice little earner and a quiet cruise now looks like turning sour and costing the poor devil a packet into the bargain. Every day he's obliged to alter course costs him, as well as playing havoc with his schedules since we reckon normally to meet our sister ship in port there," (and he pointed to a prick of light ahead), "compare notes, swap some merchandise and then set off in opposite directions until it's time to reverse the procedure. Taking wind and tides into consideration it's quite a tight timetable, which he's spent years perfecting. With his elder son captaining their sister-ship *Skorpios*, his nephew on shore to coordinate all movements and his wife in overall charge of catering, he's really got the whole thing sewn up. But it needs constant monitoring and one small slip can put everything out of synch and ruin the whole schedule. And this damn' bolt from the blue really is just what we don't need at the present moment." He paused, then added: "But he's good to work for and a considerate boss," in case it sounded as if he was complaining.

Changing the subject, Hamish decided on a long shot.

"Is there any reason you can think of that people should refer to Quellon as Chiloé's 'golden' centre?" he asked. To his surprise the First Mate burst out laughing.

"Not unless you're referring to the pawnbrokers' shop tucked away just behind the harbour on entry. With its three golden balls?" he suggested. "Everyone knows about that. It's a well-known trysting place, but," looking curiously at Hamish "I expect you're probably thinking of the antique shop with the engraving of the old gold-mines. That's quite near the harbour entrance too."

Pushing his replacement sunglasses to the top of his head, Hamish paused for a moment:

"Oh, so they used to pan for gold there, did they?" but only met with a puzzled shake of the head as the officer prepared to return to the bridge. "Not to my knowledge, they didn't. It's just an expression they use locally." He paused for a moment and then added: "They're probably referring to the goose that lays the golden eggs," and cocked his head at Hamish with a knowing look. Hamish was still in the dark but assumed he must mean the transfer of drugs which it would be comparably easy to organise in that inhospitable and difficult terrain where there was virtually no police coverage nor navigable roads inland. He decided to bide his time before pursuing this and, smiling innocently, changed the subject yet again:

"When will he announce the change of itinerary?" was Hamish's parting query. "After all, some people are bound to notice we're not in Aisén when we put the lines ashore."

"Not if we do it after dark, with any luck. When they've all got their feet under the table. Anyway, it doesn't do to send people to bed complaining. They don't sleep well and then are bad-tempered over breakfast. We'll leave it to the PR guys to sort things out for us at breakfast."

And so saying the First Mate bade him goodnight.

*　　　*　　　*

Meanwhile Vanessa and Jaime were making plans for the next day's shore outing unaware that the trip to the market in Puerto Aisén had been sentenced. Having just acquired their eighth grandchild the Fuentes were taking the opportunity to stock up on birthday presents well in advance as the toy market there was renowned and half the price for similar stock available in Santiago. With a keen nose for a bargain Vanessa was not to be thwarted when it came to keeping her brood happy and Manuel was wondering how best to break the unwelcome news to her and escape before she exploded.

CHAPTER EIGHTEEN

Although the couple from Australia, Anna and Nigel, were sharing a cabin it turned out that, as there were no single berths left on the ship by the time they came to book, this was merely a platonic arrangement which suited them both. They had met up fortuitously in LA where they had both been attending an international seminar, though speaking on different subjects. Both were determined to see something of South America before returning home to Adelaide, where they had their own pads and their own circles of friends, so, expediency determining the course of events, they had decided to take a chance. Though from quite different backgrounds, they had enough in common and easy-going enough personalities for the arrangement to work out well, so far at least. Neither snored or over-indulged excessively, so far as the other could gauge. And neither was predisposed to chatter excessively.

Having had to give the keynote paper on "Possible Beneficial Uses of Hard Drugs specifically Heroin", Anna was exhausted and looked forward to relaxing far from work and from anyone who knew her, Nigel excepted of course. She had suffered quite a bit of barracking and even some hate-mail in the aftermath to the conference and had been advised to decline appearing on a popular television chat show for fear of attracting violent reactions from the more extreme elements to be found on the fringe of the university campus. Whilst in the US she feared she had also attracted the attention of the FBI or the Anti-Narcotics & Drugs Administration. She had felt distinctly threatened, though she could not put her finger on why, and was sure she had been followed on more than one occasion when she had supposed she was on her own.

But since entering Chile Anna had been able to relax and forget this unwanted attention. The first night on board she and Nigel had slightly overindulged the Undurraga and she had slept like a top, uninterruptedly the first time in months. She was therefore hardly prepared the next morning to be accosted by a young Latin American from Vanessa's group of cousins who, turning luscious blackberry eyes on her, asked with a grin to be introduced to her and her partner.

As she focussed on the stranger she realised with a shock that he had in fact been one of the co-presenters of the Chilean paper given at her seminar, one of the more thoughtful and intelligent of his contingent, a little less verbose than his compatriots, though far younger; and one whom she had found it agreeable to discuss a particularly knotty problem with. He obviously considered Nigel and herself an "item" but had been fishing to find out more. At first he seemed hesitant about pursuing his brief acquaintanceship with her even though Anna found herself inviting him to join them for drinks that evening. She studied him covertly as he wondered whether to accept, curious to see whether he would make a pass at Nigel or whether in fact he was heterosexual. Then again she wasn't sure if it would be an asset or a hindrance to have a chaperone along! But the young man shyly declined the invitation, looking a little coy, so she decided it was all for the best. He must be quite a bit younger than her and most likely had his own relationships to think of. It was probably just inquisitiveness which had brought him round anyway.

An hour later she saw him with his arm round an extremely goodlooking flirtatious Chilean girl who kept flashing provocative smiles at him, swinging her shoulder-length black hair across her face and into his. Anna and he nodded discreetly and returned to their separate decks; she not giving him another thought until Nigel, curious, asked several seemingly innocuous questions about her 'Adonis', betraying a personal as well as a professional interest. Until now she had not thought that Nigel's interests lay with his own sex but now she began to question her assumption.

"If you're so interested why the dickens don't you find out for yourself?" Anna suggested finally, losing patience. "But you'd better steer clear of his Chilean '*pollolla*' she warned, his flirt". Nigel decided to do just that, having read about the violent jealousies young 18-year old Chilean girls were famous for, but bemused nevertheless.

Later, finding herself in conversation with Anna, Katie commented on the difference in attitude of South American men to women and vice versa, curious to find out more about Nigel and how he fitted in. She herself had wondered about Nigel's proclivities but was trying not to appear too inquisitive. Anna was intrigued by her apparent interest so

Katie went on to expound on the even more marked shift in attitudes since her mother had lived in Chile in the thirties when of course homosexuality of any kind was absolute taboo, or at least never spoken of openly, or even hinted at, not even obliquely. Indeed, it had been a prisonable offence then.

"In those days young men, rather than betray any untoward interest, would have taken any opportunity to flirt with every good-looking girl who crossed their path to deflect any possibility of suspicion. She, however, would not have dreamt of responding overtly even if their parents acknowledged each other socially," Katie explained. "In common with the Indian sub-continent and elsewhere I believe, the etiquette of *boy meets girl* by introduction only was strictly adhered to, and it was not uncommon for well-brought up *señoritas* to have a duenna. Yes, a duenna like the upper-class Spanish. Certainly no self-respecting girl of marriageable age in the twenties and thirties would have let herself be seen conversing, unchaperoned, with a young man who was unrelated (unless he were a priest or destined for the Church)."

Anna was still looking amazed but begged Katie to continue.

"It wouldn't have crossed the parents' minds that the young man's interest was faked in order to throw a false trail, and they would have been outraged had this ever become common knowledge. Indeed, I knew of a case where a 17-year old, a friend of my mother's, had been forcibly married off to someone much older, guilty only of having cast a flirtatious look at a young man not of her parents' choosing who, moreover, was suspected of having other leanings. Of which of course the girl was totally unaware. It wasn't as if she was particularly interested or even sexually attracted to him, just bored with the conventional kind her mother thought 'suitable'. But, ironically and despite the odds, she and her 30-year old husband grew to be extremely happy together even if they did end up living rather separate lives. At least they had their family relations and snobbish but well-to-do backgrounds in common; and of course their membership of the exclusive Country Clubs. And later several kids."

"But was he faithful to her, do you suppose?" Anna asked. "What about his previous girlfriends?"

"Even if he did have mistresses - and there's nothing to suggest he did - it proved to the world that he was not sexually deviant, horror of horrors. Or did it? And she had time to consort with her girl friends and her own limited circle of friends, comparing fashions and grandchildren - and maids - to their hearts' content."

"It was the norm then for girls to pretend the opposite sex didn't exist and men to flirt and treat young women as playthings, looking ostentatiously at their *décolletages*, and their legs, and indulging their 'jokes' with sexual innuendos. In fact, generally to patronise them. But they usually respected 'the fair sex' if they came from the same social milieu. Sometimes in fact they even idolised them, bringing them expensive flowers and little gifts like diamond rings…," Katie continued while Anna looked bemused. "And paying extravagant compliments. Which of course they didn't really mean. For example, I remember when I went back to Chile in the late sixties with my father, he took me to a fashionable concert in the centre of Santiago. The son of one of his erstwhile business partners was introduced to me and immediately complimented me on my '*tenu*' (they liked to show off their cosmopolitan sophistication then). I blushed and didn't know what to say, whereupon his father - not to be outdone - said: 'It's not the dress, stupid, *està la percha.*' I must have looked completely nonplussed, so he explained it was the coat hanger, ie what was supporting the dress not the dress itself which was so eye-catching…a typical compliment of smart Chilean society in those days."

Anna still looked incredulous as Katie continued: "Whereas in the house the wife reigned supreme: her word was law, except - surprisingly - insofar as the children's education was concerned (although of course she was expected to take them to church and catechism every Sunday). Yes, she was subordinate in all matters concerning schools, career and so forth, especially putative boyfriends, when it was the paterfamilias's word which counted."

"Funny, I'd always understood it was just the other way round," Anna rejoined, still a bit thrown.

"Oh no, well not in my grandfather's case anyway. He prided himself on being something of an expert on children's education. I'm not sure I agree with him, though. Certainly not in my mother's case. Furthermore, if a girl were not still a virgin on her wedding night the most awful scandal might ensue, leading so far as to the return of soiled goods in the 'best families' ie the most narrow-minded circles. Real Arabian Nights stuff. Where, like in England at this time blue-stockings could, exceptionally, get an university education and perhaps even hold their own in science and maths, even perhaps become a doctor, in Chile (and Chile was far more enlightened than most of her neighbours, the Argentine and Brazil for instance, and as for Paraguay…). Where was I?.. higher education was decidedly still only for the unusually lucky - one might even say 'maverick' few, women such as Gabriele Mistral. But even she was the daughter of a much-travelled diplomat so perhaps she was hardly typical of her generation as she had a much broader education than most of her contemporaries.

"You've never heard of Mistral our celebrated poetess? Or these days perhaps I should just say 'poet'- who won the Nobel prize? Well before Neruda too. You should read her; she's good and I think I saw a copy of her most recent anthology on the book-shelf in the main lounge. She's not as well known as Neruda of course, but still well worth trying. I'll try to get hold of the book for you…".

Anna was writing down the details when Katie resumed:

"As I was saying, my mother though gifted, was not so lucky. She was not allowed to go to art school or anything remotely like that. The best she could do was to follow a course for flower-arranging and even then she was chaperoned. There and back," Katie concluded.

When Anna expressed disbelief, Katie explained it probably would have meant going to the States or even England for art school, out of the question without a duenna in those days. "And prohibitively expensive too. Even though her parents could probably have afforded it they would only have considered spending so much money on a son's education, not a girl's where there was always the dowry to think about into the bargain." Then she elaborated:

"Far from it; all her father would say was 'she's an attractive girl with a good enough dowry, she'll get married soon enough,' - the ultimate aspiraton supposedly of a wellborn young girl at that time. After all, we're talking about just after the turn of the century - a hundred years ago now".

Anna, despite what she considered to be her own enlightened views, had never thought much about the woman's position, domestic or political, in the Chile of those days and found she was shocked. Where she came from equality of educational opportunities had been taken for granted for so many years that even her grandmother's generation had grown up expecting equality as the norm.

"Why didn't they rebel?" she asked wonderingly.

"How could they? They had no means of their own, certainly no bank account, and were tightly controlled in every way. Besides, their mothers would hardly have condoned that; and certainly their brothers wouldn't have." Katie paused and then continued:

"I'll tell you a story to illustrate how coy young girls from high bourgeois families were encouraged to be. When my grandfather fell in love with her, he sought Granny's parents' permission to pay her court and eventually arrived to seek her hand in marriage bearing a beautiful blood-red rose. Of course she was flattered, but Granny had other ideas about getting married, at least so young and to someone she scarcely knew, so she refused him. Outright. Consternation! The day after he arrived carrying two roses, again lovely carmine blooms. Again she refused him. The next day he came with three, and so on. After ten days the drawing-room was beginning to look like a hothouse and her mother was getting worried. There were no more vases in the house and the place smelt like a coquette's boudoir."

Anna was smiling unbelievingly now as she gently shook her head.

"Her own parents were bringing pressure to bear on her now but for a while that only served to stiffen her resolve. Finally, after she found a diamond ring nestling in one of the blooms together with a little love-note, she hesitated, yielded, and the rest you know. Despite his old-fashioned ideas I gather they were very happy, my grandmother's only regret being that she never did get to art school. Though she did get to dabble in water-colours later in life. Quite successfully, I believe. In fact, I still have one or two and her old paint-box somewhere."

Katie promised to lend Anna a book which illustrated the slow process of women's emancipation on the South American continent, in Peru as slow as anywhere, and to show her a passage from her own mother's diary written just before she got engaged in 1925. She also showed her a sepia-coloured photograph of the dining room of the house they lived in when they were first married. The dinner table, lavishly laid for twelve, was resplendent with ornate silver plates, solid silver cutlery and salt cellars and, in the centre, a baroque cigar lighter in the form of a silver stirrup. Light glinted from the dainty crystal champagne flutes and wine glasses, but it was the silver cigar lighter which stole the show. Elaborately interwoven flowers, all in solid silver but topped with a gold rosette resembling a Tudor rose, formed a handsome conquistador's slipper-shaped stirrup. The silver of course was mined locally in the El Teniente silver mines in which her grandfather had shares, Katie explained.

"Whew, what opulence! Did anyone really live like that in those days?" Anna asked incredulously.

"Yes, in Peru they did. And in one or two houses in Chile, in the fashionable parts of Valparaiso and Viña, as well as Santiago. As for the Argentine, I really don't know what happened there, but they were supposed to be often even more ostentatious in La Plata and some of the affluent Buenos Aires suburbs. Take the Hurlingham Club for instance, that was worse than most of the snobby London men's clubs and, like Harrods BA, proud of its English antecedents."

Anna, still looking bemused, pressed her to go on.

"I was describing the silver stirrup, wasn't I? The really amusing thing was if you pressed the rosette, taking care to point it away from you, a cutter rather like a pencil-sharpener or a silver spur jumped out ready for your cigar. All very ingenious. Oh, and I forgot to add that behind each guest's chair, when they were giving a formal dinner, stood a footman with powdered wig ready to act as waiter. Rather vulgarly ostentatious, but at least he didn't still have silver buckles on his shoes," she added, smiling. "Not by the 1930s anyway. I need hardly add that my mother was terrified all evening lest she put her foot in it by offending some pootling convention so beloved of Lima high society. Her mother's friends would have had a grand time sniggering about that the next day if she had. Or if she'd inadvertently used a Chilean word which had a different (and invariably a coarser interpretation) than posh Peruvian society. I think her husband, her fiancé then of course, would have unobtrusively backed her up if this had ever happened. He really didn't have much time for their exaggerated airs and graces either, though he bowed to convention enough so as not to offend his parents whom he adored. In public at any rate."

"There's one thing I'd like to ask you while we're on the subject," Anna pursued, blushing slightly: "Now that so many men are starting to share or even take on the traditional woman's role of looking after the children - even in some Latin American countries so I hear - with a subsequent lessening of mystique at the child-bearing role for example, do you detect any weakening of man's respect for the 'weaker sex' here?

Some men still really seem to verge on contempt, from what I saw in Lima?"

Katie hesitated. Her immediate reaction had been 'yes', but she didn't want to rush in with a snap judgement. She promised she'd think about it and let Anna know her considered opinion next time they met as it was getting on for drinks time and the evening 'copucha' around the bar. Definitely not to be missed.

"At least I envy you having been brought up with all those servants, never having to do any washing or ironing or cleaning of sinks. Or even making your own bed I suppose?"

"Now that's one thing you may not believe. All my life I've regretted not having been brought up to do housework properly or even cooking. I might have picked up a few tips if I had instead of having to learn it all the hard way. And Hamish would have been spared having to show me so many elementary domestic things…".

Anna had to admit she had never thought of it like that. With that they repaired to their respective cabins to change for dinner, Anna still shaking her head and Katie anxious to catch up on Hamish's latest news.

CHAPTER NINETEEN

Anna had just turned thirty. Her determined jaw betrayed her ambition and sense of purpose but the lines round the corner of her mouth hinted at a well developed sense of fun; she was definitely set to 'go places' and when she smiled her expression softened into an enthusiastic grin. She no longer possessed the boyish figure of her teens but her incipient curves added to her allure; at least the men in the party thought so. An excellent swimmer of near Olympic standard, she regretted she had had little regular exercise of late. However, she was determined to get fit on this holiday before returning home. And was losing no time in doing so.

'Adonis', as Anna now termed her new admirer, was obviously some years younger than her and not nearly so experienced in their particular field of research, but she found him *simpatico* and mature beyond his years in other ways. She was beginning to enjoy his company and particularly his knowledge of the flora and fauna of his native Chile, which he described charmingly to her in his halting English.

"I realise now how little I really know of my own country's natural habitats," she told him. "Certainly I would be hard put to it to describe its wildlife as interestingly as you do."

Yet where she, Anna, came from there was a far greater variety than here, at least of mammals. But this young Chilean, who had by now lost some of his shyness, was proving to be quite a wit and a good imitator of birdsong. She wished she had had the foresight to bring along a book on local wild flowers, never having imagined how they proliferated in this part of the country already as far south as Aisén - further south than her own Adelaide. Not surprisingly, there were several similarities in the flora and also in the kinds of fish she saw on display in the local market. Even Raùl did not know all their names although some she suspected were very local. There were also many exotic and vividly coloured subtropical plants she had never pictured, even in her wildest dreams, which he did know; she was especially glad of his guidance here. Through her binoculars she was gazing at a particularly interesting trumpet-shaped flower. So when Adonis sneaked up on her and tried to snatch a kiss she jumped out of her skin and pushed him away firmly. But he apparently took no offence at her rejection, just laughing it off.

"You are a very beautiful woman, you have so much vitality," he had blurted out as he hastily recovered his composure, "and I admire you very much. Please forgive me for such unforgivably bad manners. Now I must return to my group but I hope I may still see you again?"

She was surprised to be so shaken by the experience and tried to hide her confusion. His skin was olive-smooth, not a three-day stubble like Peter's back home, and he smelt of jojuba oil or something like it - probably derived from one of the native trees he was so knowledgeable about; and his eyes were so luminous. She was beginning to wish she had not been so precipitous in repelling him so vehemently; he had such allure, but she had been quite taken by surprise. Besides this would never do: she must remember their difference in age, in status and nationality, not to mention also background.

The next day as she emerged from the sulphur pools where she had gone for a pre-breakfast swim she slipped and cut her foot on the jagged stone surround. As she was wondering what best to do and how to staunch the bleeding someone appeared silently from behind the changing huts with a towel and some disinfectant.

"Hm, this looks serious; you should have an anti-tetanus as there is lots of humus and animal dirt around and…," Anna looked up and to her surprise saw it was her young beau from the previous day. She bent down to show him the wound and could feel his breath on the nape of her neck. Supporting her foot on his knee he dabbed the cut with disinfectant on a piece of gauze labelled *sterile* as he took the opportunity to run his hand up her calf appreciatively. Despite herself Anna shivered. Her scalp was now tingling with delicious anticipation. What luscious black eyes he had and how gentle his touch. She pulled herself together with a start; she really mustn't let him see the effect he was having on her.

"Oh, it's all right, thank you. I had a jab before I left home and it's well within the time limit."

He reluctantly let go of her foot. She sensed he was itching to say something more but she turned and said briskly:

"I must get some of that delicious papaya before they run out. Such gorgeous breakfasts they serve on board." With a brief thank you and avoiding his hurt look she slipped away.

It was two days later when they were all going ashore in Coinco to see the famous handicrafts down at the market before they bumped into each other again. Looking nervously round to see if anyone was watching Adonis pressed a flower into her hand, unobtrusively inspecting it for signs of a ring.

"A copihue, the Chilean national flower," he murmured. Anna inspected the scarlet trumpet-shaped blossom, limp from the heat of his hand, and held it to her nose.

"No, they don't really have a scent but they are supposed to bring good luck. How is your foot? I see you're managing to walk again without limping."

He threw her a smile and quickly rejoined his friends.

That night she dreamt a shark was closing alongside her as she swam, about to tear strips off her leg; she was drowning and the next thing she knew she was lying on the beach with a crowd pressing round her and a voice murmuring sweet reassurances into her ear. Looking up she met those limpid ebony eyes again and… And then she woke up, bathed in sweat. She fumbled under her pillow for a handkerchief and her fingers closed on something silky yet flaccid. She froze then switched on the light: a pink patch had stained the sheet and what looked like a spent carmine balloon lay in her hand. Of course the love token, she thought facetiously to herself, the copihue.

Drifting back to sleep, she was disconcerted half-an-hour or so later to hear raised voices in the corridor outside her cabin.

"Did you win the wager then, Raùl? How long did she hold out on you? What was it like, was it easy? was it cool?" and so on. At first she was merely irritated at being dragged into full wakening from a deep sleep, then gradually she became more conscious of the mocking questions. Although her command of Spanish was patchy she nevertheless had enough to follow the drift which was unmistakable. Her curiosity roused, she wondered who they were talking about and who they were teasing. Then suddenly it dawned on her. With a drumming in her head she felt a flush spread all over her body as her humiliation knew no bounds. Was that really why this gorgeous young man had been paying her such arduous attention? A childish wager, no less? It was not her imagination; he **had** been wooing her. And had she meant nothing at all to the flirt but the chance of a conquest to be witnessed by his friends? Miserably she supposed he had just been playing with her. She must be getting old and losing her attractiveness but why pick on her? How demeaning! What did he hope to gain by such callous behaviour? Let us see; two can play at that game, she decided.

But Raùl had in fact been playing his cards very close to his chest. His first intention in flirting with Anna had been to seek an introduction on his forthcoming trip to Adelaide. He had been invited to participate in an international symposium entitled "Opiates - Uses and Abuses" to be held in Southern Australia and felt sure Anna would be there too, her home territory after all. Recent research in developing opiates for beneficial use, including the possible use of cocaine for multiple sclerosis, were just her thing besides.

At first he had been rather overawed by this brilliant vivacious woman who was obviously so dominant in her subject, then he had quickly fallen under her spell: she was decidedly very attractive especially when she was roused, and he loved her freckles and auburn colouring. He had been quite sincere in telling her so. And things had gone on from there despite himself...but his girlfriend was becoming very possessive and egged the others on to tease him out of what she perceived to be his growing infatuation with someone old enough to be his mother. At seventeen, thirty seemed light-years away.

CHAPTER TWENTY

Hamish was alone in the cabin poring over his map of Chiloé trying to work out where they had taken Tony and where it was in relation to the local police station. Instinct made him glance in his shaving-mirror; he became aware of the steward entering silently and studying him intently. He stiffened as police training and a slight glint told him the young man, obviously not his steward after all, was carrying a knife.

"Who are you and what do you want?" Hamish, wheeling round, sounded as fierce as he could, hoping his inadequate Spanish would be intelligible. The fellow just grunted, his yellow eyes reflecting blank hostility. When Hamish repeated the question he spat out something unintelligible which Katie, hurrying down the corridor and finding the cabin door wide open, just caught but could barely understand. Though the irate tone left her in no doubt.

"I think he's saying he's a Peruvian freedom fighter from the *Sentero Luminoso* and you are a filthy capitalist swine in the pay of the Yankee gringos," she interpreted breathlessly. "But he seems to think you are 'Señor Tony' - a case of mistaken identity? Look out!" Her voice rose in panic as, simultaneously, the young man raised his arm, the knife flashed and Hamish swerved and ducked, kicking out sharply at the man's shin just in time to avoid the blade plunging downwards. It caught his arm a glancing blow but in his anger he felt nothing as the adrenalin surged through. Despite the gap in years, his policeman's training had taken over and after a brief struggle he had his assailant in a Highlander's iron grip. Jerking the weapon out of his hand, Hamish pushed Katie aside before the young man could retaliate, and grabbed both his arms. He twisted first one then the other behind him, viciously; and then bound his wrists together with the shaving towel draped around his neck, aided by Katie who handed him another to finish off the job, taking care to avoid being spat on by the now incandescent Peruvian.

Scrutinizing the intruder closely he realised this was no crew member nor yet a fisherman recruited to do the mafia's dirty work. But the face and its mulish expression was faintly familiar: wherever had he seen it? Surely those pointed eye-teeth he'd seen before: the teeth looked as if they had been carefully stropped so as to get a better edge and the filthy nails made it seem the owner had been clawing mud or debris, not just handling fish. For a moment Hamish thought he was dreaming again but not his habitual nightmare, something rather different this time. Deciding to play safe, he tied another hand-towel around the man's eyes in a secure seaman's knot, keeping well clear of his writhing feet. Surely he must have stolen the steward's key intending to let himself in, hoping the coast was clear. The man still hadn't uttered a word since losing his knife but he now spat expertly in Hamish's direction and swore "Son of a whore! Filthy gringo...!" still struggling to get loose and aiming another vicious kick at his captor which happily failed to connect.

He then launched into a torrent of abuse of which Katie could only understand the one word "revenge". Did he also mention the word "oro" perhaps? She explained to Hamish that the knifeman must be speaking *Quechua* interlarded with local Spanish, which she understood patchily if at all: it was the language originally spoken by the Peruvian Indians under the Inca empire and still in some of the remoter villages of the Andean foothills. Recently some anthropologists recruited by Unesco had been pressing the government to provide schooling in their native patois for the children in these villages but had met with virtually no success so far. ("Rather like the situation in Wales", she couldn't help remarking. "Or even in your Gaelic-speaking parts of Uist.") But there were obviously no votes in it since the parents were mostly illiterate and therefore under the current system disenfranchised; and which politician would be foolhardy enough to stick his neck out to insist on giving them the vote, especially when they were unlikely to support him and the reigning régime. All hell would break loose if these people ever managed to elect one of their own, the politicians well knew.

The Scot's mind flashed back to the minutes before embarkation at Puerto Montt when a knot of supposed fishermen had blocked the road down to the pier with a line of burning tyres and other rubbish, preventing Vanessa's busload of passengers from gaining access to the dockside. They had been blocked for over half an hour and had the bus-driver not managed to reverse all the way up the sinuous road and find another way round they might well have missed their departure altogether - all ostensibly over a row about overfishing by foreign boats.

Hamish had been aware that the Chilean protesters had been orchestrated and urged on by a couple of evil-looking swarthies who had kept in the shade, but the one issuing orders had borne an uncanny resemblance to the man who had just narrowly avoided stabbing him in the back. Now Hamish had time to study him, an unmistakable sickle-shaped scar over his right eye added to his sinister appearance and made him easier to recognise though at the time it had been too dark to notice it. That and his discoloured teeth and rancid breath, together with his flat nose, should make him easy enough to recognise if their paths were ever to cross again, Hamish thought. This man, who decidedly did not look Chilean, seemed nevertheless to call the shots; so what on earth could be the connection? And what could this dago (he smiled to himself as he consciously dredged up this emotive non-pc word) possibly have against him, Hamish, apart from his having been seen hobnobbing with the Interpol agent. But that was probably quite damning enough in itself. Besides, he was after all a gringo. And if the man did but know it, a churchman to boot - not that that would have cut much ice with an avowed atheist or, more probably, animist.

Reflecting on this, with a jolt Hamish recalled a moment on the quayside before leaving Puerto Montt. He remembered how surprised he was to see a goodlooking slight young man with an American-style bomber jacket, again obviously not Chilean, in a huddle with someone who had been in the thick of the fishermen's protest and who matched this Peruvian's looks. He had idly wondered at the time what they could possibly have in common; their animated conversation being punctuated by several emphatic stabbing of fingers and other gestures as they disagreed. But as they took leave of each other, after surreptitiously exchanging notes, they firmly clasped hands and clapped each other on the back in a comradely fashion.

The current incident, the knife attack on Hamish, had all happened so quickly Hamish hadn't had time to call for help. He had simply reacted on reflex and was so engrossed in tying his man up securely he even forgot about Katie until she gasped, seeing blood on his arm and the knife still gleaming dully on the cabin floor:

"Are you all right, my darling?" and in a louder voice, "You're hurt."

Even after all these years of marriage, the concern in Katie's eyes and her crooked smile made his heart bounce but he forced himself to keep to the point.

"Wheesht, woman," he hissed. "S'naething: Ah'm fine. Get the steward and quickly."

Despite all his time spent in England Hamish still occasionally lapsed, in moments of crisis, into his vernacular but Katie knew better than to hang around and was out of the door before he'd finished.

Stuffing the corner of his towel into the intruder's face, so as to silence the abuse being hurled at him, and trying to avoid his lion's breath, Hamish frisked his captive expertly for further weapons. Meanwhile Katie went at top speed to the Master's cabin, then when no answer, to the bridge. The first mate looked thunder-struck as Katie related in rapid Spanish Hamish's account of events adding that she thought the knifeman was speaking *Quechua*, the common parlance of the *Sentero Luminoso,* Peru's Maoist band of self-styled freedom fighters. Since obviously the Peruvian bigwigs in power were not going to encourage the teaching of this in the schools no right-minded person would ever admit to even understanding it. As for any right-minded Chilean it was so much double-dutch to him; the First Mate snorted his disgust and disapproval.

"Can you describe what he looked like," the Mate asked Katie.

"Well, he looked very furtive; he had the high cheekbones and flat nose and forehead of the Mapuche but with extra-ordinarily pointed eye-teeth." She paused, and was urged to go on. "Well, although his face was very swarthy he looked rather as if… as if he was a python which had just swallowed a mule and was experiencing great difficulty getting its hooves down. Oh yes, I nearly forgot, he had an unmistakable sickle-shaped scar on his forehead over his left, or was it his right, eye? Anyway, about here.." and she indicated a spot near her right temple.

Despite her scared expression, the First Mate burst out laughing. "I know exactly the fellow you mean and I can't say I'm altogether surprised. A nasty piece of work, indeed. We always suspected he was up to no good but he seems to have some powerful backers as we can never get the local police to put him inside for more than a day at a time. As soon as he's arrested some urgent message comes through from the capital telling them to release him and, bingo, out he goes again. And the police here are left to grind their teeth in impotent rage."

No sooner had Katie relayed this to Hamish back in the cabin than the Captain appeared. It was decided that Aidan, who had fortunately just arrived back on the scene too, should try to smuggle the man out of the cabin - aided by another crew member - and down the gangplank before any of the other passengers, the excitable Peruvians especially, could catch sight of him.

After a spectacular sunset most of the passengers were now happily ensconced in the bar with other things on their minds though there was no sign of the Peruvian contingent. Katie presumed that Aidan would then accompany their captive to the nearest police station for questioning: ought she not to go with them? Aidan would surely need some interpreting once there. Not only did he not speak the language properly but he didn't know the topography and no-one was even certain where the nearest police station was. Even then they might be suspicious of his police credentials assuming him to be North American and therefore interfering in their pond. It was bad enough when the Peruvians or the Argentines flexed their muscles on Chilean sovereign territory but there were limits.

"Thanks for the offer, Katie, but in fact I mustn't stop. I'm needed straight away on the mainland - I've just had an urgent message so can only come partway with you. Don't worry, that muscular crewman with a smattering of Quechua can take him provided somebody else reliable goes too. As well as you, that is, if you're willing to explain what happened and interpret where necessary. That would be a real bonus." Aidan flashed her a warm smile, embarrassed at having to embroil Katie again but impatient to get going; though also to see the intruder safely ashore, by now in the handcuffs he had resourcefully supplied. So, accompanied by the crewman, Katie as interpreter and the PR man Manuel, strongly enjoined by the Captain to look after her, they set off.

Happily they were able to commandeer a local taxi with a driver who knew where the nearest police station was. He had reason to dislike, or rather to fear, the *Sentero Luminoso* - for reasons which only became apparent later. Katie set off promising a rather apprehensive Hamish she would return to the ship as soon as she could so not to lock her out of the cabin. Persuading her to wear her sheepskin jacket was not easy but just as well, it turned out.

Hamish was still puzzled by the day's earlier events and far from convinced that it was the genuine Chilean *carabinieri* who had visited him then. Having the rare opportunity of the cabin to himself, he decided to do a little investigating of his own. Bearing in mind George Eliot's dictum "It's never too late to be what you might have been", he decided to throw caution to the winds and suit his action to Eliot's words. (It still rankled that he had been thwarted from achieving as much as he had hoped for when in the Renfrewshire police force in bringing the known chief drug-runners in Glasgow to book. Perhaps now was the moment to rectify that vicariously; maybe he could - even at this advanced stage - do something to compensate for his earlier failure.) He ran his fingers through his hair, massaging his scalp and lay back in his chair, deep in thought. His arm was throbbing and he decided he needed a drink to aid his concentration but then decided to make himself wait for Katie's return.

Looking down, he was not a little put out by discovering that his bedside Bible had obviously been manhandled since half the markers had fallen out and either been hastily replaced in the wrong place or left lying on the cabin floor. As he picked it up he realised the adrenalin was flowing and he felt rejuvenated to be back on the trail, despite Katie's misgivings over his health and his own feelings of guilt in her regard.

He reviewed the past twenty-four hours and all the incongruous, not to say nonsensical, things which had happened to him and wondered what was happening to Tony and what progress, if any, was being made in catching the perpetrators of the Inca gold heist back in Lima. It was ironic that the only person who seemed to be able to keep his finger on what was going on there was Freddie, an Uruguayan medic and nothing to do with any police or law-and-order people. Even Interpol were apparently out of the loop despite their satellite communication facilities; and it was plainly no use relying on the local gendarmerie who had shown no signs of wanting to cooperate at all so far. They made it clear they had enough on their plate with all the drug-running up and down their coastline as well as inland, very scarce resources, and were naturally hostile to any kind of foreign meddling in their affairs, especially when orchestrated by a Minister - of any hue. As if any politico cared what was going on in their remote pond, and as if they cared about any government official even if he were a so-called Minister, miles away in the capital.

Having in mind Aidan's difficulties in communicating with the local police, Hamish wondered whether the First Mate (whose English had proved far better than he had ever let on) might have some useful hints as to how best to approach the local anti-drug force with a genuine offer to cooperate, still keeping a low profile - and hopefully without antagonising them; so he went up to the bridge in search of him.

He had been reflecting on the Mate's elliptical remarks about golden geese and drug-running and a thought had struck him. Suppose these broilers which were imported weekly from the States (very often the only form of meat which the people in this impoverished region could afford to eat, even their own fish being beyond their purses since that was their livelihood); suppose these imports were not as innocent as they appeared. After all, what would it take to remove all the innards and stuff the inside cavities with ...gold? No, too expensive and it would show up if there were X-rays; besides where would the market be? No-one outside the US could afford that. With drugs of course! And then ... deepfreeze the carcases and ship them on. Bob's your uncle!

∗   ∗   ∗

A couple of hours later Katie returned breathless to recount to Hamish what had happened when they accompanied the prisoner first down to the bowels of the ship, and then later ashore to the police station. The Chilean police did not hold themselves back when it came to venting their spleen on this troublesome Peruvian and Katie was glad to leave before she could witness too many of their vituperations. The taxi-driver had been only too glad to hurry back to the ship too. On the return journey he had unburdened himself to Katie, describing the atrocities meted out to his family in the north, in the border region haunted by the *Sentero Luminoso*. When his cousins had resisted their instructions to commit acts of sabotage against the local train drivers, vengeance of a particularly bloody and uncouth variety had been perpetrated against them, leaving them completely traumatised... and devastated. So much so that they were forced to flee, with all their belongings, to safer territory further south where they later regrouped to lick their wounds and plan their revenge. The driver's eyes glittered and sweat poured off his forehead as he recounted details of their atrocities until Katie begged him to stop, but she was left in no doubt as to the bloodthirstiness of some of the sect's committed followers.

Not wishing to gild the lily, she said airily to Hamish, carefully shutting the cabin door:

"I've found out a bit more about why the taxi-driver has it in for the *Sentero Luminoso*. They certainly are alleged to have carried out some terrible things, and not all of them confined to Peru as I had always supposed. The way he described some of the revenge killings, way up in the remoter part of the mountainous area near the Chilean frontier, made me feel quite sick. Their favourite weapon, by the way, is a particular kind of curved knife, like that *kukri* my father used to have in his study, probably the kind that wretched Quechua-speaker had."

She tried to disguise the slight tremble in her voice as, involuntarily, she glanced across at Hamish's slashed forearm and its now modest bandage, which looked innocent enough. As she realised what a narrow escape Hamish had had, even though it must have arisen from mistaken identity, she shuddered, adding:

"Not even babies are immune, he told me."

Hamish quickly changed the subject. During Katie's absence he had lodged the confiscated knife with the Captain for safety's sake. He trusted it had been securely locked away: after all, he hoped it would be needed for evidence later. If they ever got that far, that is. He decided to keep his thoughts about golden geese, and also about drug-laden chickens to himself - for now; and probably not to mention them to Katie at all. She had had enough shocks for the time being and he still felt badly about letting himself become involved in the first place. Catching sight of the clock they realised with a start it was time to dress for dinner if they were not to be late. Delicious smells were already wafting towards their cabin.

"I could do with that drink first: that's one thing for sure," Hamish grunted to Katie from the shower. "Are you ready? I shan't be a tic."

"Yes, but before we go I must tell you something else. That blow-up you wanted of Jocelyn's photo - you know of the lobster pots - well, Manuel says he can get it so you can see which pots are being emptied but not so as to distinguish who it is doing the emptying. The best he can get you, and this is only after my *nicest* cajoling efforts, shows the rowing-boat alongside with part of its identity number visible on the bow. Blown up it should just about be legible."

"That's marvellous; and what is the number?"

"Oh, I've lost the bit of paper I wrote it on but I know it started with a nought and then had a six or an eight, at any rate one with a curve at the bottom, and then I think it was a letter but I couldn't quite make it out. I'll find the bit of paper and let you know for sure." Hamish sighed as Katie rummaged fruitlessly in the bottom of her totebag. Just like a woman.

CHAPTER TWENTY-ONE

Meantime Tony, transferred by police launch at dead of night to a mainland jail in Aisén, was again being grilled by the local Chilean police, but a more sinister lot this time. One interrogator in particular was restrained with difficulty by his superior officer from applying more than his habitually unpleasant strong-arm tactics learned as a young recruit when questioning some of Allende's more obstinate supporters. Tony's other questioner employed subtler but no less menacing ways of probing.

"You need not think, Englishman, that your precious Consul will save you now. From our experience in Buenos Aires we know exactly how to *aid* people in finding out your precise whereabouts, and as for what you consider your 'rights', what do you propose to do about them now? Only last week we had one of your filthy interfering countrymen here... and none of you stupid *gringos* even suspected he was right under your noses. As for your British Consul...," and he snapped his fingers airily, "what can a man more concerned with his own safety and safeguarding his property do for miserable offenders such as you? Indeed, what interest would he have in doing anything if it meant going beyond his normal comfortable pisco sour or 'whiskycito' at sundown and his five-course dinner at the Club?" He cracked his knuckles again to show he meant business.

Tony, noticing an insignia on the man's collar, realised with a shudder that this must be one of the Chilean secret police who had been sent to the Argentine for special training in some of their more sophisticated and dubious techniques. A sweaty shiver crossed his back while he wondered how the hell he could get a message to the consulate in Punto Arenas, or even one back to Hamish. By now his nail-bitten fingers were so clammy he would have been hard put to it to clasp a pencil even if one had been offered. It seemed unlikely his interrogator had ever so much as heard of the Geneva Convention and, as for letting him write a message in English, that was obviously quite out of the question. Although Tony could, just, muster a few words of spoken Spanish, his written vocabulary was decidedly limited. Besides, he had no grammar. Any message would probably be totally incomprehensible even if he did get to write it.

"It must be awkward for you now that you British have finally adopted those new passports without the convenient double pages," the interrogator leered, changing tacks.

Tony was genuinely at a loss. "What do you mean?" he couldn't help asking. The man smiled sardonically.

"*Bueno*, how do you know the going rate for each transaction then?"

"I still don't get…"

"Don't play the innocent with me, Señor Tony, or it will be the worse for you - in the long run." The whites of his eyes flashed menacingly.

$$*\qquad*\qquad*$$

Mercifully Hamish's prisoner, still at the local gendarmerie as it turned out, was to be escorted later that evening to the same jail that Tony was in. As soon as she discovered this Katie arranged to accompany Sheila when she was allowed to see Tony briefly after the *Skyros* docked in Aisén. She was able to use her feminine wiles to get a message to Tony to this effect, Manuel's assistant proving not immune to her flashing eyes and come-hither glances. Manuel himself assured her the ship's captain would arrange transport for them though, at Hamish's insistence, separately from the cabin intruder who would now, it appeared, be accompanied by a local policeman and in a less comfortable conveyance.

When finally they arrived at the jail Tony had difficulty in preventing tears from showing. Gone was the world-weary cynicism which Katie had always suspected was only a ploy to mask deep sensibilities underneath. Befuddled by the rapidity of the day's events and the totally unfamiliar surroundings, coupled with his lack of Spanish, Tony seemed totally dazed and genuinely puzzled at the turn his interrogation had taken. Realizing he had also been deprived of sleep Katie feared he was beginning to hallucinate and, in an effort to cheer him up, she started relating an incident which had happened to her on her brief return visit to Chile over thirty years previously.

To break the silence and distract Sheila who was looking around with mounting horror, Katie plunged in.

"Some forty-odd years ago, having at last finished with school in England, I was snatching the opportunity to pay a brief return visit to Chile (which, after all, I still regarded as home) together with my father. We intended to catch up with our extended family before I returned to England where I was supposed to be starting on my further training. It was now plain I would need to earn a living in Europe, there being no obvious future for me in Chile. As we surveyed the awful rundown state of our *fundos* I was distressed to detect Father trying to hide his tears; it was obvious we would never be able to return to our roots here permanently but I was young enough, at just eighteen, to regard a future in London as exciting enough to more than compensate. Besides, the cousins really were very oldfashioned and rather boring, I had to admit. England was now, in the early 1960s, the rocking country of the future and I didn't shed too many tears on saying goodbye to Santiago."

Katie told her audience she had wanted to become a social worker or a hospital almoner but her mother, who had stayed behind in England with her sister, had had other ideas. However, shortly after they returned to Buckinghamshire Katie's father suffered a fatal heart attack brought on, Katie suspected, by his distress at things in Chile. His premature death meant she could not afford to hang around. The shock of it galvanised her into making a decision as she realised there was no chance of a lengthy training; indeed, only the minimum. She needed to support herself as soon as possible since the money from her educational provision would run out shortly and her mother would then have barely enough to keep the three of them in the way they were accustomed to. And there was no other visible income. Horns were drawn in sharply and Katie learned for the first time in her life what privation meant, or at least scrimping and saving.

In an aside to Sheila, she said she now regretted having mocked her mother for all those ridiculous little economies; reusing envelopes by affixing sticky labels, hoarding rubber bands, recycling leftover food for the chickens, and sometimes even - regrettably - peeling off unfranked postage stamps to use them again. When, later, she told Hamish about this he was rather shocked and she felt decidedly chastened when he said: "But that's defrauding the Royal Mail…". Her sister had called him a prig and, although part of her agreed, Katie never forgot the scarlet on Hamish's cheeks.

That was when Katie decided to take up interior decorating in what she reckoned would be a quick fix (little did she know); at least it should bring in a bit of badly needed cash straightaway. And it had been easy to persuade the Chilean Ambassador living in Wimbledon to take her on for a three-month spell, and on absurdly generous terms, she added. And later more permanently, to her mother's satisfaction. But she was digressing in her tale to Tony, so she continued, trying to find words to cheer him up.

"While I was on my sentimental home trip to Chile with my father, I left him to go south to the farms and went myself west to the coast, to Valparaiso," she began, "to clear through customs some Persian rugs I was trying to import into the country - for a cousin. She was getting married to a Chilean doctor, a young paediatrician in Viña. Admittedly things were rather different then - 1964 - when conditions alternated between stringent austerity for 90% of the country and a glut of luxury for the oligarchs, the other 10%. Young medics, especially those who had only just graduated, fell some way between the two extremes but were nevertheless still well-off compared with the majority of people; although they always pleaded insolvency of course, particularly if they were rash enough to think of getting hitched.

"Actually there was only a slight ironing out in income levels when the Christian Democrats returned to power in 1965/66, what with their ill-fated attempts at land reform and quarrels with the Yanks and most of their neighbours. Falling out with the Argentines in particular; some little skirmish up in Bariloche with a border policeman getting shot, and the settling of old scores and so on... The memory of that and the poverty in some quarters is still pretty acute, even now nearly forty years later," Katie shuddered as she thought back to those insalubrious days. Sheila looked amazed and Tony stopped his fidgeting, urging her to go on with her story.

"Of course the medics and professional classes generally constituted the tip of the middle-class iceberg," Katie continued. "They were often the strongest supporters of Frei and his hoped-for reform programme, initially at least. But even they began to waver when they realised the implications for them of his austerity measures - new taxes on all imported luxury goods, even on food imported from the States, including broilers on which the majority of the poor depended for their once-weekly helping of "meat". It was rather ironic that these chickens were only in the shops on a Friday, ostensibly a day of fasting for all good Catholics, but that's how it worked out. So the people in the "barrios" were suddenly deprived of their once a week treat, making them even more embittered against the Chilean ruling classes. But also against the government officials. Suddenly the gloves were off and tax evasion became the flavour of the month; across the whole class spectrum, not just the wealthiest as before. And nothing can beat a smart young Chilean showing off to his peers when a question of evading taxes is concerned, especially if there is a pretty girl in tow."

"So couldn't they afford any meat at all? What about fish then?" Sheila pursued.

"Only some of the people living along the coast, and that not always as this was the fishermen's livelihood and they hoiked up the prices. Away from the coast it was only the rich who could afford to pay the transport costs inland. In fact, it wasn't uncommon to see a battered old Mercedes (cars were very scarce then) stop in Merced or one of the fashionable streets in the centre of Santiago, open its boot and reveal a whole trunk-load of live lobsters heaving up and down and crawling over each other the same way the politicos did. It would take less than a quarter-of-an-hour to clear the lot, well before the police arrived on the scene. And they weren't cheap either."

Her audience gasped and asked one or two questions and then Katie continued.

"I well recall two miserable days spent at the docks in Valparaiso with nowhere decent to stay and ending up in the YWCA, a grotty hovel two trams' rides away from the port customs. When I eventually did reach the docks I had real difficulty in understanding the local patois and the locals, my Spanish now being overlaid with a foreign intonation. I ended up being directed from guichet to guichet in the customs hall having, as I naïvely thought, correctly completed all the necessary formalities. I got advice from the little kiosk on the corner where I was warned about the daunting preliminaries - the squared paper bought at the Government stationers and stamped at a special office nearby, not once but twice, each time at the cost of a few pence; then queuing for hours for the official's datestamp, another check of my passport, another small tax to pay, another set of forms in the most incomprehensible officialese to complete, sign in triplicate, get witnessed and present at a sixth office window where on my second attempt I thought I recognised the clerk who had previously smirked at me.

"I had definitely not been prepared for all of that. Nor for the gobbledygook. When, on presenting myself for the third time at the same window this same clerk now angrily held my passport up to the light, blew through the watermarked pages making them billow out, and shook his head sadly - and pityingly I thought."

"I know just how you felt," interjected Tony, thinking of his experiences earlier with the special interrogators, but in Sheila's presence he didn't elaborate. Katie smiled sympathetically, and continued:

"On to another window with more arcane questioning; and then the whole process repeated yet again. Back to window number one - rather like the Tote I thought, (if only it had been the pay-out desk instead of this crazy rigmarole). But no. Then - finally - the penny dropped, or rather the slip of paper with the amount written on it fluttered out. Thus it would be at all the windows I supposed. I hesitated. But by now it was too late: catching sight of two of the oiliest officials smirking behind their hands, I dissolved into the most uncontrollable sobs, smudging my mascara and smearing my lipstick while hunting for a handkerchief. When finally approached by the suave Chief of Customs himself, I could only stare at him in dumb bewilderment while he asked if, '*querida Señorita*,' I liked lobster."

Two hours later, after a delicious lunch fortified by an excellent Errazuriz wine and furtively wiping the last of the lobster juice from my chin, I emerged clutching my bale of rugs. I thanked the officer tearfully while he smiled benignly but pityingly at this poor innocent gringo who fancied he winked at the head waiter as they blinked into the sunlight and he summoned her a taxi.

"Thank goodness I was better-looking in those days," Katie added, "though I never stopped wondering if I would ever be called to account or if he really was so amazed at my naïveté that it amused him to play Father Christmas. Happily, I was never to find out."

With Sheila present she didn't care to add that she feared the intervening years had scarcely improved corrupt officials' practices. Police officers in the jail at Aisén looked far more sinister and less human than the smooth Chief Customs man in Valparaiso and were almost certainly open to bribes, provided they were fat enough. But Tony seemed momentarily distracted, even mildly cheered by her anecdote. Since Sheila still looked to be on the verge of tears she wondered whether to add Ursula's story about traffic cops in the Argentine and, after some desultory chat and awkward silences, decided to give it a go. Though hardly relevant, it might serve to distract them for a moment.

"Evidently a friend of Freddie's," she explained, "a Brazilian diplomat with CD plates, had been stopped at a road intersection in Buenos Aires while driving the official car. An alleged infringement at the lights, so the policeman on point duty said. The diplomat's Spanish being somewhat inadequate, he didn't immediately cotton on to what the traffic cop (a lad 'up from the country') was saying, and it took him a moment or two to get the point.

"Pasaporte" demanded peremptorily.

"When the friend, Pedro, saw the cop peering at the writing in Portuguese, obviously unable to understand it, he made as if to explain - which infuriated the policeman, who shouted something scornful, then held up two fingers clamped together holding an imaginary cigarette and pretended to draw heavily on the fag.

"I'm afraid I don't smoke. Filthy habit," answered the diplomat, finally enlightened. And with an urbane smile he shrugged his shoulders as the policeman pointed to the car's glove compartment gesticulating and obviously demanding something or other. The glove compartment yielded nothing and the cop glowered, unable to believe it. In his experience every male foreigner who drove a smart car smoked. And every foreigner carried spare cash in the glove compartment, for the telephone if nothing else.

"There! There!" the cop stabbed his finger at a tobacconist on the opposite corner refusing to give back his passport. "Five hundred Marlboro".

"Pedro made signs as if to move his car as traffic was now building up behind him with furious horn-blaring and motorists screaming epithets out of the window. Unwillingly the policeman motioned him to the opposite kerb but still kept the passport, pretending to scrutinize it. 'Two hundred Marlboro' he ordered, gesturing across the road again.

"Pedro decided not to move his car until the impasse had unblocked as he obviously could not leave without his passport and he did not want to risk a real diplomatic incident. Slowly and ostentatiously he found a pen and wrote down the man's police number as indicated on his lapel and then the amount which he queried with a lift of his eyebrows. The scowl deepened and the demand was commuted to a hundred Marlboro, then fifty when Pedro showed no signs of getting out of his car. Finally, losing patience, the cop flung the passport down in a puddle in the middle of the road where enraged motorists were now edging past, tooting their horns and shouting obscenities at both men.

"Pick it up and give it to me," Pedro demanded in a steely voice. There was no mistaking his resolve. After a moment's stalemate the man truculently caved in and retrieved the muddy passport pretending to note the number before handing it back.

"It seems Ursula had been surprised at Pedro's laughing it off so easily but she realised that this was not such an uncommon event in the Argentine where a lot of the traffic police appeared semi-literate and, anyway, he - Pedro - had come off best. He was after all protected by diplomatic immunity and no-one, not even an Argentine official, would want an incident over something so trivial. Nevertheless, present-day Chile was not the Argentine Republic," Katie reminded herself grimly; "the régime was known to overstep the limit with impunity on occasions, but not where foreign diplomats were concerned. Yet."

However, to give herself time to think, she recounted Pedro's story to Tony as amusingly as she could, adding it to her own galling experience. At least Sheila was able to laugh and cheer her husband inbetween covertly taking stock of his prison conditions. Despite being appalled at his filthy cell, which stank of urine and stale slopped food, and was so small they had to stand in the doorway, she tried to appear cheerful and not over-solicitous.

Tony explained to them that, although his cell had only been designed for single occupancy, he had been warned he was shortly to have a fellow inmate and therefore to move his few belongings while they brought in another mattress. "Then it will likely be standing room only," he joked; "we'll have to take it in turns to lie down at the very least." Sheila tried to hide her dismay as they made their farewells.

Unconvinced of his interrogators' humanity or even whether the Prison Governor had ever read the Geneva Code, Tony looked forlorn. He had nevertheless been slightly cheered to learn from Katie's anecdotes that some Chilean officials could be human after all (if, that is, they were not thoroughly venal). But that had been half a century ago when "democracy" held sway, at least nominally. The situation now at the turn of the century was quite different and none too encouraging once the secret police got in on the act, as they seemed to have done. For one thing it looked as if Tony might be about to be accused formally of a felony, though exactly what had not yet been spelt out. There did not appear to be such a thing as a charge-sheet, at least there was none in evidence. Because of the yards of red tape involved this meant an increasing degree of the impossibility of their ever being able to reverse the situation. Or of his getting out, Tony realized despairingly.

CHAPTER TWENTY-TWO

Tony's fellow captive with whom he was later made to share his cell was a poet by the name of Felipe Lorca Vargas. Señora Lorca had been a great admirer of the Spanish poet of that name but her son did not much appreciate being called after someone who had been imprisoned under Franco. Although ostensibly for his pronounced leftwing views, it was always assumed the charge was really pederasty. In the political climate of the day this had often led to young Felipe being singled out for bullying by his more traditionalist school-mates, with painful results.

However, Tony's cell-mate had survived the bullying, some of it quite vicious, and had become extraordinarily well informed about local politics. Against the bias of the maoist set surrounding him, he developed an inclination for a law-and-order régime. This did not, however, prevent him from having a great deal of sympathy with the land reform idealists. (His enemies then accused him of having a foot in both camps.) Rather, he applauded the ideas of maximising production from the land, not all to the profit of the *latifundistas*, and if that meant giving back control to the 'rotos' (the workers and peasants) then so be it, though he would feel happier, he said, if there were some degree of responsible control in the guise of a manager; and a manager who knew his job, also hopefully was not too corrupt. But that might prove too much to ask in the circumstances, he had to admit.

Though his scimitar-shaped profile and smooth brown skin betrayed mixed origins he had no hang-up about his ethnicity. "That's the Indian in me," Felipe told Tony proudly pointing to his nose, "Mapuche of course, or as the Spanish invaders would have it, *araucano*. But I also have a Peruvian/Spanish grandmother who can trace her descent from the noblest of the *conquistadores*," (hence 'a foot in both camps' again, thought the Englishman wryly) "but I hate the more recent invading gringos, especially the Germans, the Slavs and the Czechs. They're the ones who have usurped my part of the country; and stolen my heritage. Even those pre-Nazi ones who now speak good Chilean Spanish and sing our songs with gusto but who, nevertheless, still have their own German-speaking schools and churches. They're the ones who have stolen our culture but are intent on keeping their own as well. They're the ones with a foot in both camps."

Tony was about to question him about this when Felipe continued:

"To be more precise, my paternal grandparents, the *pehuenches* were nomadic and in their part of Chile were called the *arribanos* or highlanders - 'backwoodsmen' if you prefer - as they grazed their livestock on the Andean foothills over a huge area. In fact it often stretched into what is the present-day Argentine Republic (which accounts for some of the current conflicts over grazing; and the occasional gunshot heard by the Chilean border police. Carried out by the Argentine police too). But these disputes are mainly now concentrated in or around Chaitén. That's a bit further south from here - in the volcanic region on the mainland coast opposite Queilén and Quellon, on the Isle of Castro."

"That's where our ship is supposed to be calling," Tony interrupted wistfully. "That is, if they haven't already done so. I've rather lost count of the days since I've been here."

With a sympathetic smile and comparing of dates, Felipe continued his story.

"Not surprisingly, though, my ancestors resented being pushed around and, being very bellicose, resisted the advancing Conquistadores quite fiercely all those years ago. At first they were successful and the Spaniards got a bloody nose, but eventually they proved no match for the invaders' four-footed devils, their horses, something we didn't yet know in this part of the world. **Or** the Spaniards' imported measles and smallpox either - which succeeded in killing millions of the Incas further north up in Peru. Or their syphilis either," he added ruefully.

"You mean horses weren't indigenous in South America?" interrupted Tony incredulously. "What about the *palaminos* which we've always regarded as originating here, specifically the Argentine? I always thought they …"

"No, not until later. So, not surprisingly, our native defenders were terrified of these quadrupeds, these beasts who advanced on them without mercy, trampling them underfoot when they didn't get out of the way. And the Spanish horsemen with their splendid armour looking more like centaurs were equally terrifying. The goads on their silver spurs alone could inflict a nasty injury and they didn't hesitate to lash out at any inferior in their path, ie any native. That meant us of course."

"And there was me thinking they were merely ornamental, beautiful but ornamental," thought Tony, remembering a spectacular pair of spurs he had acquired in Lima on his previous trip. Solid silver and very baroque.

"As for their so-called Jesuit priests," Felipe went on "they were held to be very fiends incarnate, particularly when they went into action forcibly baptising people, mostly already captive, by the score - into what was then a totally alien religion with quite different practices and taboos. Of course the Jesuits condemned out of hand our own native practices which my forebears had followed for centuries. Admittedly some had been a bit barbaric," Felipe added quietly, "but they formed part of our age-old tradition... And any change forcibly imposed by these fearsome outsiders was bitterly resented."

Picturing the scene, Tony couldn't help sympathising but had to admit he knew very little about the differences in tribes which still inhabited parts of Chile, and even less of the geography of the region. Though he acknowledged the scenery around Coinco to be spectacular, Felipe told Tony that the mountainous region inland along the spine of the Cordillera - particularly across the border into what was now the Argentine Republic - was even more stunning. Roughly on a latitude with Castro, for instance, the *Cerro Tres Picos* with its imposing three peaks rising up to 2,550 metres dominated the surrounding mountains and several small interconnecting lakes which glittered round it like diamonds on a necklace. Admittedly nothing like as tall as further north in the Andes proper, but these peaks were still impressive and were also surrounded by several beautifully cone-shaped volcanoes, not all of them extinct.

"In fact, the Chaitén volcano which is supposed not to have erupted for thousands of years is actually now rumoured to be showing ominous signs of rumbling again," so Felipe said. "Little telltale wisps of gassy hot air have been seen escaping, according to the locals. But way off in Santiago of course the officials just pooh-pooh this idea. It's of no concern to them. Typical northerners!"

Tony became fired with enthusiasm to inspect them for himself should the occasion ever arise but knew that, even if he ever got out of this hellhole, he would have to make a lot of money first. And that might just pose a small problem.

Horrified by Felipe's account of forcible religious conversions of the indigenous Amer-Indians by the newcomers, the Spanish invaders, Tony was further scandalised to learn of some of the other high-handed tactics which had allegedly been employed. He had never given it a thought except when he had come across some of the very stylised painted madonnas - in a roughly triangular format with lots of gold paint - mainly in the area round Cuzco. Though totally different from the Spanish style of icons, they were now fast becoming a collector's item. This had made him curious about the fusion of the two cultures and he was keen to learn more. He had heard of, but discounted, some of the bloodthirsty practices inherent in the mass baptisms.

Secretly condemning the scornful way some missionaries had acted in Africa, Tony felt this, surely, was just as bad. These people whom Felipe Lorca claimed as his ancestors had lived principally all along the coastal edge and mountain slopes of the Cordillera - further south than where they were at present. They had cherished their culture and animist traditions proudly and refused to become assimilated into the later twentieth century arrivals, the hispano-germanic inhabitants, who had eventually succeeded in predominating by the time of the current millennium. The newcomers, Tony learned, had become well-entrenched citizens with their own rights and customs, their schools and their churches and precious little trace of the original inhabitants' culture was left. Even their language had been largely assimilated and, being oral and hardly written down, was in danger of being obliterated.

Felipe, realising that Tony had only just arrived from Peru, acknowledged that his people, the Mapuche, differed markedly from the Toltecs, their sister-tribe in Peru, although they still shared certain characteristics in common. Tony was intrigued to discover this as he had made some study of the Toltecs when he had been mugging up on Nazca pottery. Though they still had certain similar facial characteristics, over years they had evolved linguistically and culturally in different directions as they had slowly adapted to their differing local terrains, and some of the tribes had fragmented into different areas. The inhabitants of the region south of Valdivia down to Chiloé, the *huilliches,* despite also being closely related, differed again. Even so, notwithstanding variations in language and costume, it was easy to see they had all belonged to the same *people* originally, Felipe said.

Most of the Peruvians Tony had come across were of slighter build and with closer-set eyes than their cousins in Chile and often had hawk-shaped noses, but this was only a rule of thumb; and he had learnt to be wary of making generalised assumptions. As he had discovered, assumptions could land you in a lot of trouble. And in any case there was a fair amount of inter-marrying between tribes and cross-border infiltration, as also was the case in the Argentine. By listening closely and not making facile "gringo" judgements or appearing superior, Tony managed to learn something of the diverse backgrounds and eventually to gain Felipe's confidence.

"A police informer succeeded in infiltrating our little group, that was obvious," the Chilean told Tony. "And instead of betraying what we assume was his original target, the leader with the communist-leaning opinions, he must have decided to go for an easier option - me. Whether he thought it was because my family was wealthy and he'd be bought off (little did he know how impoverished my poor ma was) or because he'd come to a private arrangement with the leader, none of us knew. Anyway, the end result was me fingered and landed in jail without so much as a proper charge and of course no prospect of a fair trial or anything like that, and the leader getting off scot-free. Though I suppose it would probably have been even worse if I was in Peru," he added.

"Couldn't your parents do something? Appeal to the local councillor or JP or whatever you have down in Chillán? Get word to the local newspaper. Something?"

Felipe snorted. "You obviously don't know how things work here. You don't imagine that a poor *roto* like me would have any clout or access to any of the people with influence, do you? They wouldn't even grant me the time of day and as for sticking their necks out if it meant antagonising the people in power, you must be joking." He went on huffing to himself at the naïveté of this strange Englishman.

"You mean you had absolutely no redress? No magistrate to appeal to or *diputado* or whatever you call your equivalent to an MP? No chance, rather like me it seems, of even getting a formal charge made against you so you could begin to gather evidence to refute it?"

"Not a cat in hell's chance. As far as I can see I'm destined to join the ever-increasing band of jailbirds languishing here without ever being brought 'to justice' or seeing the light of day. Don't kid yourself that your case will be any different unless you can get that Consul of yours to act speedily. As a foreigner you do have a faint chance, but as for me...," his voice tailed off miserably. "I've just learned, from the chap three doors down, that somehow damning evidence has been planted on me, 'evidence' which will effectively scupper any chance at all I might have had of a trial." Lowering his voice he continued: "They've accused me of 'homosexuality' which in their parlance means burning in hell. Even if I did prefer boys to girls, which actually I don't." He smiled disarmingly as if to allay any fears Tony might be beginning to harbour on that score.

How Felipe had sussed this out Tony had no idea (perhaps the morse code signals he thought he heard at night), but the story all sounded too horribly plausible for him to doubt, especially when his cellmate showed him the persuasive cigarette burns on his neck and thighs and hinted that he had worse marks elsewhere. He had not been able to "confess" as he had nothing tangible to confess to, but this of course had not convinced or deterred his tormentors. Or in fact made any difference for good, as it only succeeded in making them yet more implacably hostile.

Tony listened sympathetically, making mental notes where he could since his request for paper and pencil had still been ignored. Later he thought the Chilean was saying the office to himself as he kept up an uninterrupted monologue but it turned out he was reciting some of his own poetic compositions so as not to forget them. This made Tony repeat his request for writing materials, but again to no avail, the guard pretending not to understand this troublesome foreigner.

*   *   *

It was obvious the Minister of Justice in Peru, now under even more acute pressure, was screaming for a scapegoat for the Lima gold theft and the ignominy of murderous foreigners appearing to be able to come and go at will. What could be more opportune than a gringo without any obviously influential backers (whom even the British Consul had failed to contact so far) especially since his passport showed he had recently been in Lima? Not only in Lima but making enquiries about certain gold artefacts there as well. And theft on that scale might prove as damning as the murder of the fisherman, feared Tony in his gloomy state. Or even more heinous if the Minister's good name was at stake and could not be cleared quickly. It was certainly not beyond the realms of possibility that he would be framed for both. Tracked down in this not always very friendly neighbouring country, friendly to Peru that is, just the man to point the finger at, the Minister's officials might think. A gringo finding shelter in neighbouring Chile, and with no consular support, they could kill two birds with one stone; and indeed very little effort. How satisfactory.

But the Consul had been working hard behind the scenes and forty-eight hours later Tony was miraculously and inexplicably set free. Another scapegoat had been found (not one of the *Skyros* passengers) and for the time being Tony's skin was saved. He felt dazed. The unwritten charge had been shelved with no explanation and he had got off with a mere caution, though a terrible fright, and presumably a rustling of crisp notes on someone's part. It was some days before he discovered exactly what had occurred and whom he had to thank for it.

It happened that the head of the American Peace Corps working in the south of Chile, a man called Tyler, was an old college friend of Sherwin who managed to contact him by telephone from Coinco. They arranged to meet for lunch the next day before the ship sailed from Aisén. After catching up on each other's news Sherwin heard an account of the fish-farming and bee-rearing schemes being supported by Peace Corps volunteers in the vicinity. He also heard about some of the unexpected dangers they ran into from being inadvertently implicated in smuggling operations - which apparently operated quite out of control throughout the region, usually with the police totally unaware of what was going on (unless in an area where they were getting their ten percent). Or at least allegedly unaware. Having become acquainted with the local Chief of Customs, Tyler had asked him innocently who this Englishman Tony, currently in the local nick, was and his line of business as he had heard conflicting rumours circulating. At first the Chief had given nothing away but, on further prompting, had promised Tyler to look into it again.

"I think you'll soon discover there's more in this than meets the eye," Sherwin had told his friend Tyler after he'd been tipped the wink by the Customs Chief.

"You were quite right," Tyler admitted later. "Which is why my Customs Chief friend was being so cagey. If you'll fill me in on the local scenario I'll tell you all I've been able to glean on the to-ings and fro-ings of this elusive Peruvian gang. I'm sure they're up to no good; in fact are in it up to their necks. It's my belief that this 'Señor Tony' is busily being framed for one of their operations which backfired - some of the narcotrafficking which appears to be being carried out right under our noses. But possibly with the connivance of someone high up, even the Peruvian Chief of Customs himself - who knows. The two are supposed to be at daggers drawn. You mark my words."

Sherwin had described in detail the physiognomy of Señorita Ballunde and her minder, the po-faced horse; the Watanabes, their friends in the neighbouring cabin as well as one or two of the fisherfolk who seemed to be in cahoots with them, including the so-called trades-unionist from Peru who had orchestrated the strike in Puerto Montt, all the time taking care to remain hidden in the shadows.

Tyler grunted, asked one or two further questions, then promised to investigate further and relay this information to the British Consul whom he knew well and who he thought was still detained in Puerto Montt. He would be bound to know the local Chief of Customs better than himself (Tyler) and would certainly carry much more clout with the authorities. As for the initiator of the strike, he thought he might have some leads there: he would make further discreet enquiries. At least he was pretty sure he knew the man's identity and had a fair idea of who his backer might be. But he would have to tread warily here as rumour had it he was absolutely ruthless and well protected, and Tyler could ill afford to fall foul of the Chilean authorities, nor of the Peruvian. Not only *his* job but his entire Peace Corps programme was at stake.

CHAPTER TWENTY-THREE

When, unexpectedly and without warning, Tony was set free the next day, he scarcely had time to do more than memorise Lorca's mother's address together with a brief message from her son which he promised to deliver in person. Now that he was finally to be at liberty it occurred to him that it might alarm Señora Lorca less if she were to receive a visit from a woman, or from Katie *and* himself, rather than if he - Tony - went on his own. Besides, he didn't really trust his Spanish especially in his present exhausted state. So he set about persuading Katie to do just that - accompany him - and petitioned the Captain to spare one of his ship's crew to act as minder and escort to them if they managed to go as soon as they docked in Aisén early that evening.

When the Captain told him they would be sailing on the midnight tide he realised they would have very little time indeed but he was still determined to try. It was by no means certain that they would find a competent taxi driver willing to travel out of town and in the dark, but Tony felt he owed it to his erstwhile cellmate to make the effort, and Katie was agreeable to trying. The Captain finally yielded to one of Katie's most winning smiles and consented reluctantly though not without threatening to leave them behind if they weren't back on board in good time.

Having theoretically been released into the Captain's custody, Tony was anxious not to compromise him or endanger anyone else but he also yearned to confide in Johnson or, failing him, in the ex-copper Hamish before he should forget some of the particularly important details he had to pass on. He was desperate to get some decent sleep and had a job convincing Sheila, between yawns, that this errand nevertheless must take priority. Having tracked down Hamish and briefly unburdened himself of the most essential details gleaned from Lorca, he eventually succeeded in persuading Sheila to wait on board patiently until he had managed to carry out his promise. Katie could feel his wife's eyes boring into her as Tony did his best to mollify her but the situation was saved by Sheila's relief at his having been released, against all the odds.

And so the odd cavalcade set off with the Captain's warning ringing in their ears. "Remember, Señora Katie, I want no Cinderellas! Don't make me abandon you, I can't afford to leave any of my valuable crewmen behind. Midnight and no later!"

*   *   *

Meantime Hamish returned to his cabin, donned all the sweaters he could lay hands on together with a black hooded anorak and sea-boots (happily a very dark blue, not a conspicuous yellow), gloves and a scarf. Taking a rubber torch and some fluorescent tape he was able to 'borrow' from the purser, he slipped silently down the gangplank as soon as there was no-one left up top to notice, and crept down to where a couple of rowing-boats were tied up to a rusty mooring-ring. As he was trying to decipher the number on the bow to see if it matched the one in Jocelyn's photograph a voice behind him made him jump, particularly since it spoke in estuarine English.

"So, DCI Blair, what kind of a disguise do you think that is?" pointing at his rig. "Mein Gott, you haven't changed at all; even after all this time I would have known you anywhere."

Even though it emanated from a sinister-looking swarthy in dirty overalls and a fisherman's bobble hat, the voice sounded amused. It took the Scotsman a few seconds to place it and to overcome his shock. "Well, you certainly have," he thought to himself. Having dropped his torch he realised his heart was hammering as he bent to retrieve it. As he did so his eyes focussed on former British servicemen's heavy-duty boots, all the more incongruous for being tucked under fishermen's oilies, and size thirteen at that. For a moment he was reminded incongruously of one of his Jamaican parishioners back home who, complaining of her husband's cold feet in bed, said: "Trouble is, him have too much leg turn' up fe foot."

Seeing these huge feet planted directly in front of him, he knew exactly what she must mean though this man could scarcely boast any Patagonian ancestors he was willing to bet, (the Patagonians being renowned for their huge feet). Recognition having slowly filtered through, Hamish greeted Benz affably and added: "Why all the US insignia - most impressive? And why the secrecy? What the hell are you doing here anyway, Bent String?"

Realising the anomaly of his situation he looked nervously round as Tring countered:

"More to the point, what are **you** doing here?" and laughed nervously without waiting for a reply. "So you *did* get my note; I wasn't sure if it would find you in time." Benz reached out a hand and pummelled his erstwhile colleague's. "Shh. We can't talk here, we might get spotted and interrupted any minute. Follow me."

Crouched onto a pile of fishermen's nets in the lee of the nearby seawall they conversed for a moment, exchanging bits of paper then silently and stealthily withdrew, each in his own direction. But not before Tring had asked his former mate in a low sympathetic voice:

"By the way, are you still being troubled by those nasty anonymous threats you were receiving, almost regularly I heard, just before you retired from the police force?"

Hamish frowned, remembering this unhappy interlude which had marred his last year in the Force and which he had hoped would never resurface. He wondered how Tring had come to hear of it, not being attached to the same station at the time, but assured him he was not, touch wood. Then remembering himself added under his breath, "By the grace of God..." (and probably by virtue of a change in profession and removal to another area, none of which he had explicitly explained to Katie at the time). Disturbed at being reminded of such unpleasantness, Hamish did not notice his colleague's expression as he added with a sardonic smile:

"Of course you know why your mate Aidan had to leave the Force too - and so suddenly?"

Hamish looked puzzled. He had supposed Aidan was still with the Force, but under secondment. That at least was the impression he had gained.

"After killing that man..."

Involuntarily Hamish's head jerked up but Benz Tring was already sliding away into the murk. "What the hell do you mean?" he croaked hoarsely not daring to shout. But it was too late: he couldn't question him now unless he ran after him, and this would be bound to attract attention. Besides Tring, having planted the insidious doubt, was obviously not going to reveal more as he slunk away. Hamish was thunderstruck by this revelation, and very angry. How dare he insinuate such wild things and then avoid being questioned on them. Probably completely unsubstantiated too. Whatever the truth, that would explain why Aidan had not appeared to know that Benz was in the vicinity; else he felt sure it would have been mentioned. Had Benz been shadowing Aidan or was it just coincidence that they both happened to be in the same spot at one and the same time?

Hamish had to admit that he had often wondered about that incident in Glasgow's Sauchiehall Street whose fame had reached him though he had never had the nerve or, as he preferred to think, the indelicacy - to probe; certainly not to ask Aidan outright. Being a private man himself he respected the privacy of others. But he certainly did not care for this kind of smear, an accusation made in such an underhand manner, even though, on reflection Hamish realised, it did sound if not exactly plausible, at least possible. Aidan had worked in the Anti-Drug squad while Hamish had been at the Cowcaddens though they had gradually lost sight of each other during this period. For a while they used to meet up for the occasional drink or fish-and-chips when they did their best not to talk shop. There had been rumours of a fight with some druggies and Hamish had read in the press a story of one of the pushers being knifed in the arm and taken to hospital under arrest. The wound had apparently become infected (the victim was already diagnosed as having AIDS) and then turned to septicaemia. This was as far as the story went according to the general media. Had it been hushed up? almost certainly yes.

What Hamish had not realised was that, unusually, the Chief of Police had managed to impose an embargo on further details leaking out since they were still hopeful of tracing the source of the drug-dealing before the man's death became known and people panicked because of the AIDs connection and before the lead went cold. There was, unusually, no whisper of how exactly it had happened or of who was involved and Hamish had given it no further thought. Until now.

Thinking back, however, all Hamish knew for sure was that Aidan, unlike some of his earthier contemporaries, had never carried a knife or weapon of any sort unless expressly authorised to carry a gun for a special operation. But then he would not have gone in single-handed and it appeared from what Tring (alias String) had hinted that in this incidence Aidan was acting on his own. Under cover of course. But still unlikely, and even more unlikely that he went armed since he would have needed to be specially authorised to do so; and then would have been accompanied. He was after all a stickler for the rules and often enough mocked for it, so that would have been totally out of character.

So... Aidan was marked down as a killer. He found that hard to believe though he suspected there was quite a ruthless streak there hidden away somewhere. Aidan would have had to have one to survive in the Gorbels; everyone there needed steel-plated nerves, particularly the fuzz if they were to survive.

Reflecting on the rest of his meeting with Benz, Hamish had not found out anything much about his purpose in pursuing the notorious "JC" except for the obvious, that he was a Mafioso drug baron who controlled the traffic down as far as Coihaique in the Aisén Region. He obviously had extremely powerful backers as, it was rumoured, no-one in Santiago dared lift a finger against him. Hamish wondered what his drug sources were, probably the Colombian cartel which, despite all international efforts, still seemed a law unto itself with extraordinarily extensive tentacles throughout the Continent. At all events, they seemed to have all the relevant customs and excise officers sewn up, which is what mattered most to them and equally what bothered the CIA most.

Hamish had shared with Benz his misgivings about the Peruvian so-called fisherman, the Union thug purporting to be from *Sentero Luminoso,* who had tried to knife him in the cabin, and in return had learnt his full name and had his back history confirmed but not where he fitted into the scheme exactly. As an afterthought Hamish had described seeing the casually dressed young man looking rather like Jaime's nephew, young Ari, meeting up with this Peruvian aggressor on the quayside in Puerto Montt before embarkation. Benz reacted immediately by quizzing his friend for any further details which Hamish might be able to add: did he appear to be gambling on board? who did he associate with? did he look down on his luck? or was he smartly dressed? did he slip ashore at opportune moments, and so on.

Benz neither confirmed nor denied that he was hand in glove with the Americans but Hamish deduced he must be on secondment to the CIA since he did not seem to be short of funds and kept on using contemporary American expressions, larded with plenty of swearwords (which earlier in their acquaintanceship he would never have dreamt of using). On one occasion he even referred to the Miami police chief as "f...... Ed", his first name; that might just have been showing off but was not in keeping with the Benz whom Hamish used to know. Besides, why else would he bother to track down an erstwhile middling junior colleague from halfway across the globe unless he thought he could be of material help? Or supply the missing clue? Hardly friendship, Hamish reflected. Perhaps just to sow the seeds of doubt and hope they germinated? What was it he had against Aidan? Was there a personal vendetta, a girl, or was it just a personality clash? It didn't sound as if he just 'happened to be down in Chile' either. A country nearly 3,000 miles long isn't the sort of country you just happen to visit casually from a further 2,000 miles north even if the Yanks were footing the bill. Tring must have considered it worth the risk of letting the cat out of the bag - or perhaps he deliberately wanted to, to plant false suspicion in the hope it would flush some particularly canny criminal out of his lair.

Either way Hamish was mystified and not a little uneasy. Did Benz not realise that it was now more than eight years since he had severed connections with the boys in blue and almost as many since he'd last seen Aidan (until this chance re-encounter). Maybe Tring didn't believe this meeting up again with Aidan had been quite so unpremeditated and innocent; so totally beyond his control as he'd said, or perhaps Tring merely preferred not to believe it in order to further some machination of his own.

Immersed in his thoughts, Hamish was relieved to discover, on regaining his cabin, that Katie had still not returned and therefore had not been worried by his absence. But then he started to worry about her! Shouldn't she have been back by now? She had said midnight and it was now nearly 1 am...he should never have agreed to her going with that nutcase Tony; he might have known no good would come of it. Where the devil could she have got to? The Captain must be going spare as he had promised to delay their departure for a couple of hours at most but he obviously would not risk missing the tide, and time was ticking over. Hamish was just going in search of Aidan or the Captain when, to his immense relief, he heard Katie's voice bidding Tony a subdued 'goodnight' to sounds of the gangplank being raised amid the rumbling of the anchor chain.

Hamish hoped she would not realise how anxious he had been when he at last caught sight of his wife creeping aboard before hovering at the ship's rail to thank the Captain and mollify him for having delayed their departure.

"Were you successful?" he whispered urgently back in the cabin. "You mean you found Señora Lorca?" and when Katie nodded vigorously, smiling, "I bet that cost you an arm and a leg?"

"No. You're quite wrong there," she shook her head. "We managed to find the same taxi driver as we had the other day, and he refused to charge us. He turned out to be a friend of the family and a closet member of their movement, and hence a fierce opponent of *Sentero Luminoso*. What could have been luckier? *And* he gave us loads of useful information about local police corruption - actual names - who is bribing who and who is in the pay of the Minister's thugs, etc. Brave of him," she tapped her notebook. "All in all, a very good night's work" she sighed happily, yawning. "I'll tell you more in the morning when I'm less exhausted. Remind me to tell you about Señora Lorca as well - and her Peruvian forebears. Incidentally, my love, I was glad of my coat," she added by way of conciliation. "And Pablo, the crew member who came with us, was an absolute brick."

Making a mental note to seek out Pablo next morning for corroboration of the names of the Minister's thugs, and to thank him for having looked after his wife, Hamish fervently hoped that this Pablo had the good sense to be discreet.

*   *   *

Up on deck the next day Hamish wasn't sure if Jaime had singled him out for a confidential one-to-one chat or whether he was merely being a good host. Judging from his lowered voice and attitude, however, Hamish decided the former and so made himself pay particular attention.

"I feel there's something I ought to tell you about my nephew Ari," Jaime began. "As you may have observed, he thinks he's something of a lady's man but in fact most of the girls he sets his cap at seem to run for cover when he approaches. All, that is, except for that sizzling young blonde Paulina who's by way of being extremely well connected - her uncle's our Ambassador in the US, at the top of the diplomatic tree and extremely well thought of into the bargain. That makes me wonder why she's willing to spend her time with Ari, especially when she's tied up with another group and much sought after by that brilliant young scientist Raùl, to say nothing of our flashy Argentine polo-player, Tommy what's-his-name... Why, I ask myself, when she could have her pick of beaux, does she hobnob with - even though he's my own flesh-and-blood - that young ne'er-do-well Ari? He's never got two escudos to rub together and as for dress sense... I leave it for you to judge."

Hamish had caught himself wondering exactly the same thing but replied non-committally, and Jaime continued:

"When on an impulse I decided to go out of character and offer him his fare down, it was chiefly because we thought Vanessa's niece, having been let down by her *pollollo* at the last moment, wouldn't want to come on her own though she desperately wanted to see the San Rafaele glacier and needed an escort. I also suspected Ari might have been in trouble with the law, quite what trouble I didn't know, probably to do with money, though it was hinted to me it was some fairly trifling traffic offence which had set him back financially but wasn't really serious. At least to a young Chilean blade possessed of his first sports car." He grinned at Hamish. "So I thought I'd play Santa Claus for a change."

Hamish wondered where this was leading. He had himself been thinking about 'nature versus nurture' especially after Jaime had told him that Ari's mother, his sister, had been abandoned by first her husband then her lover and was now said to be virtually destitute and living in a hostel for abused women. Though they no longer spoke, Jaime obviously felt some sort of responsibility towards her wayward son, - which made Hamish speculate on Ari's background. Obviously the bad set Ari was supposed to have fallen in with had influenced his decline into first drink and then substance abuse if rumour was to be believed; but rumour wasn't necessarily always right. So had his plight been occasioned more by 'nurture' than by genes? What about the influence of his poor mother? Where did she fit into all of this? And Vanessa's niece? Hamish brought his mind back to what Jaime was saying:

"But the Captain, after talking to Aidan, seemed to think it was rather more serious than we had at first thought. All I could think of was drugs. The American cops are having quite a crack-down on cocaine and the hard stuff and had perhaps had their eye on this profligate young Latino and decided to make an example of him if and when he crossed their borders. But he'd found a crafty lawyer and was soon out on bail, put up by the drug suppliers I suspect. Certainly not by me. (Had I known I would naturally have been furious about it and come down hard on him.) But which Ari decided to skip in order to come down here and either charm - more like con - his crusty old uncle into funding him further or find some wealthy widow; or, better still, a susceptible blonde who he could convince to tide him over. At any rate, here he is and I'm not at all happy at the way he's behaving. And at what I've just found out." He stared moodily into the distance, petulantly flicking the tail of his cigar into the sea.

Though Hamish sympathised he didn't feel he could be of much help. After all, Ari was no longer a teenager, but of age and presumably responsible for his own actions however stupid they might be. But he promised Jaime to keep a weather eye out for his nephew and report back on anything untoward he might turn up. So saying he went off in search of Katie as there was still time for a swim in the pool before lunch he reckoned.

CHAPTER TWENTY-FOUR

"Hamish, you're miles away…You're not still fretting about whether Mattie will smash up the old Vauxhall or whether Barbara will forget to announce the next meeting of the Mothers' Union, now are you?" Silence. "A penny for them," Katie persevered.

They were back in their cabin after a good lunch, resting before they set off on the afternoon's excursion.

"What? Oh sorry, my darling. I was wondering…wondering what a professional fisherman like that chap - the brother of that other chap who copped it - could be doing out in the middle of the lagoon visiting his lobster pots at the dead of night. And why so stealthily too." Hamish who had really been pondering about Aidan and the possibility of Tring's sneaky accusation being justified but determined not to voice his thoughts to Katie, at least not yet, returned to his reverie and Katie to her book, a biography of Admiral Sir Thomas Cochrane, Chile's hero and Britain's scapegoat. Or, rather, being unable to keep her mind on the book, to daydreaming.

Hitherto she had managed to disguise her annoyance at Aidan's dragging her husband into this police business when Hamish had promised he wouldn't become involved - or at least would do his level best not to get seriously entangled in it. Studying her large-boned man, Katie wondered how well she really knew this enigmatic husband of hers. They had been engaged for nearly six months before she discovered that he was not even a mainland Scot, but a Hebridean. She couldn't help wondering how he would have fared had he remained for ever on his native island of South Uist farming. Seeing the hard glint in his eye as he started to talk about the local drug scene and how determined Aidan was to spike the guns of the Mister Bigs behind it all, she realized that he could never have been content without a bigger battle to fight, a larger challenge; he was too much of an idealist, a crusader. Besides, they would never have met had he not bucked the trend and gone to the mainland to university and then on into the police. So she thanked her lucky stars and returned to her book, realising that, although they had been married for nearly thirty years she perhaps did not know him quite as well as she thought she did.

In their courting days Katie had sensed an extreme reluctance in Hamish to talk about his student days as he had been so teased when he first came south to Glasgow. Teased for his accent and archaic vocabulary, his always being skint, but also for his old-fashioned good manners. Gradually, however, she managed to piece together his early story; or at least most of it. Later on they had named their firstborn child Winifred in honour of Hamish's mother who, by the little Katie could glean, must have been a tower of strength, a woman of solid unwavering principle and immense integrity. When, six months later, Winifred became a victim of cot-death Hamish's extreme grief sorely tested his faith but their shared sorrow brought them even closer; and at last Katie felt able to persuade Hamish to open up a little more on his background and upbringing.

They had been in bed when Katie finally persuaded Hamish to unbutton himself on a subject he was obviously loath to discuss, the drugs scene while at university. In the darkness she plucked up the courage to ask him:

"With all this happening around you, you didn't have a go yourself, did you?"

"Och, me - no. Ye can rest assured about that. But I knew several who did: most had the sense to quit before they got irrevocably hooked but one or two…". His voice trailed off, and after a moment he changed the subject. But Katie persisted.

"At about this time I was encouraged by my Minister at the Kirk to enquire further into possibilities of studying for entry into the police service," Hamish resumed. "I explained to my parents that I had been doing a lot of work in the slum areas but did not yet feel called to go into holy orders though, with the imminent shrinkage of the boat-building industry, I did fear that I was perhaps wasting my time at Uni."

He did not of course express this fear straight away to his parents, not wanting to alarm them unduly, but discussed it first with his Minister, at length. Notwithstanding the further upheaval and expense it would entail, he finally secured - with his parents' eventual agreement - a place at the Scottish Police College at Tullallan Castle in Kincardine Bridge over in Fifeshire. This was to be a fifteen-week basic residential training course at the end of his first three semesters at Uni. As he explained to Katie, this was called the Accelerated Promotion Scheme and was designed to turn out Sergeants at the age of 21 after a minimum of intensive training. Luckily he passed with glowing colours so his parents agreed to his abandoning University in order to concentrate on a career in the police force. Being nearly 20 now, he looked forward eagerly to earning some real money and being self-supporting at last, and able to relieve his parents of that particular financial burden at least. If all went well, recruits had the possibility of rapid further promotion (with a decent increase in salary); to Inspector by age thirty.

Recognising that this was really what he felt cut out for, Hamish welcomed the fact that he would not only be earning but perhaps able to subsidise his ageing parents later on in life when times were hard. Even with brother Sandy's help their farm was scarcely providing enough to keep body and soul together. And so they gave Hamish their blessing; and so began yet another chapter in his life history.

"I was sorry in a way not to be able to keep on my digs off the Byres Road," Hamish told Katie. "My landlady Mrs McGillivray seemed to have taken a liking to me; at least I only paid a very low rent in exchange for doing the odd job about the house, fetching the coal and mending the garden fence - that sort of thing. This way I could just about make ends meet. Together with my early morning paper round of course. Being permanently hard up, but determined never to get into debt like some of my friends,…," he stopped for a moment and then resumed.

"We used to frequent the cheapest and seamiest fish 'n chips shops, some of them really the pits, full of the dregs of the outer Edinburgh fraternity as well as the slums round the east of Glasgow, but in some you met really unusual and interesting people. Plenty of arty chappies and wouldbe poets and suchlike. Of course I was still seeing something of my Uist friends, Catriona in particular, until she… Well, she was the one who started dabbling in drugs, silly girl. Seriously dabbling I mean. At first I didn't realise and when the penny dropped it was probably already too late. It was quite ghastly. Mack and I were both sickened as we watched her degenerate. Although we tut-tutted a lot, we comforted ourselves with the thought 'she's a sensible girl with a good background, she'll soon see how much damage she's doing to herself and stop'. But she didn't. From Ecstasy to cannabis and worse; tomazepam, the lot.

And then the hard stuff. Dealers abound in the Gorbels and as soon as we rumbled one and put the squeezers on him another leapt into the gap and supplied the by now indispensable to her. It was increasingly devastating; frustrating in the extreme. And we couldn't make out where she was getting the cash from either. Heroin's not exactly cheap; you wouldn't know, my darling, but it sure isn't."

Katie sighed to show she was listening, albeit in horror.

"We debated whether we should tell her parents but, feebly, didn't want to tell tales out of school. So, shockingly, we delayed far too long. By the time word did get back to them she had dropped out of circulation. I received a terse letter from my mother asking me what in heaven I was thinking of not informing them sooner and why hadn't I taken better care of her, and so on. I really had to eat humble pie, I can tell you."

He paused. "She managed to conceal her dependency for quite a long time by begging, then nicking things, then proper stealing and worse, as she became hooked on the hard stuff, imperceptibly lured into heroin by those drug-pushing bastards."

Katie had never heard her softly-spoken husband swear before so she knew this had touched a nerve. She waited until he continued:

"By the time she was taken into rehab it was virtually too late: a very sordid and shameful story and one which does absolutely no credit to anyone. I reproached myself for years, and still do," (Katie thought of the times she had seen him staring into the middle distance with a melancholic expression and "oh, nothin'" when challenged). "What crass fools and innocents we were not to recognise sooner the seriousness of the situation. But this was way beyond our ken… we were well out of our depth and floundering. I know her parents have never forgiven us, and I can't say I blame them. I still torture myself when I remember our stupid naïveté and bumbling but each time she warned us off so fiercely for interfering in her personal domain that we feebly gave in. We had this ridiculous notion that we were adults now and shouldn't tread too clumsily within the borders of her privacy. What boneheaded idiots we were…

"To this day I shall never forget the tongue-lashing I got from the Minister when finally I asked his counsel. For not acting sooner, principally. In the restricted and conventional little world of the immature nineteen-year old I was then, too many conflicting motives were at war and I ended up not doing anything right despite my best efforts. I failed not only Catriona and her parents but my own parents too, and the whole of the island community. The memory still haunts me and probably always will."

Katie put her hand on his shoulder and stroked him, urging him to continue.

"That was one of my main motivations for joining the police force, and the anti-drug squad in particular - an effort to do something constructive and prevent such harrowing scenes in future, but, as you know, I was to be thwarted here again."

He sighed deeply and Katie recalled his desperation at the moment when his Chief had stepped in and prevented him from indicting the boss of the narcotics ring in their own area of the Cowcaddens. Hamish had always felt that, given his Chief's support, he could have nailed the bastard. But he was then to realise things were never as simple as they seemed. She knew he had nursed a grievance but had not realised until this moment quite how deep it ran or how much of a failure Hamish had felt himself to be.

Hamish shook his head, ruminating, and Katie was careful not to break the spell. She remembered him telling her how happy he had been to leave that behind when he had first gone south to England - not that there weren't drug cartels there too but by then, at his own request, he had been drafted out of the anti-drug squad so it was no longer his immediate concern. He was on loan from the Strathclyde force to enable him to complete his training - a twelve-week reconvention course at the Academy in Marlow, a blissful spot on the Thames, but it wasn't until now when he had filled in the background for her that she began to understand all the ramifications.

Marlow had proved to be his turning-point for, not only did he meet the love of his life there, but it was there that Hamish came to realise how the limitations of his background could after all be overcome by study and education in all its wider aspects. If he had not been so determined to keep himself fit, their paths might never have crossed. Although physical education and track facilities were superb at Bisham Abbey where he was based, its swimming-pool was decidedly sub-standard. So he used to go to the newly-opened baths in the centre of Marlow. And there one day, diving in without careful reconnaissance, he narrowly avoided a head-on encounter with a petite freckled brunette in a most demure swimming costume.

She turned out to be the local diving champion and hailed originally from South America, a continent he knew absolutely nothing about. Overcome with embarrassment, he stammered out his apology as he appraised her carefully. Still tongue-tied by shyness his heart swooped at her radiant smile. He felt his hands go clammy and heard an absurd knocking in his chest. Fatal meeting: he was smitten from the word 'go' by this alien creature. She might as well have arrived from the planet Venus, so different did she appear from the lasses of his previous acquaintance, but he managed to dominate his awkwardness long enough to invite her for a coffee.

To his amazement she accepted; the acquaintanceship blossomed into friendship so fast that a couple of weeks later he was invited home to meet her mother. At first he was absolutely speechless and very gauche, but gradually Katie's mother charmed him into relaxing, her younger sister stopped taking any notice of him and he learned to act naturally and unselfconsciously. His rugged good looks and height (over six-foot-two by now) together with his impeccable manners saved the day.

This attitude ended, however, when he eventually plucked up courage to ask Katie's mother (her father having already died) for her daughter's hand in marriage. Although they were into the liberated sixties Hamish knew instinctively that he had to do things by the book as, outwardly liberated though Katie's family appeared, he realised it was anything but when it came to matters of this kind. The Señora's initial refusal only served to make him all the more determined since he'd received plenty of encouragement from Katie herself: this signalled the start of a long and determined courtship which was simply not going to be defeated.

CHAPTER TWENTY-FIVE

During the early years of their marriage, Hamish, now a fully fledged police sergeant, had returned with his bride up north for a stint in the Cowcaddens. This was the area of Glasgow where he had been confronted by the fierce rivalry of the drug-running gangs which completely dominated that district. For a newly promoted Sergeant it was impossible for him not to get involved even if only on the periphery and as a virtually powerless bystander. Bribes and sweeteners were routinely offered and as routinely refused though some of the youngsters in the Force with financial pressures hesitated, he was aware.

It was later when the drug barons hit on another fiendish scheme to compromise fresh-faced keen young officers (nearly all men up there in his day) that things began to turn seriously nasty. Coming home from primary school one day young Matthew had found to his surprise and delight an intriguing parcel awaiting him on the tea-table. It was close to his sixth birthday so no-one thought to ask where it had come from. When, however, a green-and-white football enveloped in a Celtic no.7 shirt had been unwrapped by an ecstatic birthday boy, Hamish felt it time to intervene. To howls of protest, initially from Katie as well, he had whisked the offending items off, bundled them up in the original wrapping and despatched them back marked '*Return to Sender.*'

"Why can't I have one? It's *my* present," amid muffled tears. "It's not fair. All the other boys in my class have got one..." (not necessarily true, Katie noted, but almost). "Why can't I keep it? It's addressed to me." (That was true, Katie reflected ruefully.) Gradually gentle, and then not so gentle, persuasion won the day; and the reasoning for not sporting Celtic colours was borne in on both Matthew and his mother. Though this still didn't make sense to Matthew, and Katie remembered wryly her feelings of outrage when her husband high-handedly (as she saw it) had whisked off all the alluring goodies for them never to be seen again.

"Well, look at your friend Jimmy. Yes, Jimmy Lomax for example. His family is Catholic and they're not ogres or any different from us." (Hamish knew he was skating on very thin ice here as although Katie had long ceased to attend Mass, and had in fact converted to Anglicism, he risked offending her atavistic sympathies with her mother church if he trod too heavy-footedly.) "But you know Jimmy won't go to the same school as you when you both finish at St Aidan's. Is that going to make him any the less your friend?"

Matthew stared at him without answering. Thinking it over later Hamish realised it probably would make a difference for the simple reason they would inevitably stop seeing so much of each other, the two secondary schools lying some distance apart. He had hesitated while Matthew had continued to sob, and Katie furtively dabbed her eyes avoiding Hamish's gaze. But his resolve held - and the incident gradually passed into oblivion.

When, on his eighth birthday, Matthew had been given his very own *de luxe* football kit, this time by his parents (though, alas, not with accompanying Rangers shirt or scarf), he appeared to have forgotten or at least accepted the incident. But Katie, rather shamefully she felt, had not. Her face tingled as she recalled that earlier moment, especially now that she could at last appreciate what had driven her husband to take the action he had. She had vaguely been aware, even then, that the drug barons had had something to do with it but that Hamish had been loath to spell it out. When she had pressed him on it later she recognised the mulish expression which had transformed his face, which meant she might as well forget it. And so she did, for a while.

Studying him closely now, however, Katie found herself admitting that she at last understood why Hamish was so set on giving the Chilean and Peruvian drug barons a bloody nose if it proved at all humanly possible. She not only understood but found herself sympathising with his determination and could see that, by trying to prevent him from entering further into the fray, she was actually frustrating what might prove to be his only realistic chance of ever getting even with them, and thus achieving a certain peace of mind. Without explicitly giving him the go-ahead she had to acknowledge to herself that she should no longer actively prevent him by extracting unrealisable promises from him.

*   *   *

To bring her mind back to the present, Katie started an enthusiastic summary of the chapters she had read so far of Cochrane's biography. Although Hamish knew far more about this sometime Chief of the Chilean Navy than she did, she was hoping nevertheless to intrigue him into reading the book after she had finished it and thus encourage him to stop brooding on the current unhealthy drug scene. But Hamish, still thoughtful, decided to go up on deck where there might be time for a quick pipe instead before they set off.

As she joined him up on deck, a fleeting memory flashed through Katie's mind, something she had thought rather odd when she had witnessed it earlier that morning though she doubted whether it bore any relevance to the problem in hand.

"It's probably not of any importance," Katie began, "but I feel sure that Aidan, even if you don't, might find this a bit curious...".

She had been fumbling for her key in the ill-lit corridor outside her cabin when she had noticed - or, rather, heard a sound coming from Aidan's cabin further down the corridor, just beyond the Captain's cabin. Katie stood stock still listening for a minute and as she did so saw someone emerge. Stealthily. She was surprised to recognise young Ari, Vanessa's nephew, and was about to ask whether he had got lost when, seeing her and flushing guiltily, he had put his finger to his lips and mumbled, "Please don't let on to Aunt V whatever you do; she always said I had no sense of geography," and added lamely "I just mistook the deck; my cabin is directly above, you see," and scuttled away enjoining silence.

"But how did he get in?" wondered Hamish. "He must have bribed the steward or something."

"He **said** he'd picked up the wrong key," murmured Katie, "but I'd be very surprised if Aidan had left his key with the purser, wouldn't you?"

"Hmm, wasn't he the young man who knew all about Muji Gallico's secret identification mark on his stolen gold artefacts? You remember that first evening when he asked Freddie, when we were all together in the bar, something about whether a small *m* superimposed on a *g* in a rather cunning - probably unique - way matched... and poor Freddie had looked so gob-smacked?"

"Yes, it comes back to me now. But I bet it was 'cos he caught Freddie on the wrong foot. Freddie could never admit to not knowing... especially in front of such a large audience, with so many ladies in. Still, I reckon you'd better make sure Aidan knows this about Ari anyway," said Katie pushing him in the direction of Aidan's cabin.

At first Katie had attributed Ari's sheepish looks to the fact that she'd caught him picking his nose but, reflecting later, she decided he definitely must have been up to something underhand and trying to hide it by bluffing his way out.

$$* \quad * \quad *$$

While Tony and Sheila were entertaining Sherwin at the bar as thanks for his miraculous intervention with his Peace Corps friend Tyler, others were foregathering noisily for dinner. It was already a bright starlit night but the moon was being coy and hiding behind a glittery cloud and it was too cool to linger out on deck. Down in the billiard saloon noisy exchanges between the Argentine contingent and the Peruvians were skilfully scotched by the barman who brought years of experience to mediating between rival nationalities. Hamish decided he could learn a thing or two from watching and sent him a congratulatory smile. Aidan was nowhere to be seen as Hamish wondered idly whatever had become of Benz Tring and whether these two were really in cahoots or at daggers drawn. He hated the idea of being made a fool of but hated even more the prospect of rivalry or open warfare between his two erstwhile colleagues, - which could lead to nothing but disaster and loss of face all round if the chips went down. Such a fiasco would certainly send out all the wrong signals to the drug-runners, reassuring their bosses that they had nothing to fear from these quarrelsome bunglers. And Hamish still nursed the hope of bringing them to book, by hook or by crook.

Relieved to catch sight of Aidan at last, Hamish signalled to him to join them in their cabin on the pretext of showing him something in their book on birds. Once safely out of earshot of unauthorised listeners, Hamish lost no time in bringing Aidan up to date on what he'd just learnt about Ari as well as warning him of the Chilean's snooping in his cabin. He'd overheard one of the crew muttering about the crunch poker game that was to be played the very next evening while most of the passengers were ashore, and had gathered from this that Ari hoped to replenish his depleted reserves sufficiently to meet his creditors whom Jaime reckoned would be awaiting him at the next port. Not just any old creditors either. A tidy sum was at stake if Jaime's surmise was correct and the debt collectors were likely to be ruthless.

Hamish decided to bide his time and wait for developments on the poker game before alluding to the incident in Sauchiehall Street so crudely hinted at by Benz. Aidan had quite enough on his plate for the moment and Hamish hadn't yet decided how to play this one.

*   *   *

Vanessa had passed on to Katie the opinion of one of her English friends who had met Hamish for the first time, on board. On learning he was a former copper and studying his physique she had nodded without surprise, but when hearing he was now an Anglican vicar, she looked quite startled.

"I can easily see him as a policeman, he's so upright and self-contained; but to be a 'successful' vicar in the Church of England nowadays not only do you have to be exceedingly p.c. but you also have to be something of an extrovert - a showman, and that I don't believe he could ever be. He's much too shy and nice for that," she asserted. "I can't imagine him banging heads together at an unruly PCC, or standing up to the Bishop over something comparatively trivial in itself but important to him."

Katie smiled to herself, mentally comparing Hamish to the other clergy in their diocesan group and concluding she had got much the best of the bunch even if he did fail to assert himself sometimes. She had even accused him of letting the Bishop walk rough-shod over him when it came to allocating ever more pastoral duties but she had to recognise that Hamish was thriving on it. (And everyone in his parishes respected him; some even loved him.) Or he **had** been thriving until his health started to let him down, and with no forewarning too, though it was obviously partly because he had been over-doing it.

In Chile, in a nominally Roman Catholic country where the priests were still supposed to be celibate, some of the women in the pews regarded a married priest with curiosity bordering on suspicion. As if they couldn't be properly Christian. But others held it as a challenge. In Anglican England, on the other hand, one or two tried flirting though that didn't get them very far especially when the vicars' wives had active antennae and were alert. Katie pictured to herself Rosie's look of bafflement when, trying her most alluring and provocative smile on Hamish, he had appeared not even to notice that she was female. He had smiled back amiably enough but with no spark of actual recognition.

Often the crunch time was during bereavements when women especially tended to be at their most vulnerable and priests their most understanding. Then strange things had been known to happen... Katie just hoped Hamish would be wise enough to avoid this pitfall. Whenever she knew the widows herself she often took on most of the active comforting duties so as to relieve Hamish for other parochial work. (And relieve him from having to do something he had no taste for.) But she was careful not to overstep his role as priest. Some parishioners could be very touchy. Besides, wasn't counselling the man's job? Even in this day and age of enlightened feminism? Some women in their parishes obviously thought so.

CHAPTER TWENTY-SIX

The next day dawned gin-clear. On the climb up Minchinmaida, a beautiful volcano not yet totally extinct, Anna was aware of Professor Sherwin, her American fellow scientist, walking just behind her. She was going up in the hope of seeing the allegedly spectacular view and recording the volcano for posterity on her modest non-digital camera. Nigel had gone ahead to talk to a group of young Americans from deck class and Anna, whose blistered foot still made her limp, was taking it slowly and enjoying the sunshine and the chance to breathe deeply this unpolluted air when suddenly Raùl was at her elbow. Determined not to be further humiliated, Anna turned her back on him and started an animated conversation with Sherwin instead.

The young man looked crestfallen. Beseeching her attention with his eyes he whispered: "I have just received a marvellous offer of help from somewhere in Australia I've never heard of for my project. It's been commissioned by Amnesty International and it's about raising help for the orphans of political prisoners." She ignored him, turning her shoulder, but couldn't help hearing him add: "Not necessarily financial help but rather practical and moral - I mean solidarity-type aid, and hopefully help with the admin. Which is hugely needed."

Finally Anna excused herself from Sherwin to listen. Raùl, who was still hovering, thanked her and quickly went on to tell her in a low voice how he had been secretly involved with a group Amnesty had put him in touch with in the south of Chile, one of his reasons for coming on the cruise as it gave him perfect cover. He emphasized how, in the present political climate, he had had to watch his movements and be careful not to be overheard or be seen to do anything indiscreet. He knew his letters were being censored and suspected his home 'phone was tapped as well, so discretion...

At that moment his girlfriend, whom Anna was beginning to suspect might have been sent to spy on him, hove into view and, brooking no objection, bore him off to join the rest of the group for pre-lunch drinks. Raùl threw her a regretful glance as he seemed to indicate that he would try to talk again - later. So much for that, Anna smiled.

Anna realised she didn't even know Raùl's full name so could hardly put out feelers with Vanessa to find out more about him. Quite brave of him to be in contact with Amnesty though, she thought. Probably foolhardy too, in this present state of affairs that could easily invite unwelcome attention from the secret police with heaven knows what kind of awkward results. Jeopardising his family as well. However easygoing some of the new members of the Chilean government of the moment appeared to be, this still could involve some political risk especially in the event of the military junta deciding to clamp down further. Had the girl been chosen to keep an eye on her wayward young friend? The more she thought about it the likelier it seemed, particularly in view of Paulina's uncle's diplomatic connections.

Anna decided to put Raùl out of her mind and concentrate on the next day's programme which looked inviting. She had more than enough on her plate for the time being without getting involved in local politics. Besides, who knows? she might want to return to Chile some day; it would hardly be wise to blot her copybook by getting tainted with the leftwing now. Far better to keep her nose clean and concentrate on her research funding possibilities. A pity though as he was so attractive. Such a dazzling smile and that smooth olive skin.

Now she would have to think up a really convincing excuse for not joining Argos, the swashbuckling Argentine with the moustache, the one who was so pleased with himself, at dinner that evening. (The prospect of being embraced by him made her think of kissing a limp wet flannel with a fringe and made her shudder.) She would doubtless then be subjected once again to the wink-wink nudge-nudge routine about what was really in those rooms in the Lima Museum reserved for the menfolk so as not to outrage the sensibilities of the ladies. He would inevitably be joined by that doctor fellow from Uruguay who was only tolerable when he had his nice wife in tow and was not too drunk. At least Ursula made him stop preening himself in front of the ladies, winking at them in a lecherous way when he thought he was unobserved. These two were bound to be rehearsing endlessly the latest developments in that boring gold heist he seemed so obsessed with. She couldn't help betting his interest there wasn't entirely altruistic either.

✳ ✳ ✳

Jaime had been surprised to catch sight of his nephew Ari in earnest conversation with one of the younger members of the crew who doubled as cabin steward. He couldn't help overhearing Ari's farewell words: *"Addios, hasta màs tarde entonces"*. Jaime wondered quite what was scheduled for *màs tarde*, for later, and hoped it was nothing sinister. He also couldn't help noticing Ari's less than smart appearance again. Since he'd arrived he'd hardly shaved; he slopped around in a dirty T-shirt, jeans and sneakers - not at all in keeping with the dandy he used to be in Puerto Rico.

Besides, Jaime did not approve of 'designer-stubble' and couldn't understand why the young couldn't take the trouble to shave properly these days. Though etiquette on the ship was hardly formal, passengers normally tried to dress up a little in the evenings if only to impress the opposite sex. Ari having always fancied himself as something of a ladies' man, Jaime was distressed to see he had let himself go, especially when such a golden opportunity to meet a suitable girl offered. He was beginning to wonder about the boy's jaundiced look and the fact that he never seemed to surface until pre-lunch drinks, if indeed even then.

Ari meanwhile was having the devil of a job keeping from his uncle and aunt - as he supposed - all knowledge of his nightly gambling sessions down in the bowels of the ship. He was confident the throbbing of the ship's engine would drown out all sounds of any raucous disputes; the sickly yellow lighting would make it difficult for their goings-on to be observed by outsiders. But he couldn't help fearing Vanessa looked at him a bit sideways now and then.

Having decided that poker was the only way possible to repair his fortunes so as to be able to face his creditors, Ari avoided his relatives, his uncle and aunt in particular, and his sister and boyfriend and the various odd cousins he kept on nearly bumping into on board. His worst moment was when Manuel's sidekick, the young PR guru, lost quite a tidy sum to him at poker and threatened to blow the gaffe. Quite a lot of soft-soaping was needed to prevent this ugly scenario from developing further.

On this particular night, however, José had looked troubled. With this motley crowd of players Ari could hardly hope for *The Nuts*, not yet at any rate. A high-stakes *No-limit Texas Holdem* had been agreed on instead, probably the most he could aspire to in the current circumstances. Normally Ari dealt the cards like a starling voraciously attacking the birdseed, pecking at each card as if for life. Tonight, however, seated at the poker table his unusually bored expression never varied. Without appearing to move a muscle, he sized up his fellow gamblers some of whom obviously had little aptitude for bluff and certainly none for counter-bluff. He knew that, unless Fate was exceptionally unkind and continued to deal him consistently poor hands, sooner or later and certainly by the end of the night he stood to make a killing from these greenhorns. Sure enough, after three hours' non-stop play and a certain amount of wine being consumed by his opponents though none by himself, a goodly sum was due to be pocketed by Ari, everything having turned on the very last card.

Ari had kept his nerve and bet heavily on that last card, playing *on the river;* he had been fortunate enough to scoop the pot - or would have done if the wretched José had been able to pay up. To Ari's dismay and against everyone's inclination José had finally persuaded the others to 'sub' him for that last game, convinced as he was that he was going to make a fortune. Unfortunately for him luck did not go his way. Unhappily for Ari the crew's payday was not until the following Saturday so he would have to bide his time until then to be paid, he was told. This did not suit him at all since he already had a rendez-vous the following day with the vultures hovering to collect the money he still owed. He knew from previous experience what he could expect if he failed to settle on time.

A noisy fracas ensued, chairs were overturned, ashtrays upset, and through the blue cigarette smoke Ari detected the gleam of a knife. That was it then. The air was thick with insult and counter-insult as Ari swept as much as he could of his winnings off the table and into his leather pouch before making a quick disappearing act; and the evening broke up in pandemonium. But not without threats of vengeance from Ari if all debts were not settled by noon the following day.

*   *   *

Meantime Katie returned to the cabin to find Hamish in furtive tête-à-tête with Aidan. She was just in time to overhear the reason for Señorita Gonzalez-Ballunde's joining such a disparate group of fellow-passengers. The Señorita had apparently been sent down to Chile to keep tabs on some valuable cargo from Peru to make sure it reached its intended destination without mishap. Cargo on a cruise-ship was in any case a somewhat unorthodox idea; how she was to achieve this was not at all clear but Aidan seemed fairly certain that she was someone with a lot of clout and was acting on behalf of another someone even more important. However, it was only when she stumbled by chance on a clue which led her to realise that a different commodity - drugs - was also involved that she got seriously worried. Alarmed more like. Ballunde was obviously well aware she was deemed to be closely involved with the Peruvian mafia and it suited her to use this as her cover as it would protect her from other malignant kinds of surveillance, or interference, but what she did not know - or at least had not known before she set off - was that, as well as the original consignment she was to supervise, there was this additional nasty dangerous commodity in tow, probably for a different consignee, maybe an even less scrupulous one.

As soon as Hamish realised Katie was there and listening he tried to change the conversation but it was too late. She had already heard Aidan explain that Ballunde (who was allegedly the illegitimate daughter of the President's steward, a man of some substance) had seen a chance to revenge herself on her (real) father's rival - the Peruvian Minister of Justice. Aidan had discovered that the Minister was heavily implicated in the traffic of counterfeit gold artefacts out of Lima, presumably some of it the proceeds from the gold heist, and its further transit to where? no-one knew; and that her Dad was determined to exact his revenge on the Minister by exposing him. But, this news having leaked out prematurely, the Captain who always had an ear to the ground, having caught a whiff of it realised that Señorita Ballunde, his distant relation - after all -, would be in severe danger if this became common knowledge or spread any further. He was therefore doing his best to protect her, enlisting Aidan's help together with the promise of discretion.

Katie's head was buzzing. Poor Gonzalez-Ballunde, she must be in dire danger knowing the kind of people they were probably dealing with, everybody with at least one finger in the pie. And none of them with any scruples whatsoever as far as she could make out. What's more, she didn't even have her pudgy protector with her now, for what that was worth. Katie shuddered.

181

"Aidan, do you think Ballunde is party to this drug business too, because if so she'll be in mortal danger?" Hamish sounded deeply worried.

"No idea, but not unless she's completely daft - or is trying to use it as a blind to cover her interest in the gold. Which would be crazy, not to say criminal, and probably totally counter-effective too. After all, she needs to keep in with her cover - the Watanabe crowd - who will undoubtedly be aware of her reporting back to base and will be keeping a strict eye on her in the same way as she will on them. More so now in fact, now that her 'minder' has so summarily been removed," Aidan added.

"But if she needed to send an SOS for backup she would doubtless get a far speedier response than they would," he concluded, "though she would have to be discreet about how she requested it - even using the Captain's channels of communication."

Katie couldn't help chipping in. "But what if…?"

"Yes indeed, what if they find out she's been double-crossing them?" Hamish finished her query for her as he tried to contemplate the scene back in Lima with all the layers of subterfuge and backstabbing which doubtless existed there. "What's the worst they would do to her then?"

"You have to remember that the drug barons are way, way more sinister and ruthless than any corrupt government you care to nominate, even one harbouring a Montesinos as its Chief of Police, that…". Aidan left his sentence unfinished while they all pondered the horrific unknown.

After a moment's pause Aidan added: "Let me just say that in the case of a *coca* worker in Colombia who had seen enough and wanted out, not only was he found in the cane fields the next day with his throat slit, but his family was also treated to a dose of the most barbaric revenge the bosses considered suitable *'to serve as a reminder'* and left in indescribably horrific conditions. His wife, after being raped, had had her belly slit and the small plastic sachets containing their precious (deadly) white powder which she was to have couriered to Europe as a mule, retrieved. His sister had received similar treatment though she was in no way involved, and the elder of his two kids had disappeared. Presumably to forcibly join the sex trade, wherever suited them best. There was just one tiny snivelling child frightened out of its wits left behind when the enforcers had finished creating their havoc, whether by design or accident who can tell. And that poor child will be so traumatised for the rest of its life that it might just as well have been liquidated with the rest of its pathetic family. And will probably now end up as yet another teenage 'revenge fighter' in one of the *coca* gangs roaming the jungle, just another pathetic statistic."

"And don't imagine that child will ever receive any medical or psychiatric aid, will you, 'cos that just ain't on." Aidan added after a pause.

Ironically, at that moment the door to the nextdoor cabin burst open amid a great hubbub of mah-jongg and the vicious slap-slapping down of tiles. A wave of stale maize oil and garlic floated out amid the *chicha* and a woman's voice could be heard obviously giving orders above the resistance of the younger men. The door closed on the sounds of indignant protests but Hamish, Katie and Aidan were left none the wiser as to what had prompted it all.

"Whew, I wonder what that was all about? I hope Señorita Gonzalez-Ballunde isn't involved in that."

In an attempt to lighten their mood, Hamish ventured: "Remember the feline of the species…," which Katie finished for him "is deadlier than the male."

They smiled grimly and were left uncomfortably wondering for another couple of days. Not a glimpse of the elusive Señorita either, and very little stirring from her morose compatriots.

PART III

"…to the punishment of wickedness and vice…"
Book of Common Prayer

CHAPTER TWENTY-SEVEN

Johnson had looked in on his friend to find him with a glass in one hand and book in the other, apparently none the worse for his encounters of the previous day apart from a small bandage on one arm. Hamish's knife-wheeling assailant was no longer in evidence and was, he hoped, safely below under lock and key. Johnson decided to have a word with "this *dago*" (his contemptuous term for all South Americans, but particularly those with high cheekbones, hollow cheeks, and sallow colouring). He would have to persuade the Captain to provide somewhere secure for it: he didn't fancy the stuffy hold but there was probably nowhere else. Also, would the Captain provide an interpreter: if not, was there any chance Katie might perhaps oblige - if it wasn't asking too much? Hamish didn't look too happy at the prospect but Katie nodded her agreement.

While Aidan was intent on interrogating the knifeman, handcuffed for safety, aided by Katie who had difficulty in understanding him when he did vouchsafe an answer, two swarthy policemen crept on board. They were accompanied by a sinister-looking plain clothes detective with an aquiline nose and malevolent expression. Making straight for Cabin no.133 they barged in and proceeded to arrest the occupant who, looking very surprised, protested loudly in broad Scottish. Ignoring his vehement response and his wounded arm, they manhandled him to his feet, demanding "Pasaporte". The elder of them, a small man with a sinister scar at the corner of his flashing black eyes, screwed up his face in concentration, staring at the name, date and place of birth in the unfamiliar passport and finally hard at the photograph, admittedly four years old, making Hamish wonder if he, the cop, was indeed literate.

Hamish racked his brains to remember where he had seen this unsavoury individual before. He had observed a scar just like his before, but that man had been suavely literate and verging on the sophisticated. Just the opposite to the individual scrutinizing him now, with clammy hands sticking to the photo and pinpricks of sweat visible on his neck and forehead.

"You will 'ave to come with us, Señor 'Amish" he said at length.

Just then Katie reappeared on the scene totally bewildered. She had thankfully finished interpreting for Aidan and was unprepared for yet more intruders. As soon as she saw the glint of handcuffs and the expressions on the men's faces she burst into a torrent of voluble Spanish. Frightened by their menacing aspect, she explained less than tactfully how they must be out of their minds to even contemplate arresting the cousin of the President. Yes, the *President* of Great Britain (she knew that Prime Minister had no currency with such people). Could they not see the *cognome,* the surname Blair on the passport? And did they not realise the consequences to them if they arrested the wrong man? She contemplated questioning their own parentage but happily prudence prevailed. Nonplussed, they muttered among themselves, studying a tattered piece of paper on which 313 was written boldly, passing it to each other in perplexity. Undecided, they shook their heads. Katie grabbed the scrap of paper from their hands. Realising that 313 was Tony's cabin number and, knowing he was no longer there, she had no hesitation in pointing them in that direction, foolishly emphasizing that they were in cabin 133.

"Any fool could see this was not 313," her expression said. This was too much for them. To be made a laughing-stock of by a mere slip of a woman - and a foreigner at that; (Katie obviously did not sound genuine Chilean to them), a mulish expression stole over their hostile faces and they snapped the manacles shut on Hamish's right wrist before he had time to stand up again or even protest. One unclipped his gun from its holster and jamming the barrel firmly between Hamish's shoulder blades prepared to march him out of the door and along the corridor past the Captain's cabin. The officer's uncompromising expression was enough to deter Hamish from further protestation.

A half-finished game of Travel Scrabble lay on the small table alongside the bunk beds. As he was yanked to his feet by his captors Hamish had contrived with his free hand to slide three tiles so they stood clear of the rest to read Z-blank-H, unnoticed except now by Katie. Raising his unmanacled hand to his face he laid one finger to his lips and then signalled with his eyes down the corridor. Clearly he was allowing for their smattering of English so was being ultra-cautious,

Katie realised. But why the Z and why the H? She couldn't think of a single word with that letter combination unless of course he meant a *zho*, unlikely under the circumstances. Katie reflected they had hardly seen any animals at all and certainly nothing as exotic as this. The only wild beasts she had encountered so far were such unprepossessing individuals as were busy manhandling Hamish down the corridor. With some difficulty too it appeared.

Beside herself with frustration and incipient terror (there was no knowing what foolish thing they might do if goaded too much), Katie knocked frantically on Aidan's cabin door but without result. Hearing a voice nextdoor, she burst into the privacy of the Captain's cabin, knocking as she did so. No Captain, but Señorita Gonzalez alias Ballunde lolling in his chair, greeted her wild entry with an ironic "Do please come in, Señora; take your time and make yourself at home. I see you have visitors," as she watched Hamish being prodded past the door by the so-called officers. "Again?" she added dryly.

However, as soon as she had sized up the situation Señorita Ballunde abandoned her irony and sprang into action, effective action too. Without waiting for the Captain to return she grabbed the 'phone and scornfully machine-gunned the person on the receiving end. (Katie admitted afterwards how this had considerably enhanced her Spanish vocabulary). First a subordinate, and then the Chief of Police himself whom she addressed familiarly in the *'tu'* form. Action was immediate. As Hamish reported later, as soon as he spotted his captor speaking into his lapel mike, his expression changing from surly to truculent to respectful, he knew Katie must have been active. Señorita Ballunde's putdown of those who, according to Katie, had authorized the bungled arrest was an object lesson: the poor men were squirming. Despite her recent prudent lying low (wisely taking refuge in the Captain's cabin,) she had obviously lost none of her clout with the higher echelons. Katie watched her in awe.

After half-an-hour's stalling and face-saving attempts, during which time Aidan reappeared, Hamish was released but with scarcely an apology except from the embarrassed first mate, who had appeared belatedly on the scene. Then the Captain returned, furious with the bunglers but apologetic and emollient to Hamish. Each fresh invasion of his ship was making him more and more enraged and he let it be known; the mate took the chance to slip back smartly to the bridge.

Everybody spoke at once, quickly bringing the Captain up to date. After a complicitous glance at Consuelo he reclaimed his cabin and remained in private tête-à-tête with the Señorita as the rest shuffled out rather sheepishly. After a brief update, Aidan returned to his cabin and the others to Cabin 133.

Edging past the Peruvians' cabin, Hamish noticed there definitely appeared to be no sign of the bulldog minder. Curious, where could he have got to? It must be at least two days since he'd last been spotted, by him at least. Did this confirm the rumour Aidan had mentioned of the minder's having been recalled to the mainland in disgrace?

*   *   *

Back in their cabin, after a fervent embrace, the first thing Hamish said was:

"That was smart of you to work out my Scrabble clue, and so fast."

"But that's just it," protested Katie. "I didn't, or at any rate not straight away and in any case Aidan wasn't there. As you know. Not until much later, at least. I was stumped by the blank but I supposed you meant - from the tile values, ten from Z and four from H, (nothing from blank of course) - one-oh-four, Cabin 104, Aidan's cabin. It took me a good couple of minutes to work that one out and set off. But when I did charge off down the corridor I stumbled into the Captain's cabin by mistake and happily found Señorita Ballunde, who turned up trumps. She couldn't have been more effective, better even than the Captain or Aidan would have been. So it all worked out well in the end, but why...?"

"Let me get myself a drink and I'll explain." Katie, all agog, rushed to find him ice as he started.

"But what I don't understand," she interrupted, "is what this 'more lucrative' trade was, this business that they were supposed to be embarking on when you and Johnson got suspicious about it."

"You mean the Peruvian élite police, do you?" Hamish joked, purposefully not answering her question. "Or do you mean the CIA in Panama? That's what my signal was about - contacting the CIA there through Aidan. He would have known how to contact Tring and through him the whole network. And the rest would have been a 'piece of cake' but of course I was forgetting the corruption endemic in the whole South American set-up, and the delays too."

"So that was what you were really driving at with your Scrabble clue, was it? But who the devil is Tring? I've never heard you mention him before. Unless he's another of your connections from the past?" and without letting him answer, she continued: "I was with the Señorita listening to her, open-mouthed, when Aidan came scampering down the corridor to the Captain's cabin to find out what was happening. Then, thank God, you returned, still in the clutches of those morons but at least not the CIA…".

Hamish gently pushed her back into the chair, stroking a wisp of hair out of her eyes, and sat down facing her. He handed her a cold drink and holding her face in his hand for a moment, lightly caressed her cheek as he bent to kiss her.

"What on earth do the Yanks have to do with this one anyway? I thought they just concentrated on Mexico and Colombia and the main drug-running countries when they're not preoccupied with preventing Communist infiltration into Bolivia and Chile and God knows where. Oh, and Peru of course." Katie was not to be put off and was still fizzing, desperately trying to works things out. She took a large sip of her drink and was about to go on when Hamish said mildly:

"Don't forget the other side of the coin, the dollar rather - the excellent work some of the U.S. Peace Corps are doing down here." Hamish's sense of fair-play compelled him to redress the balance. "After all, if it hadn't been for Tyler, Sherwin's Peace Corps crony, Tony would hardly have been released, or certainly not so promptly. Goodness knows, the North Americans get a bad enough press as it is… at least give them a little credit when it is due."

"It's hardly surprising they're so unpopular in this part of the world," Katie rejoined. "Their brash manner when business (ie profit) is in it, combined with their naïveté, is enough to alienate anyone, even the illiterate Latinos. Or perhaps particularly the Latinos who find it hard to credit anyone being so, so misguidedly altruistic but blind to the obvious. So to stick their noses in further where they're not wanted is hardly calculated to win them any more friends - at least in this stamping-ground…,". Katie shared her cousins' mistrust of US foreign policy as evidenced in Chile. And everywhere else too in fact. *'Give a dog a bad name'* she reflected to herself: perhaps she **was** being unfair.

"With reason," Hamish said quietly. "If you were a poor Chilean *roto* with hardly enough to feed your family on you'd probably be dependent on drug-runners and smugglers for subsistence and the occasional black-market offcuts. In return for silence of course, and the odd service to be rendered. Like spying on your neighbours and reporting to the police any unusual traffic, human or otherwise. That being so, you're more than likely to believe the line they shoot. The wicked imperialist gringos out to catch the hard-done-by trader or penniless peasant and ruin him for no other reason than spite or their obsessive fear of communism or, rather, Marxism Latin-American style."

Katie put down her glass to concentrate on what her husband was saying, disgust written all over her face.

"You asked what the Americans had to do with this and that's quite a story in itself ," Hamish started to explain but Katie exploded: "You mean *another* plot? I simply don't believe it."

Ignoring her outburst, Hamish continued: "Cast your mind back a bit. You remember that very glamorous Panamanian lady I was talking to in the customs hall at Santiago airport on our arrival?"

"You mean that blonde bombshell with the ultra-smart monogrammed luggage,... do I not? Only she wasn't blonde at all. All out of a bottle if you ask me (shades of my Mama)." Katie sniffed as she remembered her momentary pang of jealousy and of how ashamed she was of letting it show. Perhaps that had been the blonde he was thinking of on arrival in Puerto Montt when he got confused with Señorita Ballunde. Ballunde had class, though, and was far better-looking, Katie reflected; better than that trollop at the airport.

"Yes, with her purple painted talons and diamonds the size of broad beans, which made you remark, far too loudly, that you bet she didn't do the ironing in her household. And you would have gone on if I hadn't shushed you." Hamish chuckled at the memory.

Katie nodded. Her feelings as she had watched Hamish seem to hang on the woman's every word and gesture were still vivid. She blushed as, despite her better judgement, her curiosity about the man-eater still gnawed. This world-weary dame had not been his usual type and she wondered what on earth he had been up to. He surely couldn't have been blinded by her sophisticated allure. Not Hamish.

"She turned out to be married to the brother of our Peruvian friend, Watanabe, and for some time they had been hatching up a nice little scheme trafficking in ... now what would you think would be the most profitable contraband to send from Peru via the Panama Canal to Britain and the rest of Europe? Drugs? or even cigarettes? a nice little money-spinner but just a cover-up for the real thing? Or even gold artefacts perhaps?"

Katie's eyes widened in wonder and disbelief as she shook her head. Hamish continued: "And who else could be better placed to issue forged passports and papers for would-be illegal immigrants than the Minister's Chief Assistant himself?"

"Stop, stop," Katie begged. But Hamish was warming to his theme. "At, say, a modest charge of $2,000 per passport, a further $500 levy for being stowed away while the ship was stuck in the Canal, and sundry other fees for extra 'services'?"

When Katie showed signs of interrupting again, drumming anxiously with her fingers on the chair, he said grimly: "And you can imagine what kind of services those would be; demanded with no chance of refusing. Far less risky than drugs, more profitable than trading in stolen works of art or faking artefacts, and virtually no risk of the valuable goods being damaged in transit or even if they were, provided they had paid the initial whack for the journey, very little capital loss to you." He paused brooding as Katie's face drained of blood, and he stared unseeingly at her.

" Of course at the time I had absolutely no inkling of this. I suppose my old police training must have taken over when I noticed her luggage tags. Something very shifty, almost evasive about her manner, and when I cheerily mentioned Lima and my 'friend' the Chief Assistant there." He stopped for a moment, ruminating. "Yes, it must have been the name coupled with her destination via Lima which set my brain racing - together with her odd reaction. Various snippets of seemingly unrelated information dredged up from my misspent past surfaced and together they added up to more than five....".

Still nonplussed, Katie murmured: "And there was I thinking you were quite smitten with the creature with her opulent tiger-skin suitcases. But," pursuing her previous train of thought, "how the hell could these illiterate penniless creatures from the '*barrios*' raise anything like that amount, let alone understand what they were letting themselves in for?"

"Not a pretty story. Those who couldn't make enough money from illegally growing coca and ganja along with their miserable potato crop either sold their daughters, or even their wives when desperate, into prostitution. Else they signed up for lifelong servitude in Latin American restaurants now sprouting up all over the fashionable capitals in Europe. Apart from skivvying the most unsociable hours imaginable, all they had to do was to appear two or three times an evening in ethnic costume playing the pan pipes or the *maraccas* or some supposedly authentic two-stringed lute, and Jo Public lapped it up. And the owners of the restaurants coined it. But *they* didn't of course. They were lucky if they were able to catch even four hours' sleep and that in a miserable ill-ventilated hovel, three to a mattress, with rats running over their faces more likely than not. And living in perpetual fear of being denounced to the immigration control."

"And that odious woman connived at that? And made millions from it I daresay?" She paused. "Still, I s'pose the immigrants were slightly better off than if they'd stayed at home on the bare mountain slopes outside Lima with no water, dying of Aids and begging for their subsistence?" Katie continued miserably, longing to be reassured. "At least they could send some of their ill-gotten gains back home..".

"Don't you believe it," Hamish went on grimly. "If they didn't pay up their instalments on the dot the local mafia got hold of their families and wreaked a terrible vengeance. Some were even forcibly infected with HIV... and word got around. So not only had they sold themselves into bondage for ever but their families were also in hock, and often considerable danger too, virtually all the able-bodied men in the neighbourhood having been conned into abandoning them for pastures new."

Tears trickled down Katie's cheeks as for a shocked moment they contemplated the bleak scenario in horror. Her manicure set had slipped to the floor without her noticing. Then she asked the question which had been nagging her: "So you mean that poor Peruvian wretch who had a knife stuck in his back in Chiloé was on the Minister's payroll and doing his dirty work? What exactly was he supposed to be doing?"

"No, no longer. He *had* been, but was now trying to escape the Minister's fixers who reckoned he was holding out on them. They thought he'd only given them half the loot stashed away in the lobster pots which he was supposed to visit daily, whereas the stuff he had in the dayglow orange pot - the one which Sheila spotted - was from an entirely different heist, and not necessarily gold either. And certainly not theirs. Not that that would have bothered them. But it sharpened their suspicions and made them even more rapacious. And vindictive towards him, in the final analysis. Poor wretch."

"And the peculiar modification you were on about - the widening of the entry-hole to the pots - was so that they could stuff more than just lobsters in the pot, I suppose? Clever of Tony to work that one out." Katie sniffed, searching for another handkerchief.

"Yes, and the stuff they…"

"Oh, you mean the erotica and all that porn? Yes, where did that originate anyway?" Katie said airily, trying not to show her revolted fascination too obviously.   Hamish, a little taken aback, decided to ignore her question - for the moment. He had certainly never before come across some of the suggestive tools whose photos had first intrigued then revolted him when Aidan had shown them to him. He wondered what kind of pervert found a use for such toys and only hoped Katie would never get to see them. But how on earth did she know about the porn anyway? His mind raced. From Sheila he supposed. No-one else could possibly have cottoned on to that - yet. At least nobody whom Katie would know, or would talk to.

Perhaps she was thinking of some of the Moche ceramics famous for depicting ceremonial sex acts in front of witnesses; or the ceremonial human sacrifice and blood-drinking, the victims being subjected to excoriation and worse. All of this was supposed to be illustrated on their pottery, but he couldn't think how Katie had come to know about it; he felt uneasy.

What Katie had not yet divulged to Hamish, and what she had temporarily put out of her mind, was a conversation she had overheard a couple of days before. She had been sitting in a secluded corner of the bar waiting for Vanessa when she heard Freddie talking, in Spanish of course, to one of his cousins unaware that Katie was within hearing distance. Perched on stools, long legs swinging, they were comparing notes about their schooldays spent in Buenos Aires and Gloucestershire respectively.

"One of the things I remember best," Freddie was saying, "from my so-called classical education in England, was a description of the curious sexual habits of the Roman soldiers, in Anglo-Saxon Britain in particular. According to my battered copy of Juvenal, or was it Pliny?, they seemed to find the fair-haired Saxon women absolutely irresistible, so alluring in fact they had no need of their weirdly wonderful sexual toys which Plautinus used to boast about."

"Oh, so that sado-masochistic stuff you were telling us about the other night," rejoined Argos, the moustachioed Argentine, "the stuff in the Gallico exhibition, those things the women weren't supposed to see…," and he mumbled something which made Freddie explode with laughter. Then, still snorting, he looked up. "Christ, I think we have ladies present. There," nodding in Katie's direction. "Perhaps we should change the subject."

Relating this now to Hamish, Katie alleged she had acted as if she hadn't heard a word and only hoped they had believed her. Not having repeated what she'd overheard to Hamish straightaway, she had forgotten all about it. Or pretended to herself she had. She quickly brought her mind back to the present. Though puzzled, Hamish had listened without comment, thankful it had not been worse, and continued:

"…the Minister's thugs got suspicious and put José on to tracking the wretched Peruvian," Hamish was saying. "This is what alerted *me* and was the moment when it all started to unravel for them especially when they mistook me for Tony - with the needless killing of that other poor wretched fisherman, my so-called arrest and everything that followed after that - with me trying not to get involved. I did try honestly." He stared into her eyes and tried to look convincing.

Katie snorted and, ignoring Hamish's little-boy plea, asked: "Is that when Tony got really seriously involved too, that after the disappearance of the first Peruvian in the Watanabe gang? Incidentally, did he ever claim his cabin after all? I know what Manuel said but did he, the one who was supposed to be travelling under the name of Lopez Jimenez, did he ever turn up?"

CHAPTER TWENTY-EIGHT

"Hold on, you're going too fast. I'm getting confused." It was Hamish's turn.

"*You're* getting confused. What about me? Whatever happened to this Lopez Jimenez character and what was *his* real name, or did he simply get cold feet and not turn up?"

"He got cold feet all right *and* turned up, poor sod, right on cue at Puerto Montt and was promptly taken for Watanabe, and so was bumped off by our Señorita Ballunde's boyfriend-bodyguard. But as it turned out he wasn't of course Watanabe: so as soon as the boyfriend realised he'd got the wrong man (we never did discover the unfortunate victim's real name) he panicked and had to dispose of the body quickly. He couldn't risk pushing it overboard, at any rate not so near harbour with lots of people and fishermen around, so he took a chance and hid it in the lifeboat under the tarpaulin... intending to get rid of it later, I suppose. Of course he didn't realise this same lifeboat was due to double, first as the outdoor fridge for the fruit and veggies on board, and then as the passenger motor launch when we all went to inspect the San Rafael glacier. You remember that hold-up when we were supposed to be at the climax of our tour and suddenly there weren't enough motor launches to get into to inspect the glacier at close quarters? So he had to think again...and damn' quickly too."

"That must have been the terrific thud we heard that first night just as we were turning in, you remember? You went back up on deck to discover what had happened while I took my make-up off, but reported seeing no-one and nothing unusual and we didn't give it another thought."

"*You* didn't, you mean. *I* did, but it didn't register with me until far too late. If instead of going up to the bridge that night I had gone on deck as I had originally meant to I might have seen something, but as it was I completely missed it, cocooned as I was with the Captain and his fascinating instruments and maps and charts."

"So you mean the minder managed to hide the body in the lifeboat hoping he could get rid of it later. But, unluckily for him, it was discovered just before we got to the San Rafaele and before he could dispose of it. Is that it? What did they do then, when they made this horrible discovery?"

"I don't know for sure. They must have trussed it up in heavy duty plastic and taken it below and stashed it somewhere until such time as the police could come on board to identify it and take it away. Meanwhile the Captain would have radioed the mainland, Chiloé I suppose, and got them to issue a warrant for the minder's arrest since it was pretty certain that's who was responsible; anyway he was caught redhanded trying to shift the body once he'd realised the lifeboat was going to be needed. So he would have been locked up down in the hold and kept there until they made landfall."

"The smell must have been something awful by that time. Dio mio! Still, if he was kept down in the hold next to it I reckon it served him right. What a maniac. *That's* why we haven't seen Señorita Ballunde's bodyguard for the last couple of days. I must say I was wondering. I was meaning to ask you," Katie mumbled, then added: "Well, at least you didn't risk having a knife stuck in you *then* anyway."

Katie shuddered at the recollection of what had happened later and continued: "So what about this last gangster, the one who did try to knife you in our cabin?" she pursued without giving her husband a chance to answer. Increasingly confused, she persisted: "Where did *he* come from and who was he working for?"

"I think he was just a lone chancer originally something big in the unions in Peru. But then he got caught up in a terrorist outfit which'd come down from Peru to stir up trouble in the fishing fraternity. They thought he would be handy for their purposes so recruited him. At first he played his role OK, but *then* he cottoned on to the trail of the Inca gold. Quite by chance. He'd had a tip-off and thought Tony knew where it was all hidden, …only he thought I was Tony. His informants had convinced him that if he threatened Tony/me with a knife he'd find out. He'd realised Johnson was in league with the CIA and he'd seen me talking to him so he just decided to have a go at me while opportunity beckoned and before Johnson returned from his shore trip. And before

I could give Aidan any more details or got too suspicious of them. Then he reckoned that if he managed to kidnap me and soften me up later he might get the info. Even if he didn't get enough details the CIA might still be willing to pay a ransom, a fat one in dollars so he hoped..."

"Some chance there, little did he know," interrupted Katie, almost ruefully it seemed to Hamish as he poured her a whisky. "But where on earth could he have taken you even if he had managed to kidnap you? He couldn't have managed on his own and, suppose he'd drugged you, the kerfuffle would surely have alerted one of the crew - or someone? Even me perhaps, not that I could have done much. I s'pose he must have had an accomplice among the crew or something."

Taking a large swig and finishing his drink, Hamish continued:

"Probably. Probably that assistant purser, the glaikit one. But what this chap didn't realise was that I had been alerted by a chance remark I heard one of the Aussies make to Johnson. You know the one who is in pharmaceuticals - or, rather, is a pharmacologist?"

"Oh, I thought he was an oenologist or viticulturist or some such long word as he told me he'd been touring the Maipo valley before coming here to inspect their wines and to compare notes with back home. He comes from Adelaide, or rather, the Clare Valley, which is why he appears to know so much about wine," Katie added for good measure.

"No, I don't mean *him*, Nigel; I mean *her*. She's the pharmacologist and a damn' good one by the sound of it. I think she's called Anna and is quite famous in her subject. At least, she's got a doctorate from Sydney University and gets invited all over the world to attend symposia and conferences; she'd actually just come from the States where she had been giving a paper in LA on ...I don't remember exactly what, but it sounded very high-powered. Something to do with the beneficial use of heroin-based drugs but ..."

"I thought *he* was the clever one and she seemed sort of unadventurous and rather pale, pale redhead I mean," Katie rejoined. "Well, how deceptive can looks be. Anyway, what *was* the chance remark?"

"The Australian, Anna, said she had overheard one of the Peruvian mob asserting I was a drug-runner but somehow with some cover-up connection to the CIA, and they were frightened I would implicate them or queer their pitch or something: quite how I don't know although they'd seen me talking a lot to Aidan and knew we must be in cahoots.

I think they must again have been confusing me with Tony. As it turned out later almost certainly they were. Then on another tack Anna told me how she and her friend Nigel had watched the vegetables, mainly sacks of potatoes and yams, lettuces, carrots, etc. and also citrus, being hoisted aboard at Puerto Montt in the lifeboats. The quantities made them curious and later they mentioned this to Aidan when he was sniffing around. Even the cranes had made heavy weather of it so they must have weighed a ton. But then if you think of having to provision upward of eighty people, if only for a couple of days before the next port-of-call, that probably takes some doing."

"And some lifting," added Katie still busy trying to visualise how many tons of potatoes would be needed. "But what a good idea to use the small boats to heave them aloft in and then have men standing by to shove them down the hatch into the storage frig, etc."

"Yes, except some of them purposely got left in the boat on deck where they were kept nicely cool by the southerly breeze and well aerated without any need to move them below."

"Which is why they didn't notice the extra bulk even when they had to shift it to get at the stuff underneath. The body being in hessian wrapping as well, it wasn't until it began to pong that anyone noticed." Katie held her nose imagining the foul putrid-sweet smell which would surely have started to be noticeable after a few days. "Think of our vegetables being contaminated by it too...ugh."

"Well, that's just it. By the time someone *did* notice we were well out to sea on the third day and not due to be near land until later next evening."

"Is that when we made that unscheduled stop to pick up 'mariscos' and other provisions and your friend Aidan slipped aboard so unobtrusively? Together with those police officers? And "Señora" Watanabe dashed ashore to make that phone call which she then totally denied making?"

"Mmm... Small wonder since she was reporting back to base - as Ballunde's minder suspected - and so was fingered to be bumped off for her pains or rather, as it happened, her 'husband' was. She escaped as she wasn't in the cabin at the time they called but they certainly intended to get her and that's why...".

A knock on the cabin door announced the steward with a small pile of laundry. While Katie dealt with the interruption Hamish hunted through his pockets for something until José withdrew.

Katie then burst in with "And there's something else rather curious, at least I can't think of an explanation for it..."

"Go on, what?" Katie wanted Hamish to show interest although she knew his mind was really already straying into other directions.

"Well, you know Vanessa and Jaime have this nephew called Ari, rather a strange boy who is always hanging around the billiard table in the saloon laying bets and losing money? The same lad who was coming out of Aidan's cabin and then pretended he'd got lost, mistaking the deck or some such rubbish?"

"Nn..yes," Hamish could just about visualise this spotty ne'er-do-well who never shaved and looked as if he slept in his clothes, although he had apparently once enjoyed the reputation of a dandy. But he found it hard to imagine him ransacking Aidan's things. It was obvious he used drugs, not the hard ones perhaps, and liked a drink or two as well, and was never without a fag in his fingers, but searching someone's cabin...

Rumour had it he frequented the less salubrious neighbourhoods of Puerto Rico when at home. On board he seemed to have struck up a relationship with some of the crew and avoided his family as if he were ashamed of them. Or more likely he saw that they probably were ashamed of him as he was permanently broke as well as scruffy-looking. An uncharacteristic relation of the sophisticated Fuentes, thought Hamish, but it took all sorts.

"This Ari," Katie continued, "appears to be hand in glove with the purser and some of the crew, at least he is always hobnobbing with them, and money - usually US dollars - seems to change hands on occasion, rather furtively. Anyway, he was obviously desperate for a fix and was trying to get hold of whatever it is he smokes - which might account for his sudden opportune dash ashore in ...Coinco wasn't it? -when..."

Before she could finish, Hamish looked up to see Aidan, glasses in hand, advancing from the direction of the bar. This, however, didn't stop Katie who was quite determined to pursue her question.

"Time for the kiss of glasses?" Aidan handed them both a drink. Katie quickly slid her first glass behind the curtain: it wouldn't do to be taken for a habitual drinker especially when she was just in the act of casting slurs on one of the other passengers' drinking habits.

"I don't know what role Ari played, if any, but I thought Señora Watanabe's 'husband' was the chap who did the underhand negotiating with the Chilean fisherman, but I'm sure Ari had some part to play there too," Katie persisted, wanting to sort it out before Hamish and Aidan got into their huddle. "The fisherman - you know - the one whose brother had been killed earlier… and who Tony then followed when they went to inspect their lobsterpots… with such disastrous results. Or perhaps it was *his* body they had somehow got hold of and trundled out that night when they thought nobody was about? Which made all that bumping noise. Oh, I'm getting thoroughly muddled. Hello, Aidan; thanks for the drink. I'll leave you two to your secrets and will join you in a moment when you've sorted everything out and can explain this mess to me more intelligibly."

She reached for the door-handle, then turned and added:

"But before I go there's just one small thing I meant to tell you, Hamish, and quite forgot until now. Aidan, you might be interested too. You remember I told you about Señora Lorca and how I discovered she was Peruvian and not Chilean at all? Just as we were leaving her she mentioned something in an undertone about her contacts in Lima. They evidently still manage to pass her the odd snippet of information hot off the press as it were. They must have some sort of secret courier or clandestine network down here. She had just received a message about Montesinos, their hated chief of police. I couldn't catch it exactly but it was something to the effect that he'd been rumbled, betrayed I think she said, and was on the run. Outside the country, Peru that is."

From Aidan's look this obviously was not news to him though he did seem surprised it had leaked out so quickly and so far away from the Peruvian capital.

"Yes, but how does that affect things in Chile?" Hamish asked.

"She'd hoped against hope that when it became known that he, Montesinos, was guilty of SS-type secret-police behaviour in Peru, (which the Chilean SS, ie the Dina, then copied here), the police in Coinco might actually get round to releasing her son, recognising that he'd been subjected to torture in Peru before coming south and realising that he'd quite obviously been framed. And releasing him soon. After all, without someone powerful to shield them, a lot of those police thugs in Chile as well as in Lima will now be looking for new sources of protection, won't they? And will probably be clutching at any straw. *They* can hardly flee the country - not like that crook Montesinos, - and may well now be desperate."

Katie was in full flow and wouldn't be stopped. "They must know Felipe's innocent if they put two and two together. At least of anything to do with the drugs. Homosexuality's hardly a hanging matter even in this benighted corner of the world. Even for that sadistic bunch of leftovers from the Dina. And what's more... Evidently before he fled the country, Montesinos had said something enigmatic to a newspaper about *"nowadays gold wasn't what it used to be - all that glisters, etc."* Nobody could quite figure out what he meant at the time but perhaps now, Aidan...? Now they've uncovered the loot in the lobster-pots... and the stolen Mujo Gallico exhibits?"

"That's just it - I can't figure it out either. There seem to be two entirely different stashes stowed out there; one the proceeds of the Mujo Gallico gold heist which may - or may not - contain some faked pieces, and the other various bits of porn, erotica and so forth nobody knows where from. They're still having to work it all out. And there's been another development and a most peculiar one, at least I'm sure you'll think so." Aidan lowered himself into a seat away from the door and in a quiet voice said something to Hamish which Katie, who was again on the point of retiring to the bathroom to change for dinner, just managed to catch. On hearing it, she couldn't tear herself away.

"Why, what's happened now? What was that?" and then she added, bossily: "don't forget it's the fancy dress party tonight. Hamish, your deerstalker and pipe are there beside your bunk and I've managed to borrow a ukelele from Manuel, the nearest thing I could find to a violin. You've got less than an hour till dinner. And, Aidan, I've got your disguise here: you'd better take it now," handing it to him. Realising she wasn't going to winkle anything further out of them, she finally withdrew having given up, but still determined to worm it out of Hamish later.

Retreating to put on her own costume of a cancan girl with froufrou skirt and hoop ear-rings, she shut the door. She congratulated herself on having persuaded Manuel to lay his hands on some so-called ostrich feathers which she had twisted together into a fetching 1920s head-dress with plenty of glitter suborned from the pastry-chef. Together with her black fishnet stockings and exaggerated make-up she felt quite confident about her costume. Quite the vamp, as she added an artificial mole on her chin. She wondered whether Hamish would chicken out when the time came and gritted her teeth. As for Aidan she despaired. He would never have the nerve, she knew. Unless she bullied him.

CHAPTER TWENTY-NINE

After a quick whispered exchange, Hamish and Aidan departed to the Captain's cabin and Katie went back to slip on the rest of her fancy-dress. As she was putting the finishing touches to her makeup Hamish returned. Deep in his musings, he hardly realised Katie was talking to him.

"Does this lipstick look too orangey to you?" Pause. "You look as if you'd been pole-axed, Hamish. What on earth's happened?" Fiddling with his pencil, Hamish ignored her first question but answered her second.

"Apparently news has just come in from Caracas confirming that the Venezuelan intelligence services have captured this man called Montesinos, Peru's former spy chief; the man Aidan was talking about earlier. He was allegedly on the run from Lima accused of embezzlement. But among his crimes he was reputed to have used 'stress techniques' - a euphemism for torture. Yes, he's the one who's been widely compared with the Soviet Union's Beria. A really nasty piece of work. This bears out young Lorca's torture allegations too of course. He should be had up for so much more than just embezzlement but I doubt if they'll ever have the nerve…He deserves a latter-day version of Nüremberg with the whole book thrown at him but, knowing them, he'll probably get away scot-free."

"My God! I suppose he didn't offer a large enough bribe so they thought they'd wheel him in and see if the Peruvian government would ante up. D'you suppose that's what happened?" Katie was agog but Hamish hesitated, distressed to see how quickly Katie had developed this cynical streak, presumably modelled on some of his own earlier reactions.

Accompanied by a thoughtful-looking Aidan, Hamish did not seem as elated as Katie expected. She herself was delighted at the news especially since it tallied with her own observations. What she didn't yet know was what Aidan had outlined to Hamish as his real motive for being so determined to nail the drug barons and how it dated back to an incident during their time together in Glasgow. Hamish also had his own grim reason for not celebrating yet; he decided to give Katie the detailed background and the further shocking piece of news later when they had more time and privacy.

"So you see, my love, your Señora Lorca was right. She obviously had advance information: I only hope - like her - this results in young Felipe being released now. Word has it that the fugitive was alleged to have undergone plastic surgery to his face, in Venezuela, making it unrecognisable. He was supposed to have been carrying millions of US dollars in a small pigskin attaché case manacled to his wrist, together with some most unusual pieces of erotica when he was 'apprehended'. So it must have been a tip-off, especially as he was so surprised he offered no resistance."

He paused looking for Katie's reaction.

"Perhaps, as you suggest, he didn't bribe somebody enough. The Venezuelans were cock'a hoop about their catch and loudly congratulating themselves; their President had supposedly proclaimed that Montesinos would be handed over to Peru 'faster than a rooster crows' - to counteract some of the nastier rumours circulating that they were hand in glove - so it looks as if the underhand bargaining is already at an advanced stage."

Aidan had known for a couple of days that the spy chief had escaped from Peru, fleeing allegations that he had masterminded a massive corruption ring involving judges, politicians and ministers and that he had laundered drugs money to the tune of some $286 million. But the Scot wondered if he really would be handed over to the Peruvian judiciary to face justice this time. Too many big names implicated and too much at stake. The politicians would be sure to close ranks to protect their own: or would they? They might just decide to pay off old scores; there must certainly be plenty of them. Or, again, they might opt to settle for some of the smaller fry and throw them to the wolves instead, men like Consuelo's bodyguard and minder for instance, who had so mysteriously vanished two or three days previously. It transpired that, as Aidan confirmed, he *had* been forcibly taken off the ship (at the Captain's insistence) during one of their unscheduled stops when not too many people had been around to see. Aidan had hinted to Hamish that this had been master-minded by Señora Watanabe who had finally become exasperated by his "bull-in-a-china-shop" antics and, financed by the mafia, her mafia, his heavy-handed dogging of Señorita Ballunde. The Señorita herself was obviously someone with enormous clout but, strangely to those not in the know, was also very much *persona grata* with the Captain, unlike most of the other Peruvians on board. She was therefore useful to Watanabe who exploited this relationship to make full use of the ship's communication facilities. But even Señorita Ballunde would have been unable to prevent her bodyguard from getting the chop had she so wished. Yet greater interests were at stake, it transpired.

Katie discovered later that the Señorita had been playing a dangerous double, not to say triple, game. Although seemingly in the Japanese mafia's pocket, she was able at the same time to keep the Captain - whose family *was,* somehow, connected to hers - informed of Chilean police progress in investigations into smuggling up and down the coast, to pass on the odd snippet to Señora Watanabe to keep her sweet; and, simultaneously, keep Lima informed of reaction on board to the gold heist.

"Yes, but you don't know the real reason why Señorita Ballunde is apparently immune, do you?" Hamish asked Katie with Aidan still there. "The reason why she gets away scot-free is because, as Aidan has just sussed out, she is the illegitimate daughter of guess-who - not the chief steward, not the Minister of Justice, but none other than the President himself! Apparently for years he had been having a liaison with a beautiful opera diva but managed to keep it hushed up so that not even his wife knew about it. The only one in the know, the President's trusted right-hand man and nominally his steward, (and wretched supposed father), has acted as go-between for years; very successfully apparently, and still does, taking the rap whenever things go wrong. So it was always believed that he was the Señorita's father, but oh no. Nothing so obvious! This so-called steward was the man who was closely related to our ship's Captain (and hence allegedly Consuelo Ballunde's distant relation too). So Consuelo had a foot in both camps; and made the most of it, exploiting when it suited her people's ignorance of the true facts."   Sensible and clever of her, thought Katie, but risky.

"But returning to Montesinos," Aidan resumed, "it looks as if he was involved in the Mujo Gallico heist as well. But at a distance, taking care to cover his tracks. After all, he *was* a crony of the Minister of

207

Justice, wasn't he? At least *he* would have been well enough placed to square off the security guards, instructing them when to switch off the laser beams, etc. - and everyone else concerned."

"Although he might then have opened himself up to the possibility of blackmail by any disgruntled underling especially later when the hue and cry had quietened down and the chips were being called in?" surmised Hamish.

"But someone else did get a whiff of it - and that someone else was … You've guessed it, yes our friend Señorita Ballunde. Who continued to play her cards very close to her chest. After all, she could only wield her influence in Peru and then only in a circumspect, rather clandestine way; whereas these events were taking place miles away in the other part of the continent - in the Argentine first, and then Venezuela. The Venezuelan President was rumoured to have set a \$1 million reward for information leading to Montesinos's capture in order to counteract accusations that he was knowingly harbouring a fugitive. This of course had still not silenced the sceptics, especially since it was after they apparently had received a strong lead about the intended final destination of the gold…," Aidan continued.

"Of course," Hamish nodded. "And the Mafia seems to have limitless funds when it comes to silencing people. The Venezuelan lot as well as the Peruvian."

Katie's eyes bulged as she listened to Aidan and Hamish exchanging further details. Aidan had emptied his pockets and was searching for something. At last he located it, a small gold coin, the size of a squashed Lima bean, and held it up for Hamish's inspection as Katie burst in with her question:

"You mean the same man who used to be in cahoots with the Minister for Justice and who was implicated in…".

"The very same," Johnson confirmed grimly, "but don't say it out loud. Even here…," and he pointed to the thin partition wall, finger on lips. Katie didn't know whether to laugh or be scared when he passed over a torn page from his diary with another name written on it. But Hamish nodded vigorously slapping his forehead.

"Of course, it all fits. Ironic that that's the same man who took as his motto *Verdad i Justicia* - Truth and Justice - from these Peruvian gold coins first minted in Lima, about 1905 I think it was. Let's see." Taking the diminutive coin in his fingers and holding it up to the light he added: "That was the Peruvian Republic of course - after they'd thrown out most of the Spanish, some of them to be replaced by opportunistic Englishmen. Like your grandfather, Katie; hence the Peruvian Corporation." He paused while Katie sniffed. "With this chap's connections small wonder they managed to get the cargo through without any excise complications and ..."

"No customs dues either to pay of course."

"You mean...?"

"Yes," (lowering his voice still further) "Vargas, the Chief of Customs himself. Who was a bosom pal of the Minister of Justice. The Minister is heavily implicated and now we've caught his henchman in the act so to speak, it'll be very hard for Vargas to talk himself out of that one, even that smarmy bastard with all his smart connections and influential mistresses. Now that the President has publicly disowned him, even he won't be able to sweet-talk himself out of it for ever." Aidan sounded jubilant.

Catching sight of the time, Hamish asked Katie if she was ready since they risked being late.

"You Presbyterians, and your punctilious punctuality," mocked Katie. An Anglican for over twenty-five years, Hamish merely smiled: he knew she was teasing him.

"No-one in Chile ever dines before 10 pm at the earliest," she added for good measure, while Aidan scampered away supposedly to put on his fancy dress.

*   *   *

Later that evening when finally Hamish had Katie to himself and there was no danger of being overheard, he gave her the piece of news he had been trying to shield her from during dinner and drinks beforehand. For a moment she sat completely stunned and then finally murmured:

"So that was why Vanessa and Jaime didn't turn up until so late and then looking completely shattered. How dire, how simply awful... Whoever could have done such an awful thing? Are you quite sure?"

"Indeed quite ghastly, but they want us to keep it under our hats for the time being - for all sorts of reasons which you'll appreciate later. So not even a word to them, my love, for now."

"There's no doubt that it really was Ari, is there? No doubt at all?"

"I'm afraid not, my darling. I know it's a terrible shock for you, as indeed it is for everyone. Just think of poor Jaime and Vanessa - what they must be feeling. And the poor wretched sister, even if they hadn't spoken in years. It's too awful to contemplate." He stopped. "And they are pretty sure they know who did it but unfortunately he's above the law, at least for the moment, until they sort this lot out."

"Poor, poor Ari. He didn't deserve that…. His throat slit you say, and then drowned?" She gulped. "Whoever would want to do that to the wretched man? Even if he did owe them money? What morons!"

She wiped her eyes, her face a deathly white.

"Of course it's all tied up with drug-running and scams but I can't say more at present. At least not until we find out more and the Chilean police clear off."

Still ashen-faced, Katie sat staring. "No wonder poor Vanessa looked so drained, and Jaime too…".

*   *   *

22nd March 2001
on board SS Skyros
   Darling Mattie,
   The briefest of notes which may well not reach you before we do. I can't get to e-mail you from here but hope you got the e-mail I sent you via Vanessa's son in Santiago confirming our flight arrival details, etc.? I thought I should warn you that we are likely to have quite a lot more luggage than when we left so don't bring your baby Fiat. See if you can find the keys to the old Vauxhall: and please check the boot's empty. Anyway, longing to see you again - but be prepared for a surprise.
   You may have read something in the press about Peru's Police Chief having been tracked down to Venezuela where he was in hiding having stashed away millions and millions of ill-gotten loot - most of it gold. Anyway, please keep ANYTHING you find in the newspapers about it; even in godforsaken old England there may be snippets worth saving. And if you are able to record any relevant news items on the telly that would be even better.
   Sorry I can't write more at present but I'll explain all when we see you again. Hope everything's on an even keel, and Barbara and

Joan are not bombarding you with problems from recalcitrant Mums
in the Mothers Union!!
    Did the swelling on your knee amount to anything serious
and was the physio able to help? We're both fine apart from a few
bruises…Dad's got a real whopper on his head, which you'll probably
see as it'll be some days before that goes.
    Heaps of love. See you very soon, I can hardly wait…
    Katie-Mum.

*   *   *

Returning to her cabin the next evening Anna found a mysterious
parcel, which Nigel had retrieved from the floor outside, wrapped up in
fancy paper. Opening it up she saw to her delight a copy of Alvarez &
Streeter's celebrated "*Wild flowers and native shrubs of Chile*", beautifully
illustrated. A note fluttered out which thanked her for her address and
many kindnesses during their trip and expressed the hope they would
soon meet up again in Adelaide at the forthcoming conference they
would both be attending. Raùl also thanked Anna for her cousins'
address at one of the Clare Valley wineries she had suggested him
visiting and finished by saying:

"I know you were (rightly) sceptical about my friend Paulina's motives
in clinging to me so. You need not have feared: I was well aware of her little
game. It suited me to string her along, as she thought she was stringing me,
in the hopes that she might give something significant away. In fact she did,
unwittingly, and it was a great bonus although I admit I was rather shocked
by what she revealed. Even more by who was implicated. Can't say more
at present: I will explain when we next meet, in your beautiful country to
which I greatly look forward, - if not before."

The note ended with a declaration of undying devotion and Anna
found herself consumed with curiosity at the maddening unexplained
hints, at the same time as grinning inanely. She carefully placed the
book by her bed, to be looked at more carefully later on, tenderly
folding the letter underneath after surreptitiously raising it to her lips.
She would definitely hunt him down at the earliest opportunity when
she would not brook no for an answer to her questions. Whatever had
Paulina revealed?

211

CHAPTER THIRTY

"Sir, a tangy Castillero del Diablo from the Concha y Toro stable? to follow the crisp Cabernet Sauvignon you had with the fish course? Yes, from the Maùle Valley. Or would you prefer a taste of this deliciously light fruity Errazuriz *pinot noir?* No, this is a new one called *Ocio* which everyone's raving about?"

The waiter filled up each guest's glass expertly. Many were feeling slightly light-headed; the conversation at dinner was flowing freely, punctuated by raucous laughter and some dubious jokes among the young who had gone to town on the dressing up. Everybody was tucking into the mountains of food enthusiastically, though some slightly hampered by their costumes.

"Wine heaven," Freddie murmured appreciatively. "Such a lingering after-taste. And no hangover, I promise you, Katie," his next-door neighbour, adding: "Have another glass; you'll need something for the toast. Or probably toasts."

"No thanks. I'm waiting for the Concha y Toro Carmenère, so much more sensual than the merlot, don't you think? Or the Bio-bio which I'm told is absolutely superb with the friandises. I'd never heard of it before this trip but even your Argentine friends on board acknowledge its superiority as a dessert wine (giving my Chilean cousins over there the excuse to be even more condescending to them!). Why don't you try it too?" Freddie managed to look suitably impressed by Katie's wine-speak, and for once was silent as his Argentine friend winked at him.

Dinner was nearly over and the fancy dress parade about to get into full swing when the Captain, resplendent in his dress uniform, rose to address the company. The gold on his epaulettes catching the light was really stunning and was reflected in the elaborate gold buttons of his high-necked white tunic which fitted snugly over slim black trousers. His insignia of office sparkled, distinctly visible in the intimate lighting, making him, with his slicked-back black hair, look very distinguished.

Clearing his throat, he started by apologising for the many small deviations from the published itinerary and any inconvenience this might have caused his dear passengers. As a gesture of goodwill on his part he had arranged that the best French champagne should be served to all on board before the final dinner the next evening, when he also had another little surprise in store for them. He felt sure that, in the circumstances, he would be forgiven any technical hitches which might have crept in and which, he added, were entirely due to *force majeure*. By this time everyone was so merry no-one felt like nit-picking, least of all Vanessa's group who had been enjoying a riotous time and had quite forgotten any small glitches which had arisen.

But the couple who entered into the spirit of the occasion the most unrestrainedly were Tony and Sheila. They had been about to lead a conga reel right round the deck regardless of the fact that the judging was not yet over but paused to hear the rest of what the Captain had to say.

The Captain had just confirmed the award of the men's fancy dress prize to Hamish for his Sherlock Holmes costume. Hamish had looked distinctly embarrassed but Katie was congratulating herself on having persuaded him, against the odds, to enter. She was delighted now to see that Sheila, who was looking more than usually flushed, had won the ladies' prize for her Swiss *gaucho* version complete with cowbell and false blonde plaits. In her dirndl she was looking even more buxom than before, Katie thought, and wondered. She decided to attribute it to the wine which had flowed copiously all evening.

Hamish looked round nervously to see if the Peruvian contingent was joining in but they were nowhere to be seen. He was glad now that common sense had prevailed and Katie had not knocked on their door earlier asking to borrow an opium pipe, if they had such a thing, for Hamish's Sherlock Holmes. Señora Watanabe for one would never have believed that she had come in a spirit of innocent fun: without doubt she would have suspected an ulterior motive. Perhaps her "husband" Watanabe would even suspect that she had come to gloat at the removal of the bulldog minder. The Señora might never have heard of Conan Doyle and his Holmes and as for the frivolity of dressing up and parading around deck looking so ridiculous, Hamish doubted whether she would have been able to fathom it. Losing face, and purposely looking foolish, simply did not figure in her book. You would have to be mad to do it.

Just as well Katie had not given in to her momentary impulse there, Hamish breathed thankfully.

Raùl, in a fetching troubadour outfit, was hovering in the background looking enviously at Sherwin who was whooping it up with Anna. Freddie and Ursula were dancing energetically and in the thick of things, Freddie in his starling-like iridescent waistcoat, looking more carefree than he had for several days. The waiters were dodging in and out trying to clear away the dirty plates without colliding with the dancers. And Aidan had disappeared. Katie had had to use all her guile to bully him into wearing a borrowed colander from the kitchen which she had skewered to his head with the aid of two knitting needles; and then added a couple of meat skewers for good measure. Happily he still had enough hair to hold it but his sandy-coloured eyes blinked unhappily at the idiot he must look. She had run up a black aerial of sorts and made him look like a rather wobbly satellite dish, the first Sputnik so she declared, but he had been so self-conscious he disappeared as soon as he felt he decently could. Katie looked round to see Hamish's large check handkerchief being swept across his forehead; that sinuous hand covered in golden hairs unmistakable.

Hamish was certainly perspiring in his Sherlock Holmes outfit even though he'd shed the thick tweed jacket and deerstalker. Almost convulsed with laughing at one of Jaime's sly jokes, he was watching Jocelyn in her blue-ribboned Alice dress and white tights as she clicked away happily with her salvaged camera. He thought of the value of her rescued photographs, about which she suspected nothing. Nor, happily, did Katie.

Katie mouthed a message across the table to him. She was thinking perhaps the time had come when she could decently remove her *froufrou* petticoat which was beginning to prickle uncomfortably and snag her tights.

"What a relief that will be! And take off some of my eye make-up too, which is making my eyes sting."

Just before she closed the cabin door Katie heard a throaty gurgle from nextdoor, which was quickly strangled. With her head against the partition wall, she listened intently but all she could make out was furtive hushed voices, in Spanish not Japanese, but even that defeating her. She put these uncomfortable sounds out of her mind as she struggled out of her petticoats.

*   *   *

By the time Katie re-emerged into the dining saloon the party was almost over and there was no sign of either Hamish or Aidan. Ursula told her that, just as she went off to change, Aidan had been summoned by the purser who had handed him a note requesting him to go urgently to investigate something suspicious on shore. She said the Captain had agreed he could have the use of the outboard dinghy provided he guaranteed to be back on board by midnight. And so, pausing only to remove his colander fancy-dress and grab his duffle-coat, he had shown Hamish the note and dashed off.

"Hamish had hesitated, looking very put out and worried," Ursula told Katie, "and then had rushed off after Aidan begging me to explain to you what had happened and to tell you not to worry! Typical," she snorted. "Men always say that when they're about to do the most idiotically foolhardy things without stopping to consider." His Meerschaum pipe was indeed still smouldering in his dinner-place. But no sign of Hamish. Katie was not a little peeved. Perhaps she only had herself to blame, she tried to think charitably: if she'd still been there he probably wouldn't have faced up to her gaze and gone, so impetuously.

Hearing the thud as the dinghy splashed down and the squeaking as the oars were noisily fitted into the rowlocks, Katie dashed down to the deck below. But too late. They were already some twenty yards out, Hamish rowing frantically while Aidan fiddled with the outboard motor. At last he got it going and Hamish was able to ship his oars as they rapidly became lost from view. All Katie could detect was the dot of his deerstalker bobbing up and down in the breeze as the earflaps spread into the wind.

Happily Katie had collected her sheepskin coat from the cabin since the evening had turned cool. She rushed up the companionway to see if she could follow the outboard trajectory from the top deck and was just in time to see from the curve of their pearly wake the dinghy coming back into sight. Although brightly starlit, the water looked black and uninviting and she shivered. A faint smell of petrol exhaust like a lawn-mower's came back to her and the feeble puttering of an outboard engine. She was about to go below when she heard a noise she couldn't fathom, a muffled cry and the indignant squawking of an unidentifiable bird obviously disturbed by the passing dinghy, amid splashing and the sound of an oar hitting the water broadside on. And then something else, heavily falling overboard with a hollow splosh, coinciding with both the boat's lights going out. Darkness; except for the reflection of the moon which glowed feebly in the distance. A great deal of cursing carried across the water, followed by a complete eerie silence as the spluttering outboard stopped. Katie strained her ears but could hear nothing more except the faint slapping of the waves. Not even an indignant seabird.

*   *   *

An ominous velvety blackness gripped them as, one by one, the stars slid behind the cloud becoming obscured like the moon. Silhouetted against the feeble shoreline lights, a shape loomed up out of the water as the last of the sparkling reflections dimmed. Hamish just had time to shout a warning to his helmsman but Aidan could not wrench the steering round quickly enough to avoid contact. A thud, a hoarse sound of ripping canvas, an oath and then Hamish heard stertorous breathing and the rasping squeak of rubber on rubber, as if a spaniel's tail had been trodden on; then frogmen's flippers slapping and squealing on the dinghy as a glistening black devil struggled alongside to seize the grabline and clamber aboard, slipping and squelching as he went. The engine having cut out, it now appeared to be flooded as Aidan made frantic efforts to get her restarted. Then another shape resembling a porpoise loomed portside. Again, a thump as Hamish, seizing the paddle out of the rowlock, spun round to confront the second menacing assailant. His shin hit the makeshift seat as he did so and he lost his balance, knocking his torch overboard; but not without catching the unknown attacker a glancing blow with the edge of the paddle, enough to unbalance him as well, making him teeter on the rounded edge of the dinghy, and finally plop back overboard with a grating screeching sound of flippers on ungrateful rubber and a huge hollow splash.

The now extinct lamp wedged in the stern to serve as a warning light fell on his foot as Aidan narrowly avoided being swept overboard too. The first frogman lunged out viciously with his weapon but Aidan's elbow managed to land him a crippling blow amidships, right in his solar plexus, at the same time as he kicked his knee. At least Aidan's foot was unimpeded by flippers whereas the frogman was floundering in his unwieldly webbed rubber feet. The man crumpled for a moment but his mate, who had now succeeded in straddling the gunwale again, came to his rescue sending the dinghy lurching perilously. Slapping the water viciously as it rocked back and forth, it sent spumes up and into the boat. A brief and ferocious struggle ensued but the frogmen being armed had the advantage. Hamish could glimpse their evilly glinting knives in the starlight but their macabre wetsuits were so slimy they gave no purchase. Intent on ducking the thrusting stabbings of the knives, he spied a gaping slit where they must have slashed Aidan's duffle-coat which in his haste he had fortuitously slipped on over his lifesaving jacket. The arm was half torn off and flicked into their faces as Hamish made a grab but he was totally unable to get a grip on either of them. If it had not been a matter of life or death he would have laughed to see his friend, after a fierce tussle, squirm out of his coat and into the briny leaving his attackers open-mouthed and baffled with just the ripped duffle coat in their hands.

But Hamish hadn't a second for reflection as they were onto him like lightening. The paddle was wrenched from his hands and before he knew what was happening he too was gulping for air in the iciest of keen glacier water. At least they had not managed to make contact with their knives, and he had avoided being hit over the head, but he wasn't sure that this was any better, draped around as he was with his heavy sports jacket and clinging trousers. He managed to kick off his shoes which were fast filling with water. His jacket too, thus freeing his life jacket. For a split second he feared for his heart as his head was plunged into the gelid water and he came up gasping but somehow he found the breath to strike off away from the dinghy and its loathsome occupants.

The slugs were obviously scanning the moonless void for a glimpse of them so Hamish avoided kicking until he was some way off, all the time calling out softly for his friend. But no sound or sign of Aidan. No response at all. Hamish fought down his mounting alarm while with an almighty slapping of the water a huge splash reverberating nearby announced that the frogmen too had abandoned the boat and dived back into the sea - though happily in the landward direction, leaving the dinghy rocking violently and shipping water. Perhaps they had been fooled by his jacket which must have trapped some air as it was still floating on the surface in the direction of the shore. Aidan, however, had spotted the floating jacket and assuming Hamish was inside it, felt heartened. At least it looked as if one of them might survive. Though he felt nothing due to the intense cold, Hamish saw with surprise that there was blood on his hand which had trickled down from a gash in his forearm. Trailing in the water, his left hand encountered something rough and hairy which he instinctively grabbed. The dinghy's painter streaming out behind gave him a spasm of hope as he clutched it convulsively, trying desperately not to succumb to the paralysing cold creeping up his legs and groin into his body.

Swimming silently but doggedly, Hamish made for the lights of the ship now brilliantly sweeping across the water. He listened intently for sounds of Aidan but could hear nothing. No noise, no squeaks, no grunts or groans, no smell, scarcely a ripple. Were they coming after him? He couldn't tell but all he knew was that he must keep moving or he would literally freeze to death, if he didn't first succumb to the weight of his sodden clothes and drown, which he presumed was what the attackers were banking on. Was Aidan, in Hamish's mind only a softie from Glasgow's gulf-stream (and unused to the Arctic cold of his Hebridean waters to the north of Stornoway), even now succumbing to the cold? Hamish's lungs were bursting and his heart was burning but he must at all costs find his friend before it was too late. He decided not to haul the dinghy in as that could easily betray his position to the marauders if they were still searching for him. Instead, he left the boat to its fate and tried circling to locate Aidan who was perhaps shielded from his view by the hulk of the *Skyros*. The ship's welcome outline was at last more clearly visible, picked out as it now was in lights.

Surfacing again, Hamish strained his ears but could hear nothing apart from the waves. He thought he could hear someone shouting but night took the words away. He caught a snatch of Chilean dance music which quickly faded as he tried to imagine Vanessa's party, oblivious to all but the fun, joining in a raucous *refalosa*.

He wondered where Katie was and decided remorsefully she would not be with the rest of the party but worriedly pacing the deck and scanning the waves. He pictured her face, crumpled with concern, the little darts into her crow's feet betraying her anxiety. He should have stayed to explain, he knew he should, before dashing off in that madcap way: but then he would have missed Aidan who would hardly have been able to survive single-handed (if indeed he was still alive). He scanned the void again for any signs, only hoping he himself would make it through so as to make it up to Katie. Encroaching numbness was lulling him, beckoning him Lethewards into oblivion. He realised he must resist it at all costs. The muscles around his heart were aching and he was beginning to feel drowsy; if only he could just give up to delicious sleep.

Drifting along and beginning to yield, he was suddenly jerked out of his lethargy by what looked like a huge submerged log floating towards him, in reality an ice-floe. It passed within inches. Now he was fully awake and aware.

CHAPTER THIRTY-ONE

Katie craned her neck staring into the black hellhole but still could make out nothing. Nor could she hear anything except the slapping of the artificially created waves against the bows of the ship. She shouted Hamish's name but to no avail, her voice ending in a screech as she stared in concentration, but still could make out nothing in the inky void. She had not realised Jaime was standing beside her staring into the nothingness too. Vanessa was obviously still in the bosom of her family and, judging by the sounds of merriment just then wafting upwards, the evening was still in full swing for those who had stayed below. The remaining revellers were obviously quite oblivious to the drama being played out in the Stygian eeriness outside.

Acrobatic bats could now be glimpsed in a stray moonbeam as they wheeled over the water, silhouetted fitfully against the reluctantly emerging custard-like moon. Their plaintive mewing, barely audible at the best of times, could not be heard against the faint strains of music floating up, incongruously, from below. The fickle moon slid back coyly behind the cloud only to re-emerge seconds later, accompanied by some stars, glittering feebly. It was now the colour of an egg-yolk with the occasional fleck of white but it still glinted sulkily, shedding little light.

The music stopped. Not a sound to be heard now, nothing except the slightest of rustlings as the fireflies brushed wings. In the void Katie was aware of hoarse breathing alongside her.

"That must be Antares," said Jaime, pointing. "The southernmost star in our Chilean sky. It's the biggest and brightest in the Scorpio constellation." Jabbing his finger into the darkness, trying to distract her, he added: "There, with that intense reddish light, a symbol for our earliest inhabitants." Jaime was struggling to find something to take Katie's mind off the enormity of the unfolding drama.

She listened with half an ear as suddenly Jaime gripped her arm painfully. With his other hand he pointed to something floating some twenty yards away. No doubt about it: Hamish's drowning deerstalker which he hadn't had the time to discard was bobbing along beneath them, the flaps spread out grotesquely like two sodden bat's ears. Until it gradually became waterlogged, releasing phosphorescent bubbles as it reluctantly sank from view.

As Katie caught her breath in a sob she sensed more activity alongside her. Someone was quickly tearing off clothes, hesitating on the brink, and then with a huge 'Splosh!' diving into the inky hellhole below. Lucky they weren't on the top deck she thought, as the glacial spray took her breath away. Whoever it was took a moment to come up and was lost from view for several agonising seconds, then he struck out in the direction of the now peaceful dinghy still almost invisible in the dark. He was obviously a powerful swimmer and in no time had reached where the action must have been. There was more splashing, then a stream of sparkling bubbles rising to the surface which pinpointed two or three misshapen black forms looking vaguely like seals half-rising from the water, only to submerge beneath it again. Yet more iridescent droplets were reflected in the waxing moonlight, faintly visible to the anxious watchers on board.

After another never-ending pause, finally "Got 'im" came triumphantly across the water, "*and* the knife," followed by frenetic splashing and an oath in Spanish.

"Great. Keep his face under water." More frantic kicking and then: "If he gives you any more grief shove him over this way. Here; let me give a hand."

She thought she recognised Hamish's voice and moaned, "Please God, let it be him." Then she recognised Aidan's unmistakable Glasgow accent:

"Look out!" in a rising crescendo of alarm.

Katie's heart was pounding as she mentally rehearsed all the things that could have gone wrong, or could still go wrong. Her darkest fears had always been centred on her children, then later, on Matthew her only son. Until now it had never dawned on her that Hamish, her dependable, inviolable Hamish, would ever become the focus of her agonising fears. She tried to force herself to be rational but failed.

"Hamish," she screamed in her anguish. "The knife. Mind the knife!" but she doubted if he could hear her. Although an excellent swimmer, with his recent heart problems Hamish would be even more severely hampered in the icy water especially with all those clothes on. Besides, his hearing was no longer as keen as it once had been. She cursed herself for making him wear his heavy tweed jacket for the fancy dress but at least he hadn't had any knickerbockers to weigh him down!

The flailing around was too far away for her to be able to see what was happening but she could now hear grunts and kicking carrying clearly across the water. And a great deal more splashing. As the moon shone ever brighter, now aided by more stars, she could make out three - or was it four? - silhouettes thrashing around in the sea and one semi-submerged black log seemingly, but no boat. Presumably that had overturned in the mêlée and floated away, minus the engine which would have dropped like a stone as it was only held on with a single bolt, so Jaime told her. He'd heard the Mate cursing earlier when the other pin had sheared off as one of the hands had brought it alongside clumsily that morning.

She looked round at the pile of cast-off clothes on the deck beside her and was amazed to notice a frilly skirt and a woman's pumps. Had any of the men dressed up in female attire for the fancy-dress, she tried to recall. In her terror her brain refused to function; she was quite beyond remembering anything which had happened earlier in the evening except for her annoyance when Ursula had told her about Aidan and Hamish dashing off so bull-headedly on their wild goose chase; and her trepidations about his heart.

Silver moonlight was now glinting on something clutched by the least bulky of the figures in the water as it progressed in a semicircle round to where one of the others was flapping feebly. For a fleeting moment she tried to picture to herself the vacuum, the empty void in her life if Hamish were no longer around to fill it. But her mind refused to grapple with the concept. It was just something inconceivable to her though, since the agony of his angina attack, she had several times tried to face the prospect. Unable to focus on the enormity of the chasm yawning before her, she prodded herself into action; she could at least do something constructive.

Dashing off to her cabin she found Hamish's heart pills and drops for angina which she grabbed, together with an old sweater. She then rushed up to the bridge and breathlessly begged the Captain to launch one of the lifeboats without losing any more time. But she found he had already done so, summoning his strongest crew members, and was having the ship's searchlights trained onto the scene. Katie just had time to hand one of the crew Hamish's heart pills with a hurried "Please, make him take one of these - immediately on contact." Meanwhile the Captain reminded them to take grappling-hooks and ropes before they were lowered with a great hollow sploosh into the depths below. If this didn't disturb the revellers in the saloon Katie didn't know what would, but still the strains of Chilean harp music drifted back up to her.

By this time the rest of the crewmen, the First Mate included, had arrived up on deck. Jaime persuaded Katie, who was shivering, to go below and organise some hot soup for the survivors if and when they came back, while he went off to ensure the door onto the lower deck was opened and crewmen were ready assembled to help them struggle aboard. The capsized dinghy could now be spotted bobbing up and down some distance away. It looked as if a great slash had been made in its side but luckily not below the waterline. Two sodden heaps resembling black slugs were being towed along in the water by a couple of semi-submerged bodies sporting half-inflated fluorescent yellow-orange life-jackets. A third slighter body in calf-length yellow zip-up oilskins and matching flippers, shining grotesquely as they were picked out in the bright lights, struck off in a businesslike crawl to retrieve the dinghy. At least it appeared to be making good progress.

"My God, it's that Australian," breathed Jaime. "The woman, the high-powered pharmacologist. I hope she knows what she's doing; those icy currents can be lethal if you're not..." his voice trailed away.

Almost paralysed by worry Katie, back on deck, was now focussing on the shapes in the water as they heaved themselves up and then became lost to view. As they loomed larger and larger coming towards her she counted first three then four. Then she lost them; her eyes played tricks on her and she could only see two, or perhaps three. Or was the third just a wave? "Hang on, Hamish, hang on for God's sake. Just another few seconds," she screamed desperately into the void as the waves snatched her words away.

CHAPTER THIRTY-TWO

The lifeboat was now alongside, thank heaven. First one then the next sodden deadweight was being hauled into the boat by the team who strained every sinew to hoist them over the gunwale and send them sprawling into the now crowded *Skyros* interior. Then silence, and Katie prayed fervently muttering under her breath while Jaime spoke words of comfort which she scarcely heard.

Jaime had helped her down to the deck below where the door already stood open ready to receive its strange cargo. Like a whale, thought Katie incongruously, preparing to ingest plankton. The rest of the crew together with one of Jaime's sons had already assembled there. Suddenly Katie felt arms thrown around her and Vanessa, covered in glitter and smelling strongly of wine, sobbed convulsively: "Is it true? Jaime told me about Ha...?" and her voice trailed off.

"What do you mean? Is what true?" Katie was confused, and even more alarmed by Vanessa's hysteria. She wheeled round to Jaime for explanation.

"That Hamish...First Ari, and now Hamish...?" She gulped as if trying, but she couldn't get the words out. "I'm so dreadfully sorry," she finished as an icy hand clutched Katie's breast. As if through a fog she was aware of her temples thumping furiously and then vaguely of more movement swirling around her. She found herself hanging on to Jaime as she heard one of the crewmen shout to the skipper:

"Hold on! Another body here - a deadweight and long enough to be one of the gringos, heavy enough too," his voice trailed off.

Katie sank to her knees. "Let it be him," she prayed, but no sound came.

*   *   *

Nigel, mystified by Anna's sudden disappearance from the fancy-dress party, had also arrived at the scene.

"Don't worry, Katie. Anna is an excellent swimmer, very strong and almost Olympic standard. I'm sure she knows what's she's doing," he reassured her, so for a moment she felt calmer though her fears still centred on Hamish.

He couldn't have drowned - not yet anyway. And where was Aidan? Then Katie started worrying about Hamish again and dashed off to the cabin to make sure she had the right cardiac pills ready for his return. Meanwhile Raùl, ghostly white, was lurking in the background looking agitated; he soon went away when it was obvious there were enough people milling around and getting in the way. By now, thank God, the crew were beginning to take charge and bustle people out.

Lit by the searing searchlights the lifeboat at last, after an eternity, began to discharge more flotsam. Tensely waiting, Katie snapped her eyes shut and found herself clinging on to Jaime again as she played back in her mind a mental translation of what she had just heard a crewman shout.

"Hold on. Still another bod here; this one's an absolute deadweight. I'd say he's probably snuffed it - or else he's full of seawater…whatever. No sign of life here yet."

Still on her knees Katie groaned "Oh, God! Not him". But the body still lay inert in the blackness of the hold as it was manhandled away from the spotlight's reach, a slippery black cylindrical shape quite motionless.

The other bodies floundered like eels and stank like the Puerto Montt fishmarket. Grim work, and smelly. Even in these pure glacial waters. It was extremely difficult to get hold of their elusive cargo but at last the welcome party, now with stout gloves on, succeeded. After the first three bodies had been safely gathered they lay heaving in a heap with pungent rivulets of water streaming off them. By now Katie, almost blind with panic, and still praying hard as she watched the men haul in the fourth deadweight, gave a convulsive sob of relief as she recognised Aidan. The lengthy body just lay stock still until it was turned face down, but at last something twitched and a faint moan could be heard. Then water started to seep from his mouth, and then trickle out, the shoulders shuddering then lying eerily still again. But where was Hamish? Was he dead? And what was that other black shape now being hauled aboard by the exhausted crew?

Katie, sobbing now, could hardly bear to look. An even lengthier and bulkier body than Aidan's, glazed under the unnatural light, was being laid carefully down almost at her feet. It lay totally inert until Jaime pushed her away and got to work on it together with a member of the crew. She just had time to glimpse the unmistakable face.

Though the total episode had only lasted quarter of an hour or so, it seemed an eternity to the onlookers. The tension had been as palpable as waiting for the final wicket to fall in an evenly poised test match. It was some time before the shocked and shivering corpse-like creatures, now shrouded in blankets, gradually revived with hot drinks. The comatose one, however, scarcely responded and only showed the faintest sign of animation when the kiss of life was applied by a reluctant crewman. Aidan sat hunched in the corner with glazed eyes, his teeth chattering uncontrollably. Jaime had helped Katie prop Hamish up (for the last one hauled in was indeed her beloved) and put him into the recovery position after he had finally appeared to come to, partially anyway, having spewed out quantities of salt water.

Realising the crewman would not have been able to, she quickly slipped some drops under Hamish's tongue and stroked them down his throat watching him swallow instinctively. At least he was still alive - just. She watched his unmistakably lengthy figure first stretched out on the deck and then hunched in a corner, and wondered how his heart had stood up to all its exertions. Thank goodness he had had the sense to put on a life-vest (only semi-inflated) under his jacket and to kick off his shoes. She peeled it back with sweaty fingers, his sweater and Viyella shirt, then his aertex vest, and laid her head on his chest. Not a sound: hypothermia must have set in. She listened again, silent tears streaming down. Just the merest suspicion of an irregular heartbeat, very slow and feeble. Searching feverishly she thought she detected a faint pulse in his neck; he still appeared to be breathing, albeit almost imperceptibly. Then he groaned and rolled over again, sliding on the slippery deck. By this time the ship's doctor had appeared on the scene and all was hustle and bustle. Katie heaved a long juddering sigh. He was going to make it: surely he was. He must.

Aidan too had had a life-jacket on which had enabled the crew to hoist him out of the water into the life-boat. The two assailants had been wearing wetsuits so at least they did not suffer such extreme cold. But the slipperiness of the rubber had made it extremely difficult to fish them out, especially as one was unconscious, and they had landed in an undignified sprawl upside down on the decking where they still lay inert. Like two revolting black slugs, thought Katie, glistening in the artificial light. How she would have loved to stamp on them and grind them into the deck.

She was frantically chafing Hamish's stiff icy neck and shoulders, whispering endearments to him without much hope he heard her. Massaging his back with neat alcohol, willing him to come back to life, she again felt a slight pulse near his collarbone. She was about to rub it again with her strong hands when the doctor intervened: "I'll take over now. You go and find him some soup." She noticed with relief one of Hamish's toes twitching, and then another. 'Pisco does have its uses,' she thought as she rubbed harder before yielding to the medic.

Remembering how she had often cursed his icy feet in bed in their impoverished early days together, she smiled ruefully. She had not allowed herself to imagine what the future would be like without him. Indeed, would life - could life - have any future for her without? She had often cursed his obdurate obstinacy as it seemed to her. His mother used to call it firmness of purpose, but then she would, wouldn't she? But now she was willing him to show some of this unappreciated characteristic.

She suppressed a sob as the enormity of the situation began finally to seep into her consciousness. What if he didn't make it after all? How could she face the emptiness ahead, existence devoid of all meaning, of all sensation? A hole bigger than the whole universe; an unfillable void would open in her heart which no amount of substitutes could ever replace. True she had Mattie and her friends to think of. But her son would soon be flitting the nest for good, her friends and parishioners were fine but they had no conception of what Hamish meant to her, and besides… She couldn't remember a time without the love of her life, his friendship and companionship, his dependability and unfailing devotion to her, his sense of humour - rather dour at times admittedly, impish at others; his compassion and love of humanity and sense of family.

As she listed his many qualities to herself she felt totally blank and hollow. There would be no-one to tickle her legs in a certain spot which reduced her to helplessness and made her melt into total non-resistance. No-one to murmur sweet endearments into her ear and make her feel dreamy. No-one to remind her to take her keys or her gloves, or the short-cut to avoid the inevitable roadworks. No-one to sing his favourite hymns slightly off-key in the bath or spout his beloved *Rubaiyat of Omar Khayyam* just when she was trying to get to sleep. ('What Lamp had Destiny to guide…' indeed?). How could she even begin to think of life without him? He was so warm and protective. She just couldn't envisage a future without Hamish.

Back with the soup she watched anxiously as the doctor continued to sound with his stethoscope, probing gently with his hands, helping Hamish to sit up and cough. By now his eyes were open and he was blinking in the strong light of the torch beamed in on them. Then his sinewy hand crept out and sought hers and she knew the worst was over.

Such a gush of relief enveloped her that her eyes went prickly and she thought she would faint. "Thank the Lord," she murmured.

"Aidan?" he croaked. She smiled reassuringly pointing at the heap in the corner. Jaime was directing operations to oversee ministrations to Aidan who now began to show distinct signs of slowly reviving. Meantime Anna, having retrieved the dinghy minus its outboard, had been hauled aboard complete with flippers. She disappeared almost immediately together with her bundle of clothes before she could even be thanked. Despite her heaving chest and goose pimples she had appeared to be not greatly the worse for her experience and Katie waited gratefully to thank her for her intervention which had undoubtedly been crucial.

On her knees beside Hamish, Katie was immensely relieved to hear him splutter again and spew out more sea water. Instinctively she put her hand to his forehead and held him while he coughed. Then he put out a hand again to grab hers and whispered "Katie? Thank the Lord. Are you all right?" and then after a minute, "My binoculars?"

"It's not your binoculars you should be worried about. Besides, it was already dark and you wouldn't have had them with you. If anything, it's your new good shoes you had to kick off and your lovely deerstalker." She paused to see how much he had taken on board, then continued: "Are you thinking of your heavy rubber torch? That probably saved your life: it stopped one of your visiting mermen from stabbing you in the arm, and you were able to give him a good clunk over the head with it, at least according to what that crewman said."

She discovered later that it had at least knocked right out of his hand the fearsome-looking knife with which the invader was preparing to slash them and the rubber dinghy once again, perhaps to more purpose this time. Most likely after he had disposed of Hamish and/or Aidan under the waves.

∗   ∗   ∗

It looked as if Hamish's heart had stood up to its exertions pretty well all things considered, as his breathing slowly returned to normal. His face under the bright lighting still looked the colour of porridge but at least his teeth had stopped their convulsive chattering and he had stopped clamping the spoon as Katie tried to force the warm soup down him. She noticed that one of his front teeth had been chipped and assumed that was when the paddle had hit him full force. He would have a lovely bruise in the morning. Already she could see the beginnings. She glanced at her watch and saw to her amazement that it was already 3 am so quite time for bed! If, however, that was the full extent of his injuries then she should be thankful indeed, she realised, provided his heart had not been further damaged. The doctor was reassuring but still looked worried. Since the small sickbay was already full to bursting with other casualties and Katie seemed so competent, he was persuaded to let Hamish return to his cabin for the night. He made her promise, however, to summon him no matter when, should the need arise. He made a note of all Hamish's medicaments before returning to his cabin, leaving her with his strict injunctions.

Two crew members were about to help her along to the cabin with Hamish, an unwieldy man to manoeuvre at the best of times, but especially in his semi-comatose state. Luckily there was only one short flight of stairs to negotiate and all was going well when suddenly Katie became aware of someone weeping noisily. Stooping over the inert body of one of the frogmen, to her surprise she recognised Vanessa, white and aghast. Jaime's arm was around her heaving shoulders and he too looked amazed, pale and stricken, as together they studied the face of the young man who appeared to be dead. The body was now being examined by the doctor who, straightening up, shook his head regretfully, extending his hand in sympathy to Jaime.

"If he hadn't been so partial to the bottle and substance abuse," opined the medic removing his stethoscope, "he might have stood a chance. But as it is I'm very sorry to have to tell you that he's had it. The combination of his excesses, the icy water and over-exertion on top of a full stomach and plenty of alcohol, have proved fatal. On top of the effects of, shall we say, an 'irregular' lifestyle."

He paused; Vanessa sniffled and Katie shuddered as the full impact hit her. The man with the knife who had assaulted first Aidan and then her own beloved was none other than Ari, the spotty and putty-faced young Fuente nephew whom she had supposed, erroneously, was already dead. The one who had allegedly been knifed and then thrown overboard to drown. But who must obviously have been misidentified; only later to become involved in this nasty fracas. But why? What on earth could he have held against the two Scotsmen whom, as far as she knew, he'd never even spoken to and certainly had no dealings with? She racked her brains but still couldn't believe it as she went over to extend her sympathy to the two Fuentes. Silently they embraced before she rushed off to catch up with Hamish. They stared after her with vacant eyes.

Still shaking, Katie returned to her cabin and to a prostrate Hamish. She couldn't be sure until the next day of course but she was confident he had suffered no irremediable harm, his breathing having returned to normal and his heart having stopped thudding and resuming its usual deliberate beat. She was reassured when she saw that his eye had resumed a faint twinkle as he attempted to joke with her. But it closed again quickly as he seemed to drift off into a deep sleep. The doctor had seemed relieved that he had apparently not suffered worse but cautioned her strongly, warning her that he was still not out of the woods. Struggling to get his trousers off him, and his other wet clothes, she was appalled at the bruises but managed to contain her questions until a night's sound sleep should restore him, and fell into bed herself completely spent.

CHAPTER THIRTY-THREE

Late the next morning Hamish looked more himself again and was able to talk, slowly but rationally, having nearly slept the clock round. He was ravenously hungry so Katie rushed off to find him some 'breakfast'. Glancing out of the porthole as she went she glimpsed one of the smaller albatross just skimming the waves and then rising into the air with an exuberant thrust which perfectly matched her soaring heart, the sun just catching the tips of its wings. It swooped up in a heavenly arc and then was lost to sight as she gazed, silently thanking God for Hamish's deliverance and his return to her.

She was looking forward to finding out several interesting and unexpected details of the night's events but first went to see how Aidan was. She found him sitting, fully clothed, in his cabin in the process of interrogating Manuel (who doubled his public relations duties with that of purser). Aidan had discovered that Manuel's assistant José had been pestering him for an advance on his wages. Manuel had difficulty understanding why it was so pressing since they weren't about to berth anywhere and there seemed little call for cash. But the previous day José had been insistent, looking repeatedly over his shoulder nervously as he tried to persuade Manuel to pay up. When it was explained to him that they needed to call at the bank in Coinco before any of the crew could receive their wages, he threw a despairing look at Manuel, muttering direly under his breath and dashed off looking like thunder.

From questioning other crew members Aidan soon heard about the ill-fated card game the night before the drowning incident, Ari's apparent recklessness and his intransigence about being paid what was owed him immediately without waiting for the ship to dock. It was obvious someone was after him and not someone who would show mercy if the loot weren't forthcoming on the nail. From his previous researches Aidan had guessed about the drug-runners and the extent of their network but still couldn't be certain who their Mr Big was. He was loath to jump the gun but really had no option now but to persuade the local police force to wheel in those implicated locally, whose names were mostly well-known. The police would be very reluctant, he knew; some of them had grown up together, gone to school together, maybe even fished together, but he had no leeway if he was to fulfil his Interpol mandate and not risk their jumping ship on docking. He knew the Captain would be furious too as he was already short of hands and would be unable to recruit further manpower until Puerto Aisén at the earliest.

Aidan did have the added bonus of the list of names which Katie had culled from Señora Lorca, most of which tallied with his own previous information. But the scent had gone cold after the Santiago contact was checked out. He was, however, absolutely determined to follow up on who was controlling the contents of the lobster pots and who was arranging the counterfeiting of the artefacts which had been found to be faked. He was also more than a little curious as to the identity of the man, allegedly Ari, who was killed in the earlier fracas. Had he been detailed off to collect from the lobster pots and if so, who by? Aidan knew he would have to persuade the local police to put a discreet watch on whoever collected the goods from those suspect pots: if need be, he would have to bludgeon them, he saw he had no option. They would be unwilling to do it and even more to inform him of the results if it was someone they knew, but essential if he was to trace the trail back to its origins. Surprisingly he found an unexpected ally in the First Mate who at last seemed to be warming to him and anxious to help. Perhaps he had his own agenda, thought Aidan, remembering his kinship with Señora Valdemar. But any port in a storm…

∗   ∗   ∗

The next evening saw Aidan and Hamish, accompanied by Katie and Anna, all seated in the Captain's cabin. Although Hamish's eyes still looked sunken his heart had returned to normal and his appetite was back. Aidan, whose sinuses had - amazingly - benefited from their seawater immersion, thanked the Captain most warmly for all his support and apologised for the lost outboard engine from the dinghy which of course he would arrange to have replaced.

To his surprise the Captain, waving his apology aside, reciprocated the thanks. For some years, he revealed, he had been held to ransom by these drug traffickers up and down that stretch of Chilean coast (all under the sway of the notorious 'JC'). Not only had they threatened to put his mini-cruisers out of action but also to harm his family if so much as a breath of suspicion or accusation was voiced to anyone in authority in Coinco or Santiago. The local boys were all squared off, or so it was implied, but if anyone from the capital were to come snooping and anything untoward be hinted at, even if it led to no arrests or sanctions, then vengeance would be wreaked. And everyone knew what that meant. Almost all the inhabitants along the shoreline were involved in one way or another and those few who weren't knew better than to spread any rumour or try to interfere. Too many examples of instant "justice" had been meted out for anyone to be left in any doubt as to the reprisals which would be taken. Hence when he, the Captain, heard that a foreigner - a gringo - had been enlisted by Interpol to come snooping and that the Minister of the Interior, no less, required his immediate assistance his heart had quailed. This could only spell trouble, and trouble on a gargantuan scale he feared.

Sure enough, trouble was not long in coming. It had all been sparked off by the discovery of that first body, the fisherman's; then the next - even though it had lain there for a good four months, supposedly undetected, and was in fact sufficiently decomposed to make identification difficult, or at least very slow. The Captain's entourage had been lucky to escape the immediate consequences of this - a matter of fortuitous timing rather than judgement. But the Interpol agent had arrived, satellite messages had begun to come in thick and fast (he had never been so popular); the Englishman had been arrested and carted off to jail on the mainland to sighs of relief from the locals...and all the rest of the sorry story - which by now they all knew although some not in its entirety.

"The two anonymous wet-suited attackers of the previous evening turned out to be in the pay, the clutches I should say, of the drug baron who had apparently got the wind up after he got word of CIA interest as well as Interpol's," the Captain then told them. "They, the wetsuits, had been deputed to dispose of this nasty nosey Scotsman (and anyone else who aided and abetted him) and to this end had concocted the urgent summons from the mainland just across the sound, arguing that since it was known the *Skyros* would be sailing on the very early tide next day the Captain would not want to hang around long. And they could do their dirty work in the black of night without anyone being any the wiser. (They had miscalculated the moon's phases but even so they nearly got away with it.)"

So Ari *was* in the pay of the drug barons, thought Katie mournfully, - more shame and sorrow for Vanessa and Jaime. Her heart went out to them at the realisation of this double-whammy. Poor Jaime for his distress, his shame and for having misjudged Ari so completely. And for the death of one of his relatives even if he had turned out to be a bad 'un. He was still family after all.

"But they had reckoned without his having an associate in tow and a doughty one at that," the Captain resumed. "More than that, the heroic and entirely unexpected public assistance shown so courageously by our Antipodean friend," (and here the Captain bowed gallantly to Anna) "could be said to have tipped the balance. Two young and agile frogmen in wetsuits, armed with knives and expecting and ready for action, against two er..less young and perhaps not quite so fit older men even though both - happily - were strong swimmers and ...reasonably er…". Here the Captain's eloquence deserted him for a moment. So Aidan took up the tale.

"It was obvious their plan was to immobilise the dinghy with their knives and then hit me over the head with the paddle, forcing me into the water where - without the benefit of a wetsuit or even any very serviceable clothes - I would shortly either drown or freeze to death. And they could pass it all off as an accident. But, as the Captain said, they had reckoned without my gallant friend here (sincerest apologies to you, Katie, for dragging him into this) who not only disconcerted them but managed very effectively to distract their attention from me, even sending one of them overboard. The other nasty piece of work, though small by our standards, was not so easy to dispose of but…we managed, finally…," he finished modestly. "With the invaluable help of our friend from 'down-under'. She not only grabbed the paddle from the water and hit him on the wrist when he had the knife inches from me but she was able, God only knows how, by rocking the boat to make him drop into the drink to join his comrade. So that Hamish here could deal with him and sew him up nicely ready for the tow back to *Skyros*. Meanwhile, in the dark and freezing water our heroine located and then pushed back to base our errant rubber boat. It must have been creasing - absolutely exhausting; and to cap it all, she escaped before anyone could thank her.

A real Amazon, I can tell you. Thank you again, Anna, from the bottom of my heart." Aidan seized Anna's hand and in a totally uncharacteristic gesture kissed it.

There were murmurs of thanks and congratulations all round, and they all took the opportunity to hug her. The Captain promised her a free trip the next time her travels took her in his direction and everybody summoned up a hooray of sorts albeit rather a hoarse and croaky one.

On her way out of the cabin the First Mate took Katie aside and whispered to her: "You remember you were so intrigued by the jewel-studded collar of that albino guard-dog in …Coinco, belonging to my cousin Señora Valdemar?…Yes, you might like to know I've just discovered some more about it. Her son's just told me - in the strictest confidence naturally. Inside the collar, cleverly hidden away flush with the interior moulding, was a tiny key - gold of course- but not a conventional key. Oh no; it had a four-digit number inscribed on it which you would need a magnifying glass to read. And even if you did manage to decrypt the number you wouldn't necessarily know what it was for…".

Katie, mystified, urged him to go on.

"It turned out to be for a strongbox. Not a box held locally; one eventually located in the Peruvian capital - in one of the Ministry strong-rooms - in which apparently the customs officers found more, duplicate, keys to all the safes and security laser beams controlling the Lima Museum. At first they couldn't make it out at all. Then they couldn't believe it. What would the master-key (of which allegedly no copies had ever been made) to the keys to somewhere in Lima be doing in a backyard way down the remote Chilean coast?"

Katie blinked as she pondered the significance of this piece of intelligence - and its ramifications. She wondered whether Aidan had already worked it out. She also knew she wouldn't be able to prevent herself from telling Hamish despite her promise to keep it under her hat. Thanking the First Mate with a deep smile, she slipped away quickly.

CHAPTER THIRTY-FOUR

Back again in Santiago two days later, they were gathered outside the Waldensian church, which bore a striking resemblances to the Nonconformist church of Hamish's childhood. Jaime laughingly said, "You two had better come back again soon. It's obviously the only way I can get Vanessa to come with me on a Sunday and she actually quite enjoys it when she does make the effort. At least she meets a lot of her friends here, a lot of whom have come today specially to see Hamish. And today she can ride on the crest of her recent success. And of yours too, of course."

"That was a good sermon." Hamish did not want to discuss recent events and felt an urge to change the subject. "I'm not sure our own church would have taken quite such a forgiving stance; or, indeed, that I would have encouraged them to. Laymen cheating the customs and excise is one thing but government ministers cheating their electorate is not exactly the same, at least not in the eyes of our so-called democracy. Or my view either, I feel I should add. As for ministers who themselves cheat, unfortunately that is no longer such a rarity, even in Britain." Katie gulped on hearing Hamish say this: how things had changed. She noted Jaime's reaction with amusement.

"But I can't imagine it done in our country on quite the same scale or with such panache. It's not so much that we are more law-abiding, or even more moral, as the notion that we probably have more of a civic sense of duty. At least I hope so. And probably our gutter press is more active in ferreting things like that out into the open. Besides, we're more likely to get caught - with pretty dire consequences. Our police may not be the most efficient in the world but at least they're more honest than most and would be less easily bribed. Most people realise that if we cheat the government of its taxes someone else has only to pay more in the long run. Unless the government is absolutely craven. It doesn't necessarily stop them, the cheats, of course but... Or we go without. I know you don't have a welfare state here as such but nevertheless things do seem to be going in that direction." Not before time, Katie thought to herself, glancing involuntarily at Jaime who had looked away.

"At least State employees are starting to have pensions," Jaime agreed. "And the trade unions are becoming much more powerful. And assertive. Whether that's a good thing or not...but no unemployment benefits. Yet. Over my dead body - that would be the passport to all the *far-nientes* climbing onto the bandwagon; all the *mapuches* and layabouts." He grinned. Jaime reckoned he had a reputation to keep up. You had to have a few hard men around or the place would go to the dogs. "Or at least not for women: they've got their men folk toiling away to keep them in luxury," he added, looking provocatively at Katie, Vanessa being deep in conversation with her friends.

But Katie wasn't going to rise to this bait.

"Anyway, in Britain somehow the money has got to be found if we want to maintain our welfare state *and* our National Health Service with all the extra workers coming in now from the rest of Europe, not to mention Asia and the Baltic states." Hamish, warming to his theme, added: "...not that that affects our get-rich-quick boys, granted - or the foreign mafia," thinking of the lack of social provision he had seen in the poorer districts of Santiago but not wanting to be insulting, particularly so near the end of their holiday. He remembered both Vanessa's and Jaime's sensitivities and took his cue from his wife. Any imagined slights to their beloved Chile and Hamish would find he had put his foot in it again. Katie also was beginning to show chauvinistic tendencies about her native country, Hamish was amused to note. Obviously time he took her back home, and quickly.

To make amends he had found in one of the craft markets a huge replica of the Inca golden manikin which, against his nature, he had managed to bargain down to a reasonable price. He then presented it to his hosts in gratitude for their hospitality. They had appeared deeply touched by his gesture, warmly embracing him and extending repeatedly renewed invitations to them to return to Chile. And Katie had secretly been most impressed. This Chilean experience had had unlooked for consequences.

Just before they left for church Vanessa had taken Katie aside to thank her for her help. Her constant cheerfulness and good temper throughout the trip, and Hamish's huge, indeed heroic, contribution towards bringing the culprits to book had been vital to its success. Everyone had said so. And then she made this confession:

"When I first met Hamish at the airport he seemed so quiet and shy, so solemn and unforthcoming, and unassuming, I must admit I wondered what you saw in him. In fact I wondered why you had married him at all - except he's a goodlooking macho sort of bloke. It wasn't until I got to know him a bit better that I began to realise. He was so content to let you do the talking; he never tried to impress or leap in with facile judgements, I just thought he was rather dull and uninteresting: in fact I totally under-estimated him, I admit. I'm so happy we had time enough to find out what he is really like. I can't tell you how much Jaime likes him, and admires him; and me too. He's marvellous - and quite different from most Latinos. But well worth the effort of getting to know…I think you're really lucky, and you well deserve it. And I hope his health hasn't suffered too much from all the excitements and things?" she tailed off.

Katie was gratified. She had at the outset detected a slight coolness on Vanessa's part which had thawed as they went along. But to get this encomium was truly worth while. And it had sounded utterly genuine. From Jaime too, even if only at second-hand! To hide her embarrassment she mumbled, "I'm so dreadfully sorry about Ari; it must have been simply ghastly for you both. What a horrible shock for you all, in fact," and then embraced her cousin warmly, hiding her face. She hadn't wanted to break the spell but felt she had to show that she and Hamish knew all the sordid ramifications and were genuinely sorry about the turn of events. Ari was after all a relation even if he was a ne'er-do-well druggie who did try to kill her husband.

She had just had it confirmed by Aidan that, despite the earlier confusion in identifying the culprit, Ari was indeed one of the two knife-wielding assailants set on them by the Peruvian drug chiefs. And this was undoubtedly with malice aforethought since amongst the effects found in Ari's cabin was a piece of dog-eared paper. And on this paper were two columns of figures, one in black and the other in red in some kind of elementary code. Aidan had worked out that each number corresponded to one of the suspect lobster-pots and to the specific loot stashed in it together with its supposed market value and ultimate destination.

Discussing it with Aidan earlier, Hamish had been extremely puzzled since he was certain he had seen the unfortunate young man after the time of his supposed demise. This was when poor Vanessa and Jaime had been, erroneously as it turned out, informed of the ghastly throat-slitting accident which was supposed to have accounted for young Ari. Hamish had in fact been quite right, but this hadn't saved the wretch from his wrong-headed and crazily criminal intentions later. Although it had so nearly been touch-and-go Hamish couldn't find it in his heart to rejoice at the idiot's demise; he had in fact been sickened to have his identity confirmed.

Katie knew that both Aidan and Hamish had pleaded for clemency in the police's dealing with the other prisoner, obviously on the payroll of the Minister too, but it was anybody's guess as to what would finally happen to him. She preferred not to speculate but turned her thought to how, that morning, Hamish had apologised most humbly to her for having "put her through purgatory and back" during and after his illness, particularly the episode in the water. To show her how contrite he was he had presented her with a little gold brooch inset with lapis-lazuli, a peace offering. She found it absolutely enchanting and, since in her opinion he owed her no apology, it was a gesture made all the sweeter for its spontaneity and surprise. But this was a private affair and she didn't feel like sharing it with anyone, at least not just yet.

Thinking back to the eve of their departure on holiday Katie realised how Hamish had mellowed since his attack. In the earlier days of their marriage he would have been quite unable to make such a gesture, let alone admit he had been at fault in any way, but now...now not only had he gained in confidence but a lot of his rough edges had been honed in the process. And to concede that Chileans might be right and his compatriots wrong in anything, no matter how small, this was a new Hamish.

*   *   *

Noticing a very unusual sunset that evening, Katie reminded Hamish of the extraordinary sky on the first evening when they arrived in Chile. Perhaps she should continue to believe in omens after all. Not willing to appease her superstitions, Hamish just grunted and gently steered her back indoors.

Departure the next day saw them all gloomily at the airport where they had first met a fortnight previously. It seemed like a lifetime ago. After fond farewells and vowing to keep in touch, the Blairs went to the check-in desk.

"There must be some mistake." Hamish shook his head at the attractive airline employee who sported a waxy copihue in her buttonhole. "We're travelling cattle class; certainly not First, nor even Club - unfortunately."

"No, no Sir. You are definitely upgraded to First, I have it here - on the orders of the Minister himself, no less. Come with me. Is this your entire luggage?" and she cast a disparaging eye over their motley assortment of bags which Katie had been so afraid would be over the weight limit. "Just leave it all to me: here are your luggage reclaim tags, six in all," as she tried not to sneer.

Sweeping past the other tousled looking passengers queuing to present their passports, some hostile, some merely curious, Katie thanked her lucky stars she had had the good sense to leave behind in Vanessa's fridge a last-minute gift from Jocelyn. Several kilos of frozen mariscos! Even in double-duty plastic the huge block of ice they were incarcerated in would scarcely last the journey before beginning to drip on some poor unfortunate's head or, if she managed to smuggle them into the hold, onto someone else's luggage. Tempting though the idea had been, good sense had - unusually for her - prevailed. Thank goodness.

Half an hour later, still astounded by their good fortune, Katie wondered which Minister as she settled herself into her luxurious seat, having made good use of the VIP lounge in the interim. Sipping her champagne, she watched the other poor passengers lumbering on board trying to cope with infants and hand luggage and dropped carrier bags while they vainly sought their seats. She was intrigued by the little presentation packs they had been handed by the air hostess on settling into their lavishly appointed seats and stupefied by the amount of in-flight entertainment apparently on offer. Hamish stretched out luxuriously in his roomy seat-cum-sleeping-berth imagining Vanessa giving Jaime hell again or perhaps just enjoying her triumph to herself. After all, despite the mishaps it had mostly been a triumph of organisation, if not a total triumph in what had actually transpired. Poor Ari, he thought and poor Vanessa and Jaime. And the poor sister too, even if they had been at loggerheads. She hadn't even had the time to make it up with her silly misguided brother.

Hamish felt a little sorry for Aidan too, who would doubtless still be trying to persuade the authorities in Lima to put sanctions on the villains responsible for all the recently unveiled atrocities but in particular for those involved in the drug-running. Since most of them had been in high-up positions he had little hope of any very great success there but, knowing his tenacity, Aidan would be bound to persevere until the Interpol agency in New York decided it was time to call him off. A truly thankless task he had set himself, Hamish knew, and one in which he had really wanted to collaborate with Aidan - as much for his own satisfaction as anything else. But this time he didn't fancy stretching Katie's patience beyond its limits.

Katie was amused to note that Hamish was wearing the garish new socks she had given him as a joke. She had found them at the airport and, having made sure they were the correct family tartan, thought what the hell, "even though he's far too conservative to be seen dead in anything other than his regulation plain grey or beige or, at a pinch, pale blue," she muttered to herself. A year before he would have thought his new socks vulgar and never have dreamt of putting them on; she would have found them a year later at the back of his sock-drawer smelling of mothballs. But he had mellowed...She put her arms round Hamish's neck and whispered something to him. She was amused to see him blush which even *his* weatherbeaten complexion couldn't hide.

"And to think you promised me a peaceful holiday," he countered, "the perfect rest after that ghastly hospital experience. Just as I was beginning to believe what that Frenchman Molière's supposed to have said about 'unbroken happiness being a bore; it should have its ups and downs'. And then you go and do this to me," he teased. "However, I have to admit I shall really miss those beautiful Chilean snowy mountains with their amethyst reflections in the sea; and I even quite *like* some of your Chilean compatriots...and some of the Aussies and other passengers were halfway towards being decent too! What's more, I found the food quite palatable, most of it, the seafood especially. And as for the wine - that was a real revelation. I had no idea Chile boasted such a wide variety of really drinkable and top-rate wine, reds in particular. I shudder to think how much they must have cost."

"We'd better pass that commendation on to Jaime," Katie smiled.

But as if he hadn't heard her he continued, "It was a real bonus, as well as a coincidence, running into my old mate Johnson - but a huge surprise. I almost didn't recognise him at first. But I could have done without Bent String as well, that's for sure. And his insinuations. Anyway, I've promised to look him up - Aidan I mean - when I'm next in Glasgow, unless he manages to get down to Cheshire first. Strange such a nice chap as him is still a bachelor. We, meaning you," (smiling at his wife) "will have to see what we can do about that…".

"So much for the confirmed xenophobe," she thought, "You surely don't expect me to recommend any of my friends, English ones at that, to marry a policeman!" Mentally adding 'matchmaker' to her role-list, she listened as Hamish went on to list the new friends he wouldn't mind seeing again, - in her role as entertainments officer.

"But what do you mean by insinuations?" she pursued looking puzzled, in her best 'stepping-stone' manner.

"That business about Aidan's having supposedly killed a man in Glasgow - as insinuated by Bent String. It all turned out to be a nasty smear, I was relieved to have it confirmed. Apparently, shortly after we'd finished our initial training, Aidan's younger brother was involved in a horrific car accident when he was run over by druggies high on a mixture of heroin and booze. While he was lying on the road with blood streaming from his head wounds the driver responsible was taunting the fuzz, Aidan and his mate who'd now arrived on the scene, with particularly choice epithets and threats, refusing to cooperate and move the car from off the young lad's foot. The driver's female companion high on drugs, was screaming obscenities and letting out a stream of invective so strident that Aidan could not hear himself think over the din. And Aidan was quite unable to persuade them to move, short of physically manhandling them. The wretched lad lay moaning, obviously seriously injured, and all they could do was to continue hurling insults so Aidan, barely able to contain himself once he realized it was his own brother lying pinioned, after moving the car dragged them off and clouted them for good measure before jamming iron bracelets onto their tattooed wrists.

"Shortly after the youth expired it turned out a photographer, a paparazzo, was 'opportunely' on hand. He managed to sell his stolen picture for an exorbitant amount and then decided to capitalise on it by claiming the lad had been killed by the fuzz: and this is the story which made the rounds. Fortunately, there were enough honest witnesses nearby who came forward and testified to the true events for Aidan to be cleared in the court case which followed, several months later. But poor Aidan not only lost his kid brother in harrowing circumstances but was apparently severely traumatized by the whole affair. I suppose all this must have happened while I was down at Marlow (and had other things on my mind); otherwise I don't know how I could have missed seeing it in the papers. Anyway, that's what that vile creep Tring meant by it all. And to think I was nearly fooled by him into harbouring doubts about poor old Aidan."

Hamish gazed out of the porthole as Katie picked up the paper again. She was distracted by the headline in the newspaper handed her by the flight attendant. "*Minister of Justice to taste his own medicine: jail sentence for corruption and larceny, drug-dealing,... of Justice.......*" A dazzling crimson sunset now fired by streaks of orange and vermilion made it impossible to read more.

"You mean the *Minister* himself really was behind it all? I don't believe a word of it. I thought it was the spy chief or at least the Chief of Customs. But *he* had so much already. Why ever did he want more, that's what I can't understand."

"Ah, my sweet innocent darling, you probably never will. But you must realise that not everyone is as unworldly as you. Or as easily contented. There will always be people motivated by power and greed, insatiable greed, in this case a sort of "gold-lust" knowing no bounds - verging on paranoia, in fact. The more they have, the more they crave."

"And in his case I've no doubt he was egged on by that dreadful wife of his always wanting to outshine all her rivals by wearing the latest line in ostentatious jewellery. I suppose that would necessitate melting down some of that exquisite Inca gold. Oh, it doesn't bear thinking of. I really can't believe that anyone could be so...so.." She was lost for words.

"Philistine?" he offered.

"I was going to say 'crass' or even 'evil'," Katie rejoined. "To think he was Minister for **Justice** too: there's the irony." she continued. "But why would one Minister in Venezuela shop another in Peru, that's what I would like to know. It's not even as if the countries were at loggerheads."

"No, not exactly, but the two Presidents were. And apparently there was quite a back-history of antagonism and personal dislike going back decades. What could be a handier way of discrediting one within the auspices of the ECLA - that's something like the Latin American branch of the UN - than attributing to him the shadier dealings of another, say Peruvian politician, all the time pretending to be 'holier-than-thou'?"

Katie thought for a moment and then: "But to replace some of those artefacts with replicas, some of them very crudely done, seems absolutely crazy. Surely he knew some expert would spot them sooner rather than later."

"Well, read this." And Hamish passed his newspaper over to her where she read:-

"Art crime is a thriving industry: on the roster of international illicit trade, art crime is now number three, trailing only drugs and illegal arms."

"Well, we knew about the drugs and probably the illegal arms but this takes the biscuit…".

"Yes but read from page 5," Hamish urged. "Read from: " *Some, ceremonial daggers, etc…*". And she read: *"ceremonial daggers, Inca crowns and ritual ornaments on display at the private museum are replicas of pieces that once featured in its collection; very obvious fakes whereas others are finely made replicas of the original artefacts,"* stated Paloma Carcedo, *one of the expert archaeologists from Lima's Universidad Catolica, which has been analysing the museum's pieces. "The collection was known abroad as Peru's trove of pre-Columbian treasures; now it seems it's just made up of thousands of forgeries…. Originally owned by the Manuel Muji Gallico Foundation, the collection was once known as the world's biggest and most prestigious assembly of pre-Columbian art treasures. Amassed originally from the Spanish Conquistadores in the 16th century, it has travelled to exhibition halls all over the world to global renown,"* and so on. Look, there are even some illustrations of the pieces Freddie was talking about that first evening. You remember?"

"You mean *he* stole them, the Minister for Justice - or rather got his own security guards to, having first switched off the security - and then replaced them with fakes he'd already had made up in his own workshops. But in the case of the ones Freddie was telling us about it seems they weren't quite quick enough to replace them before the alarm went off and, rather than be caught red-handed, he the Minister had to invent that cock-and-bull story about thieves breaking in and eluding the laser beams, etc. etc. Then he didn't know where to go from there so he had to have them spirited out of the country *pdq*! And down to neighbouring Chile! What a mularkey. And he was still left with egg on his face. I wonder what he'll do now to brazen it out. I gather his wife has already disowned him: not much future there I suppose…or at least no more gold dinner services. So she's abandoning the goose that lays the golden eggs, though who would ever take the likes of her on, I can't imagine."

"But how on earth did he think he'd manage to flog them on the international market? Even on E-bay that would be a bit dicey, wouldn't it? He must already have had someone lined up to…," Katie added after a moment's pause. Hamish had anticipated this question and showed her an article which Aidan had cut out of the Police Gazette describing in detail all the internet ads, aliases and all, for disposing (for high prices) of priceless stolen artefacts on the international scene. It appeared it was already big business, expertly organised, and with the added virtue that it was virtually untraceable even by Interpol. Her eyes bulged.

"Was this what Bent String was supposed to be on about?" she asked and received a non-committal reply. She looked at Hamish curiously but he had already retreated into his book, or pretended to.

Some minutes later Katie, shaking off her gloomy reverie, picked up the paper again and her eye was immediately caught by something new. "Look, Hamish, a review of that young Lorca's book of poetry. Hurray, it's come out at last: he must be thrilled. I wonder where we can get a copy…"

"You don't need to wonder any more. Have a look at this." Hamish emerged from his reverie. "I'm sorry, I forgot. Tony slipped it to me for you just as we were boarding. He felt certain you would want to see it before all memories of the holiday had faded. It has the loveliest dedication I've ever seen inside. From Tony. Mind you, that was the least he could do after all the interpreting you did for him. And the dangers you ran…".

"And the number of times Sheila wept on your shoulder," she rejoined, examining the poems. "And to think young Felipe should now be back home with his poor mother who must be recovering from their ordeal. I only hope he'll manage to find another job; or perhaps he'll make enough from his poetry now that he's become famous?"

"You know they found evidence of disguised torture all over his body except, of course, on his face. He looked exactly as if he had a strawberry rash, the pinpricks of the torture stick were spread so evenly over every part of his body, and his genitals were purple with bruising."

"So senseless. What did they hope to get out of him? It's not as if he knew anything compromising, is it?"

"No, but they were systematically gunning for the country's literati who were all suspected of being extreme leftwing fanatics in the footsteps of Allende. That is, if they were not actively pro-Pinochet's government. Even when not Communists or Maoists, if they were still not verbally in favour of the régime, they were suspect and on DINA, the secret police's, list. Almost as bad as the Stalin régime's purge of artists and writers in the fifties, or was it the sixties? And if they were ever heard to criticize the government even in private… This of course all formed part of the State's good scare tactics. And don't think there weren't informers everywhere 'cos there were, even in the most unexpected places. I'd say it's all to Chile's credit that it didn't really work, at least it didn't cow the literati, and they're now at last set back on the road to a democracy of sorts." He paused and rubbed his eyes. "Though it will take some time for a complete volte-face."

"In fact, in some respects I'd say their government was really more enlightened now than ours. And they're reintroducing civic controls and a lot of other things to safeguard individual liberty which we could do with…"

"Or at least more effective - which is not necessarily the same thing. But I never thought I would live to hear you say that….". Katie looked at him, amazed.

"But Felipe's rave reviews," Hamish continued, changing the subject, "should really set him up now in the literary world and prevent any more unwelcome attention from the secret police…".

"Did I tell you that Tony has accepted a job at the British Museum liaising with the Museum of Mankind in tracing stolen artefacts? Which virtually makes him a civil servant! Imagine - Tony, after all the things he said about the inefficiency of…".

"Perhaps his experience in jail will make him see things from the other side now. At least this means that young Tony junior will have some stability in his life, especially if Dad manages to get his millionaire backer to pay up after all the hassle he's been through."

"So that **was** what Sheila was being so coy about. I'm really pleased for them both and would like to keep in touch with them. After all, London's not so far away. "

"And with some of the other members of our group too. Freddie and Ursula have promised to visit us when they are over in London next month and we have a pressing invitation to pay a return visit to Jaime and Vanessa, rather surprising in the circumstances I would say."

Hamish was not so sure about wanting to keep up with Freddie now that his secret was out but he hoped that his wife was still unaware of the less savoury details and therefore said nothing. As Katie was about to yield to the effects of the champagne and nod off she sat bolt upright and said: "That reminds me, whatever happened to Freddie's isotopes? Do you know whether he ever managed to get them through? They would hardly allow them through customs legally and Ursula explained to me that they don't last for ever. Something about their half-life…".

A sly grin spread over Hamish's face. "Ah, the isotopes…I was wondering when you were going to ask me about them. Well, it's a long story but the upshot is - as I reckon Ursula must have suspected - they weren't really isotopes at all but a solid gold priapic manikin. Yes," as Katie gasped. "Freddie must somehow have blackmailed one of the guards into letting him lift it from the Minister's haul of the Mujo Gallico heist, one of the star exhibits, having cottoned on very quickly to what was happening. In return for his (Freddie's) silence, he was allowed to acquire one of the smaller supposedly less significant pieces as they - the guards - thought. Little did they know, it was probably one of the most valuable pieces in the entire collection, being one of the few to survive from a looted archaeological site some twenty years ago."

"You don't mean one of the pieces which were stolen from the Royal Tombs of Sipàn when they started excavating? I suppose Gallico got to hear about it and…"

"Yes, well, however he got hold of it… It was one which was to have been hidden undetected in the second lot, in the lobster pot with the dayglow orange pennant hoisted. One of the lobster pots which, as Tony spotted, had had its tapered entry-hole modified so as to be able to get something larger than a lobster in. Which made me and Aidan think it came from an altogether different source. But how Freddie actually got hold of it still remains a mystery. And how he managed to smuggle it out I can't imagine - it must have weighed a ton - but he was probably facilitated in order to silence him about the larger theft which I reckon he clearly must have figured out somehow. Hence his great interest in keeping tabs on progress in the Minister's 'search' for the offenders."

A picture in the newspaper of a very sheepishly grinning Freddie caught her eye. And then she saw the caption *"Philanthropic doctor decides to spread it around"*.

"I wonder if Ursula will ever forgive him…", Katie chortled until she fell asleep.